THE POLAND TRILOGY BY JAMES CONROYD MARTIN

Check out The Poland Trilogy: https://goo.gl/93rzag

Based on the diary of a Polish countess who lived through the rise and fall of the Third of May Constitution years, 1791-94, ***Push Not the River*** paints a vivid picture of a tumultuous and unforgettable metamorphosis of a nation—and of Anna, a proud and resilient woman. ***Against a Crimson Sky*** continues Anna's saga as Napoléon comes calling, implying independence would follow if only Polish lancers would accompany him on his fateful 1812 march into Russia. Anna's family fights valiantly to hold on-to a tenuous happiness, their country, and their very lives. Set against the November Rising (1830-31), ***The Warsaw Conspiracy*** depicts partitioned Poland's daring challenge to the Russian Empire. Brilliantly illustrating the psyche of a people determined to reclaim independence in the face of monumental odds, the story features Anna's sons and their fates in love and war.

06-24-2017

THE BOY WHO WANTED WINGS

To JoAnn

Best,

James Conroyd Martin

JAMES CONROYD MARTIN

HUSSAR
QUILL PRESS

The Boy Who Wanted Wings

First Print Edition: August 2016
http://www.JamesCMartin.com

Edited by Mary Rita Perkins Mitchell
Cover and Formatting: Streetlight Graphics
www.streetlightgraphics.com

ISBN: 978-0-9978945-0-9

Art:
Front cover: ***Husari Szarza***
Back cover: ***Husaria***
Interior: ***Husaria.Polska duma***
By Halina Kaźmierczak
http://www.kazmierczak.netgaleria.eu

Title page:
Polish Eagle, drawing
By Kenneth Mitchell

Interior art:
Wycinanki, Polish folk papercuts
By Frances Drwal

While some charcters are based on historical personages, this is a work of fiction.

ALSO BY JAMES CONROYD MARTIN

The Poland Trilogy:

Push Not the River
Against a Crimson Sky
The Warsaw Conspiracy
and
Hologram: A Haunting

ACKNOWLEDGMENTS

I wish to express my deep and sincere appreciation to those who have given of their time, expertise, and enthusiasm along the road to this novel, especially Lorron Farani, Judith Sowiński Free, Scott Hagensee, Linda Hansen, Halina Kaźmierczak, Leonard Kniffel, Kitty Mitchell, Mary Rita Perkins Mitchell, Faye Predny, John Rdzak, Radosław Sikora, Miltiades Varvounis, Cheryl Wolgamott, and loyal members of Portland's 9-Bridges Downtown Saturday Meetups.

~For my loyal readers,
with sincere thanks~

THANK YOU for reading ***The Boy Who Wanted Wings***

PLEASE sign up for an occasional announcement about freebies, bonuses, booksignings, contests, news, and recommendations. http://jamescmartin.com/announcements/

LIKE me on **Facebook**: James Conroyd Martin, Author https://www.facebook.com/James-Conroyd-Martin-Author-29546357206/

Follow me on **Twitter:** @JConMartin

Follow/add me on **Goodreads**:
https://www.goodreads.com/author/show/92822.James_Conroyd_Martin

E-mail me at: JConMartin@gmail.com

HISTORICAL NOTE:

On the eve of September 11, 1683, a massive Ottoman horde was besieging the gates of Vienna and had been doing so since the previous July. Now, however, they were just hours from capturing this capital of the Holy Roman Empire. The Turks' intent was to bring Islam to all of Europe, and this city was seen by East and West alike as the gateway. They had already achieved success in Greece, Bulgaria, Romania, Hungary, and Serbia. With the window of time closing for Vienna, the walls were about to be breached on September 12 when the vastly outnumbered Christian coalition, led by Polish King Jan III Sobieski and his famous winged hussars, descended Kahlenberg Mountain to engage the Turks in an attempt to lift the siege.

Is it merely coincidental that Al-Qaeda terrorists chose September 11, 2001, for their horrific attack on New York and Washington, DC? Or had the Battle of Vienna—as seminal in human history as the 1066 Battle of Hastings—inspired a symbolic message that the time had come to resume the struggle of 1683?

GLOSSARY

Dog's blood!: Damn, Damn it!

Dniestr—Dnyehstr: a river in Southeastern Poland, now in the Ukraine, that empties into the Black Sea

Dwór—dvoor: manor house of the Polish nobility

Halicz—Hah-leatch: a historic city in Southeastern Poland, now in the Western Ukraine

Hussar—hu´-zar: (Polish hussar or Winged Warrior) a heavily armored shock cavalryman, often a lancer

Husaria—hu´-zar-ia: plural of hussar, the elite of the Polish cavalry

Janissary—an Ottoman infantry soldier

Kołacz—kaw-watch: a special decorative wedding bread or cake

Kontusz—kaw-ntoosh: a long, robe-like, decorative garment worn (over a *żupan*) by noblemen of the Polish Lithuanian Commonwealth

Kraków—Krah-koof: a city in Southern Poland on the River Vistula; from the twelfth century to 1595 the national capital

Kwarciani—kfah-rchia-nee: elite hussars assigned to the "Wild Fields" on alert for unrest and raids from Tatars and Cossacks

Pacholik—pa-ho-leak: military retainer; plural: Pacholicy—pa-ho-lea-tsi

Rotmistrzr—rot-measts: military company commander, usually a nobleman

sipâhi—sipâ-hi: an Ottoman cavalryman

Sukiennice—su-kie-nnea-tse: the Cloth Hall, centerpiece of the Market Square in Kraków

Szlachta—shlach′-ta: the Polish gentry; minor nobility (six to eight per cent of the population)

Towarzysz—tova-jish: military companions, or knight-officers, accompanying a company commander (rotmistrzr)

Wycinanki—Vih-cee-nahn-kee: Polish folk papercuts

Żupan—żhu′-pahn: a long, lined garment worn first by noblemen of the Polish Lithuanian Commonwealth, then by males of all classes

Halicz

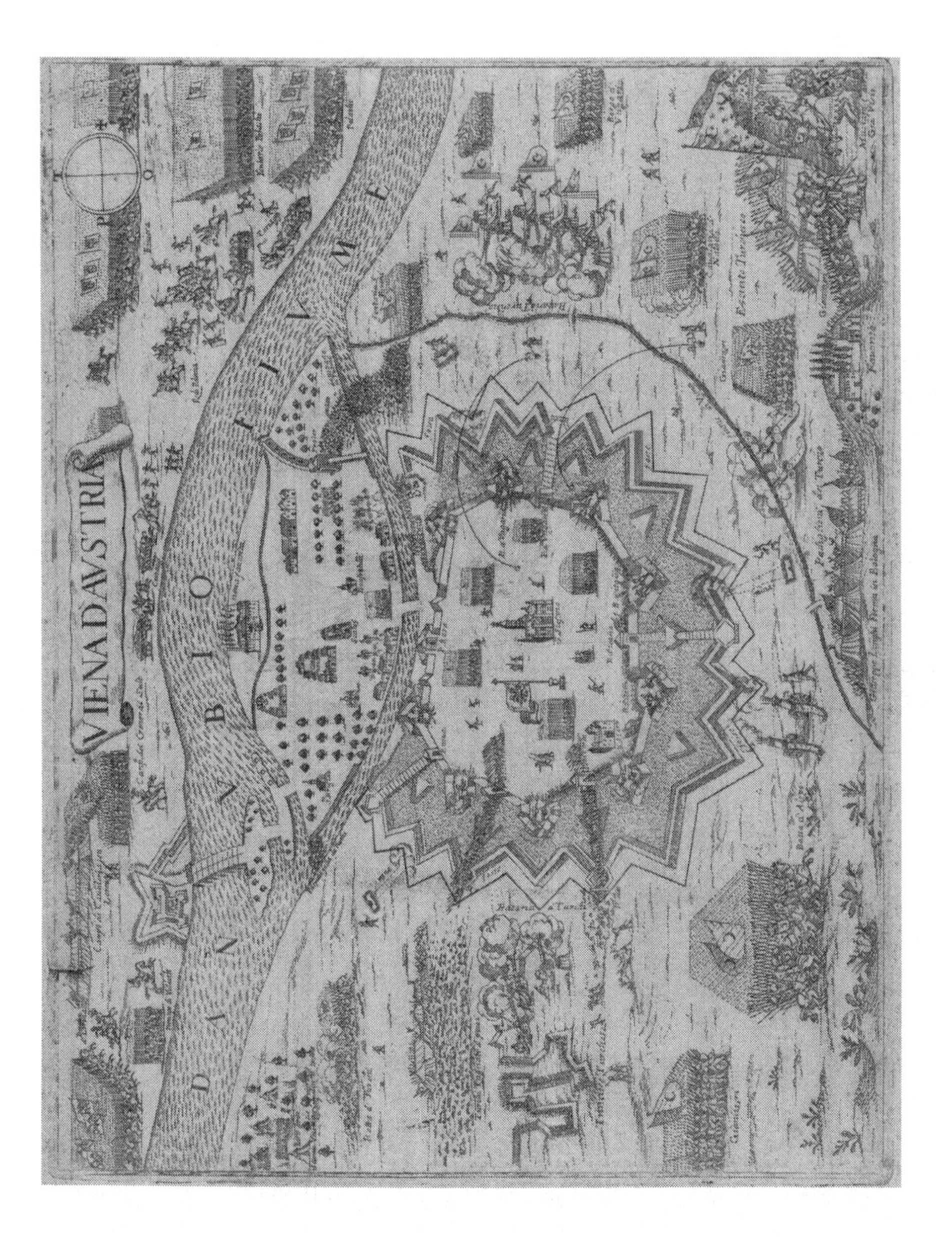

Viena d'Austria By Giuseppe Longhi

The Relief of Vienna, 12 September 1683 By Frans Geffels
Wien Museum/Courtesy of Wien Museum

ONE

Southeastern Poland
May 1683

AS THE COACH TRUNDLED ALONG, days out from Warsaw, Krystyna took little notice of the passing countryside, wondering instead how Mother Abbess Teodora reacted when she opened her underskirt drawer only to find a dead rat.

"What the devil are you smiling at?" her brother asked.

"Nothing… Oh, I do wish Papa had you bring the open carriage."

"The open carriage?" Roman's mouth gaped. "Between Warsaw and Halicz? Are you daft? Did you learn nothing at convent school?"

"I did," Krystyna snapped, eyes flashing at her brother, who sat rigid on the padded bench across from her as the coach rattled on. "I learned that after five years there, I should be very glad to come home."

"Why, on the way to Warsaw the rain fell in torrents for two days running," Roman said, persisting in his own line of thought. "Did you wish me to arrive drenched to the skin? The open carriage would have been a bucket on wheels."

She gave out with a little laugh. "But it's sunny enough now. Oh, Romek," she said, employing his sobriquet, "it was a wish, nothing more."

He looked at her as if puzzled, shrugged, and settled back against the cushion.

She smothered another laugh. He had taken her literally, as had so many of the Carmelite nuns. At sixteen, she was—at last and for good—coming home to Halicz. It had taken some doing. She sat back now, tilting her head toward the window, watching the landscape glide past as she had imagined so many times in her cell: the strong, evergreen sentinels on the slopes of the Carpathian Mountains, the verdant green fields, the herds of oxen, and the gentle turns of the sparkling, elegant River Dniester. They were nearing Halicz. It was all too wonderful. The week's grueling travel and dreary lodging places were forgotten. She glanced back at Roman, whose eyes were closing despite the relentless racket and jarring grind of the carriage wheels. He couldn't understand that she would have liked to be in the open carriage, sans bonnet, the wind slapping at her face, the scents of spring lifting her, and the sights of Southeastern Poland flying past her. The freedom was at once her nectar and ambrosia. She had been recalled to life.

As the coach came around a turn, her gaze fell upon Castle Hill and followed the winding, weedy path up to the ruins that sat atop it. Her heart caught. She had climbed the heights years before, a lifetime ago, wandering through its broken walls and dilapidated interior, stumbling among stones and splintered glass, richly imagining herself as sovereign of the land, the rabbits and red squirrels her subjects. Those days came back to her like found gold coins. Her holiday visits home in recent years had been short, affording no time for the castle, and the previous winter had been the harshest and snowiest in decades, precluding any visit for nearly a year.

Castle Hill faded into the distance. The perfume of May lilac enveloped the coach, a scent redolent of springs past and childhood. Summer was on the horizon. Shivering, she pushed from her mind the memory of how cold and damp her cell was throughout the long, dark winter behind convent stone walls and allowed herself to slip into a reverie as scenery sped by in a dazzling blur.

The carriage had only just passed through one of the villages owned by her family when her eyes lighted on something and she shouted out for the driver to stop at once. Jumping up from her seat, she called again, louder, as her brother roused himself from a sleepy trance.

"What are you doing, for God's sake?" Roman growled.

"It's the flowers—the white and the blue wildflowers—here, near the road. I want some for my room." The carriage ground to a halt and Krystyna flung open the door, ready to tumble out without benefit of the drop-down steps when her brother grasped her upper arm, holding her in place.

"Let me go, Roman!" she cried, holding to a post, disallowing herself to be directed back to safety; neither did she strain to leave the coach. Her gaze became fixed on two men—boys, really—in the field, not far from the road, farmers who had been readying the soil for planting, but who were now staring back at her. They stood, these young men, still as scarecrows, their straw hats in their hands. Had they doffed them for her? Her gaze was drawn to the dark-complexioned one, so striking was his smile and look of surprise.

The moment hung fire. She stared, as did they.

At last, Roman loosened her grip and forced her safely back into the coach, dropping her unceremoniously onto the bench, her yellow gown billowing about her like a flower in full bloom. She noticed that as he reached out to pull closed the door, he paused for a moment, his eyes narrowing, forehead crinkling in disapproval. He was taking note of the two young men.

Suddenly he slammed shut the door, gruffly urged the driver on, and slid closed the leather window shades. He sat now across from her, his mouth a flat line of seriousness, his eyes—a midnight blue—honing in on hers, the emerald green eyes over which a few of the nuns had marveled. Not Mother Abbess Teodora, however. "Reckless," she would have hissed, had she borne witness to this little episode. "You are a reckless girl, Krystyna Halicka." Well, she would not have to hear that husky, grating voice again. Not for talking during morning prayers. Not for stealing down into the cold room after bedtime for something sweet. Not for peering out the window at a group of passing cadets. She sighed in relief.

As for her brother, she could read his smug expression. He was relieved, but he was also congratulating himself on having avoided a scene that would have marred her homecoming and no doubt brought blame down on his curly blond head.

"Wildflowers, indeed," Roman intoned with the sarcasm of a school master.

Krystyna knew she should thank her brother, her elder by three years. She drew in her breath now—and extended her tongue as daintily as if she were to receive Holy Communion.

TWO

Southeastern Poland
Halicz

Aleksy Gazdecki sat at table, absently watching his mother, Jadwiga, remove dark bread from the bread-oven, a built-in necessity in every cottage, no matter how poor. Hungry as he was, even the tantalizing aroma of bread direct from the white oven—coupled with the sharp whiff of bigos that had simmered all day in a pot above the kitchen grate—could not stir him. He was lost in thought about the unusual scene that had unfolded that afternoon.

"Aleksy!"

His mother's raised voice propelled him to the present. He hadn't heard the high-pitched whine outside the door, but his mother had. Her large frame was turning toward him. "That dog of yours is not welcome here. It should be with the sheep. No beggars here—we have little enough."

"The sheep are tucked in, Mother."

"And who's to protect the hen house from that fox that took our fattest hen the other night? Tell her to be off, Aleksy." His mother turned back to the business of ladling out the bigos, the hunters' stew containing scraps of pork from their Sunday meal four days earlier. Sauerkraut, mushrooms, onions, apples, and peppercorns produced its heady scent.

Aleksy rose from the table and started toward the door, but at that moment it opened and his father and brother entered, allowing Luba to make a mad scramble for safe harbor under the table near Aleksy's chair, well hidden from his mother's eyes and swift broom.

Damian's hungry gaze was glued to the steaming bowls so that he was oblivious to the dog's movement, but Aleksy's father seldom missed the flight of a fly and didn't miss Luba's covert entry. He nodded for Aleksy to abort his mission and return to his seat. Above his broad nose and grizzled moustache and beard, his eyes glittered with blue mutiny. Aleksy retreated to his place, allowing Luba, a Polish lowland sheepdog of medium size with a long shaggy coat of white with gray patches, to place her muzzle on his boot.

No sooner had the meal commenced than Damian spoke: "We saw a strange sight today—didn't we, Aleksy?" He did not wait for a reply. "Seems Lord Halicki's daughter has come home from the convent school in Warsaw."

"Really?" Jadwiga asked.

Without further prompting—and with as much relish as for his plate of bigos—Damian launched into the telling of the incident of the girl in yellow who had nearly fallen into the ravine.

"It's been five or six years since I've seen her," his father estimated. "I imagine she's grown to be a young lady."

"It happens in a heartbeat, Borys Gazdecki," Jadwiga told her husband. "I was a mere fifteen when you set your cap for me." Her gaze shifted to Damian. "So you were taken by the sight? Remember, she's of the *szlachta* and not meant for the likes of you. "

Nor for me, either, Aleksy thought. He had been taught early on to watch his step with members of the *szlachta*—the lower nobility. He sent up a fervent prayer not to be brought into the conversation.

Pulling on a piece of bread, Damian chewed, the light blue eyes considering his mother's words. The short span of time expanded for Aleksy, who knew what was to come—Damian always talked too much—and grew uncomfortable by the moment. A heat came into his face. He held his fork but had yet to use it.

"I'm spoken for, as you know, Mother," Damian said.

"Indeed—but boys are boys and your Lilka is way over in Horodenka," Jadwiga said, "so there's nothing to keep you from ogling a yellow dress hereabouts, is there?"

"But I'm not the ogler—am I, Alek?" Damian pronounced Aleksy's diminutive in an exaggerated and accusatory tone that served to heighten the drama—and Aleksy's embarrassment. Huskier in build and two years older, he enjoyed a bit of fun at his brother's expense.

His parents' eyes moving to him now like search lanterns, Aleksy became tongue-tied. His ears burned. He wished he could give Luba a tug and make for the door with her. He looked down into his bowl. "Hold your tongue, Damian," he murmured.

"*You* were taken by her?" his mother asked.

Aleksy looked up, attempting to decipher the smile on his mother's face. Did she understand? Or was she amused? Might she be implying that he was even more of an unlikely admirer? The thought hardened like a stone inside him.

"It was his *wish*," Damian interjected, "to be taken by her." His laugh allowed for a bit of stew to fly out of his mouth.

"Enough!" Jadwiga snapped.

"Swa!" Somehow their father could make a growling sound out of a shushing word.

Damian hushed.

Borys' attention turned on Aleksy, eyes as sharp as his words. "You didn't say anything to the girl, Aleksy?"

Aleksy could only stare at his father. The mood at the table had turned, quick as lightning.

"Nothing forward? Nothing improper? Tell us, Aleksy!"

"I did not."

"I had better not hear otherwise. She is the lord's daughter, his only daughter, and if he were to hear that one of his tenants' sons had dared—"

Jadwiga interrupted, attempting to steer the conversation. "There, there, Borys. He said he did nothing improper, didn't you, Aleksy?" Directed at him, her amber-flecked blue eyes radiated warmth.

"We both removed our hats."

"You see, Borys. Tenant farmers but gentleman-like in the presence of the lord's daughter."

"Had she fallen," Aleksy blurted, "I would have caught her."

Damian laughed. "You aren't so fleet of foot, Aleksy, and we weren't standing that close to the road."

Before Aleksy could contradict Damian, their father's fist came down upon the oak table, causing a clatter of pewter plates and rattle of utensils. "You would do no such thing, Aleksy! Do you hear? If such an event occurs again, you are to keep your hat on and your eyes on the task at hand. Both of you! Is that understood?"

Damian spoke: "Father, it was just that—"

Aleksy saw his father's powerful arm move up and then come down in a wide arc, his huge hand clouting Damian across the face, nearly forcing him from his chair.

"You are to learn, Damian," his father said through clenched teeth, "and you too, Aleksy, that there are rules to live by!"

The meal was finished in icy silence. The plate of saffron wafers went untouched.

"You won't tell?" Aleksy asked again.

"I said so, didn't I?" Damian called back as he struck out for home and the mid-morning meal.

Aleksy had to trust that his brother would get the story right: that he was staying in the fields to take a nap instead of returning home for breakfast and that he had with him some cheese and leftover bread to tide him over until supper, the only other meal of the day. The bread and cheese part of the tale was true. The rest was fiction. He smiled to himself, thinking that Damian would not gamble taking another clout in his brother's stead.

Gathering up his bow and linen quiver filled with lovingly fashioned arrows made of ash, Aleksy mounted Kastor, the family horse, and directed him toward the road to Mount Halicz, his thoughts not on what he was about to see, but on what he had seen the day before—the girl in yellow. She was a sight to behold. Her blond, braided hair coruscated in the sun like a halo. He had gone to sleep thinking of her, had awakened thinking of her. It was foolish, he knew. Why, they hadn't even spoken. He knew nothing of her except that she was exceedingly beautiful, like the personification of a springtime daffodil. And she had looked at him, too—well, at *them*, him and his brother. Maybe it was Damian who drew her attention. Wasn't that more likely? His heart faltered. *Why should she be interested in me?*

Kastor meandered on, sure of footing but slow as sap from a tree in winter, for he was but a plow horse that had aided in many a spring planting. His gray hide was freckled with brown, like age spots. Aleksy's father had often commented that if the world were a fair place, Kastor would have been put to pasture by now. When they came at last to the foot of Mount Halicz, Aleksy's thoughts were still on the girl. He looked down at his hands, his arms. How dark they were, severely so in contrast to the porcelain white of her face and hands, dark, too, in contrast to the whiteness of Damian's skin, especially in winter, when the browning from the summer sun had faded. While his own skin darkened somewhat in the summer, any fading in the cold months was almost imperceptible. He thought of her eyes. What color were they? He had not been close enough to determine. They were light, no doubt, blue like Damian's—or green or gray. They were not nearly black like his; nor were they almond-shaped, like his.

The differences stung like a serpent's bite. Of course, he had always known—or so it seemed—that his parents were not his parents, that his brother was not his brother. And there had been myriad times when the differences mattered, as they did now. Still, the poison had never seemed as toxic.

Borys—Aleksy called him Borys rather than Father—had told him years ago that they had adopted him and that his parents were of a Tatar tribe of nomadic herdsmen south of Halicz, on the Budzhak steppe that stretched to the Black Sea on either side of the River Dniester. Borys had been an infantryman under Lord Halicki in a military company assigned to protect the Polish-Lithuanian Commonwealth from the incursion of Cossacks and Tatars on the southern and eastern steppes. While supplying no real details, Borys had told him that both of his parents had been killed, adding that his father had been a leader of some distinction, a detail that Aleksy clung to like the air that he breathed. One day he would insist on more facts.

When he was seven years of age, his mother had suggested to Borys that he be allowed to visit a nearby village of Tatars loyal to the Commonwealth so that he might study and learn their language and ways. The local parish priest protested, however, fearing Aleksy would take up the Muslim faith and Borys sided with him.

Despite sometimes being labeled "the Tatar" by his peers, as well as by some adults who snarled at him, Aleksy had been content to stay within the cocoon of Polishness he had come to know. Even though as the years went by and he became less fearful of venturing away from the family that had taken him in, he was afraid that doing so would hurt them. And so he had embraced Christianity and the Polish way of living.

But then there were times like these when he felt removed from every thing and everyone around him. Oh, he knew that the boundaries of class set a rich lord's daughter upon a pedestal and well out of a tenant's son's reach, but he realized now that the fortune of his birth—his coloring, visage, and Eastern ancestry—made the chasm between him and the girl in the coach impossibly wide and deep. It escaped his logic, and yet somehow he deemed it a fault of his own.

He was caught between cultures. Still, he thought, his acceptance of things Polish could be providential—should he ever have the opportunity, slim as chances were—of meeting the girl who had so entranced him.

About halfway up the mountain, he came to a clearing that jutted out over a bare field. He dismounted. His eyes fastened on the activity below. This is what he had come for, and so he put the lord's daughter from his mind. Brooding on what cannot be, he determined, would come to nothing.

The company of hussars on the field far below seemed larger today, at least fifty, Aleksy guessed. They were being mustered into formation now, their lances glinting in the sun, black and gold pennants—each with a white eagle—flying. There would be none of the usual games, it seemed, no jousting, no running at a ring whereby the lancers would attempt to wield their lances so precisely as to catch a small circlet that hung from a portable wooden framework. Today they were forming up for sober and orderly maneuvers. He wondered at their formality.

Aleksy took note of the multitude of colors below and the little mystery resolved itself. Whereas on other occasions the men, some very young and generally of modest noble birth and means, wore outer garments of a blue, often inexpensive material, today they had been joined by wealthier nobles who could afford wardrobes rich in their assortment of color and fabric. These men—in their silks and brocades and in their wolf and leopard skins or striped capes—gathered to the side of the formation to watch and deliver commentary. Aleksy caught his breath when he suddenly realized that some of these must be the Old Guard of the *Kwarciani*. They were the most elite of hussars permanently stationed at borderlands east and south of Halicz—in what was called the Wild Fields—to counter raids by Cossacks and Tatars unfriendly to the Commonwealth. Their reviews would be taken, no doubt, with great solemnity and likely nervousness by the young lancers. Every soldier would make the greatest effort to impress the legendary men. According to Szymon, Lord Halicki's stable master, in recent years the numbers of the *Kwarciani* had been reduced by massacres, and talk had it that they were eager to replenish their manpower. No doubt a few of the local novices below would be chosen to join the heroic elect.

Some place at his core went cold with jealousy. If only he were allowed to train as a hussar. He could be as good as any of them. *Better.* No one he knew was more skillful at a bow than he. He could show those hussars a thing or two about the makings of an archer—even though he had come to realize fewer and fewer of the lancers bothered to carry a bow and quiver. The majority now disparaged the art of archery in favor of pistols, relying on a pair of them, in addition to the traditional sabre and lance.

Naturally enough, there was no disdain for the lance, the very lifeblood and signature weapon of the hussar army. Aleksy smiled to himself when he thought of his own handcrafted lance.

His thoughts conjured an elation that was only momentary, for he thought now how he had had to hide away his secret project under a pile of hay in the barn—and unless he should happen to be practicing with it one day in the forest when a wayward boar might meander his way, he would never be able to use it. His spirits plummeted. And the thought of mounting a plow horse like Kastor with it instead of riding atop one of the Polish-Arabians strutting below made him burn with—what? Indignation? Embarrassment? Humiliation—yes, he decided, humiliation was the most accurate.

Inexplicably, the thought of the girl in yellow once again seized him, lifting him. Would he bargain one dream for the other? Life as a hussar in exchange for life with her? His breaths became shallow. He thought he just might risk anything to succumb to her charms. Almost at once his own bitter laugh stifled all thoughts as he grappled with the fact that he had no opportunity to become a hussar and no opportunity to even address such a young lady.

"Silence!"

The order travelled up the mountain like a clarion call. Below, the young lancers were being ordered to muster and were readying themselves for a practice drill.

At the far end of the field two columns of the sleek *Turks*—Polish-Arabian horses—began moving down the narrowly marked twin tracks, the formation so tight as to make it seem the riders' stirrups must be touching. The butts of lances held steady in their toks, boots that were strapped to the right side of the saddles. The hussars lowered the lances parallel to the horses' heads, the pointed ends aimed at the imagined navels of the enemy. Two by two, the hussars put spur to their Turks and the beasts fairly flew down the track at full gallop—as if shot out of twin cannons. Aleksy had witnessed the usual maneuvers a dozen times and they had never failed to excite him, but today the sight was many more times thrilling because, attached to the steel backplate of each hussar was the apparatus that held dual wings rising vertically, each with dozens of eagles' feathers whipping against the wind like palm branches. Szymon had told him about these soldiers' wings, but this was his first sighting of them. "They're meant to scare the life out of the enemy and the enemy's horses, my boy," he had told Aleksy. "And they do a fine job of it!" Until today—at this very formal exercise—Aleksy could only imagine the splendor of the sight. The sun was warm on his arms, but nonetheless his skin turned to gooseflesh as he watched the hussars cover some four hundred paces and come to the end of the field, each line forming an arch as they turned outward—their horses' hooves expertly kept from stepping out—then flying back to the point of departure. From above, the outline of colorful uniforms and wings formed a most perfect and beautiful figure—appearing as one magnificent, moving pair of wings. The vision took his breath away.

Szymon, a riveting storyteller despite his gravelly voice, had enflamed Aleksy with tales of the hussars and the King of Poland, detailing the military exploits of Jan Sobieski that led to his being named Grand Hetman of the Crown, the equivalent of the Commander-in-Chief of the Polish Army. Szymon had been a *pacholik*, or retainer, for Lord Halicki during the most recent wars with the Ottomans a decade before and had witnessed Sobieski's initiative to increase hussar units, a move that accounted for a string of victories that led to his being elected King Jan III Sobieski. In a speech to the Sejm, Szymon recalled, the king designated his hussars "the hardwood of the army."

Still in a trance inspired by what he had just witnessed, Aleksy goaded a nervous Kastor down the uneven mountain path. Not far from the foot of the mountain, the horse stopped suddenly and a slight shiver alerted Aleksy to possible danger and brought him up short. A movement in the brush caught his ear. The beat of his heart accelerated as reaction trumped thought. He drew reins, his eyes raking the thicket. It was then that he spied the cause. His hand seamlessly reached back for an arrow, nocked it to the bow cord and loosed the shot. The goose feather-fledged shaft flew true. He let out a little whoop as he jumped down and went to take up his prize. The arrow had pierced the plump rabbit at the neck, allowing for the body to fully serve the family's table. His mother would light up at the sight, for meat was a rarity at table. They usually had to trade or sell his fowl or game in order to afford various staples such as pots, utensils, sugar, mustard, black pepper, nutmeg, and salt ; often, too, larger game—deer, elk, or wild boar—became part of their tithes owed to Lord Halicki.

Aleksy withdrew the arrow, wrapped a strip of cloth about the wound, and tied the animal to his saddle. He remounted Kastor, thankful for the little body tremor that had alerted him to the presence of the rabbit. Before continuing down the mountain, he carefully unstrung the bow and placed it in the soft linen bow case he had fashioned. To preserve the strength and tension of the weapon, he never left it strung for more than three or four hours at a time.

He was not long on the road home when he heard horses' hooves behind coming toward him at full gallop. Turning, he sighted two riders. He directed Kastor off to the right, allowing room for them to pass.

In but moments one rider was there at his left while the other pulled up on his right, brushing up against Kastor and forcing him more to the road's center. Both had slowed to his pace. The two were young hussars that had just come from their maneuvers. The horses were breathtakingly beautiful stallions, to be outdone only by the magnificent wings of eagles' feathers fastened to the backplates of the soldiers. Even before they spoke, Aleksy was seized with a presentiment of danger. He was certain he knew the identity of these young soldiers. He did not pull up Kastor, allowing the horse to plod slowly on. He loved old Kastor and yet he burned with embarrassment to find himself hemmed in by the pair of elegant high-stepping Turks.

"Well, what have we here, lord brother?" asked the hussar on his left. Then, to Aleksy: "Who are you, boy?"

Aleksy turned to him. The soldier was no more than a year or two older than he, taller in the saddle too, and handsome. The blond curls, dusted by the afternoon's activities on the track reached the low collar of his red *żupan*. Beneath this long, sashed garment, white linen trousers were tucked into yellow leather boots. He had seen this one recently—but not in uniform.

"I said—"

"I was on the mountain watching."

"Watching? Watching us?"

"Yes, milord."

"Spying, were you?"

"No, milord."

"And what were your impressions?" This question—friendlier—came from the soldier on the right. Even though the term "lord brother" was commonly used among military comrades, Aleksy realized these two were indeed brothers. The family resemblance to the first speaker was evident, but he was younger, less confident, and not as striking in looks. His long, straight hair was more of a brown, rather than blond and, like the other, he wore neither helmet nor cap. He wore a blue *żupan* with leg wear and boots similar to his brother's.

Aleksy halted Kastor and the soldiers on either side followed suit. "I did miss the jousting and running at the ring, but—"

"But what?" the older one demanded, his gaze seeming to alight on Aleksy's bow, which protruded from the bow case.

"The wings made up for the missing games. Are the devices heavy on your back?"

"So this *watching* is a pastime of yours, is it?"

"Yes, milord." Aleksy hated using the epithet for this peacock but hoped the courtesy might take the edge off his belligerent attitude.

"Would you like to be a soldier, boy?" He smiled meanly. "A hussar?"

Aleksy's mouth tightened. *Of course,* he wanted to shout, but the impossibility held him silent. He managed a slow nod of the head.

Laughter came from both sides. "Where's your lance, then?" the elder brother asked. "Maybe it's at home being polished by your squire?"

"I do… " Aleksy thought better of his intended retort.

"You do what?"

"Nothing."

"That's a fine stallion, too," mocked the one in blue.

Aleksy turned, focusing for a moment on him. Matching his light brown locks was a wishful wisp of a moustache that he was twisting. His nose had been broken.

"Damned if it isn't," said the other. More laughter.

"He's a plow horse," Aleksy said, turning to face forward.

"And you are a plow boy, I would guess. Where is your plow, boy?—And what is this?" The soldier in red prodded the rabbit with his boot, still in its stirrup.

"A rabbit."

"Why, if we hadn't left our lances in camp we could have had some good fun playing running at the rabbit instead of running at the ring." He winked at his brother and they shared a guffaw. He then continued the interrogation. "And where did you shoot the little beast? Why, it looks quite fresh!"

"There." Aleksy motioned behind him. "On Mount Halicz."

"Indeed? And do you have hunting rights for those grounds?"

The unexpected challenge stung. "No, milord."

"Then you are in violation of the owner's rights."

Aleksy was nearly certain that, like him, the brothers hadn't a clue whether Mount Halicz even had an owner. And so he dared to question, "Who is the owner that I may plead my case?"

The soldier's face pinkened. He stammered for a moment, then asked, "How did you kill it? It looks cleanly done."

Aleksy's left hand lifted to touch the tip of the horned tip bow that protruded from the bow case slung on his right shoulder.

"Let me see it!"

At the order, an alarm went off inside him. Aleksy thought of spurring Kastor into movement but knew that was useless. They could run him down in twenty seconds flat. Heart pacing, he drew in a silent breath, removed the bow from the case, and gave it over to the soldier in red, who examined it closely.

"I'm surprised at the workmanship," he said, turning it over in his hands. "It's good. It's a bit longer than what I've used."

"Five feet, eight inches. The perfect length, I'm told." Aleksy waited for the next question.

"Who made it?"

"I did."

"You?" He harrumphed. "A plow boy?"

Aleksy's expression and the slightest nod was his response. He was nearly certain that the soldier meant to take it. Would he allow him to do so—without a fight? Where would that lead—challenging members of the *szlachta*? Especially these two. His spine tightened. Come what may, he would not stand by and see the bow he had labored over for months taken. Yew was the best wood, Szymon had told him, and for the length of yew needed, the stable master had troubled himself to send all the way to Henryków, in Southwestern Poland where the oldest yew trees grew.

"Let's have a string," the soldier ordered.

With misgivings, Aleksy withdrew the hemp cord from a little pocket in the bow case and surrendered it.

The soldier fastened the noose to the nocked horn at the lower part of the bow. He placed that end of the weapon on the toe of his boot and attempted to bend it now so that he could stretch the eye of the cord up to the nocked horn of the slightly longer top part. He surprised himself when he couldn't do it. He tried again.

Bows made of yew could be a challenge to the strongest of men and trying it while mounted made for a serious challenge. Aleksy had seen strong and sturdy men struggle with such bows.

With each new try, the soldier's once pink face reddened until it nearly matched his crimson *żupan*.

Aleksy held out his hand to retrieve his property.

The soldier shot him an angry look and tried again—to no avail. "I can't manage it atop this horse," he admitted.

"It's difficult," Aleksy said.

"You can string it?"

Taken aback by the foolish question, Aleksy nodded, resisting the boast that he could string it right there and then—atop his horse. Over the past ten years he had created ever stronger, more resilient bows, all the while strengthening his arms and adding muscle and volume to his back and shoulders.

"Give him the bow," the brother said. "We don't have time for this."

The soldier hesitated, the knuckles on the hand that held it going white. Clearly, he coveted it. Frustrated, he took either end of the bow and attempted to bend it in the opposite direction. It was evident now that he wanted to break it.

Aleksy's heart pounded. In his mind he could hear the snap that would come with the breaking of the beloved bow. "Give it back," Aleksy shouted. "Now!"

The soldier's face was contorted with exertion.

The yew held.

At last he slapped it into Aleksy's hand. "What are you? A Turk?"

So this is what it all came to, Aleksy thought as he placed the bow and cord in the bow case. "Tatar." He felt his spine stiffen.

"Ah, Tatar. You're dark like a Turk. And you have the eyes of a Mongol. What are you doing around here—spying on our maneuvers?"

"Not spying, milord. I live close by."

"In whose household?" The question was voiced as a challenge.

"That of Borys Gazdecki."

"So!—You're the one he took home from the battlefield a few years ago?"

"Seventeen—seventeen years ago."

"People said he did it because his second son died."

"We should go now," the brother cautioned. "I remember him. He was underfoot in the stable often enough before we left for our training."

The soldier in red nodded but kept his eyes on Aleksy. "Then, you're the changeling all grown up, are you? If you know what's good for you, you'll stay out of our way." He spat in the direction of Kastor.

"Come on, Roman," the other urged.

The two gave spur now and were soon in full gallop, stones and clumps of mud flying back like buckshot. Aleksy glanced at the spittle that had struck his boot but the insult did not register.

Roman, he was thinking. *Roman*, he was called. He had seen the face of that one before. And he had heard his name the other day at the roadside, spoken by the girl in the coach, the girl in yellow. These were her brothers. Worse, they were the sons of the lord who owned their tiny village, the nobleman who owned the *dwór*—manor house—called Poplar House, and who all but owned the Gazdecki family themselves.

THREE

"DAMN!" ROMAN SPAT. "THERE'S NOT one longbow here that rivals that dark devil's bow. The nocked horn at the ends doesn't compare in workmanship. And none of the bows have the same spring to them. A cholera on him!"

They stood in a small room off the manor house kitchen called the weapons room. Marek was returning to its place on the wall one of the bows he and his brother had been inspecting. "What does it matter? We've got fine pistols. The finest! And you know that to aim with a bow from atop a horse is impossible."

"Evidently not so for our new friend with the rabbit." Roman was examining a bow his father had once carried.

"Forget it. Concentrate on our chances of being called up to join the *Kwarciani*."

"Did you see the wound on that rabbit? A perfect shot through the throat! I should have just taken it."

"The rabbit?"

"Don't be an ass, Marek—the bow! What could he do to stop me? His family is one of ours."

Marek was chuckling at his little joke. "Let him have his damn bow. To hell with him—think about your lance. It's perfection! What chance does he have of ever lifting or owning a seventeen-foot lance?"

"For once you have a point. Still—"

"Yes, one with seventeen feet behind it." Marek laughed. "Come on, we'll be late to supper and the old man will bark at us. You know that we've got to get back to camp afterwards. More maneuvers tomorrow, remember?"

"We're no more than two minutes late," Marek said.

It was their mother who chastised her boys for holding up the supper.

"Oh, Zena," Konrad said, playfully intoning the diminutive for Zenobia, "you should have seen our boys out there today. They were magnificent!"

Two maids commenced with the first of the courses, mushroom soup.

Roman had no appetite. He gave only the appearance of following his father's proud detailing of the day's maneuvers at Mount Halicz, omitting the less than splendid errors made by his elder son. And to make him more disconsolate, the incident with the bow still rankled. Sitting at his side, Marek joined in on occasion. Across from the brothers, gowned in cornflower blue, sat Krystyna sipping at her soup, her eyes going from Marek to her father and back again as the descriptions unfolded.

"Have you nothing to add, Roman?" his mother asked.

"No."

His mother rested her spoon. "Nothing?"

"It went well, Mother. Perhaps we'll be selected for the *Kwarciani*, perhaps not."

"That's a devil-may-care attitude," his mother said.

"I expect there isn't much drama to maneuvers," Krystyna said, drawing all eyes to her. "No risk and therefore no excitement. Isn't that so, Romek? I should like to see a joust. I should like to see a real battle!"

"Krystyna, that's enough!" His mother pursed her lips as if tasting something sour. "I told you I have no patience with you. A battle, indeed! War is not a mazurka in a music room. You'd faint dead away."

"Not I," Krystyna said, spoon raised and green eyes riveted on her mother as she made what seemed a deliberate slurping noise.

"Well, I have a good feeling about our chances, Roman," Marek said.

"Good feelings don't fetch water, lord brother," Roman said, his annoyance with his sibling overshadowing for the moment his nagging disdain for the Tatar. "Now, if Papa had said but a word or two—" He silenced himself, wishing he could retract the half-statement.

His mother's gray-eyed gaze locked on to his father's across the length of the table. She had caught the meaning. "Why Konrad, do you mean to say you didn't identify your own sons to the Old Guard. Why, you know them all!" Using her fingers, the bone-thin woman plucked from her teeth an inedible bit from her mushroom soup, grimaced, and pushed the bowl to the side.

Lord Konrad Halicki's round, fleshy face darkened and his eyes, all blue fire, went from his wife to his son. "You dare bring this up at table, Roman. We've been through this time and again. It's your *skill* that is to get you a place with the *Kwarciani*. And Marek's. If it's meant to be." He leaned against the back of his chair, his hands interlocking against the orange brocade *żupan* that restrained his large belly. "Without proving yourselves, you don't deserve a place on the border. It's too dangerous!"

Conversation ceased for several minutes as the maids came into the dining hall with the main course, a shoulder of venison spit-roasted in the Hungarian style and dill-speckled boiled potatoes.

His mother resumed the conversation once the maids had passed through the swinging door to the kitchen. "Ah, well, I'd just as soon have you both close to home, not out wandering the Wild Fields."

Roman was about to protest and Marek, seeing his intent, dutifully chose to change the subject. "We saw that Tatar today—the one from the Gazdecki family."

His father seemed irritated. "He's not from the Gazdecki family, Marek. His name is Aleksy Gazdecki. He is one of their family."

"Still, it's odd that he should have a Polish name," Marek said. "He's Tatar, Papa."

Roman's father spoke with a stern formality. "His adoptive parents are Polish and his adoptive country is Poland. This is what matters."

"What was it that made Borys Gazdecki adopt him, Papa?" Marek asked. "After all, he's from the savage Wild Fields, isn't he?"

The count's gaze went with lightning speed down the table to his wife. Roman turned, too, and realized that she had stopped eating and had paled. Her hands were in her lap. She seemed to be deliberately avoiding her husband's glance. He had the impression that at any moment she might jump up and run from the room. An odd current of electricity ran the length of the table. Was it his imagination, or was there some secret his parents shared about the Tatar boy?

"He hardly seems a savage," Krystyna said.

The table went quiet. Krystyna drew a piece of venison into her mouth and slowly set down her fork, aware she had turned the conversation upon herself and relishing having done so.

"What?" The countess had come to attention as if from a trance.

"When did *you* see Aleksy?" the count demanded of his daughter.

Roman bit down on his lower lip, an old habit. It dawned on him now that the Tatar was one of the two boys in the field that he and Krystyna had seen from the coach. She had made the connection at once. His stomach tightened out of fear that the near mishap in the carriage was about to come to light. He was certain that the fact that he had saved his sister from falling into the ditch would be eclipsed by the precarious danger he had somehow allowed to occur.

Krystyna took several beats to finish chewing before she spoke. "Oh, I do think I remember him as a boy hereabouts before I went away to convent school. He shadowed Szymon in and around the stable and barn." The green eyes suddenly went to Roman.

Roman gave her an almost imperceptible shake of the head, imploring her to be silent on the subject. Only *he* stood to lose. Her lips formed an enigmatic smile. Her eyes fluttered. Had the silly fool failed to read his cautionary signal? What more would she say?

Her reply mollified his father, but his mother spoke now. "Ah, you have a good memory," she said, a tremble in her voice. "That was years ago." She reached for her wine goblet.

"And he's grown to be an interesting young man," Krystyna said, eyes on Roman.

She was going to tell after all, Roman realized, steeling himself to deal with his father's anger. He silently cursed. She was taking delight in this little game.

The eyelids flickered again. "Of course, I'm merely assuming."

Damn her teasing!

"He's become a good farmer and helpmate to Borys," the count said.

"But not," her mother advised, her eyes colorless stones above the rim of her goblet, "someone you're at all likely to have any sort of exchange with. He is a peasant, after all. Stay clear of him, do you hear?" She drank, leaving unsaid the fact that he is a Tatar.

"But if he is a good farmer, Mother, as Papa says, isn't he in part responsible for the rye that made this good bread? Isn't that a sort of *exchange*?" She held up a piece of black bread and bit into it.

Krystyna's questions shut down the conversation completely. Roman could only marvel at Krystyna's nerve. How had the Carmelite sisters put up with her?

Roman and Marek left for camp well after dark, leaving their wings behind in the weapons room, for maneuvers the next day were to be informal. Marek wanted to gallop and issued a challenge. Although Roman agreed to race, urging his Turk into a canter, he lost interest before achieving a gallop and found himself lagging behind, lost in thought about his chances of being chosen for the *Kwarciani*. He had made light of it at supper, but in truth he was serious as the gallows about his chances of being inducted. Unlike his brother, he had little optimism. The maneuvers had not gone so perfectly for him. He knew that at the turn-around at the end of the track his horse had stepped outside the path markings. It was just for the briefest moment and only a few steps—chances are the judges wouldn't have seen the error—but the misstep had so unnerved him that he attempted to direct the stallion with his left hand on the reins, and in so doing he lost his concentration, allowing for the lance in his right hand to shake and falter. He steadied it almost immediately, but he had violated the first rule of carrying a lance: never direct a horse with anything other than your knees at its flanks. He knew that was a blunder that could not have gone unseen.

Chances were better his younger brother would be selected. His performance had been perfection. *Damn him for his good luck if he is chosen.*

His thoughts lighted upon the Tatar and his incredible bow. How he would like that bow for himself. It would assuage a part of the humiliation he would feel if he is not chosen. He cursed himself again for not taking it. Would the boy sell it to him? Perhaps, if the devil were offered enough. Even as he called him a devil in his thoughts, there was no denying that he was indeed a handsome rogue, what with his swarthy complexion and almond-shaped black eyes. He wondered if his looks had had an effect on Krystyna. He scuttled that thought almost immediately. If her eyes had gone to anyone, surely it was to the Polish brother, the truly Polish one—and yet he could not recall the brother's face.

Roman reached the forest now and drew up. He listened for Marek's horse. Nothing. Little expecting they would be separated, they had not discussed whether they would take the shorter route through the birch forest or the longer but more clearly delineated path around it. Without giving it much thought, he goaded his horse forward with the pressure of his knees. It took just fifteen minutes to regret his decision, for the forest became black as pitch and while his horse could sense the path if they moved slowly, there was no glimmer of the moon or even a star shimmering through the high tree-top openings. Like ghostly fingers, low-hanging branches brushed against his plumed cap.

Roman was thinking of turning around at the very moment he heard the noise. His horse heard the baying of a wolf pack, too, and halted at once. The animal let out a fearful snort, and a shiver ran through horse and rider. Even at some distance, the howling of wolves curdled his blood; it always had. Being torn apart by wolves made for an unspeakably gruesome death and one not uncommon, no matter the season. He had seen the grisly remains of a three-person hunting party once and the sight remained seared in his memory.

Roman's decision came quickly. He attempted to turn and retrace their steps, but the horse stubbornly stayed in place. He abandoned the use of his knees, instead employing both reins and spurs, none too gently. The horse turned, turned again in confusion or fright or pain, and turned yet again. Roman lost his bearings.

The shrieks of the wolves heightened to a deafeningly clamorous pitch. They had found their prey. An elk? A deer? And then the incomprehensible occurred to Roman—Marek? *Had* he gone on ahead? Roman's stomach roiled. He thought he would be sick. *Chrystus Jezus, let it be that Marek took the route around the forest.* Why had his brother allowed such a distance to come between them? But he knew at once that it was *he* who had allowed it. What to do?

He listened to the sickening, echoing sounds that came from—where? Behind him? The horse whinnied, its worry borne out by its ears that were flattened back and little convulsive tremors in the hard muscle beneath its mane. "Steady, Flash," Roman murmured. The stallion snorted, slowly pumping its front legs, as if in readiness for his command.

Getting his bearings, Roman was about to spur the horse away from the sounds of the wolf pack when he heard noises—the breaking of twigs and the rush of something or someone through brush and low-hanging tree limbs. More wolves? *Holy Chrystus!*

He felt as if his heart would come through his chest. What seemed an eternity passed. The sounds grew louder, the terror more intense.

Finally, moments after he recognized the padding of horses' hooves on the soft forest floor, he heard his own name called out. "Roman!"

And then Marek was there, drawing close, their mounts snout to snout, his brother's face barely visible in the dark. "It's you, Mareczek—thank God!"

"Were you so frightened?" Marek asked. "Ha! You must have been! You never use my diminutive anymore."

Before Roman could reply, the wolves' cries rose to a shrill crescendo, drawing Marek up short. "God's bones!" he hissed.

"Better His than ours—let's get the devil out of here!"

Marek paused for a moment, mesmerized and listening. "They're feasting."

"And no doubt battling each other for the best pieces. Let's go!" Roman said, certain that his younger brother was gripped by the same fear—that it was no animal being torn to pieces.

"God's bones!" Marek repeated, shivering at the sounds. "I couldn't wish that on the worst Turk in Constantinople. Well, perhaps on the Sultan."

"Oh, I could think of a Tatar I would wish it upon. If I believed in wishes."

FOUR

"WHAT DO YOU THINK OF it, Idzi?"

Aleksy bent to retrieve from the straw-strewn surface of the barn the lance he had created. He turned the unwieldly weapon over in his hands, admiring it anew. Years before, he had made friends with Lord Halicki's old stable master, Szymon, under whose tutelage he had become an expert in woodcraft, fashioning his own yew bows and ash arrows. Szymon had pronounced him an excellent bowyer and one magical day the year previous had allowed him to examine an old lance once used by the count. Aleksy took the measurements of the lance and carefully replicated it from a seventeen-foot length of fir-wood cut in halves and hollowed out as far as the rounded handguard at the lower end, thus reducing its weight. The shorter section managed by the lancer was left solid wood for leverage. The town blacksmith that provided Aleksy's steel arrow points forged the lance point.

"It's a beauty, Aleksy. How did you manage to fasten the two pieces together after you hollowed out the wood?"

"Just by chance. One day Borys made an off-hand comment about a Mongolian formula using a tar made from birch bark. I tried it and it worked just fine, as you can see."

"Why is it you call your father by his Christian name?"

"He's always had me call him *Borys*. I guess it's odd to most folks."

"You don't call your mother *Jadwiga*, do you?"

"God help me if I did."

"So what now?" Idzi asked. "About the lance."

Aleksy interpreted the question as, *You've created this thing—now, what's the likelihood of its doing you any good?* He ignored it, posing one of his own. "Can you lift it?"

"Who the hell do you think moved it to this side of the barn so that the cow or Kastor wouldn't trample it? Just because it's four times longer than I am tall doesn't mean I'm a weakling, my friend."

"Indeed," Aleksy said as he gently returned the lance to its place of safety. "Why then, you could be of value to the army." He stood up, unable to contain a mischievous smile, and turned to Idzi. "You could run at the horsed enemy with the lance and he wouldn't see you coming until you jabbed him in the toe from below."

"Or—if he's on foot—his codpiece," Idzi said, his smile wide. "You're a bastard, you are."

The two fell to laughing now as they sat cross-legged in the straw, the lantern between them, the muted thrum of rain on the thatched roof. Aleksy felt as if he could make a bit of fun out of Idzi's dwarfism, such was their friendship. And Idzi took it in stride and could return in kind with Tatar jibes. The barn was his home, along with the family horse, cow, and a variety of farm animals. He had come to the family seven years before, at the age of ten. He showed up one day, an orphan looking for work and he stayed on to take care of the barn, hen house, pigsty and the like, worming his way into the hearts of everyone, especially Aleksy's, with the exclusion of Aleksy's mother, who insisted on calling him by his full Christian name, *Egidiusz.* She said she held nothing against the lad who refused to grow, but she never invited him into the house unless it was to deliver eggs, a slaughtered chicken, or on some other errand. Idzi had been nearly as tall as Aleksy when he had come to the farm, but now he was no taller than the height of Aleksy's waist. He had a large head offset by a mass of sandy hair, a keen mind, and unapologetic sky-blue eyes. Aleksy thought him a handsome little man, one who minded his manners in front of Borys and Jadwiga, and yet when Aleksy asked his parents if his friend could partake of a Sunday supper the previous winter, Borys went silent in deference to Jadwiga's glowering expression and adamant refusal. Aleksy wondered sometimes why *he* had been adopted and accepted into their home as son and brother to Damian while Idzi—of Polish blood—was relegated to servant status with lodging in the barn.

For food, Idzi fended for himself, but Aleksy often brought him leftovers in the night—a bit of meatless stew and bread this night—when they would converse while whittling out of linden wood the figures of animals or people. Although Aleksy loved his brother Damian, he found a deeper connection to Idzi.

"Aleksy..." Idzi said tentatively, his eyes on his own sculpture of a dog meant to be Luba, who lay sprawled on her side close by, a fluffy mound of white and gray.

Aleksy grunted.

"You've carved enough soldiers to make your own army should you somehow bring them to life."

"And to life-size."

"Which means taller than me, I'll wager. You're working on an animal now, yes? Is it a goat?"

"Hah! It's not a goat, fool. Soldiers have to ride, yes?"

"A horse, then. And when do *you* plan to ride?"

Aleksy looked up and even in the lantern light could see the sharpness of Idzi's gaze. He shrugged and felt his face heating.

"You know what I mean, Aleksy. You now have your lance. When do you make your move? Ever since I've known you, you've had soldiering on your mind. So, when?"

"I don't know. It was easy to think about, easy to talk about, but not so easy to do."

"Why?"

"You know very well. Who will take me? Yes, I have a lance and I'm a damn good archer, too! But I have no horse, for God's sake. And I've never even ridden a good horse, a really good one. A Polish-Arabian, a "Turk," like the mounts I saw the Halicki brothers with, damn them."

"Still, someone should give you a try."

"Why should they? I hear that a Turk costs over one hundred and twenty złotys." Aleksy fell silent for several minutes. "I should get back to the cottage. Can't afford to be tired in the field."

"Unless you find a nice shady spot."

"Shady spots don't get the weeds pulled or baby plants set upright after tonight's rain."

"Aleksy, is there something else?" Idzi's eyes were on him again. "To keep you here?"

"Like what?"

"Damian says you were taken by that girl—the one in the carriage."

Aleksy's mouth fell open. "Damian said what?"

Idzi just stared, searching, a dormant smile playing at the corners of his mouth.

"Curse my brother! His mouth runs like a springtime mountain brook." Why should Damian meddle so? First with his parents and now with Idzi. He sighed. "Damn! She's a noble's daughter, Idzi! Do you take me for an idiot? I'm not to even talk to her. And yet—*why* should it make such a difference?"

"I don't know, but it does and it's something you can't change, like my size. The girl's high-born and you're not. They say, 'Those born for the cap should not crave the crown'."

The answer was not to Aleksy's liking. He said nothing.

"So if nothing's holding you here," Idzi said, "why don't you go—take a stab at soldiering?"

"Maybe I will. Are you so anxious to see me off and away?"

"It's just that you've spoken of nothing else. I thought it was in your blood. And now the lance is finished and it is a beauty. Why, I'd go with you myself if I thought—well, I'm not an idiot, either. Just a dwarf."

Aleksy found no suitable reply. *And maybe I am just a dreamer*, he thought. Standing, he tossed his sculpture into the corner and gave the facsimile of a sleepy stretch. "I'll see you tomorrow. You should sleep, too. That rooster will have you up before you know it."

Idzi laughed. "The cock is the village clock, no?"

"Heard you had a little clash with the Masters Halicki," Szymon said within moments of opening the tall doors of the huge Halicki stable so that Aleksy could enter with his horse and dog. His milky blue eyes twinkled above a wildly full and grizzled beard.

After Sunday Mass at the little village church, Aleksy often visited Count Halicki's stable master at Poplar House. Their initial relationship had been struck years before when Borys had business at the manor house and Aleksy had trailed along and been amused by Szymon in the stable. Their friendship was truly sealed when he learned that Szymon had been held captive for five years by Tatars not friendly to the Commonwealth. Here was a man—Polish to the bone—who could tell him something about the

Tatar people to the east, Aleksy's people, something more that the cryptic Borys had told him. Aleksy learned that his ancestors originated in the extreme climate of Mongolia's Gobi Desert. After centuries of migrations and subjugations, the Tatars came to form a piece of what was called the Golden Horde, one that controlled the Eurasian Steppe. From that tapestry came the Budzhak Tatars and a particular tribe Borys had told him about—that of his parents—who tended cattle and roamed the land south of Halicz, on the plain that followed the River Dniester toward the Black Sea.

Szymon's statement about the Halicki brothers brought Aleksy up short. "The one had a mind to steal my bow.—Who told you?"

"That sounds more like Roman, I can tell you. Puffs like a toad. The trick is to treat him like a tadpole. He was a regular little miscreant as a child."

"He hasn't changed."

Szymon laughed. "Ah, Alek," he said, using the diminutive, "they seldom do. Once a slyboots, always a slyboots. His brother Marek told me about seeing you. I guess they were surprised to see you almost all grown."

"Almost?" Aleksy feigned an affront. "Evidently not surprised in a good way."

"What would you have done had he taken it?"

"I would have taken it back and probably broken it over his head." Later, in bed that night, Aleksy would wonder whether his own statement wasn't a bit of bluster.

"Ah, then it's best ended as it did. Don't be so impulsive, my boy. Had he absconded with it, we could have pleaded your case to the count."

"And what would his father do?"

"Hopefully the right thing, Alek."

Aleksy made a grunting sound. "Maybe."

"I've thought of a few new expressions for you today. Put Kastor over in the stall and come sit."

Aleksy did as he was told, then passed the count's horses, lingering for several moments at the stalls of the Halicki brothers' Polish-Arabians, stroking their fine manes.

"Some beauties, huh?" Szymon said.

"I've never seen the like."

"The boys were well rewarded for their successful military training.

Their father spent some money on that horseflesh, I can tell you. They had better appreciate them. Now, hurry, boy!" Something in his throaty tone made Aleksy think Szymon harbored a bit of jealousy for the advantages of the brothers' births, as well as for their youth.

The two sat at a small rough-hewn table. Luba settled into a mound of hay. "How did you get away—when you were a captive?" Aleksy asked.

"Lord Halicki missed my expertise as a retainer in our fighting years, I guess," Szymon said, laughing. "He paid the ransom."

"Ransom?"

"Yes, my boy. It goes that way often enough. If an enemy thinks you might have value, they'll seek a reward for your return. The bartering took years, but here I am. Now, do you wish to learn or not?"

Aleksy's interest in his own personal history had led to Szymon's teaching him Tatar customs and phrases. The phrases, in turn, had led to Aleksy's learning how to write the phrases. Szymon, having studied to become a priest years before, had an education more advanced than the average stable master. He had not blinked two years earlier when Aleksy told him he could neither read nor write. What peasant could? "Well, I shall teach you what I know," he said, "not that it's so much, mind you, but it will do. And I will teach you the Tataric *and* the Polish."

And in that way the tutorials had begun. Aleksy dared not tell his family he was learning to read and write. He could imagine no positive reaction and suspected Damian would be jealous. He had, however, trusted Idzi with the secret.

Two hours passed with Szymon's quizzing Aleksy on phrases he had already learned. After acquitting himself well in speaking the phrases in Polish and then Tataric, Aleksy used a stick to spell out the phrases in the dirt floor of the stable. Szymon could teach only the written Polish. He had not mastered the written Tataric.

Today Szymon taught several new sayings. The one he saved for last played tricks with Aleksy's mind: "At home with their friends, all men are soldiers."

Aleksy thought about its meaning as he repeated it back in Polish, then in Tataric. Then came the Polish writing in the dirt, all the while his mind working. Was that phrase alluding to bravado? *Is my dream nothing more than bravado?*

Evidently Szymon's mind was working in the same direction. "Have you thought more about your joining the colors, my boy?"

Aleksy cursed his own tongue. Why had he told people about his foolishness? Why? Now they had expectations of him. First Idzi—and now Szymon. He was filled with shame. "Soldiering? I have no horse."

"Not all soldiers have horses."

"A foot soldier? Never!"

"The infantry is nothing to be ashamed of. And, who knows, maybe the King's Army will supply you with a mount once you show them your fine bow and fine lance. I had some doing in that, you know, making of you a fine bowyer and allowing you to copy Count Halicki's lance."

Luba's head came up from the straw at that moment and she began to growl. Aleksy and Szymon turned toward the door that led to the path up to the house. There stood Szymon's apprentice, Gusztáf, eyeing them peculiarly. Szymon stood and took two steps forward so as to make the soldier saying in the dirt illegible. To keep the lessons secret, they were conducted only on Sundays because Gusztáf went home to the village of Horodenka for the day.

"You're back early," Szymon said.

Gusztáf nodded, his eyes shifting from Szymon to Aleksy and back again.

For a few awkward moments nothing more than the shuffling of a horse in its stall could be heard.

"Gusztáf," Szymon said, managing a false smile, "will you be a good boy and take the bucket there and fetch some water?"

Blond, with hazel eyes above a sharp nose, Gusztáf was a year younger than Aleksy and not one to hide his emotion of the moment. Today it was suspicion. He resentfully picked up the bucket and made his exit.

"What did he hear?" Aleksy asked, scrambling to his feet.

"I don't know."

"About the soldiering?" Aleksy's heart was racing. "About Lord Halicki's lance?"

"Not to worry, my boy. You know, I did try to teach him to read a bit. He wasn't interested. Too bad for him."

"But if he heard—if the count should find out—or my father!"

"I can handle the likes of Gusztáf. He's a homely lad and not so very bright, but I'll make a decent groom out of him in the long run."

"He doesn't like me. He never has."

"Don't take it personal. Now, let me teach you a new phrase, yes? *Scratch a Tatar and you'll find a Russian.*"

Aleksy grasped his meaning. "So Gusztáf hates Russians? Most Poles do!"

"No doubt." Szymon spoke quickly. "And many connect Tatars with Eastern people and with Russia. Enough of that—now listen to me closely if you wish to avoid the infantry. Even without a horse, you can leave Halicz with riding skills."

"On what—Kastor? You're joking!"

Szymon took Aleksy by the shoulders, the pale yet keen eyes on him. "I said, listen to me, boy, so that you might one day be a man! Milord and the countess are on their way to Warsaw to celebrate the wedding of someone or other related to his lordship's friend, General Lubomirski. Roman and Marek were not about to sit in a carriage for days, so they went by horseback. I suspect they want to get to the capital early and have a bit of fun. Those family things go on for days, not that you or I would know, but they do! And then there's the travel time. They will be gone for at least the next several Sundays. You are to come earlier than usual on those days. Gusztáf sets off for Horodenka before dawn, so come right after."

"I have Mass—"

"God will forgive you for a few Sundays. Make up some excuse for your parents. The Almighty will forgive you that, too."

"But—why?"

"Listen, Alek, and I'll tell you why! You come at dawn and I'll let you ride one of the boys' Turks."

Aleksy had to shake his head. Was he understanding this clearly? His heart beat fast. He peered into the dark—toward the horses' stalls. "Why didn't they take them?"

"And waste prize horseflesh on a wild ride, not to mention trusting someone to care for them in Warsaw? No, they took a couple of hearty but ordinary stallions. They're impatient, too, especially Roman, so they'll trade them off a couple of times at outposts along the way." Szymon gave a conspiratorial wink. "Now, on those Sundays I can teach you plenty about horsemanship."

Aleksy had more questions, more protestations, but at that moment the door behind him creaked open. Luba started to growl again. Gusztáf entered with the water.

Sunday came at last. The night before, Aleksy told his parents he was to help out old Szymon and that he would attend early morning Mass at a church in Halicz rather than the village chapel. Regret for lying and missing Mass was eclipsed by the sheer excitement of riding a Polish-Arabian. He scarcely slept. This was the immediate and reachable goal. The other—soldiering—remained so elusive a thing for a peasant and non-Pole that its achievement seemed unfathomable.

Aleksy had always approached the Halicki *dwór* from the rear because that gave closest access from his village and because his business had always been with Szymon, but today—well before dawn—he took the road leading up to the house, walking Kastor down the long, poplar-lined drive so that he would not call attention to his arrival. The columnar shape of the poplars offered little concealment for a man and horse, so as he neared the house he took up a position behind a belt of tall bushes. From here he could see the comings and goings of the household. He would be able to witness the leave-taking of the groom for his family cottage.

Aleksy knew Poplar House and its outbuildings from its back end, but now he studied the building, taking in the size and the grandeur of the façade. He had seen little of the Commonwealth and so to his mind this could have been the residence of one of its mighty magnates, those wealthy-beyond-measure nobles who numbered no more than perhaps forty in the nation. Rather, this was the home of the Halickis, a *szlachta* family. There were estimated to be many hundreds of these lower nobility families. And then, of course, there were the multitudes of the peasantry, folks like his family who were all but tied to the land.

Day was breaking gray but the starkly beautiful white of the three-storied *dwór* fairly glowed in the gloom. Huge windows fronted the center of the building on the ground and first floors, slightly smaller ones gracing the two wings running to the left and to the right. Aleksy's gaze was drawn at once to the huge columned portico at the center—Polish symbol of hospitality—then taken up to the balcony on the roof above it and the tall mullioned French doors that provided access. Above the second level, he took in the attic level, the whiteness giving way to the dark evergreen shingles of the deeply sloping roof. Here the windows were like half-coins beautifully incised into the roof. Almost like Eastern eyes peering out, he thought. *Like my eyes.*

Amber candlelight glowed from one of the eye-windows at the far right. A servant getting dressed to start the day?

Aleksy was jarred from his conjecture when he heard a horse clip-clopping along the path from the rear of the manor house. He drew back and stroked Kastor's forehead to keep him quiet. The rider urged his horse into a canter as soon as he came to the drive fronting the estate. They flew past and by the time they came to the main road they were at a gallop—and gone. Gusztáf was on his way home, to Horodenka.

Aleksy glanced up. The window had gone dark. "Come on, Kastor," he said, remounting and proceeding to the stable.

"You may choose between the two," Szymon said, ushering him to the stalls of the two Polish-Arabians. "On second thought, I would recommend Miracle, Marek's Turk."

"Why?"

"Roman's mount is more spirited, like him. Perhaps next Sunday for that one, yes?"

"Who am I to quibble?" Aleksy held his breath as Szymon led Miracle from the stable. He had had little opportunity to observe the Turk when the Halicki brothers accosted him so that only now was a good appraisal possible. The chestnut coat shimmered in the early morning light. The animal's dark, observant eyes regarded Aleksy beneath a forelock that was fully black, as was his mane and tail. Aleksy went to his side, noticing now that the legs beneath the knee were dark, too, but the fetlocks were white as milk. In no time he was fully mounted, aware of the strength of horseflesh under him and experiencing a thrill each time Miracle responded to his cue.

For several hours they worked in a corral far from the house and away from the eyes of house servants. Szymon had cut markings into the dirt similar to the ones Aleksy had observed at Mount Halicz. The horse had been schooled well and knew the drill, so it was just Aleksy doing the learning, all the while imagining a lance in his hand.

"I have things to tend to," Szymon said at noon.

"I see," Aleksy said from atop Miracle. Assuming they were done for the day, he started to dismount.

"Stay right where you are, young Alek!"

"But, why—"

"I don't expect either you or Miracle is tired out. You've got to get to know him—and him you. Go out on the road and give yourselves a workout."

Aleksy inhaled deeply. "Truly?"

"I said so, no? Take the afternoon."

"But—but what if someone sees us? Polish-Arabians are not common around here. They'll recognize him and you'll be in trouble with his lordship."

"Ah, well, take back roads then. In fact," he said, pulling at his salt and pepper beard, "take that road up to the castle ruins. There are some long stretches along the way. No one's likely to be there. Folks think the place is haunted."

Aleksy didn't have to be convinced.

"And next Sunday—oh, you see that contraption on the right side of the saddle?" Szymon was pointing to a rounded leather holder attached to the saddle. "It's called a tok. It's a Hungarian word. Do you know what it's for?"

Aleksy nodded. He had seen it used often enough. "The butt of the lance."

"Damn right. Now, next Sunday I want you to bring your lance. Can you manage that?" Without waiting for an answer, Szymon swatted the hind of Miracle and he took off at once, as if he were anxious for the outing.

Aleksy had no opportunity to respond. He would have been speechless anyway. What could Szymon mean—other than it was his intention to teach him the use of the lance atop one of the Polish-Arabians? The horse moved easily, transitioning quickly into a full gallop, and a kind of joy Aleksy had never known pumped through him.

The horse was aptly named.

"No water, my friend." Aleksy stood next to Miracle, his hand stroking the high forehead. He had given the stallion a good workout and deeply regretted not having taken a waterskin for himself and, more especially, for the horse.

But this outing had been anything but planned. They stood in the bailey of the castle, having carefully crossed the broken-down drawbridge, its chains long in disuse from time and rust. "We'll go back soon," he promised his charge. But for now he wanted to explore the ruins; he had not been here for several years. While some people thought it haunted, Aleksy thought it the stuff of dreams. He looked about him at the stone and timber ruins of gatehouses, kitchens, stables. He searched for a post to tie up the horse, and finding nothing suitable, placed the reins under a large stone.

He then made his way to the castle keep which rose up from a raised shelf of land near the rear wall. Standing just inside the four-level structure, he found the stairs in fairly good condition. With a glance out at the patiently waiting horse, he took the stairs, floor by floor, carefully stepping over boards, bricks, and shards of glass that lay strewn about. The remnants of the timbered roof had given way years before so that on the fourth level the sun streamed in upon him. He walked to what had been a crenelle, a narrow window slit meant for archers—like himself, he dared to think—but time had rendered it a huge gaping hole with no lintel.

He looked down at the bailey, not seeing the lone horse nibbling on some sweet grass but imagining instead what this castle had been like in its days of use when men patrolled the gatehouses, blacksmiths worked in their smithy, grooms in the wide stables, servants came and went on errands, some toiling in the kitchens, the huge fireplaces lighted and the scent of roasted meat in the air. And in the rooms of the keep below him the members of the noble family entertaining and being entertained. Time yielded to his imagination.

Absently, he noticed that Miracle's head had come up, his ears on alert. The imaginings fell away. Even at this distance Aleksy could see the horse grow tense. His head was moving from side to side, one ear flattened back. What was it? A snake there in the overgrown brown grasses of the keep? It very well could be. Sweet Jezus—and here he was four floors up in a tumbling down structure.

He had only just turned to make for the stairs when he heard the neighing of a horse. He pivoted back to the window. Miracle was growing restless, his right front leg pawing at the dry ground.

The neighing came again and Aleksy's worst fear was realized: it was the neighing of another horse, somewhere outside the front of the castle.

There was no time to theorize who it might be. Aleksy dumbly stared as Miracle pulled at his reins in an effort to escape. The stone was not so heavy it would restrain a horse that had the will to pull free. Miracle—this magnificent treasure of one of the young Halicki lords that Szymon had placed in his custody—would be gone before Aleksy could pick his way down four rubble-filled floors.

Heart pounding, he went for the stairs. His descent to the third level was unimpaired, but on the second level the edge of a stair gave way and he fell. He picked himself up and ran faster, fearful first for the horse and then somehow certain that his life was about to change.

FIVE

When Aleksy came out from the castle keep into the bailey, he saw that Miracle—valuable beyond measure and not his to lose—was gone. "Dog's blood!" he cursed. He felt suddenly dizzy. His temples began to throb. "Miracle!" he called, running for the bailey gateway, thinking how, unguided, the horse could easily have a leg crash through the rotten bridge over the dry moat. A broken leg was a death sentence. Or—was someone attempting to make away with a valuable bit of horseflesh?

"Miracle!" he called again even as he slipped on loose gravel and stumbled, his hands breaking the fall. He ignored the pain in his right wrist as he started to push himself up from the ground, but in mid-effort a commotion in front of him drew his attention.

Two horses were now entering the bailey. The rider on the lead horse held the reins to Miracle, who stepped obediently to the side.

Aleksy opened his mouth but no words came forth. He stared.

"You are a bit careless with an animal that does not belong to you."

Her voice—if not her words—was as he had imagined. Sweet as honey. And yet projecting the authority and, yes, haughtiness of the nobility.

She drew her horse up to within a few feet. He managed to stand now, his face burning with humiliation. And yet, his heart raced at what he saw. Today the girl in yellow wore a brown trousered riding outfit that looked to be soft as satin. Beneath a fur-trimmed riding cap, her hair was plaited into twin braids that spilled down her back. He noticed now how the sunlight brought out a reddish cast to her blond hair. It was a color his mother had called strawberry blond.

"Well, don't you have a tongue? Can't you speak, boy?"

Were these words, still honeyed in sound, meant to sting in their meaning? Aleksy dug for a reply. Should he offer an excuse or beg forgiveness? Both? Should he introduce himself, knowing how improper that would be considered. Improper on two counts: he was not of the *szlachta*—the minor nobility—and a proper introduction called for a third party.

"Perhaps you are dumb," she said. "Are you?"

"No, milady."

"Are you hurt, then?"

He shook his head.

"Ah, good!" She had ridden astride the horse, but now one leg came over the side. She meant to dismount and held her hand out to Aleksy.

For a moment Aleksy could not fathom what was happening and he stood rooted to the ground. "Come along, now," she urged. "What kind of groom are you?"

So that was it. She thought he was the family's groom. He moved forward, reached up, took her proffered hand, little calculating how far off the ground she was—and it wasn't until she was falling forward that he realized she meant for him to catch her.

The dexterity of an archer surfaced now as both hands moved to the softness above her hips, taking hold, swinging her in a half circle, and depositing her safely on the ground. He found himself staring down into her eyes. His question as to their color was answered in an instant. They were like a pasture in a rain-heavy June—the greenest he had ever seen.

"I am quite safe now, boy," she said. "You may unhand me."

"What?—Oh, yes, of course!" He felt a great rush of heat rise to his face. Was she offended by his forwardness? Or amused? He averted his eyes and his hands fell to his sides as he backed away a couple of paces. Excitement coursed through him at the sight—and touch—of her, and yet her use of the term *boy* roused irritation. Oh, he was used to Szymon using that appellation; he had done so for years. But this—her use of it—was something different.

She watched him for a moment and gave a little indecipherable laugh. She adjusted her belt to which a sheathed knife was attached.

What should he say? Did this unexpected situation release him—them—from the usual strict propriety expected of her class regarding first meetings?

"I am not a groom," he began.

"Then who are you?"

An opening: "Aleksy Gazdecki."

"From the little village at the border of our estate?"

"Yes."

"I knew that."

He blinked. Did she recall seeing him the day she had nearly fallen from the carriage? "I did not take Miracle without permission."

"Indeed." She appeared amused. "Do you suppose you can find something to which you can tie the reins of the horses?"

"I'll take them into that stable."

"Do that, will you? You did bring water?"

"No, milady."

"You wouldn't make a very good groom, would you?" Another laugh. She reached up and took down a waterskin from her saddle. She uncorked it and took a drink.

"If you cup both of your hands, I'll pour so the horses can drink, Miracle first, then Flash."

Absently, Aleksy did as instructed. He forgot his own thirst and turned to stare at her horse—or rather, Roman's stallion. Until this moment he had not even realized that she had taken the Turk that, according to Szymon, was too spirited for him to take today. The animal was even more beautiful than Miracle. He was black as midnight, but for his mane and legs below the knees, which were swan-white. Also predominantly white, the tale had a streak of black running through it that made for a blurring effect as it swept back and forth.

Aleksy's gaze came back to girl and he could see by her slight smirk that she had read the surprise on his face. Her expression, in return, seemed to say, *Yes, I can manage Flash quite well.*

When the horses had drunk, their long, rough tongues tickling Aleksy's palms, the girl said, "You must be thirsty, too, yes?"

The question came as if it were an afterthought but to look into her eyes made him wonder. He nodded. She handed him the waterskin and he held it up over him, drinking from the opening without his lips touching it. He spilled but a few drops. "What am I to call you?" Aleksy asked as he handed her the waterskin. If this was an improper moment for an introduction, so be it. "Lady—"

"Krystyna."

"Lady Krystyna," he said, wishing to tell her it was a lovely name but words failed. He performed a little unpracticed bow.

She laughed, a bright, tinkling sort of laugh. What did it mean?

He felt very foolish.

Her head was turning this way and that as she assessed the castle, the braids following. "It's been years since I've been here. I was so eager to come back. Come, I want to show you the keep."

Aleksy wasn't about to tell her he had just seen it, and that he, too, had been to Castle Hill years before. As she bounded forward, he followed, his mind in ferment.

They walked through the doorless ground floor entrance. "This was the reception room of those long-ago days," Krystyna said. "I would hide here and my brothers would try to find me. I was often able to elude them completely. Oh, look, I got myself into that fireplace once and stayed there, listening to them call out. 'Krysia!' they called. 'Krysia!' That's what they called me then. It got so very dark outside and we had been overdue at home for ever so long. I gave them quite a scare, I can tell you. How I enjoyed that!"

"I don't think you would fit inside anymore," he said.

Her head whipped around in his direction and the gaze of green fire said it all.

Jezus Chrystus, he said to himself. *Now I've done it.* But he had no words to explain, no breath to speak.

Krystyna regarded him as if with curiosity and let the moment pass. She removed her cap and tossed it onto the base of the hearth. With both hands, she reached back and pulled her long braids forward so that they graced her shoulders and fell to well below her breasts. She glanced at him again, her gaze no longer sharp. "Let's go upstairs!"

Aleksy's breath came back and he followed.

Krystyna had a story for every level, sometimes two. The structure rang and rebounded with her animated and mellifluous voice and Aleksy thrilled to it. He wished the castle possessed a hundred floors.

They came to the top level. "Oh, look!" Krystyna cried, pointing to a great piece of a stone cornice that had fallen in through the collapsed roof. "I do remember this!"

Aleksy came to where she stood and studied the words that had been chiseled on the cornice.

"Do you know what it says?"

It was the question Aleksy dreaded. He stared at the words, temple throbbing.

"Oh!" she said. "You don't read, do you?"

Aleksy stiffened. "I *do* read."

"Really?" Her eyes went wide. "Ah, but you don't read Polish, do you? You must read Tataric, then? You are a Tatar, yes?"

Even though he could detect no meanness in her tone, their differences were now spoken aloud. Had he for a short time forgotten?—Had she?

"I cannot read Tataric," he said, his eyes fastened to the cornice. "I can read Polish—a little." He stared at the chiseled stone letters. "Kubacki is the name of the clan," he said, attempting to sound more certain than he felt.

"It is," Krystyna said. "And the other words?"

Had he impressed her? Another word was familiar and he racked his brain until he recalled the saying Szymon had made him learn. "Hearth," he said, haltingly.

"Yes," Krystyna said, waiting for more.

Overcome with embarrassment and hoping to divert her from the rest of the wording, Aleksy blurted, "I know a saying with *hearth* in it."

"You do?"

Not only was he certain she saw through his attempt to stall for time, but he was now afraid how she would react toward a generalization about women. Would she take offense? He hesitated. He could tend the land, ride a spirited horse, shape perfect lances, bows, and arrows from wood, and yet here—with her—he felt a helpless, hapless fool.

She stepped around so that she faced him. "Well? Out with it!"

"The saying goes, 'When two women rule a hearth, the sparks fly and the thatch burns'." He drew in a breath, waiting for—and fearing—her reaction.

Krystyna drew her head back a moment taking in the meaning. Had he offended her? The moment hung fire.

Suddenly, her hands flew to her cheeks, the fingertips pointing north to eyes that sparkled and danced. She laughed heartedly. "I lived in convent school for five years, do you know?" she asked, catching her breath. "And I can vouch that the thatch was always burning!"

Aleksy joined in the laughter, more in amazement that he had made her laugh!

"And look there!" she cried, pointing skyward. "No roof to this hearth!"

He had only just started a reprise of laughter when she suddenly stopped and turned again to the cornice.

"The word you're missing is 'heart.' It reads: *Kubacki Hearth and Heart*, rather nice, wouldn't you say? Now, let's go back down."

She had left him no opportunity to respond. He trailed her. It seemed her feet moved as quickly as her mind.

Once again on the ground level, Krystyna ran toward the stone base of the hearth and sat. "I used to sit here imagining that this was *my* castle. Come forward, boy, you are to be my visitor. I shall receive you."

Aleksy smiled, ready to play the game, and moved toward her.

"Ah, but you are a Tatar—I forgot."

He halted at once.

"My fortress has repelled Tatars for hundreds of years! How shall it be, then?" The question was not meant to be answered. She spoke as if thinking aloud. Her face brightened. "You must be here to call for terms of peace, yes?—Or—perhaps you can portray a captive? A slave, would you mind that so much?"

Stunned, Aleksy felt some intrinsic part of him falling away, falling to dust, the magic of ruined castles gone. His temple pulsed with humiliation and anger. In a momentary flash, he recalled fishing at the river one particular morning when he was about eight and three boys from another village chased him away, calling him names and throwing stones. He went home empty handed, without the two prize fish he had caught or his fishing pole. He was so put to shame that he told no one. Similar incidents occurred with regularity, but he never spoke of them.

"Well?" Krystyna asked, retrieving her cap and stroking its fur trim. "This could be my crown."

He found himself staring at her. Was her barb—camouflaged by a smile—any better than those who hurled outright insults?

After she adjusted her cap, her eyes fell on him. "Yes? You don't wish to play?"

Had she no clue that her insult had cut him to the quick? Aleksy turned and made for the door. He headed for the stable. He could hear her footfalls behind him. Was it his imagination—or did she softly call his name? Did she mean to apologize?

"I should leave first," she said crisply, following him into the stable. "Besides I shall need a boost."

No apology. She was of the nobility and could say what she liked.

Aleksy readied the horses and coupled his hands together, providing the lift. He would remember that her boots were of the finest, softest russet suede and that she was light as an angel, but he neither spoke nor looked at her. Within him hurt and anger collided with attraction, rendering paralysis.

"Give me fifteen minutes' start," she said, urging Flash to move. "It's best that way."

He knew, of course, that they could not be seen together. By the time he had mounted Miracle, he saw that she had halted her horse at the gateway. She turned her head to her right shoulder, and in her honeyed voice said, "Oh, boy—you can ride Flash next Sunday. I'll take Miracle."

Aleksy could only stare after her, stare and wait the fifteen minutes, pondering what she had meant.

Krystyna expertly dismounted and threw open the stable door. "I've brought Flash," she announced.

Szymon appeared. "I see," he said, approaching the horse. His eyes narrowed as he lifted one hand to stroke the shimmering black flank. "He's worked up a good lather. You've had him at a good gallop."

"I have, yes."

"I did tell you, Lady Krystyna, that he is a powerful animal."

"I can handle him."

"Speed can be a dangerous thing, milady, to you and to Flash."

"You need not worry, Szymon.—Oh, I told the Tatar boy he could ride Flash next Sunday."

The stable master's mouth fell agape. "You saw Aleksy, milady?"

"I did—and a good thing, too! You sent them off without a drop of water. I trust you'll not do that again." Krystyna turned and started toward the house.

"You talked—the two of you?"

Krystyna pivoted to face Szymon. "Yes, we talked. Isn't that what people do?"

"I—I just mean… well, your parents would not approve."

"Oh, Szymon, who's to tell them? They disapprove of so many things, you know. Why, I doubt they would consent to your teaching the boy how to ride, don't you?" She paused for effect. "And if my brothers should learn you've been lending out their prize warhorses?" Krystyna smiled at the stable master, whose face had gone as serious as a doctor's. She turned now and took long strides toward the house.

She entered the manor house through the kitchen.

"There you are!"

The tone of the housekeeper startled Krystyna. "Hello, Klara. Have you been looking for me?"

"Have I? I've been up to that attic room three times this afternoon."

"Oh, sweet Jezus, you've made *szarlotka*!" Krystyna made a beeline for the kitchen work table where the large-framed woman in her white apron and cap was applying meringue to the apple cake. Her finger was in the large crockery bowl before Klara could bat it away with a wooden spoon.

"Just wait, milady!"

"Yes, Klara." Krystyna licked the light confection from her finger.

"Now, where is it you ran off to? I nearly fainted when Szymon told me you had taken off on one of the boys' warhorses."

"Don't worry about me."

"I will worry, what with your parents gone." The housekeeper waved the spoon in mock threat. "Riding a warhorse and unaccompanied! Szymon and I will both be homeless when your parents get wind of this."

"Then we will have nothing but windless days, dear Klara, when they return, wouldn't you say?"

The woman grunted. "Indeed. It's no wonder..."

"Wonder? About what?"

Klara's face folded into one of shared confidence. "The convent school."

"Oh, that. You don't think I *wanted* to go back, do you?" Krystyna gave out with a little laugh and again dipped her finger into the bowl. "No one there made *szarlotka* like you do, Klara. It's heavenly!"

Klara sent her a glance of disapproval but was nonetheless charmed. She went back to her artistry with the meringue. One more sortie by Krystyna prompted the housekeeper to release a large breath in exasperation. "Well, I guess you'll be coming down to earth soon enough."

"What does that mean?"

"Nothing—I meant nothing by it."

"Oh, yes, you did!" Krystyna moved around the table to face the housekeeper. "What?"

"There, I'm finished. The bowl is yours, Krysia."

"Never mind. What did you mean?"

The woman sighed in defeat. "It wasn't my place to say anything, but..."

"But?" Krystyna wished she could lay hands on Klara and shake the words out of her.

"Well, you're to be married."

"Oh, Klara, that's a year away."

The housekeeper vigorously shook her head, the ruffles on the white cap catching wind. "It's to be moved up."

Krystyna felt as if she had been slapped. "What?"

"Your mother had a letter before they left. I heard her talking to your father. The other family wants it moved up."

"Moved up to—when?"

Klara shrugged. "I don't know. Now, you'll bite your tongue when you mother speaks of it. You don't want to get me in trouble, do you? No more apple cakes."

Krystyna turned around and headed for the servants' back stairway.

"Krysia," the housekeeper called, "the bowl!"

Krysytna was already halfway to the landing of the first floor.

In her attic room she dropped down onto the side of the narrow bed. She had won her freedom from the nuns only to learn this news from a servant. She had meant to enjoy herself during the year before the marriage. It was little enough time, little enough freedom. Days like today—riding horseback at breakneck speed with wind lashing her face and furrowed paths flying beneath her—would be but a memory. Freedom would be a memory.

And then she thought of Castle Hill and the boy. What was it about him that had caught her attention? On that day in the carriage her eyes had gone to him even though the other boy—the Polish boy—was tall and handsome enough. She lay back against a pillow, the thought of marriage receding for now.

What is it, she asked herself, *about this Tatar boy—this Aleksy?*

SIX

ALEKSY SAT ON THE EDGE of the hayloft, hands testing his bow string, feet dangling. Presently he heard the door below open and close. Moments later the figure of Idzi appeared, smaller than ever when seen from that height. He was whistling. The sight of Luba lying in the mound of hay that made for Idzi's bed caused his large head to do a sweep about the barn looking for her owner.

"Where have you been?" Aleksy asked, announcing his presence.

Idzi's blond head ceased movement, and the eyes, glinting darker now in the shadows created by the lantern below, peered up at him. "And I thought my mother had abandoned me."

"I've been waiting."

"So sorry, Your Majesty." Idzi made an exaggerated bow. "Come down, come down. Did you worry about me?"

"No. You come up." Aleksy set aside his longbow.

Idzi sighed but put up no argument. He climbed the ladder, his foreshortened legs straining with each rung. At the top, he swung around with surprising litheness and sat on the edge next to Aleksy, who felt his gaze in the semi-darkness but did not return it.

"You're still moonfaced," Idzi said. "About the girl—his lordship's daughter?"

"Idzi—"

"Yes?"

"What's it like?"

"What's what like?"

"To be you?"

"Ah, you mean strong and virile, clever and fast as a greyhound and twice as handsome?"

Aleksy scoffed. "You forgot *humble*."

"I didn't wish to seem conceited."

"You're just mad, you know that?"

"And you're madly in love, you know *that*?"

"How can I be? One meeting that's all. And she—"

"Is of the gentry, yes?"

"Not to mention as Polish as—well, you."

"Hey, you're right," Idzi said, feigning surprise. "I *am* Polish! Do you think *I* should have a go?"

"Stop joking around."

"You're right. I probably would have but half a chance."

"Egidiusz!"

"Sorry. But don't call me that. I'm Idzi."

They sat in silence for a full minute, sparring done.

"It's hard sometimes," Idzi said, "being—like I am. But one has to get along."

"How do you do that—get along?"

"I don't know. It's my fate to be small. There's nothing I can do about it. What I hate most is that people sometimes treat me like a child because of my size. Or because I can joke, they tell me I should become the king's fool at court."

"I hope I haven't treated you as such."

"No, you haven't." Idzi let out a sigh. "But I've my home here and my jobs to do. It's a simple life." He struck Aleksy in the shoulder with his fist. "And I have friends."

"And what of those who jeer and make faces at you?"

"And trip me or knock me down?—I've learned to stay out of their way. This is my lot in life. I figure it's their lot in life to be ignorant asses. They have the problem, not me."

"Have you not longed for more?"

"Once upon a time, but as I see it—life, that is—there is the changeable and the unchangeable. I once yearned to live in a fine house. Now, I'm happy with my little corner of the barn."

Aleksy fell silent.

"So" Idzi ventured, "you think I'm telling you to stay away from the Halicki crowd? All of them, the pretty young filly included?"

He had read his mind. "Aren't you? Shouldn't I? Our roles in life—hers and mine—are unchangeable, no?"

"Well, someone once told me that the most important things in life happen only once. I wasn't there last Sunday. What was she like—besides being the most beautiful female you've ever beheld?"

"Ah, if I knew, I could tell you. There was no introduction, no proper one. I had to ask her name at one point. It's Krystyna—but it wasn't until after she left that I realized she had not used my name even once. She kept calling me *boy*."

"Oh."

"I know. Not a good sign, but she chattered on and on, took me around the castle keep as if she was a tour guide, and there were moments when I thought she saw me as an equal, as if I was light like you and had those round blue eyes."

"Back to my handsomeness." Idzi checked himself. "Just moments?"

"Yes." Aleksy wanted to tell him how she spoke of him as her captive or slave, but the words just fell away. It was too humiliating.

"Tell me again, how were things left when she rode off?"

"She said that I could have the more spirited horse—Flash—come Sunday and that she would take Miracle."

"Implying that she would meet you there again?"

"Yes—no!—I don't know. It's been driving me crazy."

"Crazy in love, like I said."

"Love doesn't come so fast—does it?"

"In the legends it does."

"What should I do?"

"You go on Sunday, but—"

"But what?"

"You don't give up your soldiering idea. You take your lance and let Szymon teach you what he may. It's your dream."

"And one just as unlikely to fulfill."

"You know that there are ways."

"Ways?"

"Well, in difficult times, I've heard, times such as the Swede invasions of a few years ago, men without noble status and even some with questionable parentage were accepted as *pacholicy* for soldiers. Should your friends, the Halicki brothers, be inducted into the *Kwarciani*, they will require three such retainers each."

"Me, a *pacholik*? You mean—like a squire? To one of *them*? Not on your life!"

Idzi ignored Aleksy's protestation. "In those dark days, some of those common retainers performed commendable service to the Commonwealth and were made fully fledged soldiers. Some were even ennobled. And now they say dark days are coming for the entire continent."

"Poland seems to always be facing dark days. Oh, I would beg to be a retainer, Idzi, but I would not beg the Halicki brothers."

"Is that unchangeable?"

Aleksy laughed. "It is."

On Sunday Aleksy arrived at the Halicki *dwór* with lance in hand. Unlike the saddles on the Halicki Polish-Arabians, the old and worn saddle on old Kastor had nothing to anchor the butt of the lance so that maintaining the lance's balance had been difficult, making the ride in the dark slow and awkward. He dismounted. Secreting himself behind the same belt of bushes as the week before, he waited, noticing that the corner third-level window was again aglow with amber candlelight. He managed just a quick glance before the three-beat gait of a horse's canter drew his attention toward the stable. Gustáf was leaving. Aleksy stroked Kastor's forehead to keep him quiet. At the very moment the groom's horse moved past him, breaking into a gallop that would speed Gustáf to Horodenka, some instinct—some sense of being watched—deflected Aleksy's notice. He looked upward, squinted. There was a motion at the attic window. The arched valance was fluttering.

Below it, a pale face in the flickering light seemed to float there.

He blinked and it was gone, swift as a specter. If it were a ghost, it was that of a young girl. The Sunday before he had guessed that room to be a servant's quarters, but today he wondered if it might not be Krystyna's—Lady Krystyna's. His heart caught.

Aleksy stared to see if the figure would return to the eye-shaped window. After several minutes, he cursed himself for being foolish and made short work of getting himself to the stable, where Szymon awaited him.

"You weren't here when I came back last Sunday," Aleksy said as he led Kastor to a stall.

"I had other things to do. Good God, I expected you knew how to stable the horse."

"I wanted to ask you—"

"What?"

Aleksy approached Szymon. "Last Sunday—did you say anything to Lady Krystyna about me before she left with Flash?"

"Lady Krystyna, is it now? Mighty familiar with the *szlachta*, hey? She told me she saw you."

"Szymon—"

"It was a surprise to me. She came in wanting me to saddle Miracle for her. She had been riding him every day since the count and countess left. I wouldn't agree to it at first, saying how it would get me in trouble when the count gets back. And she says she'd get me in trouble for sure if I didn't saddle him up right then."

"And you did."

"No choice. She looks like a fine piece of marzipan, that one, all sweet and pretty. But she's got a mind of her own and seems to enjoy seeing someone make a fuss or making a fuss herself. And to top it, I had to give her a few pointers, but just that first day. After that, it was like she grew unto the saddle."

"And so last Sunday with Miracle gone, she insisted on riding Flash?"

"That she did."

"Did you tell her about me and my practice with Miracle?"

The old man shrugged. "She asked me where Miracle was. What could I say? The horse was out for repair? No, I told her I had a boy take it out for exercise."

"Did you tell her my destination? That I was headed for Castle Hill?"

"Let me see, now—I don't rightly remember. Might have, but I don't recall. Are we going to jawbone all morning, Alek, or are we going to teach you how to run a lance?"

They left the stable, Aleksy atop Flash, Szymon walking alongside carrying the lance. Another time, Aleksy would have been solely focused on the enjoyment of this pivotal point in his life, but for the moment he could do nothing but wonder whether the girl in yellow had sought him out the week before. Had she remembered him from the day she nearly fell from the carriage?

They advanced to the rear corral. Aleksy saw that Szymon had set up a wooden apparatus that held a small ring suspended on a string. It was a game and yet it was practice for one's marksmanship. He had seen it done many times watching from Mount Halicz. He thrilled now to have his chance at it.

"Here's your lance. Now, place the butt into the tok."

Aleksy obeyed.

"Good. Now, the most important thing for a lancer," Szymon said, his weathered face and gray streaked beard upturned to Aleksy, "is leverage as you attempt to balance both your mount and the lance. It can be a difficult dance."

It was a predictable thing for him to say, as predictable as it was true. Aleksy had to combine what he had learned last week—keeping the horse on a defined track and managing the turns—with mastering the lance, the speed, and the aim. It took a good dozen attempts before he tore the ring from the post. That done once, he was able to achieve it every third or fourth try.

At midmorning Aleksy's thoughts strayed to Krystyna. Would she be riding Miracle today? Had it been her intention to go once again to the castle? Dared he think that it had been her purpose for him to meet her there? And if that had been her sincere intention, might she not have changed her mind over the course of a week's time?

"Now, my boy," Szymon announced, interrupting Aleksy's thoughts, "we need to practice with you pulling up the lance at a moment's notice. When you're a hussar on the practice field you'll be divided into two groups facing one another. The approach will begin with the butt of the lowered lance secured in the tok and the point aimed at the very spleen of the soldier coming at you. On the track next to you, he'll be coming at you full tilt, mind you. I've seen the king himself oversee this formation, and from a distance it looks as if the fight is real as rain. And at the same precise moment—the very last moment—you must pull up on your lance in unison with the soldier on the approaching lane so that no fellow lancer is wounded."

"Szymon, what happens—in real battle, I mean—when you make contact?"

"When you spear someone? With luck that's the end of him. Why, in the thick of battle I've seen a big brute of a man skewer two devils on his lance."

Aleksy blinked in wonder.

"But, remember, double or nothing, after the initial charge, it's the end of your lance. Time to drop it. It's no good in up-close combat. And it's a rare lance that gets used twice. You have to hope your company has a good supply for the next day, the next battle. In the meantime, whether you've got someone on the point or not, you drop the lance and it's time for the sabre."

"I don't have a sabre."

"And you're not yet a hussar, are you? All in God's time."

All in God's time, Aleksy thought.

Practice at this event went on for more than an hour, Aleksy responding better and better to Szymon's croaking cry of "Pull up! Pull up!"

The phrase that would keep coming back to him, however, was *when you're a hussar*... This was the coin of encouragement, a coin that now held company in the purse with the coin invested by Idzi. If these two envisioned him as a hussar, could he do less?

As they returned to the stable, Aleksy was struck with the deflating thought that Szymon would think Flash too tired—and perhaps he was—to be taken on an outing to Castle Hill. His heart beat fast upon entering the stable, his head turning toward Miracle's stall. It was empty.

"I see she's taken Miracle," Szymon said. "Bring Flash here for a bit of a drink. Could use one myself—ale my preferred choice."

Aleksy's fear that he would not be allowed to ride Flash accelerated. His heart quickened. That Lady Krystyna had taken Miracle raised the stakes. He looked over to a stall where Kastor stood. He would take the plow horse and he would suffer the humiliation with a smile. Hell, he thought, I'll walk to the castle if necessary. She was there. She had to be there.

Szymon turned to him now, his face dark. "About you taking Flash out, Alek—"

Aleksy drew in a big breath and held it, prepared for disappointment. He would not argue with Szymon. He already owed him too much.

"I want you to make sure you bring a waterskin this time. Last Sunday Lady Krystyna railed at me good for sending you off without one."

From a distance, the decaying castle atop the hill appeared like a black and gray chalk painting. It was eerily silent, too, as he drew closer. Was there anything to the widespread notion that it was haunted? Then, from beneath, came the reverberating sound of Flash's hoofbeats carefully treading the rotting drawbridge and in moments they were passing through the gateway of the structure and entering the bailey. Here Aleksy allowed the horse to prance majestically in large circles while he took in the revolving facades, eyes darting about, searching. It seemed deserted.

He dismounted, listened. Nothing. He felt foolish for thinking she would be here, for thinking she had intended a meeting. Maybe it was her little joke on him, one she would share with her brothers. He took hold of the reins and led the horse toward the dilapidated stable. Flash suddenly tossed up his head and neighed. He had caught wind of something. From inside the stable now came another neighing in return greeting. Miracle—he was sure it was Miracle.

Aleksy felt a rush of blood come into his face. *She has come. She is here.* He led Flash into the stable. His hands worked nervously at the knot that would tether Flash in the stall next to Miracle.

In moments he was outside and in the bailey again, listening. All was silent as a cloister. Where was she? Why hadn't she let her presence be known? It occurred to him then that she might have fallen, that her boot had become lodged in broken boards or the crevice of a stone step—or a half dozen other possibilities. He looked to the keep and moved toward it thinking that he could be her rescuer, as in the stories—not her slave. He would be well rewarded by a thankful and generous father. He would be asked his heart's wish—and that would be to have the hand of the rescued maiden.

All of these thoughts vanished at once upon entering the keep. What nonsense, he would think later.

Her riding habit today was slate gray. She sat on the low flat stone that she had called her throne the week before, looking up at him from under her plumed hat as if—what? As if she had expected him? As if he had kept her waiting? As if his presence had disappointed?

"What is your name, boy?"

Has she forgotten? "Aleksy," he answered, nearly certain that she did recall but pretended otherwise.

"And did Flash ride well? Did he give good service?"

"He did."

"This morning, from my window, I noticed that you brought a lance."

Aleksy immediately thought of that third floor half-coin shaped window. He nodded. It had not been a servant's room. It had been hers.

"And can you use it?"

"I am learning."

"In secret, it seems. You waited for the groom to leave, didn't you?"

Aleksy's stomach churned. This seemed more an interrogation than a conversation. What would she do with the information? He affected a smile.

"Isn't it the case, boy, that you don't want my parents or my brothers to find out about any of this? Isn't that true?"

Aleksy stiffened. "It is true."

She smiled as if she had cleverly cajoled a murderer into confessing his crime.

Well, he could play at this, too. "And you, Lady Krystyna, would you have them learn about *any of this*?"

His arrow flew true. The smile vanished and for the first time he saw that her face colored, if only slightly.

The moment passed quickly. She drew herself up, her eyes flashing a petulant retort. "You think not? Why, it would amuse me greatly." She was suddenly standing and moving out into the bailey, expecting him to follow, chattering on about how things at the castle had fallen into even greater disrepair since her girlhood days. He did follow, and they came out into the sunlight. "There is one tower with a stairway that is still passable. I'll show you."

He followed her into the tower at the right front of the keep. "It doesn't look safe," Aleksy cautioned, noting the cracked and crumbling condition of the open spiral stone staircase with its winding narrow steps. But she was already climbing it, much too quickly, he thought.

"I've already been up here this morning," she called back, her honeyed voice echoing down into the well-like void. "You needn't worry. Now, hurry along."

She was staring out at the panorama when he caught up to her. The battlements were in relatively good condition. "It's so beautiful looking out from up here," she said. "You can see for miles."

Aleksy wondered if she had been up here watching for his arrival.

"You brought your bow, as well."

"What?"

She turned away from the scenic overview and faced him, her heart-shaped face all seriousness. "Your bow and quiver? I did see them, too, I think, here at the castle. "

"Yes, I left them in the stable. Why?"

"Well, isn't this where the archers took their aim? From these very openings, I imagine when they were under siege in those days that they killed many a Tatar." She seemed to realize what she had said the moment the word *Tatar* finished her thought. But she made no comment, no apology. She turned again to look out.

Had the word been an arrow, he would be lying at her feet. He tried to assess her expression from her profile. Had she meant to insult? To inflict hurt? Her visage was one of innocence, not malice—why, she hadn't even colored in the least. How to figure her?

"I should like to learn how to use a bow," she said.

"Why?"

"I should like to go to war. There's talk of nothing else back in Warsaw. I should like to protect my homeland as much as the next person, man or woman."

"I could teach you."

When her eyes focused on him, he saw in them green laughter and he became certain—for the moment, at least—that she had been manipulating him for her own amusement.

"What an interesting offer," she said.

"You had only to ask.... But women don't go to war."

Her perfect forehead furrowed and her tone soured. "Well, then we shall forget it." She pivoted away from him and stared into the distance through the crenelle.

Aleksy regretted not playing along. At first mention of her interest, he had imagined showing her how to hold the bow, place the arrow, draw, take aim, and loose. How could he do so without placing his arms around her, without touching her?

He surfaced from the little fantasy to see her moving down the stairs without so much as a by-your-leave. Had he lost his opportunity—or had she been teasing all along?

He quickly followed, coming to the ground level with a little jolt. She had turned, waiting for him, and stood now but a foot away, her eyes on his. She lifted a hand to his face and her fingertips lightly brushed back a lock of his hair. "Why are your eyes shaped as they are?" she asked.

The touch of her thrilled him, but then the sense of her question came home to him. Was this meant as another arrow? he wondered. In any case, it had the sting of one. He had never been asked such a question. And yet her face pleaded innocence. "I was told once," he said, "that my lineage goes back to the Golden Horde."

"The Mongols?"

He nodded. "Far to the northeast. They say that the eyes are shaped to protect against the sun and snow." When she didn't react, he added, "It is very bright there."

Aleksy could not tell whether Krystyna was processing this information and allowing it to pass without comment, or whether she gave his words any thought at all.

"And you said you can teach me the art of the bow?"

"Yes. I could show you now." Aleksy started for the exit into the bailey but she placed her hand on his arm, detaining him.

"No, not today." The green eyes flashed with some sudden change, some hidden emotion. "I must go now." Her voice was flat, its honey gone. "Help me mount Miracle." She hurried toward the stable.

Aleksy followed. When he brought the horse out and helped her to mount, he looked up into her serious face.

"Wait half an hour," she said and gave spur.

"I'll teach you next Sunday, my lady!" Aleksy called.

Krystyna was nearing the gateway and gave no response.

"Next Sunday!" he shouted, praying her family did not return before then.

Szymon wasn't in the stable when Krystyna returned with Miracle and she was glad for it. In the kitchen Klara wheeled about with a look of reproval on her face, but Krystyna hurried past her, her own cautionary expression holding in check any comment from the housekeeper.

In her attic room, she seated herself in the window seat, absently observing the drive that led from the house—poplar trees lining each side—to the main road. Sparrows flitted from tree to tree.

That boy, she thought, *that boy*. Almost immediately it came to her. He was not a boy. Not any more than she was still a girl. At school she had flirted with boys—the cadets that would pass while she took good time sweeping the portico, the two grooms in the convent stable who vied for her attention, and Tadeusz, the nephew of Mother Abbess Teodora, who visited more often than his aunt thought seemly. She was the one always in control and she regarded moments with those boys moments of harmless, flirtatious fun. But, today, when she lightly touched Aleksy's face, some strange, startling fear ran through her like a current. She assessed in those dark eyes a young man whose attraction to her ran deep. And so she had abruptly left and come home. There was danger here—for both of them. There would be no more Sundays.

Sometime later, the sound of knocking jolted her. One of the maids was calling her to supper. "Coming," she replied, glancing out the window. Summer was at its height, and yet the sky had darkened. A storm was on the rise.

SEVEN

Warsaw
June 1683

"God's wounds!" While Roman's curse was voiced at a normal volume, amidst the lively strains of the mazurka, the sounds of boots and slippers on the dance floor, the hubbub of socializing at the wedding reception, only Marek, standing beside him, heard the words.

"You're bored, Roman?"

"Standing here watching the well-heeled of Warsaw parade and prance about? Yes, bored and irritated beyond imagination." He drank down the goblet of mulled wine and motioned a serving boy over to refill it. "At least the liquor is first rate."

"We saw the public rooms of the Royal Castle today. I thought that was interesting, especially that secret passage leading from the king's private rooms through an elevated tunnel all the way to St. Jan's Cathedral. Keeps the great man safe, yes?—And this is no cottage, either." They were in the ballroom of the magnificent Lubomirski Palace.

"Bah!" Roman scowled. "Who gives a damn?"

"Well, there are many pretty girls. So far I've danced with four. And you?"

"Two—very proper ones on the lookout for husbands—sons of magnates their targets, no doubt."

"Won't you marry someday, Romek?"

Roman sighed, annoyed by Marek's solicitousness. "Someday, yes, my lord brother." He drank deeply. "But first there's the—"

"The *Kwarciani* and the excitement of the Wild Fields, I know."

"What if we're not selected this year? I want to be there at the border, keeping the Tatars at bay."

"Cossacks, too, but the real threat may not be from the southeast. From what I've heard here in the capital, it's the Turks that are the real threat and that they mean to march right through Europe like it's their parade grounds. Just the same, Roman, I told you I feel good about being selected."

Roman harrumphed. "*Your* horse didn't step off the path. *Your* lance didn't falter."

"They were little enough mistakes."

Roman turned and with his free hand shoved at his brother's shoulder, causing a bit of red wine to splash out of Marek's goblet. "Big enough to lose the chance! And look at your father across the hall, talking away, reminiscing, no doubt, about the old days at his borderland fort at Bracław."

"You're bitter."

"Chrystus, yes! All he had to do was point us out during maneuvers and we would have been commissioned in the *Kwarciani* by now."

Marek accepted a cloth from an alert server and wiped at the spattered wine on his hand and cuff. "Why is it, Roman, that sometimes you say to me *your* father instead of *our* father?"

"Because it's true!" Roman drank deeply. "My father is dead—killed by a Tatar on the Wild Fields."

"You were a baby, Roman. You didn't know him. And that man across the way—*our* father—raised you."

Roman could not deny these things.

Marek returned to the original thread of conversation. "Father has his reasons. He wants us to be inducted on our own merits. So this is what irritates you?"

"No, do you want to know what irritates me?" Roman drank again. "I'll tell you! That group over there!" He pointed to a group of men, most in military attire. "Damn Tatars!"

"They are Lipka, Roman, here from Lithuania. They *are* Tatars and by all accounts as good winged horsemen as any. In a three-day battle Jan Sobieski held Warsaw from the Swedes at Brandenburg with two thousand of the Lipka lancers. After that, he won battle after battle and received one promotion after another—until he was given the throne. He sets great store by the Lipka."

"I don't care what Jan Sobieski thinks—"

"Lower your voice, Roman. You're not being respectful. He's the King."

"King or no—those men are dark dogs who kneel on sheepskins and pray to the East."

"You don't think they can be Poles at heart and still be Muslims? They have been accepted into the Commonwealth and some have been ennobled for their service to the Motherland."

Roman drained his goblet. "Matters not to me. And you know as well as I there have been a good many renegades among them that have turned tail and fight now with the multitudes of their kind that murder and take Christian slaves for the Sultan. They're slant-eyed devils."

"Roman!" Marek hissed. "You'll be heard."

Lord Konrad Halicki sat at a richly draped round table, his wife at his side and friends all around. Placed next to him was a uniformed general, Prince Hieronim Lubomirski. The reception celebrated the wedding of the prince's niece, Marianna. It had been a good enough excuse to bring together old comrades, Lubomirski had said. Konrad had served the younger man at the siege of Chocim, ten years earlier. He took note of the general who was recounting with great animation a particular skirmish. At thirty-five, his dark brown hair was receding, but neither it nor his dramatically drooping moustache had a trace of gray. The dark brown eyes, wide and laughing now, on the field were narrowed with discernment and decision. Konrad chuckled to himself, remembering the battle a little differently—but with victory the outcome what did a bit of embroidery matter? What mattered—making this reunion with military friends more bitter than sweet—was that the capital here was on high heat with talk of the Sultan's ignoring treaties and amassing fighters from a dozen regions for an attack that would push westward. How far west? Charles of Lorraine had been named field commander for the Holy Roman Empire and Lubomirski himself had been given command of twenty-seven hundred soldiers north on the River Váh. Such were the details of a council of war the Holy Roman Emperor Leopold had held some six weeks earlier, at the request of Pope Innocent XI, who was calling for Christian nations to form a Holy League against the Ottoman infidels.

Every so often, Konrad turned to the dance floor and—between the ebb and flow of the dancers—caught sight of Roman and Marek standing on the other side of the ballroom. He thought how they might be drawn into a war as massive and daunting as the anticipated one Lubomirski had told him about earlier in a private moment. It seemed a far different and more deadly conflict than if they had been taken into the *Kwarciani* and assigned to manning the eastern forts against groups of marauders on the edge of the Wild Fields, Cossacks mostly, that seemed to follow the spring locusts westward, out of the steppes and toward the Commonwealth.

He now leaned in toward his wife, who sat on his other side, and spoke in a confidential tone. "Zenobia, your son seems to be imbibing to excess."

"*My* son? You mean Roman, I take it?"

"Shush! You're too loud."

"And I suppose Marek is not drinking—or is he drinking milk?" The countess laughed at her little joke.

Konrad forced a laugh, too. "I did not mean to start a holy war between us." He took her delicately veined hand and kissed it. "If I say your son, you know which one. There—admit it."

"His name is of two syllables, like yours, Kon-rad. Now, where are they? I suppose you want me to say something to him?"

"Best to say something to both, Zena," he said, hoping to assuage her pique by using her diminutive.

Just as Konrad directed his wife's line of vision across the chamber to where the boys stood, one of the Lipka soldiers stepped through the opening between the brothers, inadvertently jostling Roman, whose wine splashed out of his goblet. Roman turned on the young Lipka. Words were exchanged. Roman, his face red as the wine, dropped the metal cup and drew his arm back, ready to strike. Like quicksilver, Marek grabbed hold of his brother's arm and stepped out in front of Roman, face to face. Strong words and spittle flew between brothers. Roman dropped his arm and Marek turned toward the Lipka soldier. After a brief exchange, the dark-complexioned soldier bowed contritely and with great grace moved off. Roman glowered after him.

Konrad, whose stout form was half out his seat as he prepared to push through the dancers, saw the situation resolve itself and so sat. "There,

Zenobia," he said, "*there* is the reason I will not speak up for the boys and have them hustled off with the *Kwarciani* to the Wild Fields."

"You mean his impulsiveness, I suppose."

"You put it delicately, Zenobia, as a mother would. I call it rashness. He's capable of great anger. He's all mouth and trousers. Who's to say where it will lead?"

"Would you rather he was all mouth and no trousers? Perhaps this rashness—or is it boldness?—will lead to success for him in the Wild Fields."

"Yes, and it could lead to a quick death. Quick tempers must be mastered. A good soldier demonstrates equipoise. And he needs to know that Tatars serve on both sides."

"So will you stand in their way if they are chosen?"

Konrad would not take this occasion to tell her that they might soon be called to serve in positions far more dangerous than the *Kwarciani* face at the Wild Fields. "No, I'll not interfere. Even the raven must release its fledglings to the sky."

Zenobia gasped. "Raven? What a mean thing to say!" Her stormy face materialized. "Am I then a scavenger?"

Konrad's mouth clamped shut, regretting at once his analogy. If he kept on, his wife wasn't likely to speak to him for the duration of the trip. Her memory was long. He tried to think of something to say to sugar over his own impulsive—however accurate—comment.

It was at that moment that King Jan III Sobieski was announced. Amidst much fanfare, he entered the hall. Chairs screeched loudly on the marble floor as those seated rose, the men bowing and women curtseying, while dancers halted in mid-twirl and the cleats of soldiers' boots clanged dully in unison just once on the wooden dance floor.

Roman and Marek had come to attention, as well.

After an exchange with Prince Lubomirski and the others at the host's table, the king began to make his rounds among the tables, heels thumping the floorboards and spurs ringing sharply.

Roman scoffed. "Did you see how Father bowed and scraped?"

"I saw no scraping." Marek said. "Should he come by, what does one say to him?"

"Well, lord brother, you might ask why he's losing his hair, or why he's getting so fat around the middle."

Marek dared a little laugh. "He is a man in his fifties."

"Exactly! I doubt that there is another Battle of Warsaw in him now. He bought that little village of Willanów on the Warsaw outskirts and has started a fine palace for himself. I imagine that will keep him busy. He'll ponder over what statue of himself is to be placed where—and the like. And it will take men like *us* to hold off the Horde."

"I wouldn't count him out yet. But I do wish Krystyna had come. She'll be so disappointed to have missed the king."

Roman turned to his brother. "Why didn't she come, Marek?"

"You don't know? It was her punishment."

"For what?"

"For disobeying the convent school rules. You really didn't know? The nuns expelled her. Why, Mother was furious."

It took a couple of beats for Roman to process this news about Krystyna, but before he could pursue it, Marek nudged him.

King Jan Sobieski was but a step away from them. Roman searched for words of greeting. What *would* he say to the King of the Commonwealth of Poland and Lithuania?

"Politeness," Marek urged.

Roman grunted.

EIGHT

Halicz

"We'll be taking Flash out to the rear corral soon enough," Szymon said, "but for now there is more to show you."

Aleksy was staring in amazement at an impressive array of shields, single and double-edged sabres, daggers, and war hammers laid out neatly on the straw. "You'll need to know more than how to use a lance, my boy. Once the initial charge is over, whether you've managed to impale some poor enemy soul or not, it's time to drop it and go to other measures."

And so the morning ran long with weaponry lessons and then the riding and work with the lance. When they returned to the stable, Aleksy immediately looked to Miracle's stall. It was empty. While that did not necessarily mean that Krystyna had taken it to Castle Hill, he took it as a good omen, noticing nonetheless that Szymon had processed the same information and that his expression had gone dark.

Halfway to the castle, Aleksy met with an ill omen coming toward him in the form of a boy on horseback. It was Gusztáf returning early from his visit home, much too early. There was no time to veer off the road and having no wish to engage him in conversation and allow for questions, Aleksy spurred Flash into the quickest gallop he could manage. Nonetheless, he had no cloak of invisibility to cover himself and his mount so that despite the breathtaking speed, the groom likely recognized them both immediately. What would come of it? In a little while Aleksy reined in the horse, his sight undeterred from the castle, his mind praying Szymon would spin Gusztáf a good tale and somehow swear him to secrecy.

The thought of Gusztáf vanished when he led Flash into the castle stable and found Lady Krystyna standing near the stall where she had placed Miracle.

"You must have just gotten here," Aleksy said.

"Actually, I was just about to leave."

Aleksy hid his disappointment. "But now—you'll stay?"

"For a short while," she said, moving toward the doors.

Aleksy placed Flash in a stall and followed her, miffed by something in her tone. What was it?

"I finished late with Szymon."

"Oh, I saw the weapons there in the stable." Krystyna turned toward him, her hand shading her eyes from the sun. "I imagine he enjoys talking about his old days with my father at the border of the Wild Fields. I've heard the stories a hundred times."

Aleksy resisted telling her Szymon was preparing him for service in the King's Army. It was an unlikely possibility and she would see it as such. Instead he said, "I—I brought my bow today."

Krystyna was silent for a few moments, then said, "Leave it here for now. Let's go into the tower again." She didn't wait for a response.

Inside, she immediately started the climb.

Upon reaching the battlements at the top, Krystyna went to look out one of the crenelles. Aleksy posted himself at the opening next to hers and stared out at the landscape, praying she would not say anything about killing Tatars.

Faces forward, speaking as if to the air, rather than face to face, they carried on a long conversation, commenting on buildings in the far distance, arguing whether wolves were to be found in the nearby forest, and having imaginative fun with the formations of clouds. The better part of an hour passed. Then they went quiet for what seemed a long while.

Krystyna broke the silence at last, still speaking through the crenelle, her words directed at the far-off woods. "I had not planned to come today, you know."

"No?" He directed his reply through his crenelle.

"This is the last time."

"Must it be, Lady Krystyna?"

"It's a serious matter—my being here with you." The words came as if disembodied.

"Your parents would not approve."

She sent her little giggle out over the landscape. "No, they would not."

"Neither would mine."

"Really?" she asked. She laughed again as if the thought had never occurred to her.

Aleksy drew in a deep breath, expelling it now in the form of two words: "Do *you*?"

"What?"

"Approve."

Silence.

Face forward, he waited and a few moments multiplied into many. His heart beat fast. He had been too bold. He had embarrassed her and his spirits dropped like a stone.

Another minute and he sensed some movement in his peripheral vision. He turned and saw that she had shifted in place and was facing him. Her plaited hair flashed gold in the sunlight. "It's a serious matter," she repeated. "Aleksy," she said tentatively, her head angling down a bit as she gifted him with a smile, not a wide one—but a sweet one, a real one. "I approve."

Aleksy took the three or four paces toward her and halted. He had little experience at this and silently prayed that he could accurately read her expression. Later, he would wonder where his store of nerve had come from, but for now he had to bend only slightly to kiss her.

Her lips were soft and yielding. He didn't attempt an embrace and yet the kiss held some moments. She withdrew then, concern clouding her face. He thought for a moment that her temperament had shifted and she would slap him, but as if something had gained her attention from without, she turned to the crenelle, her eyes narrowing as if finding focus on something in the distance.

"It is a serious thing, Aleksy, as I said." Suddenly, she wheeled back to him, her expression dark as winter. "My brothers are here."

It was true. Aleksy heard the hollow sounds of hoofbeats hitting dry earth now and looked out to see three figures atop steppe ponies climbing Castle Hill. He turned back to Krystyna, but she was already nearing the stairs. He hurried to catch up.

Outside, in the bailey, the blinding sun made the three riders appear faceless and dark, like *wycinanki* figures—papercuts—against a brilliant yellow foil. Aleksy shaded his eyes against the sun in an attempt to make out the identities. Two were her brothers and they were glaring hatred in his direction. The third was Gusztáf, who had no doubt led them here. *God's teeth!* He had played that card badly. The surprise early arrivals of the groom from Horodenka and the Halicki brothers from Warsaw—what worse coincidence could he have imagined?

"Filthy swine!" spat Roman.

"Get away from her, Tatar!" cried the other brother.

The brothers threw themselves down from their ponies now. Roman raced toward them. "You'll hang for this, Tatar!" he shouted. "You'll hang if we don't kill you first."

The threat was not idle. Aleksy knew of a man in the next village—a Pole by birth no less—who had been brought before the *starosta*, the local constable, on charges of rape and even though the woman professed his innocence, within a fortnight he was supper for buzzards.

"He did nothing," Krystyna said in the few seconds she had before being seized and lifted onto Marek's shoulder as if she were a Persian rug. Then, as she was being hauled over to where the groom stood by his horse, Krystyna called out the most extraordinary words: "Aleksy, you did so much as promise, you know."

Was she so naïve that she didn't understand the seriousness of his situation and that her brothers could interpret her statement in ways having nothing to do with the art of archery?

Roman was pushing him now, both hands repeatedly striking his chest, propelling him backwards, toward the doorpost of the tower. Once Aleksy's back abutted the post, Roman cuffed him hard across the face. If they had been of the same well-born class, the confrontation would cease and a duel would be arranged. As it was, however, Roman struck him again. He went to use his other hand—his left—for the third strike, but in doing so released his hold on Aleksy's shoulder. Aleksy made the most of the blunder, pushing him forward so as to give clearance for a powerful fist to the jaw. Roman went down.

Aleksy regretted the impulse at once. There was no telling what might befall him or the Gazdecki family. Roman would not forget. The next thing Aleksy's senses fastened onto was Krystyna's calling out. He couldn't determine what she was yelling. Was she concerned about Roman? Or about him? He allowed Roman to pull himself up but failed to notice that Marek had been coming at him. Had Krystyna's cry been a warning?

Both of his arms were taken now and pinned behind his back. Roman's bloodied face was coming toward him.

Marek called out to the groom orders for him to start for home at once, leading the steppe pony upon which Krystyna had been placed.

Aleksy looked toward Krystyna who struggled with the groom, but her hands had evidently been tied to the pommel of the saddle. Suddenly Roman was cursing and Aleksy took a strong blow to the face, then another, and another. He struggled to stay conscious, to hold himself up. "We could drop you from the tower, Tatar, but we'd rather see you hanged." A punch now to the stomach took the wind from Aleksy and he bent over. "You'll see what becomes of defilers!" Roman's leg came up suddenly, his knee slamming into Aleksy's groin. Marek released him and he fell to the ground.

He lay on his side, his body folded up like a grasshopper's, his eyes clenched tight in pain. He felt a darkness closing in, a painless vacuum, and he welcomed it.

Someone kicked him now, squarely in the ribs.

"What did you promise her, Tatar?"

"What?"Aleksy opened his eyes. One would not fully open. With the other, he saw Roman glowering high above him.

"Unless you want to die now, tell us what you promised her."

Aleksy struggled for the words, for his mind to work. "Nothing."

"Liar!" Roman kicked him in his stomach. "Tell us."

"You want to live, yes?" This was Marek's voice.

"She asked—"

"What—what did she ask?"

"To learn the bow."

"The bow?" Roman asked, incredulously.

Those were the last words he would remember before slipping into unconsciousness.

When he awoke, hours later, it was to the gritty-gravelly—yet somehow soothing—voice of Szymon, who had come to fetch him home. He was being settled into a wagon. He attempted to lift his head from his supine position. "Szymon—"

"What is it, lad?"

"My bow and quiver?"

Szymon had to assure him twice over that nothing had been left behind. His bow and quiver were gone.

NINE

THE NEXT THING ALEKSY WOULD recall was seeing shadows of treetops passing overhead against a night sky dotted with stars and a half moon. Szymon was taking him home in his wagon. He was laid out like a corpse. How had the day so rich with promise and excitement come to this? As the vehicle rattled on, every rut, every pit in the road shot currents of pain ripping through his body. I should pray, he thought. He had once asked Szymon—who did not attend Sunday Mass—if he prayed. Attempting to soften his croaky voice, Szymon said, "I do pray when I breathe, my boy. And when I breathe, I pray." Aleksy had not understood his answer then, thinking it a kind of word puzzle—and it remained one. He closed his eyes against what was happening to him and welcomed a kind of emptiness that had no need of prayer or thought. Only breathing.

He awoke much later, sensing he was on his cot in the alcove off the kitchen area of the cottage. The familiar sharp but sweet scent of fresh dill—for his favorite soup—and caustic smell of cooking cabbage comforted him. He could hear voices in the kitchen but the sense of the words eluded him. His father's voice sounded angry, his mother's querulous, and Szymon's placating. There would be hell to answer for, sooner rather than later.

Aleksy slept undisturbed through the morning and intermittently during the afternoon, occasionally aware of his mother close by for brief moments, her lips whispering prayers, the scent of onion in the air. The interrogation started in the late afternoon with the arrival home from the fields of his father and brother.

The little family gathered at his bedside. "For the love of God, Aleksy, what possessed you—daring to ride the young masters' horses? Szymon be damned for allowing it" And so began the litany: Did you not know the risks? The situation in which you placed yourself? The family? Have you lost your senses? And to be found with the count's daughter? What is the meaning of this? What went on? Nothing? You could be executed for such a nothing. Was this a planned meeting between you? What do you mean you're not certain? It was not the first meeting? Did you lay hands on her?

Admission of the kiss caused his father to blink in disbelief, turn away, take a few steps, halt, pivot and advance toward the bed, his voice building. "By all that's holy and the wounds of Jezus Chrystus, no matter what she may have implied, you must know your place, do you hear?" He stopped just short of the bed, his face aflame. "And you struck the count's son, for God's sake!"

Aleksy put up no defense, and so his father tired after half an hour and left, his orders that Aleksy stay clear of Lady Krystyna vociferously meted out. His mother lightly touched his hand before leaving his bedside to go about the preparations for the evening meal. Damian—a kind of amazement in his blue eyes—was left to help Aleksy hobble outside to the privy.

Aleksy was made to convalesce for two days during which time the family moved about with nerves on edge, fearful that at any time a summons might arrive from the *starosta*—or if not from the Lord Constable—from Count Halicki himself.

On that second day, Tuesday, he reached a conclusion. He would not sit around waiting for things to happen to him. A few more days and he should be in good enough health and appearance to take to the road. He would not spend his life toiling in the Halicki fields, living in a cottage and village owned by others, occasionally being tormented by the sight of the girl in yellow. No, he had made up his mind, settling on Saturday to set forth. He would take his fate into his own hands on Saturday.

By Thursday, Aleksy's bruised ribs allowed him to move about slowly, and while he was nearly free of real pain, his father insisted he stay indoors so significant were the bruises and lacerations about his face. Questions from other villagers would not be welcome.

At mid-afternoon, a knock came at the door. Aleksy was alone. His mother was working in her garden and Borys and Damian were in the fields. He stood, heart thumping, certain that the moment had come—and resolved to face up to what might come. He had done nothing so terrible. He would accept his fate. He went to the door and threw it back. His gaze was drawn downward.

Idzi had not yet seen the results of Sunday's outing and so he stared at Aleksy's face for a long moment. Then he whistled. For once he was at a loss for words.

"Looking for me, Idzi?"

"Did you get hit with a board? That one eye is a badge worthy of veneration. Like the rainbow, it is."

"Never mind. What do you want?"

"Someone's looking for you."

"Jezus Chrystus—who?" This was the summons, he was certain. Would Lord Halicki vent his spleen on him—or on the entire Gazdecki family?

"In the barn."

"Who?"

"Can't say." Idzi pivoted now, his short legs pumping quickly as he made his way toward the out-buildings.

When Aleksy reached the barn, he looked back to see Idzi across the way, at the corner of the hen house, his tousled head turned in his direction, his expression impossible to read. Aleksy blinked and the little man was gone.

Uncertain of who or what awaited him, Aleksy drew in a deep breath, opened the barn door and entered. The door swung closed behind him. Idzi had been too serious for this to be a joke. What if the Halicki brothers were here, eager to take further revenge? He peered into the semi-darkness. All was silent. Aleksy trusted that Idzi was too good a friend for this to be an ambush.

"Hello," he called in a hoarse, tentative voice.

A rustling sound came from the darkness at the rear of the barn. Aleksy shifted his eyes, straining to focus.

"Who's there?" he demanded.

Luba came bounding forward, circled around him, leaning into his legs. "Hey, girl, what's the excitement about?"

Someone who had been hidden in the shadows moved out into view now, the light blue gown and wide-brimmed sun bonnet taking shape as the figure moved toward him. Amidst the usual smells of the barn, he now caught a whiff of perfume—hibiscus, he guessed.

"Lady Krystyna!"

She moved forward quickly now, the bell-shaped gown gliding as if she were a specter. It was clear even in this light that she was struck by the damage to his face. She let out a little gasp. "What have they done to you?"

Aleksy's heart thundered in his chest to think she had come to him. "It's nothing," he said.

"It is something. Why, I would not have one of our farm animals treated in such a way."

"Another day or two and no one will notice. Listen, this is dangerous for both of us. We can't be found here. If your brothers should—"

"They've gone off on their maneuvers. Oh, I am so ashamed of my brothers, Aleksy—they were fools to think—"

"Think what?"

"That you and I—" Was she coloring? It was impossible to determine in the dimness.

"I know." He *did* know, too, and the knowing hurt.

Krystyna gave a little laugh. He could not tell whether it was at the abridged topic at hand or at Luba, who collapsed in a heap as if bored. "Beautiful," she said, nodding toward the dog.

"Beautiful," Aleksy repeated. He was not looking at Luba.

Krystyna glanced up at him, eyes assessing. His forwardness was not lost on her, but—dismissively—she returned her attention to the dog. "She's like a great gray and white pillow gone all to shreds. How old is she?"

"Just three." He was thankful for the dim lighting of the barn because he felt his face flushing. It seemed that only he was embarrassed.

Her eyes, dark now in the gloom but etched green in his memory, took hold of his. "I came to tell you that they will not harm you—any more than they've already done, at least. It took some doing. Now you must keep to your bargain."

Aleksy stared in silence some moments before giving a subtle laugh laced with irony. "It will be some little while before I could hope to teach you. I'm embarrassed to say I have neither bow nor quiver. I've made a good number of bows, but I've sold or given them away. That is, except for a child's bow I made when I was eight."

Krystyna countered with her own unique giggle. "What is that in the corner by the door, then?"

Aleksy shifted his eyes to the door. His jaw dropped. There to its right, leaning against the doorpost, stood the bow and the quiver.

"They took it," she said. "That is, Roman did. I heard him say he had never seen one as fine. I thought it should be returned."

"Thank you, Lady Krystyna. Won't they be angry?"

"I hope they are! I hope they are mad as Hell is hot! I'm not afraid. When shall you give me my lesson?"

"Right now, yes?"

"Here?"

"Why not?"

"Wouldn't it be better in a few days? When you are feeling better? I could meet you in the forest. On Sunday!"

"No, I can't." Forgetting the random muscular spasms in the area of his ribs, as well as the admonitions of his father, Aleksy was already rushing to make an archery butt out of a cylindrical hay bale.

"Are you certain?"

"Yes," he snapped cavalierly. "Now, we'll need light." He went to open the double doors, allowing entrance of a great shaft of sunlight. Picking up the bow and quiver in one fluid movement, he returned to her and touched her gently at the elbow, directing her where to stand. "Let me show you first." He stood at her side. "I must warn you that if you persist in learning how to shoot properly you will acquire two calluses on your bow fingers."

Krystyna took his hand and inspected his fingers. "A small enough sacrifice," she intoned, "but it so happens I have my riding gloves." She turned and ran toward a far stall that held a dapple-gray horse that Aleksy had not noticed. "I brought Daffodil today," she called back. "Too tame a creature, but the Turks were ruled out by my father and I wasn't about to walk."

Her touch had set off a flow of electricity that ran up his arm and rippled through his whole body. His face flushed hot.

"You didn't think I walked, did you?" she asked as she hurried back. Coming to stand before him, she looked him in the eye and said, "Well, maybe I would have, who's to say?"

Could this be anything other than flirtation? Both heart and mind faltered. He had no words.

"Do I need both?" she asked.

"Both?"

"Both gloves, Aleksy. Do I need to wear both?"

He looked down at the brown kid gloves. He felt foolish. "No, just one. Do you do most things with your right hand?"

"Yes."

"Then wear the left one. The arrow could damage the leather, however."

"I don't care," she said. Dropping the right-hand glove onto a little heap of straw, she drew on the other.

He took the end of a length of hemp cord from a compartment in his linen quiver, picked up the longbow and attached the cord to the nock in one end, bent the weapon—with the ease of an archer who had spent years strengthening his back, shoulder, and arm muscles—and attached the cord to the other nock. "The tension in the cord is essential," he said as he withdrew a homemade arrow made of ash, just to make small talk. "For strength, the nock on the arrow and the ones on the bow are made of split elk horn. Now, I'll show you how to load. You stand erect with feet shoulder length apart. Keep the bow lowered at first and nock the arrow. You'll be using three fingers. Then you bring the arrow up, like so, extending the bow a bit, and draw, bringing the cord back to your ear if possible—with all your might—aim and let fly."

Aleksy loosed. The shaft's steel head—purchased in Halicz—was so sharp and propelled with such force that the arrow completely disappeared into the bale. They heard it strike the wall behind the target.

"You killed Lord Haystack!" Krystyna trilled.

Aleksy laughed. "A blunter tip is more appropriate for practice lest you really kill a person, but I hadn't planned on practice today. I hadn't planned—"

"My turn," Krystyna said.

Aleksy nodded, handed her the bow, and stepped behind her. He offered her an arrow. His heart beat erratically at the thought that a moment he had dreamt of was about to be realized. Correctly finding placement for the three fingers of her gloved hand, she nocked the arrow. He prepared to place his arms around her to instruct her in the proper hold and stance. And she would likely need his strength for the draw. He well knew that it took years for the novice archer to draw the cord of such a yew bow back to the ear.

Holding the arrow point down, as he had done, Krystyna started to lift it, evidently thought of a question, and swiveled about to face Aleksy.

He laughed and gently pushed the arrow back down and away. "Did you suddenly think to kill me?"

"No, I want to know why you cannot meet me in the forest on Sunday next."

"I won't be here. I'm going away on Saturday."

"Away?… Away where?"

"You should take aim now, Lady Krystyna."

"No! Tell me where. You will come back?"

"Someday, perhaps."

"I won't shoot until you tell me!"

"I'm going to join the King's Army—if they'll take me."

"You aren't serious."

Aleksy bristled. "I am."

"What do you have to commend yourself?"

"I have what you are holding in your hand. I thought I would have to fashion another one, but now—I'm grateful to you for returning it."

"Had I known, I wouldn't have done so! Why, you don't even have a decent horse. Did you plan to steal one of my brothers' Turks?"

"I don't steal!"

"You're offended—I'm sorry."

"My legs are sturdy enough."

"They say there's a war in the near future!"

"Exactly."

"You'll likely be killed!"

"We all have our fates to fulfill."

Krystyna stared at him for several moments, as if assessing his sincerity. She then drew herself up and threw down the bow and nocked arrow. "I think you are a fool, Aleksy—a fool, do you hear?"

"I thought I heard you say on two Sundays ago that *you* wanted to be a soldier. Didn't you mean it?"

"No—well, maybe—at the time."

"For you it was a whimsical wish. It wasn't real.—But I do mean it. I have nothing to hold me here."

"You want to prove yourself in the eyes of Poles, is that it? People like my brothers?—As if you are a Pole yourself?"

"I *am* a Pole!"

"Is there no mirror in your little cottage?" She paused allowing the comment to do its damage. "Can't you at least see your reflection when you bend over a basin of water?—You do wash, don't you?"

Aleksy suddenly wanted to strike her across the face. The urge surprised him and he drew himself up. "Nonetheless, I will be gone come Saturday."

He was not alone in his impulse, for she stepped forward and drew her hand back as if to slap him, but seeming to accede to a second thought, she sighed and let her arm drop to her side. "You're a fool, Aleksy Gazdecki, and we're well rid of you." With both hands to his midsection, she shoved him aside.

He stood stiff as a stone statue as she made for Daffodil's stall, reeling from the pain to his ribs—but so much more from the sting of her words. He was stunned by how quickly things had gone awry. That was the way with her, it seemed.

He did not, would not, call her back. She hated him.

The mare was moderately small so she mounted it herself and was soon directing it out of the stable, with not a look back in his direction.

The fantasy, tender as a spring shoot—yes, he had dared to imagine it in the nighttime hours—that she would allow him to care for her, had been crushed like the bud of a flower under her boot. She was right: to think for a moment that ancestry, complexion, and title did not matter was to be a fool. The greatest fool in Halicz.

Luba was up and rubbing her gray and white shagginess against him. Mindlessly, he reached down to pet her. He could pray now only for forgetfulness—and finding a place in the army. Saturday could not come fast enough.

He noticed now the brown glove clenched in Luba's mouth.

TEN

"Aleksy!" His father's gruffest voice awoke him on Friday, long before the sun had come up. "Aleksy, get up!"

He had had trouble sleeping and longed for another hour of sleep, but his father had never awakened him in such a manner before. Something was wrong. He twisted on his cot and bolted upright, a searing pain at once reminding him of the tender condition of his ribs. More slowly, he swiveled and placed his feet on the floor. "What is it, Borys?" he asked, rubbing his eyes, taking great care with the bruised one.

"It's Count Halicki," his father said, "that's what it is."

"What?"

"You heard me. We've been called up to Poplar House. No doubt it's about what you did last Sunday. We'll be lucky if we're not evicted."

"Evicted?" The word was spoken only to himself. His father had already stormed out of the cottage.

He dressed quickly and went into the kitchen. He was startled to find his mother sitting in a chair, weeping.

He knelt down in front of her and took her hand. "If this is my doing, Mother, I will make it right."

His mother was slow to bring her eyes to him, but as she did, the blue had softened. She seemed to focus on his bruised face, her hand moving to gently brush against his cheek. "What God brings, God brings."

Aleksy took her callused hand, kissed it, stood and made his exit.

Outside, Borys had hitched Kastor to the wagon. Aleksy climbed aboard and they moved off.

Neither father nor son spoke for the duration of the ride. Aleksy tried to imagine what was about to transpire, regretting he had not left the village the day before. He knew that, years ago, his father had served with Count Halicki in the wars against the Russian and Cossack armies, as well as against the incursion of Tatar tribes on the Wild Fields southeast of the Commonwealth, on the steppes extending from the River Dniester as far east as the River Don in Russia. His father rarely spoke of those war years, but it seemed he held the count in good esteem, and the count must have been of similar mind, for he had been generous to his father in the years since. Could what happened at the castle ruins have placed their relationship in jeopardy? Had the Halicki sons taken the situation with him and Lady Krystyna and from it fabricated a story that impugned the honor of their sister—at the hands of a local Tatar? It was a hanging offense and often the evidence against peasants was slight.

Krystyna had said she had convinced them not to bring charges against him. But what if they changed their minds? What if Roman sought revenge for losing the bow he had so coveted?

Or—what if Krystyna herself was lashing out at him? He had not for a moment forgotten how she had become consumed with anger when he told her he was going away. What if she had accused him of things that didn't happen? What then? She was an enigma, indeed. So very changeable, like a weather vane.

At the Halicki stable Szymon took hold of Kastor's reins as Aleksy and his father alighted from the wagon. No one spoke. Szymon cast a dark, knowing look at Aleksy. Was it one of sympathy? Empathy? Or was it fear that he himself was to be implicated for having supplied the horses on the previous Sundays?

They entered through the rear of the manor house, where several house servants gawked at them, and were shown to the count's library. Count Halicki sat behind a great oak desk in his *żupan*, the long red robe resplendent with gold buttons down the front. A wide Turkish sash of russet and gold cinched his considerable girth.

"Welcome, Borys," Count Halicki said, coming to his feet with some difficulty. His smile seemed genuine. His hair was thinning but his black moustache was expertly manicured. "And this is the boy—Aleksy. My, nearly grown!"

"It is, Lord Halicki."

"How tall he is since I last saw him playing about the stable!"

Aleksy bowed, and when he stood erect, he saw that his facial bruises and lacerations had not escaped notice. And yet the count turned to speak to his father. Aleksy let go an inner sigh that he made no mention of his appearance. He had not prepared a response should he be asked about his injuries. He felt blood rushing to his face. What could he say if the count pursued the issue?

"Ah, Borys," the count was saying, "we have been through too much for you to maintain such formality, yes? Ridden stirrup to stirrup through many a campaign!—It's Konrad to you, my friend."

Aleksy relaxed a bit. Lord Halicki's affability was encouraging. His mind wandered as the count continued to engage his father in conversation. Where was Krystyna? Did she know of this meeting?

At that moment he heard footsteps behind him. Was this perhaps Krystyna?

But the count's little announcement smothered that thought at birth. "And here is one of my sons—Marek."

Aleksy's heart dropped within his chest as he turned to see the younger brother enter. Marek smiled as the introductions were concluded, a smile Aleksy could not decipher. The count directed Borys and Aleksy to take the upholstered chairs in front of the desk while Marek repaired to a couch at some distance behind them. He would be silent for most of the meeting, but Aleksy could not for a moment forget his presence.

Count Halicki cleared his throat and launched into a review of the state of affairs in the Commonwealth and the dangers posed to Europe by the Ottoman Empire, beginning more than a century before with the Ottoman's unsuccessful siege of Vienna in 1529. He moved on to recent history: how he and Borys aided Sobieski in defeating their western push just ten years before in a great battle at Chocim; how just a year ago Sultan Mehmed IV was advised by Grand Vizier Kara Mustafa to consider the peace treaty with Habsburg Emperor Leopold I nonbinding; how the Ottoman army, culled from every corner of the Islam world, had amassed at Adrianople and then moved on to Belgrade. The spies and intelligencers were convinced the sights of the Ottomans were set on Vienna—and on all of Christian Europe. Both Muslims and Christians viewed the seat of the Holy Roman Empire as the gateway to Western Europe.

Aleksy listened to the monologue with great interest because the Commonwealth was evidently in great peril, but also because a war might bring his main chance—to become a soldier. The possibility was there. All the while, too, relief poured like a spring waterfall into him. For the first time that morning he felt as if he could breathe freely without a sword at his throat. He had not been brought to the Halicki manor house to be accused, tried, and sentenced.

Throughout the speech, the count's searching dark blue eyes came back to Aleksy now and then, pausing as if reflecting on something other than the content of the moment. It was the strangest sensation, one that he was to puzzle over as the days passed. For now, he could only wonder *why* he had been summoned.

The count came to what seemed the end of his history lesson. "Borys, I should like nothing better than a campaign such as we forged against the Turks—when was it? 1669?"

"It was 1668, Konrad, and we weren't finished until '73."

"Ah yes, well, I am forty-five now, damn it, but I'm awaiting my orders."

"I would have a go again, my lord," his father said, "if you would allow me."

"I know you would, but you are needed here. At least for now." He turned his gaze to Aleksy. "Has your father told you how he saved my life?" The count didn't wait for a response, his gaze returning to Aleksy's father. "Borys, you are what makes that little village tick. You've done your duty and acquitted yourself proudly." His eyes darted to the back of the room where Marek sat. "My sons, however, are chomping at the bit to fight for the Commonwealth. They were hoping to be inducted into the *Kwarciani*, but the danger at Vienna's gates is much more serious than defending stray marauders wandering in from the Wild Fields. The Turks called the Christian city of Constantinople the 'Golden Apple,' and they took it more than two centuries ago. Today they call Vienna the 'New Golden Apple' but I'll go to hell and back before they take Vienna and start transforming cathedrals into mosques."

"Praise God!" Aleksy's father said.

The count nodded and continued: "Now, I met with Sobieski at a wedding I attended not long ago in Warsaw. Our standing army is just eleven thousand, but he has issued a General Ban, calling on us nobles to take up our military duty. While I await my orders, my sons will continue the Halicki service as hussars. They are to be *towarzysze*—companions—for a company assembling in Kraków next week. They say Sobieski is on his way and that his main forces will coalesce there."

"God go with them! My compliments to you and to your sons," Borys said, turning to nod in Marek's direction.

Aleksy sat immobile, as if a serpent had stung him and left him paralyzed. *Marek is to have my dream, my chance,* he thought with no small amount of resentment. *And Roman, too? Dog's blood!*

"Personally," the count was saying, "I think they are too green to get involved in something like this. Thus far it's been mostly parading around in their feathers like knights of old."

His father spoke: "Weren't we all green before the Turks, when it was the Russians and Cossacks—and before that, the Swedes?"

The count laughed. "Indeed, indeed. One wave after another and yet we endure. Poland endures. You're saying they have to start somewhere."

"Yes."

"Good man! And that brings me to my reason for asking you both here today." His attention shifted momentarily to Aleksy, who sat thinking he would forego the impossible dream of becoming a hussar. Why he would be most needed, if only as an infantryman, should he show up at a post as planned—or better, at Kraków, where the King's Army was gathering. That it seemed possible filled him with a light-headed elation.

"I've hired drivers for the two wagons of equipment, but these are old men whose fighting days are in the past.—Now," the count continued, "while the usual custom calls for each *towarzysz* to have two or three *pacholicy*, along with horses, I find that I am able to afford one *pacholik* for each of my sons.—And for Marek I have selected as retainer your Aleksy."

Retainer! Aleksy thought he would go wild at the thought. He wanted to strike out at someone, something. *Retainer!* A lowly servant to Marek! Suddenly he was surprised by his own voice: "But I can fight, Lord Halicki!" His voice echoed loudly in the room. "No one is better with a bow than I, it's true! And I've fashioned my own lance—it's a beauty, too." He sensed his father's head turn at this news, but he pressed on with his case. "I've dreamt of nothing but soldiering. I can be more than a retainer! I can fight!"

The count smiled slyly. "Evidently," he said.

Aleksy remembered his bruised face and burned with embarrassment.

"And he *evidently* can ride, too, Father!" The irony-drenched line came not from Marek but from the doorway. Borys turned to look but Aleksy didn't have to do so. It was Roman's voice.

"Ah, Romek," the count said, winking at Borys. "A late sleeper. No luxuries like that when you're on the march, are there, Borys?"

His father stood and nudged Aleksy to do the same. Roman seemed quite pleased with himself. The needling sarcasm in his comment about Aleksy's riding made no impression on Lord Halicki; if he had been informed about the outings with the Polish-Arabians, the transgressions seemed not to be an issue. What did the count know? Were there to be no accusations against him concerning Krystyna?—Or was knowledge of his meeting with her going to be used as an implicit bribe to make him accede to any demand, such as bind him like a thrall to Marek? It had been a meeting with the young countess, or rather three innocent meetings, and nothing more, nothing licentious. Well, there was the kiss, but could that be called anything more than a flirtation? And then there was the incident in the barn. He and Krystyna seemed to be at odds most of the time. She was an impossible girl.

"Now, my boy," the count said to Aleksy, much like a tutor to a restless child, "not everyone can be a soldier. There are invaluable jobs to be done in a camp that greatly contribute to a company's success. Your father can support me in that. He was a true and loyal retainer—as you will be. And there were times when he was called upon to fight side by side with me."

"But—"

The count's raised forefinger and stern expression shushed him at once. His father had surreptitiously gripped his elbow in warning, as well. There would be no more arguing his case. And yet—there was still some satisfaction to be had here. Was a retainer not a soldier of sorts? And Marek had a more poised temperament than did Roman. Might he and Marek actually get along and work well together?

"Now, our business is done." Count Halicki stood. The meeting was over. "The departure is set for Thursday. You'll have one of our steppe ponies, Aleksy. Perhaps Marek will allow you to do the choosing."

"I've already chosen it, Father."

Roman again. Aleksy froze in place.

"You see, Father," Roman said in an obsequious tone, "Marek has decided to take Ludwik on as his retainer, leaving me with Aleksy here."

His face aflame, Aleksy turned to Roman, making no attempt to hide his hatred.

"Fine, fine!" the count said. "I knew you boys would work things out. Come here, Aleksy."

Silently seething, Aleksy obeyed. The count took a gold cross on a leather lacing from his desk. "You are tall," he said. "Here, bend your head a bit."

Aleksy did so, feeling the lacing fall about his neck and the cross swing to and fro, falling into place just below his collarbone when he stood erect.

"You're Christian and those you travel with must know you are Christian, my boy. Remember—it's the cross that will prevail in Europe, not the infidels' crescent."

Aleksy and his father were silent much of the way home. The quiet was unnerving.

"Now, what's this about making your own lance, Aleksy?" his father asked, breaking the silence just before their arrival, as if just remembering the boast. "Was that a lie?"

Aleksy told him how Szymon had shown him Count Halicki's lance and how it had inspired him to create his own.

Borys grunted and said nothing.

No doubt, his father was relieved the family was not in jeopardy, but beyond that—what were his feelings? He seldom allowed his emotions to show. Would he miss his son? Aleksy wondered. Would he miss him as if they were of the same flesh? Would he worry for his health, pray that he not be wounded? Or, was he regretting most the loss of another hand in the field?

So his father had saved Count Halicki's life—but kept it secret. Keeping wartime stories secret—is that what returning soldiers did? What else from those war years had he kept hidden? Aleksy remembered his father telling him some years ago that he was too inquisitive and that when he turned eighteen he would tell him more about the circumstances of his wartime adoption. What was there to be told? He was not so very far from that age now. Would he tell him before he left for the army? Did his father even remember the promise?

"Did you have a choice?" The question came from Damian. The family sat at the mid-morning meal that had been delayed because of the summons to the Halicki estate. "After all, the Halicki brothers—no one has a good word for them. And what they did to you—"

"That's enough," Jadwiga said. "Things will be different and those boys will pipe a different tune now that they and Aleksy are all on the same side.—Don't you think so, Borys?"

"What?—yes, I expect that's right."

Aleksy looked at his mother, who seemed to have wished for stronger support from her husband. Upon hearing details of the visit to the Halicki estate, she had expressed her relief to hear nothing had even been said about the incident at the castle ruins, but when told about his induction as a retainer, she fended off tears and lines of worry returned to her tired face.

"You'll need a change of clothes and a warmer cloak," Jadwiga said. "You can take Damian's with the sheepskin lining."

"What?" Damian protested, bringing his fork down on his plate. But a severe glance from his father made him think again. "Oh, very well, he can have it."

"Thanks," Aleksy said although he was less than invested in the details of his having to leave home.

He lay on his cot that night tossing about, his mind teeming with thought. If the count had delayed but another day, Aleksy would have been gone on his own adventure. Might he have been accepted into service? Surely he would have if the Commonwealth and the whole of Europe were in as desperate a state as the count related. He could have fought. He could have been his own man. But now he was to render service to Roman, who so clearly hated him. As a retainer! How was he to endure it? His life would be made hell.

Aleksy thought about staying true to his plan and leaving in the middle of the night without a word to anyone. It was a consideration that did not go far. People would not believe he went to fight. They would deem him a coward, thinking that he ran from a challenge. His father would be humiliated in the eyes of Count Halicki. The relationship between the two compatriots going forward would never be the same. To leave would shame his family. And having brought shame on them and himself, he would fear a homecoming. No, if he were to leave on his own, he could not return.

Suddenly, mindless of the pain, he pulled himself up and sat on the side of the bed. He had a terrible thought. *What if—Sweet Jezus, what if Krystyna had warned her brothers that I meant to leave come Saturday? Is it possible? Would it have been unintentional? Or would she do so intentionally, expecting that they would stop me? Was it mean-spirited revenge? She could not have imagined this outcome. Or could she?*

She had been so angry with him. Aleksy recalled now Szymon's telling him that Lady Krystyna seemed to enjoy having a fuss made. A fuss? This was much more than a fuss.

Aleksy stood and quietly left the cottage. Anyone hearing him would think he was making a night-time visit to the privy. He walked the grounds, Luba beside him. The full moon lighted the clear night. Stars were hard to detect. Fate had cast the die for him. He was to be a retainer. So what? Slowly, the realization came upon him. He would not be tied to the land at this young age. How he had wished for an escape. *This* was his escape. He would be a model retainer. Might there be advancements for men who could handle the bow as well as he? Create arrows as straight as his? Every man would be needed when the Ottomans thundered west across the steppes. He would be among soldiers and perhaps in the thick of battle. And he would learn to handle the Halicki brothers. He would make them see that dark skin and black eyes make little difference when one's nation is in the fight of her life. Besides, there would be Tatars fighting on both sides. Everyone had heard of the bravery of the Lithuanian Tatars, the Lipka. Roman and Marek would learn to trust him, depend on him, and although they might never love him—or he, them—they would learn to co-exist, confining their targets to the coming Horde.

Aleksy returned to the cottage and settled himself on the cot, curling into an old familiar position. He thought about Idzi's notion of the changeable and the unchangeable and he found himself at peace with what seemed his fate, his unchangeable fate. Luba yawned and settled on the dirt floor. "I'll miss you, friend," he whispered.

Still, he could not fall asleep until he admitted to himself that he would miss Krystyna. He felt an ache he had never experienced before. He leaned over and stroked Luba's thick fur. "Will *you* miss me?" The whisper this time was not meant for his dog.

ELEVEN

ROMAN ENTERED HIS FATHER'S LIBRARY and stood before the large desk. Count Halicki looked up from a document he was perusing. "You asked to see me, Father?"

"Yes, Roman, I did." His father glanced up. "How are the preparations going?"

"Fine. All will be ready come Thursday." Roman shifted from one foot to the other as his father's attention returned to the paper. He was anxious to get back to his archery practice. His anger that someone had taken Aleksy's bow and quiver had not cooled, and he vented his frustration by shooting at small forest animals with his inferior bow. He had not discovered who had taken them. He suspected Szymon, but to accost him about the matter would be an admission of his own guilt in the original theft. Had they been returned to the Tatar? The boy himself wouldn't dare sneak about the estate. "Is that all, Father?"

"No. I want to remind you of my indebtedness to Borys Gazdecki."

"He saved your life, I know."

His father put his signature to the document, carefully blotted it, and looked up. "What you can't know is how that changes things. How you see the world differently."

Roman nodded.

"He sets great store by his son Aleksy."

Roman shrugged. "He's not really his son, Father. He's a Tatar."

"That does not preclude the fact that he is loyal to the Commonwealth."

"Borys or Aleksy?"

"Both!—Don't be impertinent! And you may happen to be of the *szlachta*, Roman, but you are to afford respect to those deserving of it despite their lot in life. Be respectful to him always."

"Very well," Roman mumbled. He was unimpressed but knew not to argue. It was a small enough issue. He had something more important in mind. "Father, have you seen to Szymon—for his having given our Turks over to my sister and the Tatar—Aleksy?"

"I have. I've spoken to him."

"Spoken to him?"

"As for Aleksy—"

"Isn't Szymon to be dismissed?"

"No, Roman, I am not going to dismiss him for being generous."

"Generous!" Roman grew dizzy with anger. "He was generous with our thoroughbreds, mine and Marek's! How dare he!"

"And who sent for them? Who paid for them? I did. Now I told you that I talked to him about it. It won't happen again."

Roman bit down on his lower lip. He longed to curse, but he knew that would not bode well the next time he wanted something. He turned to leave before his resolve to keep silent could weaken. "If that is all—"

"No, about Aleksy—"

Roman turned again to his father.

"I said at the start that he was to be Marek's retainer and I meant it."

Roman's breath went out of him. "But Marek and I decided—"

"It doesn't matter what *you* decided. He's Marek's."

Roman struggled for control. "May I ask why?"

"For the same reason you want him as a retainer, I suspect. You would lean too hard on him. You seem to have a personal vendetta."

"Who told you that? If Krystyna—"

"Never mind. I can see that you do."

Roman opened his mouth but a denial failed him. He nodded to his father and left the room.

Krystyna sat in the window seat. She could hear her mother calling for her on the floor below. She did not respond. Would her mother climb the steep steps to the top level? Krystyna felt secure here. This had been the schoolroom for her and her older brothers in their early years when they were under the care of Henrieta Bakula, a strict but sincere governess whom the children called Yetta. On her rare visits home from school, Krystyna had transformed it into her own little kingdom complete with a red velvet high-back chair and needlepoint footstool. She shunned the wide canopied bed in her bedchamber below for the former governess' narrow iron-framed bed that was situated in the corner where the roof sloped. What she loved most was the window seat beneath the semi-circle window from which she could watch the changes in the sky. Here she could dream.

There was an agitated knocking at the door, and then it was thrust open.

"Mother!" Krystyna jumped to her feet.

Countess Zenobia Halicki stood in the open doorway, breathless from the stairway. "I—I don't know why you spend your time up here, Krystyna. These many flights are hard on me. And you have a lovely room three times as large below."

Krystyna smiled. They had had this conversation before.

"We've had a letter from Lady Nardolska, Krysia," her mother announced, still catching her breath.

"Yes?" Krystyna felt a little chill come over her. Her mother seldom used her diminutive so that when she did, Krystyna was put on guard.

"Come and sit down near me." Her mother entered the sacrosanct room and sat upon the red velvet while Krystyna dropped to one of the children's chairs close by. "Your marriage that we set for next year was arranged years ago."

"I know." She felt a kind of vertiginous movement in her stomach. She knew at her core that Klara had been right. It was no wonder that people said servants know more about what occurs in a household than does the master.

"Well, with things in turmoil as they are in the country, it seems that Fabian, your intended, will be called to serve in short order, like your brothers."

"And?"

"They want us to come to Kraków so that everything can be arranged and the banns announced."

Krystyna felt herself paling. "The banns—a year early?"

"No, dearest, they want the marriage to take place within a month."

"A month!"

"It can be done. I can supervise your trousseau and—"

"I'm not concerned about a trousseau, Mother. I'm concerned that I have not met Fabian since before going to school. Six years!"

"You and he got along splendidly."

"We were children!"

"This trip will allow a meeting."

"A *meeting*?" Her stomach threatened revolt.

"Yes, dear."

"A meeting and then marriage?"

A shadow passed over her mother's face. "Yes, dear, it's been planned this long while."

"Not by me."

"And so? Your parents have arranged this marriage. This is the way it is done. We have your best interest in mind."

"Do you?"

Her mother's face folded into a scowl. "Of course—and, might I say, this could be a blessing coming at this time."

"This time?"

"I just pray to God that—wind of whatever went on at that castle doesn't get to people like Lady Sylwia Dulska. That witch would likely send out runners with the gossip."

"Mother, there is nothing to gossip about."

"We didn't send you to the good sisters so that the minute you arrive home you could have your good name dragged—"

"Stop it, Mother" Krystyna interrupted.

"While you may have convinced your father it was innocent, and it may be so, it's a matter of how people perceive things."

"They want a child, yes?"

"What?"

"They're sending their heir off to war and they want the seed of his child in his wife—in case he does not return. That's it, isn't it?"

Her mother's mouth fell agape. "Krystyna, what a way to talk! The nuns didn't teach you such notions."

"I did learn history and the concerns of dynasties, even lesser ones."

"Don't be flippant! The Nardolski family is a significant one, just a step or two away from magnate status. You've known about this union most of your life. It is the best possible match. Or did you think you could snare a future king?"

"Mother! I'm not attempting to *snare* anyone!"

The countess affected empathy. "My little Krysia, you're frightened to have this come upon you so suddenly. That's understandable, darling. I'll see you through it."

"What if I don't like him?"

"You'll learn to like him. Some of the best marriages start out this way. Love often blooms."

"What of your marriage, Mother? Did you come to love Papa? I've heard you say to Papa that you don't understand him, never have."

"Ah, your ears are big and your tongue is tart, Krystyna. We have our differences, your father and I, but you can love someone you don't quite understand." The countess stiffened in the chair, the gray eyes hard as flint. "We leave next Wednesday. Your father is seeing to the arrangements." She stood now. "Oh, tomorrow you are to say your goodbyes to Roman and Marek at the morning meal and then you are to go to your room."

"What? While everyone sees them off from the front portico, as is customary?"

"Yes." The countess shifted in her chair.

"Why is that?" Krystyna rose.

The question gave her mother pause. "Because… because I say so." She stood and started for the door.

"Is it because of the Tatar? Aleksy?"

Her mother halted and when she turned about, Krystyna could see that her face had reddened. "No."

"It is. He'll be there, too, with the other retainer. You've listened to the boys and what they've told you. You haven't believed me—that everything at the ruins was innocent. He would make a good friend, perhaps. That's all."

"A friend?" Her mother gasped, the redness paling. "As you said, Krystyna, he is a Tatar. He's not our kind. And I find it unseemly of you to be calling him by name."

"Why?—It's a Christian name."

"I'll wager his first name was not."

Krystyna was at a loss to counter this statement but her conundrum was rendered moot by the closing of the door.

She moved to the window seat and sat, looking out as dusk fell. "Oh, Yetta," she whispered, "if only you were here to guide me."

TWELVE

ON THE MORNING OF DEPARTURE, Roman entered the stable and found Szymon at the rear tossing hay over some object. "What is that?" he asked, quickening his steps.

"Nothing, milord, just an old lance."

"Let me see," he said, pushing the stable master aside. He leaned over and lifted it, shaking off the hay. "It's not old and it's not one of ours, is it? Although it does look much like father's old relic." He took stock of it. "It's a good weight. Leverage is excellent. Where did it come from, Szymon? Where?"

"Just found it there among the muck, milord."

"You were then going to hide it? For whom? From whom? Don't lie to me!"

Szymon did not respond.

"Ah, then if I break it in half it should be of no matter to anyone, yes?" Roman moved one hand up to the narrow end of the lance and lifted his right knee.

"Milord!"

"You know as well as I that it's the Tatar's!"

"I told him I'd stow it away."

"For what? He didn't make it himself?"

"He did. I gave him no help."

"To what end? He'll never be a lancer. The stupid fool! I would break it, but I'd rather put it through some Tatar cousin of his in the Sultan's horde. Put it in the wagon with our others."

"But, milord—"

"Do as I say—hey, wait a moment! You're the one who put it into my father's head to go light on the Tatar! You're the reason why he was taken from me as retainer."

"Your father has his own good sense."

"And you are a busybody, always have been!" Enflamed to think a stable master had stymied his plans for the Tatar, Roman lifted the lance to strike Szymon. He brought the shaft of the weapon down on the stable master's shoulder, dropping him to the ground. That he didn't cry out galled him. He lifted it again, bringing the lance up and back into a wide arc.

But he could not bring it down. A strong hand had taken hold of it, and then the lance and a powerful force behind it were propelling him forward in a twisting motion, forward and downward. He released the lance and was sent sprawling into a muck-filled stall.

He stared up at Aleksy Gazdecki, unable to make out the Tatar's expression.

"You would fight the stable master for my lance? Does it make you proud? Take it, Roman! Take it. Use it with my compliments against the enemy of the Commonwealth." Aleksy bent to help Szymon to his feet.

Aleksy was leaving the stable by the time Roman pulled himself up. "We leave in twenty minutes, Tatar!" he shouted, his rage impotent.

Aleksy pivoted, his eyes moving up from Roman's soiled yellow leather boots to his face. "I'll be there in front."

Roman looked down at his *żupan*, trousers, and boots. Even the ends of his sash had been dirtied. He himself had but twenty minutes to get clean of the filth.

At the kitchen door of the manor house, Aleksy glanced behind him, fearful that Roman had followed him. He hadn't. He ventured a guess that he was probably at the well trying to clean off the muck. He smiled to himself. Whatever the payment might be for tossing him into the filth would likely be worth it. He opened the door and listened. All of the sounds came from the front of the house, where things were being carried out to the horses and wagons that would comprise the cavalcade to Kraków.

Aleksy slipped into the kitchen and quickly found the servants' back stairway. He took the stairs two at a time, passing the first level, and arriving at the top floor. He took his bearings, ascertained the corner room from which he had seen the glow of candlelight on two occasions, and stepped lightly in that direction.

He rapped quietly at the door. Nothing. His heart sank. The danger was all for nothing. Then he thought he heard something, maybe the creak of a floorboard or wooden chair. He rapped again. Soft footsteps now. Advancing. Coming closer. The door slowly opened inward.

"Aleksy?" Krystyna stood, rooted to the floor as if she were seeing a long dead ancestor. She wore the yellow dress and it seemed that his memory of it—of her—had not done justice to the incandescence he now imbibed. There was something different about her, too, but her reaction left no time to search it out. "Hail Maryja!" she was crying, again and again.

"And Józef, too," Aleksy said, smiling at her reaction. "May I talk to you?"

"Who—who showed you up here?"

"I showed myself."

The green eyes went wide. Krystyna stepped out into the hallway looked down the length of it, as if for a spy. Satisfied, she pulled him into the room. "What are you doing here? My God, if my parents find out you'll be killed outright and I'll be flayed alive."

"So I'd be the lucky one?"

"I'm not joking. It's not funny, so wipe that smirk off your face!"

Her anger seemed real enough, Aleksy conjectured, but he was almost certain that the danger of the situation somehow pleased her beyond measure. "I overheard your father say that you were not coming down for the farewells." Aleksy paused, his heart beating fast. "I... I wanted to see you."

Krystyna's brow lifted, furrowing slightly. "Why?"

"I... I don't know—well, to give you this." From the inside pocket of his *żupan*, Aleksy withdrew the brown riding glove he had retrieved from Luba.

Krystyna stared for several moments, then gave one of her little laughs as she took it from him and tossed it onto the child's desk nearby. "That wasn't necessary."

"I know, but it gave me an excuse if I was stopped on the stairs." He paused, allowing for her to laugh again as he chose the words that would draw closer to the truth. "Actually, I wanted to ask why you were angry that I was about to leave for the army."

Krystyna cut short her mirth and turned her head away, as if to look out the window. "I don't know what came over me. It was wrong. I was wrong."

Aleksy realized at once what was different about her. Her unbraided blond hair had been loosed so that it fell down her back in shimmering waves of red-gold. A simple pink ribbon held it back from her face. Her hair would be unbound like this on her wedding night, he thought, and the breath went out of him. He reached out, wanting to gently turn her around to face him, but his hands fell away. "It seemed to matter to you—that I was about to leave."

"And now you are." Krystyna turned back to him, her face devoid of emotion. "You see, Aleksy, you were my little divertissement at the ruins."

"What does that mean?"

"It means I was entertaining myself." Her chin tipped upward. "That's all."

Aleksy's eyes narrowed as he tried to read her face. Did her visage match her words?

"And now you are to leave to fight for the Commonwealth," she said, all lightness, "along with my brothers. Farewell."

"Did you have something to do with that?"

"What do you mean by that?" Pinkness appeared in her cheeks.

"Did you tell Roman that I was about to leave so that he might get the idea to have me as a retainer? You did, didn't you?"

"Why, that would have been a spiteful thing for someone to do."

"Yes, but—from my view, to the good."

"Good?" She seemed to take offense. "What do you mean?"

"Had I gone off on my own, it's doubtful I would have been inducted." He grinned. "Now, I will be certain of having a way to serve. If not as a hussar or a common soldier, then as a retainer."

"I did tell—but not to get you killed in the bargain." Her petulant tone tempered the concern the words implied.

"A small blessing," he said.

Either she did not process his reply or she failed to sense his irony. Her mind took another path. "You must watch out for Roman. You must have noticed Marek's crooked nose. That was Roman's doing. He doesn't play fair—never has. I did do you one good turn."

"What?"

"I had my father make you Marek's retainer instead of Roman's."

"I see. A second blessing." Aleksy performed a mock bow. "Thank you."

"I've grown up with both of them. Roman makes his own rules."

"I understand." He also understood that she was concerned for him despite the mask she wore. "I'll survive," he said. "And I'll come back."

Krystyna turned aside. "You'd best leave now."

"I said I would come back."

"To teach me the bow? I won't be here, Aleksy."

"What do you mean?"

"You must leave now." Without a glance at him, Krystyna moved to the door and pulled it open. "They'll be looking for you."

"Krystyna!" The call resounded from the front stairwell and struck them both silent. They listened and it came again.

"It's Mother. Sounds like she's already come up from the ground floor. She hates making the climb. If I go to the head of the stairwell, I'll call down and keep her from coming up. Now, go!"

"I won't—until you tell me—"

"What? Until I tell you what?"

"That it matters to you—my going."

"Krystyna!" The call from her mother was louder, closer.

"Jezus Maryja!" Krystyna hissed. "She's coming up! There's the back stairwell, that way. Go now or we're both of us cooked." She looked up at him, her eyes dilating as she focused.

He saw that she was taken aback by what he had only just realized himself: that tears were forming in the tails of his eyes. He little cared if they were to spill. It was likely that he would never see her again and that thought overcame his pride. "Does it matter?"

"I see my father has given you a cross to wear so you won't be taken for a Turk who wears the crescent." Before he could respond, she reached up, untied the pink ribbon holding back her hair, and held it out to him. "Perhaps you'll carry this, too."

"I will," he heard himself say, knowing he had his answer.

"Now, you really must go!" She had her hands on his *żupan* now and was about to push him toward the servants' stairwell when she stopped, the emerald eyes suddenly true, the mask torn away. She pulled him toward her, leaning into him, face upward. She kissed him. His arms went around her, tentatively at first, then tightly. The kiss seemed to draw into a full minute, neither of them caring if Lady Zenobia Halicka reached the top level landing or fell backwards to her death.

The next thing, the thing he would remember on a host of solitary nights, was the sight of Krystyna and the glow of her yellow gown racing away, down the hallway toward the main staircase, away from him.

Krystyna stood at the semi-circle window cut into the roof of the manor house, looking not out, but inward. Her life had changed in an instant. And in just weeks—or days—the remainder of her life was to be set in stone: wife, mother, grandmother and then a headstone on her grave. She had only just been emancipated from convent school, imagining that there were to be months of freedom—parties, masked balls, flirtations, and her favored *kuligs.* How she would miss those wild sleighing outings. None of that was to be now, it seemed. In no time at all she would bear the name of Nardolska and if that family were to have their way, in the blink of an eye she would be bearing the next son in their noble line. She grew dizzy with despair at the mere thought. Her youth would be spent.

Oh, she could not blame King Sobieski and his war. She had learned in convent school the seriousness of the threat from the East, how the Sultan—and those who came before him—had vowed to remake all of Europe in the image of Allah, decimating any vestiges of Christianity in the process. Thoughts of those who would die—Christians, Poles, friends, family—tempered her personal sense of loss.

The sounds of a great commotion below caught her attention. She glanced down from her window to see that the train of horsemen and wagons had already formed and was beginning to move out, down the drive and toward the road. Her eyes honed in on faces now. Ludwik's and Aleksy's families were there to see them off, the little dwarf among them. A half dozen servants attended the fledgling soldiers. These men would come back soon—all but the two that would drive the wagons along the march—but the futures of Aleksy, Ludwik, Roman, and Marek were more uncertain.

Her eyes raked the parade of riders. She was instinctively searching out—not her brothers—but Aleksy.

Aleksy! How could someone so different matter to her? He was as different from her as fire from ice. What was it about him that made her kiss him? Was it the depth of those dark, dark almond-shaped eyes that told her so much? He loved her. This she knew.

But the kiss—the enormity of that impulse struck her. Had someone witnessed it, she would be ostracized. She felt her face flush with heat at the thought. And yet some little pleasure brewed within her that she struggled to contain.

Krystyna knelt on the window seat, her nose to the glass. The perimeters of the panes had yet to be sealed with wax against the winter winds so that she could inhale the sweet summer scents.

Her eyes caught Aleksy now. When the steppe pony that he was riding left the poplar-lined manor house drive—at some little distance from her vantage point—turning into the road, Krystyna saw him tilt his face up and toward her window. He gave a slight wave now, slight but unmistakable.

Krystyna shrank back, away from the window. She put her fingertips to her lips and she suddenly heard Mother Abbess' voice: "You are a reckless girl, Krystyna Halicka!"

Had she been reckless? As her meetings with Aleksy flashed through her mind, her sense of time blurred.

When she looked again the little cavalcade was gone, as were the well-wishers. Why hadn't she waved? She was about to turn away when a motion below drew her eye. The rushing movement of an animal—a dog. The animal loped along the drive, slowed, sniffing the ground, came to the road and halted. It was Luba, Aleksy's sheepdog. It was there that Aleksy's scent went cold. His loyal dog sat now, as if confused, looking one way then the other, her gray patches like unmoving clouds in a white sky.

Krystyna turned, raced out of her room and, grasping the folds of her gown, bolted down the stairs.

THIRTEEN

"DID YOU COME FREELY?" ALEKSY asked. He had seen Ludwik on occasion, but he was from another of the Halicki villages so that they were not well acquainted. He was close to twenty, Aleksy guessed, with blue eyes, shaggy blond hair and a stocky physique just short of corpulent. They had been riding side by side on the road to Kraków for more than an hour without speaking, and he was determined to break the ice with this fellow who, like himself, was to be attached to the Halicki brothers for who knew how long. After all, they were to be comrades.

"To serve Roman?" Ludwik grimaced, started to say something, thought better of it, then gave a slight shake of his head, allowing his hair on either side to fall forward and nearly cover his eyes. He spoke in a confidential tone. "No more freely than in my village where we work three days a week for the Lord Halicki and make sure that he gets his share of wheat and fowl and the tithes from the pigs, sheep, bees' honey and the rest."

"And beef from the slaughter every third year?"

"Yes."

"Same in our village," Aleksy said. "He's a consistent landlord, you must admit."

"So you did not come freely, either?"

"No, but I will make something of it."

"What do you mean?"

"I want to be a lancer," Aleksy said. "I want to wear the wings."

Ludwik turned to him as if he had just started speaking Swedish. "And… and you think as a retainer…" Ludwik laughed loudly. "Marek might allow you to clean his lance, or hand it to him—but carry a lance into battle? You are a dreamer!"

"I want to fight!"

"Oh, they might let you die, you can wager on that. Unprepared and unsuspecting retainers fall to the enemy all the time, so I'm told. The stable master at home calls such deaths unintended damage."

"I have my bow and my arm is not complete without it."

Ludwik laughed again. "A bow?—not very good in hand-to-hand combat."

"I'll buy a sabre in Kraków," Aleksy said, though he had far too few coins for that.

Ludwik scoffed. "Our lords might not sleep so well on the night you go to your pallet with a sabre as a bedmate."

Aleksy laughed now.

"And," Ludwik added, "won't you be afraid that you'll be thought one of the enemy?"

So there it was: his race. With their situation so similar, their differences had slipped his mind. He felt the muscles in his neck tense, his face flush. Was a friendship out of bounds?

"Well?" Ludwik persisted. "You're Tatar, yes?"

Aleksy's spine tautened. "Yes, and you may not know that the Lipka are Sobieski's best lancers. They are Tatars."

Ludwik shrugged. "I didn't know."

Aleksy noticed that up ahead Roman observed them talking and was now detaching himself from several other riders and approaching the wagon behind which Aleksy and Ludwik rode. He was placed on guard. "Are we not allowed to converse?" he whispered between clenched teeth.

There was no time for Ludwik to respond.

Roman seemed as if he was about to hector them for something, but then his gaze fell on Aleksy's horse. "Who gave you *this* steppe pony?" he demanded.

"Gusztáf," Aleksy said.

"Gusztáf, my *lord*!" Roman bellowed.

"Gusztáf, milord."

At Kraków, Roman and Marek had had the sides of their heads shaved in warrior fashion so that the angry red rush of blood to his head was made all the more apparent. He turned and shouted for the groom, who rode at the tail end of the caravan.

Gusztáf's face was bone white by the time he drew his steppe pony up close.

Roman was so angry he could hardly speak. "Is this the steppe pony I picked out for the Tatar here?"

"No, milord."

"And *why* isn't it?"

"I was told the other wasn't healthy, that it would not survive the trip."

Roman nodded toward Aleksy. "By him?"

"No, milord, by the stable master."

"Szymon? He dared to countermand my order?" His eyes went to Aleksy.

Aleksy recognized the disappointment in his face. Roman had hoped *he* was the one, he realized. In that case, he would feel free to take some measure against him. As it was, any other infractions Aleksy might commit were to be handled by Marek. It was a favor from the saints—and from Krystyna—that he had been made the younger brother's retainer, rather than Roman's. Had not Lord Halicki intervened at Krystyna's request, Roman would have had complete freedom in his behavior toward Aleksy.

His face aflame with rage and his mouth closed so tight as to make his lips seem but dark lines, Roman turned and hightailed it toward the front of the procession.

Less than an hour later, Gusztáf made the mistake of riding too close to Roman's horse. Roman leaned over toward him and with both hands struck him with enough force to jolt the boy from his saddle. At first one foot caught in his stirrup but when it came free, he tumbled headfirst to the ground. Oblivious, the caravan continued on. Only Aleksy and Ludwik halted and dismounted to aid the disoriented and bleeding Gusztáf.

Aleksy empathized with the boy. He had been Roman's victim by proxy.

God's wounds, he silently swore. According to Szymon, it was two hundred and sixty-eight miles to Kraków. Travelling at fewer than twenty miles per day, it would take them a fortnight.

It was not an auspicious beginning.

On the second day, as planned, they met up with four more *szlachta* soldiers and their retinue of grooms, servants, and retainers, tripling twice over the length of the caravan. Each noble soldier had two or three retainers and Aleksy suspected such extravagance piqued Roman and Marek, who had—other than paid drivers for the two Halicki wagons—only one each.

On the positive side, however, Aleksy's skill with the bow meant there was no campsite meal without fresh meat or fowl—and often enough to share with the other nobles and their retinues. Roman's eyes had widened and he glared with hatred at Aleksy when he saw him with the coveted bow for the first time, no doubt wondering how he had come by it. He said nothing, however, and a few comments overheard in the ensuing days made it seem as if Roman was proud of the fact that one of their retainers was by far the best shot and able to provide bountiful game. Ludwik proved himself best at arranging the fire and turning the spit. It came as a surprise to both retainers that things in the Halicki group began to run rather smoothly.

On two occasions the cavalcade came to inns for the night. The *szlachta* soldiers took rooms while their retinues took shelter in barns and other outbuildings and were pleased to do so. One slept with an eye open for thieves or wolves when sleeping in the tents or in the open.

It was on his short, diversionary hunting forays—those times when Aleksy had to become single-focused—that he felt a purpose and a power. At other times of the day and night the thought of Krystyna was on his mind or a hair's breadth away.

He replayed in his imagination every instance of their meetings, every word spoken between them. For each thoughtless comment, glance, or laugh she had shown, there were points in time when she seemed to understand and even connect with him. But for the most part these were unspoken moments, moments he had recounted so many times that he could not trust his memory that they even occurred. The only occurrences he could rely on as true were the two kisses. He had taken the initiative at the castle ruins, but it was the kiss she had given him that stayed with him. He could still conjure the pressure and moistness of her lips, the closeness of their bodies, and the faint scent of violets about her person.

She kissed him! Might it portend something? Would she see him when this war with the Ottomans passed into history? Just the slimmest possibility that this could be lifted his spirits. He passed his hand over the hidden pocket of his *żupan* that held the pink ribbon she had given him. He felt hopeful. And then—like the sword of Damocles—would come the realization that he was nothing more than a peasant in one of her father's villages, a retainer to her mean-spirited brothers—and a Tatar with dark-hued skin and slanted eyes. There was that, always that.

He mentioned nothing of Lady Krystyna to Ludwik. If he had laughed at his notion of soldiering, mention of his love—and it was that, Aleksy had come to admit—would send him howling as if mesmerized by a king's jester.

As the days wore on, Szymon's estimate of travel time proved accurate. In a fortnight they arrived at their destination.

Kraków was a marvel to Aleksy and Ludwik, neither of whom had been to a town larger than Halicz. After days of travel their fatigue evaporated at the sight of the Wawel Royal Castle and the great cathedral—where for centuries Polish kings had been crowned and buried—their foundations rooted to a great rise of limestone called Wawel Hill. These edifices sat safely enclosed by wall and tower fortifications. Dwarfing the lesser structures and humble homes to the north, Wawel Royal Castle—wreathed in a morning mist—seemed to float in space like some unearthly land of enchantment, the Vistula bending and winding through the lower part of the city, south to northwest, like a loosened sash on a rotund noble.

But it was not a city asleep.

The center and environs teemed with citizens, soldiers and their retinues, animals, wagons, all in motion, all reverberating with a great racket. In addition to the many Christian churches, the city was home to several synagogues and a good number of Jews.

The components of the still amassing army took over huge fields south of the city. On the absent king's orders, companies were streaming in from the northern and central areas of the Commonwealth, as well as from Podolia, Moldavia, and Galicia. The makeshift quarters in the fields were shrinking with each influx. The newly arrived and comparatively tiny Galician contingent from Halicz found a spot just large enough near the river. The servants who had helped with the move would return to their homes within a day or two. The soldiers and retainers would stay and await orders—and the arrival of the king. Rumor had it that King Jan Sobieski would reach Kraków by the end of July.

Aleksy and Ludwik were afforded a little lean-to tent attached to the larger one the brothers used. The two wagon drivers who would stay on, Bogdan and Jacek, somehow found space in their crowded wagons, as well as canvas to protect them from the elements. Once the other servants departed, it would be the responsibility of the two retainers to hold every inch of space they had claimed, and as act as grooms, bargainers, hunters, cooks, as well as guardians of their goods, food stock, armor, and weapons. The two drivers were old and of little use other than manning the wagons, so it came home to Aleksy early on just why many of the nobles had three retainers each. It was no extravagance. Aleksy and Ludwik were doing the work of six.

Early on the morning Gusztáf and the other servants were to leave, Gusztáf reached into the tent and tugged at Aleksy's booted foot. Aleksy crawled outside and stood, wiping at his eyes. The summer morning's mist swirled around their feet. "What is it?"

Gusztáf, never a talker, was tongue tied at first. "I... I never thanked you for helping me up that first day, you and Ludwik."

"Ah, you're welcome, Gusztáf. You'll want to thank Ludwik, too, yes?" Aleksy started to lift the flap of the tent to call out Ludwik, but Gusztáf restrained his hand. "No, I have more to say—to you only."

Aleksy turned back toward him. "Yes?" He looked into the serious hazel eyes, and the quip he was about to make died in his throat.

"I'm sorry—for that day I told Roman that I saw you heading for the ruins."

"Ah, well, you couldn't have known their sister was there, too."

Gusztáf's eyes went to the ground and slowly came up again. "I did know. I put together things that Szymon had said."

"You thought Lady Krystyna was in some danger then? It was a reasonable thought."

Gusztáf shook his head. "No, the young miss has a mind of her own and needs no bodyguard. I misjudged you. Oh, I didn't think you a danger... but I was jealous."

"Of me?—Why?"

"That Szymon sets such store by you."

"I see." Aleksy took Gusztáf's hand in both of his. "Thank you, my friend."

Was it the mist or were there tears in Gusztáf's eyes? The groom withdrew his hand. "Before we wake Ludwik, I want to wish you well and to be careful to always safeguard yourself."

Aleksy chuckled. "I'll be in danger, Gusztáf, you can count on that, but no more so than are those thousands you see here who have come together for the Commonwealth."

"You are." Gusztáf drew him farther from the tent where Roman and Marek were sleeping off a night of drinking at the taverns. When they stopped, he leaned into Aleksy. "I've heard him talk."

"Roman?"

Gusztáf nodded. "More than once. Beware."

At that moment Ludwik pushed open the tent flap, making his appearance and cutting short Gusztáf's warning.

The sights and sounds of Kraków wore off in short order for Aleksy. Mornings were spent hunting. Whereas he and Ludwik had started alternating days for venturing into the city center for an hour or two, Aleksy—so taken up with his thoughts of Krystyna—allowed Ludwik to see the sights three or four days to his one. He stayed to watch over the campsite and maintain the personal armor of the Halicki brothers.

Every night since his arrival, he dreamt of Krystyna. But this night, the fifth, was scored into his memory by the time morning came. They were in the castle ruins and she was running from him, flying up the stairs of the castle keep, calling his name and laughing. Upon his arriving at the top level, he quickly ascertained that she had vanished. From the gaping window, he looked down, afraid of what he might see. The courtyard was empty.

"Aleksy!" she called. Dreams need not conform to spatial rules so that when he looked across the courtyard, he spied her at the door leading into the east tower. "Aleksy! Come find me," Krystyna called in a childlike voice. She disappeared into the tower and he went racing down the keep stairs, out into the yard, then to the tower. Round and round he climbed the open, crumbling stairwell. He was dizzy by the time he reached the top. He moved out onto the battlements. She was not to be found. He leaned out over one of the broken crenelles, surveying the landscape, as archers must have done for centuries. Then his eyes moved down, looking into the waterless, rocky bed of the moat.

Krystyna lay on the ground, her body mangled, lifeless.

Aleksy took in the sight. This is not possible, his heart cried. And then he called out, again and again, "Krysia! Krysia!"

His cry was suddenly interrupted by a violent shaking. He awoke staring into Ludwik's wide, blue eyes.

"What is it, Alek?" Ludwik asked, addressing Aleksy informally, for a fine friendship had developed between them.

"What?—nothing, Ludwik. I'm sorry I woke you."

"You were calling out in your sleep."

"Was I?—I'm sorry."

"Who is Krysia?"

"What?" Aleksy felt his heart contract as if a hand had grasped it.

"Krysia. That's the name you called out."

"Shush, Ludwik, shush! Are Roman and Marek back yet?"

"No, they're probably good for another hour at the taverns."

Thank the Lord Jezus! Aleksy thought. He had been calling out the name of their sister. What struck him as bizarre was the fact that he had used her diminutive, a privilege she had never afforded him. She had mentioned the nickname at their first meeting at the castle ruins, but in all his daydreaming of her he had never even thought of her as Krysia—it was always Krystyna. What did it mean? Dreams were unfathomable.

"Who is she—this Krysia?"

"A girl."

"Really? I guessed as much." He gave out with the facsimile of a laugh. "You'll have to say more than that before I let you fall back asleep."

Aleksy didn't intend to do it—tell him—but the story spilled out of him like waters from a sluice gate. He spoke of his meetings with the enigmatic Krysia, the contrary signals she sent, and the final goodbye kiss. What he withheld from his friend was the fact that she was the daughter of the landowner, sister of Roman and Marek, and—of course—that she was of the nobility.

"So you were—are—infatuated with a girl from the village, huh?" Ludwik asked. "If it were me, I'd be more direct. I'd let her know how I feel. But then again, I'm twenty. You'll know for next time with the next girl. Don't be so damn delicate." He paused a moment, as if refiguring. "Ah, but then again, you probably feel like you do because of your Tatar blood, yes?"

That again. Funny how sometimes I forget. "Yes, there is that."

"Still, if she doesn't require too much of a dowry, I suppose her parents would be happy to have you take her off their hands."

The confession had gone far enough. Aleksy was suddenly filled with regret for revealing any details. It could prove dangerous. "You won't tell them, will you?" Aleksy nodded in the direction of the brothers' tent. "I mean, we are friends now, yes?"

"Yes. It's just between us." A long moment passed. Ludwik's gaze moved in the direction of the Halicki tent, as if considering the little vow he had taken, as if suspecting there might be something worthy of being hidden from them. In another moment he seemed to brush off the notion, saying offhandedly, "Oh Alek, anytime you need advice about love, just let me know."

"I will," Aleksy said, rolling to his side, his back to Ludwik, and all but certain that his fellow retainer had never been in love.

"Or," Ludwik said as an afterthought, "maybe you can consult a gypsy. There is an old wagon farther down at the water's edge that belongs to an old crone. For a złoty she's at the ready to tell the fortune of a soldier."

"But I'm not a soldier. I'm a god-forsaken retainer!"

FOURTEEN

KRYSTYNA STOOD AT THE WINDOW on the top floor of the Kraków town house belonging to the Nardolski family, the July sun streaming in. She wore the white gown of Indian cotton that her mother had insisted upon. Her own preferences ran to colors—reds, blues, greens, yellows—but she had to admit that it was a cool garment in what promised to be a scorching day. The Nardolski city residence was not far from Market Square so that she watched the city swarm with animals, vehicles, and people of all races, classes, and occupations. The sight held her transfixed for many minutes before she turned around and took stock of her rooms. The night before, she and her mother had been given a warm welcome by Count and Countess Nardolski, and she had to admit that with the plush velvet sofa and matching bed hangings, as well as a French vanity table with silver combs and brushes laid out, she had been given a most luxurious suite. She had been provided with a sitting room leading into the bedchamber that featured a separate dressing area with massive wardrobes. Her suite faced the street while her mother's was on the same level but at the back of the house. The luxury impressed her. A far cry from her cell at convent school. And yet skepticism closed in.

A light rap came at the door and her mother entered without pause, passing quickly through the sitting room and onto the brilliant Persian carpet of the bedchamber, her gray eyes alight and scanning the room, like search lanterns. "My! We arrived too late last night for me to get a good look at your chamber. It's lovely, dearest, isn't it?" No reply was expected. "The tapestries are exquisite!"

"And how is your suite, Mother?"

"Mine? Nothing like this," she whispered, "if one might even call it a suite. It may have belonged to a maid.—But it doesn't matter, does it? It certainly seems they wish to spoil you."

"You needn't go on about that. It's you they wanted to impress."

"What do you mean?"

"I mean, Mother, that last night I overheard you speaking with Lady Nardolska after you had viewed the rooms. You insisted they reverse their arrangements. The maid's room was the one intended for me, wasn't it? They wanted to pamper *you*. I'm merely the property they are acquiring."

Her mother's face ran red. "Krystyna, that's no way to look at it—"

Krystyna gave a dismissive wave of her hand. How she dearly loved to outwit and provoke her mother. "Never mind, Mother."

"Oh, I do wish your father had come. I thought at his age he was done with war."

"Will our host, Count Nardolski, serve in the army?"

"The elder? Why, I don't know. Nothing was said."

"Perhaps he's too wealthy."

"Krystyna! What do you mean? What a thing to say! I'm sure he'll serve if called upon."

"Perhaps. But Papa said *his* call is from his conscience."

"What are you saying about Count Nardolski? Hush! I don't like this conversation—and in their own home! Their son, your betrothed, is serving for this household."

"So they said."

Her mother looked askance. "Fabian is in his company's camp outside the city. He's to be here for the betrothal supper."

Krystyna felt a fluttering in her breast. For years her parents had talked about Fabian Nardolski as her intended, but to her their union seemed a distant, nebulous thing. Now the word *betrothal* conjured up a thing of substance, something that shook her insides, something that made her cower. Krystyna looked to her mother. She wanted to run to her, to be held, but chose to keep her distance. There was no safe harbor there.

During the two weeks and two days' journey by carriage, her mother had spoken only of the advantages of this marriage. The Nardolskis were so wealthy and influential that it would advance the status of the Halicki family. "You will have only the best," she had said. "Your children will have only the best. Indeed, they will marry into the families of magnates and perhaps even kings."

"But if the Sultan has his way with Europe, Mother," Krystyna countered, "I'll be just one of many wives—or a slave. Come to think of it, one fate is like the other."

Her mother's face radiated shock and her thin form went rigid in the rocking coach, and if at that moment its wheels had not happened to negotiate a series of jolting pits in the road, Krystyna was certain she would have reached across and slapped her. As for the Nardolski name and influence raising the Halicki clan status, Krystyna had been cut short of reminding her that the root of her intended's family name meant *downward.* Did her mother understand the concept of irony?

"You will behave tonight, Krystyna," the countess was warning now. "No statements meant to stir things. This city is already astir." She passed Krystyna and went to the window. "Good heavens, what a sight out there! You're not to go out unattended. Is that understood? Promise me."

"Are you afraid I'll be wrapped up in a Turkish rug, sold, and sent east?"

"Krystyna!"

"What is he like—now, I wonder?"

"Fabian? His parents boast of his good looks."

"They would."

"You saw the painting they have of him downstairs. Quite lovely!"

"I wonder who paid the artist."

Her mother glared at her.

"And his character?" Krystyna persisted, "Flawless, I suppose. A perfect knight, like Zawisza the Black?"

Her mother gave out with a deep sigh. "Perhaps, my darling, but without the black hair and black armor. I'm going downstairs. When you come down, I want to see the Krystyna smile your father treasures."

Krystyna forged a grin that did not qualify.

Her mother's mouth tightened as if with purse strings. She turned and made her exit, the slight train of the green silk day dress lapping at the arabesque design of the carpet.

Krystyna threw herself on the sofa, the crimson upholstery a blood-like foil to the billowing white cotton gown. Years ago she had accepted the fact that her marriage had been decided, but it had always been something she would experience later in her life. That the marriage had been moved up because of the national peril had thrown her off kilter. She felt herself teetering at the edge of a vortex that would swallow her whole. She had thought she had another year, either to decide this was what she wanted or to scheme against the arranged marriage. In the latter case, she would have found a way, but the speed with which things were happening made the marriage appear an incontrovertible reality. Now, even the cell at the convent school seemed preferable to what lay before her. There, restless as she had been behind the high convent walls, she knew that a life with unknown bends and turns awaited her. But she hadn't known it was toward *this fate* she was being jettisoned. It was customary for the daughters of the magnates and the *szlachta* to be educated in the convent schools so that when they returned home they would lead dignified lives into a dry and wizened old age. Krystyna grew dizzy thinking how the years would whip by like the winds off the steppes. And she would be tied to a man who was not her choice.

Agnieszka, her best friend at school, had chosen not to go home where her parents meant to marry her off, electing instead to stay at the convent and take the vows of a Carmelite nun. Krystyna shivered. No, that had never been an option for her.

What *does* he look like? she wondered. It had been so very long since they had met. She had been—what?—ten years old. Six years ago he was affable enough, but his physique was soft and fleshy, his round face riddled with pimples. And what of his character? Oh, he had sworn to fight for the Commonwealth, but wasn't that expected of a young noble who might one day serve as a legislator in the Diet? According to his parents, that was his ambition.

Dear Mother of God, I have a mere handful of days left to myself. Just days.

Aleksy picked his way down a steep, stony slope toward the River Vistula. He found her draped in black, old but agile enough to be sitting cross-legged under the weeping willow, as Ludwik had described. Her eyes, blacker than his, seemed to pierce him.

"Come for your future, soldier?" The gypsy drew in on her pipe.

As Aleksy moved closer, the searching eyes squinted. "Ah, are you a soldier? You're not, I see."

"No, I'm not. I am a *pacholik*—a retainer. But it's my wish... to be a soldier." The herbs the woman was smoking tickled his nose.

"And that's why you've come to me. To see about your wish?"

"Will it come to pass? I want to know."

"Two złotys."

"But you charged my friend just one. The big fellow in the light blue *żupan*."

"Big boy, blond hair, dirty brown boots—very muddy?"

"Yes." Aleksy nodded, laughing.

"He had no specific wish, as you do. Two złotys." The gypsy tapped the pipe's bowl against the tree to empty its contents, then placed it to her side.

Aleksy had to undo the loops from the buttons on his *żupan* in order to withdraw the coins from a secure inside pocket. He tossed them onto a cloth she had laid out.

"Sit down." Almost by sleight of hand the coins and cloth disappeared in the moments it took for him to sit on the hard ground.

As he sat, tucking his legs into a cross-legged position, the leather lacing with the gold cross Lord Halicki had supplied slipped from the opening in his *żupan* and swung like a pendulum to and fro across his chest.

The gypsy's widening eyes followed it. "Ah, the cross—and not the crescent."

"No, I'm not Muslim. I'm Christian!" Wrong on her very first observation, he thought. Not a good omen.

"I see. Give me your hand."

Aleksy did so, feeling more and more foolish. She took it in both of hers, leaning close, head down, so that he found himself staring at the dirty gray kerchief on her head.

"You see how all the fingers are of different sizes? So much the better for their usage. The thumb is the strongest, but I see your index finger and its taller companion are heavily calloused."

"I'm an archer."

"Ah, I see. Now, here is your Life Line, moving from between your thumb and index finger in an arch across the middle of the palm to the base of the thumb. You will fight. I see many weapons, many deaths."

"Will I be a lancer?" The question, only half-serious, flew out of his mouth. She could not know anything, not anything real.

She ignored his question. "Just above the Life Line is the Head Line, you see." Her finger moved horizontally across his palm. "You have a strong love of adventure and enthusiasm for life. The Health Line, here, moving from the little finger to the base of the palm is nearly invisible and that can be to the good. Now—the Heart Line. It is here," she said, running her finger from beneath the index and middle fingers to the edge of the palm beneath the little finger. She looked up, grunted, changed her hold, ran the fingers of one hand over his as if erasing what she had seen, and grunted again. The black eyes came up once more and she said, "You are not truthful."

"What?" He pulled his hand away.

The gypsy pointed her finger at him. "You have *two* wishes."

"What? What do you see?"

"A heart—yours—easily won. And a second wish, just as close to your heart as the first, perhaps closer."

Aleksy sat paralyzed. He had come only because Ludwik had badgered him to do so. What prescient powers could this withering old prune truly have? His skin prickled. "What do you see?"

She put out her hand, palm up. "I see two more złotys. Two wishes, four złotys."

This was the moment for him to leave. Her method was as crooked as her spine. The initial two złotys were as good as thrown into the Vistula. Was he to throw another two in after them? Moments passed as he considered. When next he looked, the cloth was placed again on the ground.

"You want to know," she said, the tilt of her head drawing up the loose skin of her neck in a posture of supreme confidence. She'd been at this game for many years.

He did want to know. He withdrew another two coins, dropped them onto the cloth, and watched her skillfully seize them.

"Your hand."

He obeyed. He would cuff Ludwik for getting him into this situation. This time she did no tracing of his lines; instead, she held his hand, closed her eyes and seemed to go into a trance.

Two full minutes must have passed. "The other wish?" he pressed.

She looked up, eyes bright, and smiled, revealing three or four widely-spaced, moss-colored teeth. "A woman, a very young woman."

Aleksy was not impressed. A wish regarding a woman might fit most every one of the nearly twenty thousand men already assembled at Kraków. He knew, too, his expression gave away his disbelief.

"She is not Tatar," she said.

"No."

"A complication. There are others, too."

"Women or complications?" he asked, his tone mocking.

She gave a wry smile. "Complications."

"Yes, there are complications."

"I'm talking about people, people… working against you. There are lies."

"Lies?"

"Yes. She is very beautiful. Hair of gold. She is Polish."

Aleksy felt knots forming at the pit of his stomach. How could she know this? And then he thought of Ludwik. He must have given her this information. Was this a big joke being played on him? But, then again, what lies had he ever mentioned to Ludwik? What did she mean?

The woman looked into Aleksy's eyes as if she could read his mind, and she drew back as if stunned, her sentence flying out like an arrow to its mark: "The woman—she is high-born."

Aleksy went numb. He had not dared to reveal that significant detail to Ludwik. To tell him of his love for the sister of the Halicki brothers would invite scorn and ridicule. He would think him a ridiculous person. And there was the matter of trust: What if he was to speak of it—knowingly or not—to the brothers?

Aleksy's thoughts came back to the gypsy. What powers did this woman have? A shiver ran through him. He swallowed hard. "What of these wishes?" He hardly recognized his own voice, it quavered so.

"You want to know the outcomes, yes? I cannot always see my way to the outcomes."

Aleksy stared at her, waiting, suspecting she would ask for more coins.

Her face folded into an expression of what appeared to be empathy, her voice seemingly sincere. "There is another line on the palm, one that not everyone possesses—the Soartă."

"Soartă?"

"It's Romanian for Fate—the Fate Line."

"Do I have one?"

"You do. It runs from the wrist to below the middle finger. It passes through the others in its path."

Aleksy stared at his palm.

"You see that it also crosses through several other shorter lines," she continued. "These are obstacles. Your path has many bends. The danger is not always on the battlefield. But I cannot see what is written."

Idzi's words about the future came back to him now. "You mean the *unchangeable*? Is that what you mean by *written*?"

"The unchangeable? That is a mystery for the scholars, my Tatar friend." A laugh seemed to gurgle up her throat. "And truth to speak, I've had a score of scholars come to me for guidance. For myself, I can only hope that there is no such thing as the unchangeable."

Krystyna sat nervously running the tip of her index finger in half-circles over the base of her crystal wine goblet. This was to be the celebratory supper at which the betrothed parties were to meet for the first time in six years. The tension was palpable. Her mother, gowned in aqua and uncharacteristically quiet, sat on her right. Fabian's parents sat at either end of the long table of polished oak. Countess Irena Nardolska had been a beauty once, as evidenced by her delicate features and still shapely form. Into her mid-forties now, she wore an abundance of jewelry, her black satin gown a foil to diamond bracelets, pins, and a two-tiered necklace. Her perfectly coiffed hair was a bold shade of red that Krystyna had never seen before. She found herself absently wondering if it was a wig. Robed in a scarlet *kontusz*, Count Ryszard Nardolski was a tall man with a long face, moderately pitted, that accented his height. His dark hair and moustache had started to silver. His hooded eyes now and then would surreptitiously sweep to the tall clock in the corner of the dining hall. Across from Krystyna and her mother sat an empty chair. The young Count Fabian Nardolski had yet to arrive.

Krystyna's memory of him was crisp in her mind. Six years before he and his parents had visited Halicz. He had been pleasant enough as she showed him around their estate, exploring everything from the root cellar to the schoolroom on the uppermost level that she had so recently transformed into her sanctuary. Was he still plump and clumsy? Was his round face still pimpled? At the time Krystyna had no idea that while they were playing at some children's card game at the top of the house, their parents were below in the reception room plotting their nuptials. And now she sat waiting to see what had become of that unattractive, gawky boy. Time was running out on the little freedom she had gained since her expulsion from convent school.

Krystyna had observed a water clock once and she imagined herself now as a condemned criminal watching the steady fall of the drops, listening to the relentless, nearly noiseless, plops, knowing that when the water was done, life would be over.

It seemed that while the wine had not run out, polite conversation had, and an uncomfortable lull ensued. Already on two occasions Krystyna had noticed a maid peek out from the door to the kitchens in an effort to see if the courses could commence and twice she had been turned back by a subtly severe look flashed by Countess Nardolska. On these occasions Krystyna noted that the woman had a tic in the form of a twitching beneath the right eye.

Krystyna's mother now dared to venture into the void, addressing her host and hostess. "Your town house is superb, I must say. Why, Krystyna's suite is unparalleled!"

Countess Nardolska cleared her throat. "It is not much in comparison to our estate at Opole. Isn't that right, Ryszard?"

The count grunted in the affirmative.

"I daresay," the countess continued, turning to Krystyna, "that your rooms at our castle at Opole will please you beyond measure."

Krystyna was reminded of a proverb: "He who buys a cage will then want a bird." She rendered the facsimile of a smile. "Will we"—she couldn't bring herself to say *Fabian and I*— "not have our own estate?"

The table went quiet. Krystyna felt a sharp pinch to her thigh. Such was her mother's method when Krystyna spoke out of turn at table, but it had been years since it was employed. Refusing to acknowledge the reprimand in any way, she kept her vision fastened to Countess Nardolska's sharp gray-green eyes, thus keeping the question in play and putting the woman's tic into motion.

"There will be time for that," the countess said. Krystyna knew that her future mother-in-law thought her bold and presumptuous. It was her clipped tone that did the pinching. Nevertheless, Krystyna rather enjoyed the minor clash. She smiled and did not push further. However, she knew instinctively that it would be a battle with this woman for years on end. The countess would live well into her old age, and Krystyna would be as a prisoner in the Nardolski household, watching the years drip, one by one, dropping like tears in the water clock.

A little commotion arose in the kitchens and then a young man dressed in a teal blue *żupan* emerged through the swinging door, wine glass in hand, his handsome face alight with the impropriety of his entrance. Lord Ryszard Nardolski stood, his face registering indignation at the tardiness and execution of the arrival, but beneath the disapprobation, Krystyna recognized relief that his son had finally arrived at his own betrothal supper.

Bringing the heels of his boots together, Lord Fabian Nardolski provided a brief apology for his tardiness and bowed toward his mother and father, turning from one to the other with enough grace to avoid spillage of the red wine, but sans reason for his lapse in manners. Lady Nardolska forced a smile and reintroduced her son to Krystyna and her mother.

"Welcome to our humble town house, Lady Halicka and Lady Krystyna!" As he took his seat across from them, he went on for a while, reminiscing about his visit to the Halicki estate six years previous. More than the particulars of what he was saying, Krystyna would later recall the motion of his mouth and the glittering white teeth.

Krystyna's mother had gone into fits of anger when one of her three were late to the table, but one glance at her smile now told her that Fabian's charms had worked magic on her.

So this then was Fabian Nardolski, her intended. She found herself staring. He was not unattractive. He was not fat. His skin was flawless, his eyes the blue-green of the sea, his smile contagious. He was looking at her now, smiling, seemingly impressed—and somehow, she sensed, exhibiting a kind of possessiveness of her.

Disappointment enveloped her, followed quickly by surprise. She had prepared herself to be—what? Put off? Perhaps even repulsed? Like a lawyer, she had prepared a case against the marriage, a case that she would lay out to her parents with heartfelt tears. She would refuse to marry an overweight and ugly brute of a man. Now—what argument did she have? That he was tardy? That he, like most men—soldiers especially—drank?

She must think of something. There must be a chance—however slim—that she could convince her mother that this union would bring only unhappiness. Given time, she was clever enough to manipulate her parents, but the blessing of time had vanished with the coming of the Ottomans. *Damn them!*

And now—given the adoring gaze her mother was bestowing on Lord Fabian, as if he were Konrad, the hero of Danzig, or some such handsome knight stepping out of a fairy tale to win the day, as well as the lady—what could she say to prevent the inevitable?

That she loved another?

Do I?

FIFTEEN

THE WAWEL CATHEDRAL BELLS RANG out the fourth hour. Aleksy sat in camp, cross-legged, whittling at his figure of a horse. He had abandoned the first one, the one Idzi had thought was perhaps a goat. This was his third attempt.

He had done his hunting early, bringing back an array of rabbit, squirrel, and pheasant, all of which were hung close by, prepared for the fire. The cooking would be left to Ludwik, who was off exploring the town. Roman and Marek, blessedly, spent little of the daytime hours in camp. This time was Aleksy's.

He was thinking again of the gypsy, regretting the four złotys he had lost to her—without gain to himself. He would not allow Ludwik to goad him into such a venture again. The woman had failed to render a single hint at his future. It was no wonder the priests preached against such tellers of fortune. And yet—she had realized he held two dreams. And she had honed in on his love for a high-born woman. How was that possible?

Ludwik appeared out of the ever-shifting streams of soldiers, retainers, servants, and camp followers passing by the campsite. "How's the horse coming, Aleksy?" he asked.

Aleksy looked up. "Almost done, my friend. Now it's just a matter of infusing it with life."

Ludwik laughed. "And did you plan to shrink yourself to fit?"

Aleksy grinned. "Ha, tomorrow we'll awake to find him full size, you'll see, tall and sturdy, just like Flash and Miracle over there."

"I saw something else today."

"What now? A gypsy, by chance?"

"Something better. A young lady, by chance."

"Really? Did she stalk you? Did she wink at you? I have no more złotys to lend you, should she rent by the hour."

Ludwik dropped down beside Aleksy. "I'm serious. It was the girl!"

"What girl?"

"The girl you dream about."

Aleksy's lightheartedness soured at once. "Not funny, Ludwik."

"No, really. It was at the cathedral. She was just as you described—long blond braids and beautiful beyond compare."

"Don't be ridiculous. You don't know her. You've never seen her. And she's at home in Halicz."

"No! She's here, Alek. It was her, it was."

"Green eyes?"

"I don't know—I didn't get close enough."

"Then how could you… and I suppose she was wearing a yellow gown? You see a pretty girl in a yellow dress and you think it's the same girl? How naïve you are, Ludwik."

"It wasn't yellow. Do you think girls always wear the same dress? *That's* naïve! It was blue."

"Then what possessed you to think—"

"Her name is Krystyna."

"What?" Aleksy felt a flutter in his chest.

"It is."

"Ha! Why, there must be a thousand Krystynas here in Kraków alone."

"But this one is yours!"

"You're daft, man.—What makes you think so?"

Ludwik's smile was all smugness, as if he were laying down his last card, the card that would win the game. "Because I followed her out of the cathedral and on the steps there she met with her brothers who were waiting for her."

Aleksy felt as if all his breath had been suddenly taken from him. His head spun. "Roman and—"

Ludwik nodded. "Roman and Marek, yes."

Aleksy sat back, allowing his dizziness to pass, the news to be absorbed. Krystyna Halicka was here in Kraków. How was it possible? In a few moments another thought sparked. "Ludwik, how did you know—that is, I never told you—"

"That your Krysia is their sister? Give me some credit. I may not read and write like you, but I'm no fool either. Last week I overheard Marek mention his sister's name, and it took about two seconds to put things together."

Aleksy jumped to his feet.

"Not so fast, young lover! She's gone."

"Gone? How do you know? She may still be in the square."

"She's not. I saw Roman and Marek escort her out of the square."

"Where to?"

"Alas, that's where my knowledge hits a stone wall. They went down Grodzka Street which had few people and I dared not be recognized by Roman. He'd thrash the living hell out of me."

"Damn, Ludwik, you could have thought of *something* if they saw you!"

"But I didn't. Sorry." Silence ensued. Ludwik then ventured a thought. "Couldn't you find out her whereabouts from—"

One dark look from Aleksy aborted his sentence. There was no way he could broach the subject of Krystyna to her brothers.

Aleksy had been told by several Krakówians that their Rynek Glówny was the largest and most beautiful Market Square in all of Europe. But as the days of his search for Krystyna wore on, he began to wish the square were a little smaller. Bordered by countless town houses, palaces and churches, the Market Square had as its focal point the massive Sukiennice—the Cloth Hall—the center of commerce. The roof of the building had a parapet embellished with painted masks that Aleksy came to feel were mocking him as he made his hourly rounds that took him through and around the hall, squeezing then through the teeming square that smelled of spices and unwashed bodies, up the stone steps into the colossal architectural hodgepodge that was the Wawel Cathedral, passing through the vestibule, the nave, the transept's crossing, coming at last to the sanctuary boundary, no longer impressed by the Herculean columns, ornately vaulted ceilings, sculpted figures, or daunting tombs.

So often had he passed by a priest, Father Franciszek, who stood at the cathedral's entrances selling little medals of Saint Stanislaus of Szczepanów, Poland's patron saint—for the maintenance of the building, he said—that they had struck up an acquaintance. "In and out like a light," the priest joked today. "Plentiful but brief are your orisons. Alek, I'll give *you* a złoty if you tell me what you're praying for."

Aleksy favored him with a smile. "A miracle, Father."

Retracing his steps, he repaired to where Grodzka Street met the square. Here, on the spot where Ludwik had last seen Krystyna, he rested, watching the colorful beehive of activity before him, his eyes ever alert, his heart despondent.

It was on the seventh day of his afternoon routine that he stood at the corner of Grodzka Street, leaning against a town house. There was no time for making his rounds again. He would be expected back at camp. He came to a decision. On the morrow he would ask Ludwik to switch his free time to the afternoon hours, allowing him to search in the morning. Perhaps Krystyna came out in the earlier, cooler hours of the day. And then, again, perhaps she had not returned to the Market Square at all. Perhaps this was all for nothing. She might already be back in Halicz.

Ready to plunge into the hive once again, he was moving away from the stone building when someone tapped him on the shoulder and said, "Aleksy." He turned about, but he had recognized the honeyed voice at once.

Krystyna was dressed in a gown of deep green that made Aleksy notice her emerald eyes first and then her expression, one that he deciphered as playful delight. On her head she wore a gold scalloped scarf of Eastern design, one of her red-gold braids eluding it and spilling down her bodice. He took in a big breath. She seemed to be waiting for him to say something but words would not come.

"I thought I might find you somewhere about," she said.

"You were looking for me?" Her animated expression made him think she had been doing just that.

"Well, not really searching, but I thought I would tell you something if I were to find you." Krystyna seemed to be tempering her initial excitement—joy?—upon seeing him.

"What are you doing here, Krystyna?"

"My parents brought me. They… we came to visit family friends."

"It's a strange time to go visiting, what with the fate of our nation in the balance."

"Well… they had their reasons."

"I'm glad that they did."

"I'm not."

"Why?"

"Oh, I don't know. They're an uninteresting family."

"They live here on Grodzka Street?"

"They do." She gave a little shake of her head. "What about you? When will you be leaving?"

"When the king finally arrives from Warsaw. We hear he's travelling with a huge entourage and it's going very slowly."

"I see."

The conversation continued in this way for several minutes, touching on the Ottoman threat and approaching storm of war that could change forever the face of Europe. It seemed to Aleksy that they had started to exchange bits of information in a formal sort of way and that the excitement of the initial informal and more personal meeting was deflating. It was as if they were strangers. Had she really kissed him on his day of departure from Halicz—or had he imagined it? "You said you had something to tell me," he said. Did he dare think she would share her feelings? Was it about the kiss?

"What… oh, it's about your dog."

"Luba?"

"Yes, just after you and the others left, Luba went down our drive to the road, following your scent."

"She did?"

"Yes, she must love you very much."

"She does.—And you?" The bold words were out of his mouth as if the gypsy had possessed him. The heat of embarrassment rose up into his face.

Krystyna misinterpreted—deliberately, he was certain—the abrupt question. "I once had a terrier, but he formed no special bond with me. Quite independent he was. Oh, he warmed up—to anyone who had a piece of meat or cheese to offer him."

"Luba got home all right?" This thread of thought was disconcerting. Of course, he was concerned for his beloved dog, but what if she had brought Luba to his home? What would she have thought of such a spare cottage and the simple way his parents lived?

"He did. I found your dwarf Idzi talking to our stable master Szymon, so I had him take her."

"Thank you, Krystyna."

"Krysia."

His heart beat fast. "Krysia, then." It seemed the line of formality had been breached.

"Would you like to walk around the square?" he asked.

"I dare not. If I were seen—"

"By your brothers?"

She shrugged. "And others."

"Who?"

Her expression went dark and her tone sharpened. "It doesn't matter. Others, that's all."

He felt the moment of closeness slipping away. Impulsively he took her hands and pulled her a few steps to the side of the building where a doorway arch sheltered them from only the most curious eyes. He drew her close then and kissed her.

For a moment he thought the kiss would go on, as had the one she had initiated. But she pulled back, her face contorted and grim. "No!" she cried.

"But I thought—that is, you kissed me—in Halicz."

"That—that was—"

Aleksy bristled. "What, a mistake?"

"No," she said. "But this is a mistake." She was backing out from the embrasure. "This is a mistake. I must go now, Aleksy."

He tried to hold on to her hands, but they pulled away, one and then the other. "Stay a moment, will you?"

"We're not to meet again. We can't."

"Because I'm a Tatar?"

"No, that's not it."

"Your family, then?"

"Yes, of course. And—"

"And *what*?"

"Goodbye, Aleksy. Do not follow me. It will be dangerous for you." She turned her back to him and started to move off.

"Wait, Krystyna! Meet me here tomorrow at noon—please!"

Still in motion, Krystyna turned her head to him for a moment. "I can't, Aleksy. I can't—you must forget me!" She slipped now in and among the crowd on the street.

For a moment he wished he had not found her here in Kraków, that she had remained what she had been to him: a wonderful, impossible dream.

But this wish was eclipsed by the sight—just seconds before—of her green gown and her porcelain face beneath a scalloped gold veil turning to warn him away. Those emerald eyes were streaming tears.

Aleksy stood transfixed, watching until the last bits of green and gold dissolved into the tapestry of the teeming street scene. She was gone.

SIXTEEN

ROMAN HAD ONLY JUST MOVED out of the Market Square and into Grodzka Street when he nearly collided with a young man who wasn't watching where he was walking.

"Aleksy!"

Aleksy's head jerked upright. He halted.

"Looking for lost coins, Aleksy?"

"No, milord."

"You were walking with your head down. Have you lost a złoty, then?"

"No, milord."

Roman realized the Tatar's dark complexion was unnaturally pale. "What is it? Are you all right?"

"Yes, I am."

What had put him out of sorts? Roman looked up the street toward the Nardolski town house. Could he be aware of Krystyna's presence in Kraków? How? Not very likely, he decided. But just the slightest possibility sharpened his tone now. "Just what are you doing here, Aleksy?"

"It's my free time, milord. Like Ludwik, I enjoy exploring the city."

"Indeed?" Roman noted how very little he seemed to be enjoying anything. "What are you doing on Grodzka Street?"

"Is that the name? I didn't know. I've explored all the streets leading from the square. I'm on my way back to camp now. Did you see the fat pheasant I brought in this morning? I don't want Ludwik to char it on the spit."

Roman watched some shift go on behind the Tatar's eyes, as if he suddenly realized it was to his own benefit to mask his sour mood with a light and friendly tone. Roman's impulse was to throttle the truth out of him, but he knew that would do little good. Aleksy was a stubborn one.

And here on the public street, he hesitated to make a scene. Besides, he was Marek's retainer, so according to custom only Marek could take physical action. It was a custom he would easily disregard, but his gut told him he would need greater motivation than merely finding him on the street where the Nardolskis live. "You'd best move, then, hadn't you?"

Aleksy pivoted and moved away.

"Aleksy!" Roman called.

The Tatar stood still and turned to look back, his face opaque.

"Marek and I won't be there for the late meal. Be certain to save the full breast of the pheasant for us."

Aleksy nodded, turned away, and melted into the crowded square.

Roman moved up Grodzka Street, toward the Nardolski town house. The Tatar's placement in this street and his behavior were too much to ignore. Was it merely coincidental? He would bear close watching.

In the evening, while escorting his mother in to supper, Roman whispered to her. "Did Krystyna leave the house today?"

"No, she did not. Why?"

"Are you certain?"

"Yes. She has had explicit orders not to leave the house unattended."

"Mother, be certain she obeys. There are dangers out there to be found." The tête-à-tête concluded as they entered the dining room, where five others were seating themselves: Krystyna, Fabian Nardolski, his parents, and Marek, who had arrived in the late afternoon.

Roman watched Krystyna, who added to the conversation when addressed but in the interims seemed distracted. He thought her behavior the likely result of being thrust into a marriage that up until recently had been set for the next year. What had seemed remote was now days away. She was behaving as well as might be expected. He had to admit to himself she was in a situation he himself would not appreciate.

He watched Fabian Nardolski, too. The man was personable and handsome—and he knew it. Even in the conversations he didn't initiate, he seemed to dominate, so great were his knowledge and opinions—and so straight his teeth, their whiteness exaggerated by his tanned complexion. He was trying hard to impress Krystyna, it seemed. Whether his effort was having any effect remained to be seen, but by the end of the meal Roman was impressed that Fabian's goblets of wine outnumbered his own.

The clock on the mantel out in the suite's sitting room gently chimed two o'clock. In her bed, Krystyna turned on to her side. She had yet to fall asleep. The events of the day played and replayed in her mind. She had tried to live up to expectations at supper. Had it appeared that way to others? She was the princess consenting to marriage to a prince so that two nations might be united, to the benefit of the many. According to her parents, that was the object of marriage. Except that she was not a princess—although her parents did see the union as a political one that would unite two families, a union that would elevate one—theirs—to new heights.

How was she to escape her fate? Fortuna's whimsical wheel was turning. There would be no arguing with her mother. Lord Fabian had enchanted her, that was clear, and the same would be true of her father once he arrived. Fabian had drunk quite a bit at supper, but that was the way of things for young men, especially men in the military. Besides, he seemed to hold his liquor well. She remembered now how during the meal his sparkling turquoise eyes would move surreptitiously to her, holding her gaze with such boldness that it seemed as if he were holding her at the waist, drawing her near. As if he were kissing her with his eyes. These moments played out quickly, for he meant no one else to notice. He no doubt thought that they were welcome flirtations and that she would respond in kind. She, however, felt nothing in these moments and she hoped her own gaze relayed exactly that. It was only now, in retrospect, that she realized that she did feel something. It was neither attraction nor love. It was a sense of violation.

And yet she was fated to marry this man, to spend all of her days with him.

Her mind moved back to the afternoon—to Aleksy. In having told him that she had not been searching him out, she had lied to him. She had sneaked out of the Nardolski servants' door three days running so that she could scour the Market Square. But it wasn't until she tapped him on the shoulder and he turned around that she realized how desperately she had been searching. For in that moment she knew she had dropped all the decorum that a young lady was supposed to exhibit, so infused was she with exhilaration to see him again. He—with his sharp dark eyes and sharper mind—could not have missed what she felt. Oh, she had attempted to switch to a more impersonal persona but doubted her acting skills had been very convincing. At their parting, how could he have missed the tears in her eyes?

Krystyna sat up to throw back the summer quilt and draw up the lightest of covers. She lay back, eyes on the ceiling that had been painted like a sky—blue, with a myriad of tiny stars, invisible to her now in the darkness. That was the moment, she thought, that split-second when she turned her head for one final glance and caught the depth of hurt in his dark eyes, that she knew she loved him. That was mere hours earlier. And yet it was a lifetime. Sadness, emptiness, and despair enveloped her. She would never look upon those almond-shaped black eyes, never taste those dark lips again. He was on a different path. No!—she immediately corrected herself—it was *she* who was on a different path. *If only I were a peasant, free to marry the man I love.*

The lightest knock came at the door, arresting all thought and emotion. It was the middle of the night. She was about to call out, asking who it was, when she heard the door's latch lift and the door creak open. She immediately deduced it was her mother, whose calling card was just that: a light knock and then entry without waiting for a welcome.

The spidery play of someone's candlelight from the sitting room reached into the bedchamber, shadow chasing shadow.

"Mother?" Krystyna whispered. Then, louder "Mother, is that you?"

No response.

Krystyna waited, heart racing. Slowly, she sat up, bringing her legs to the side of the bed, dropping her feet to the floor. Stricken dumb with thoughts of an intruder, she tried to think of something nearby that could serve as a weapon. Why hadn't she thought to have one within reach? This wasn't a walled convent school, nor was it their provincial country estate where doors were left unlocked. This was Kraków—like all great cities, a place of great wealth and culture, but also one where evil might be found lurking in alleyways or in one's own home, and it was especially abundant now, with great multitudes of soldiers and their hangers-on gathered to drink and game and—

The figure was moving out of the sitting room now and coming forward, into the bedchamber. The shadowy silhouette was much taller and huskier than her mother's thin physique. It was a man.

"Who is it?" she cried. "Tell me or I shall scream the house down."

"No, don't do that, Krystyna!" He moved the candle close to his face then.

"You!" she cried.

"In the flesh," he said.

Krystyna stood, covering herself out of embarrassment for her thin nightdress. She backed up a pace as he advanced.

"You wouldn't want to wake the household, would you?" The words fell in the most casual and charming fashion from Lord Fabian Nardolski's lips that one would think the middle of the night entry into a maiden's bedchamber nothing other than an ordinary appearance at breakfast in the dining hall.

"Lord Nardolski!"

"Ah, so formal, Krystyna, so formal."

She saw that he was disheveled but fully dressed. He must be drunk, she thought. Her fear recast itself into pique. "What are you doing here?"

"I thought that if we were of like minds, you would not be able to sleep either."

"I—I was sound asleep."

He laughed. "You must be a light sleeper."

"This is—"

"Inappropriate, I know that.—Did I frighten you?"

"No." She strived for a bravado she didn't feel. "I'm quite used to men stealing into my bedchamber."

"Oh, really?" Laughing, he set the candle down on a table and moved two steps forward, halting when he saw she had taken three back so that she stood pinned against the wall. "I just thought that we could become more acquainted without the presence of others always about."

What had he in mind? Krystyna tried to hold her voice steady. Fear returned. "There will be time for that."

He nodded. "Alas, after we're married. That is true, but I wanted to crack the enigma that is Lady Krystyna Halicka before I marry her."

"There is nothing puzzling about me. We could meet tomorrow in the garden. I shall see to it that we are alone."

"Sadly, my duties will take me away for the duration of the day."

How to answer this? Just what are his intentions, Krystyna questioned, her mind holding panic in check.

"You *are* a puzzle, Krysia.—You see, you just flinched when I dared to use your diminutive. I've watched you and opened my heart to you and in return, I see nothing beyond the startling green of your eyes. Your eyes are like sentinels, always watching, always on guard. What are they guarding, Krystyna?"

"Nothing, Lord Nardolski." He was completely sober, more so than at the supper table.

"That's what I fear—that there is nothing in those eyes for me. Is it still *Lord Nardolski*?"

"Fabian."

"Better. Have you had a suitor at home? Is that it?"

Krystyna felt blood drain from her face and was thankful for the dimness of the candlelight. "No," she said.

"And even though the marriage has been moved up, you do agree to it?"

Krystyna's back stiffened involuntarily and she sensed one of her old moments of recklessness coming on. "Has it been moved up so that I might bring the family a Nardolski heir?"

"You mean, should something happen to me? *Now* I see a glimmer of something behind those emerald orbs. Honesty! How I do appreciate that! While my mother may have such morbid thoughts about my survival in mind, I do not. That may be my parents' reason for the hastiness, but it is not mine. I will return from battle, you may be sure."

Krystyna stood speechless.

"I understand, too, from my father, that you voiced some concern about where we would reside. We have what we call a hunting lodge, but its eighteen rather luxurious rooms make it much more than that. I can assure you that we'll take residence there. I promise. Believe me, *I* know my mother can be overbearing. You'll be witness to her ways only on holidays.—Agreed?"

Krystyna could do nothing but grudge the slightest nod.

"Good! I'll take that admission as a little victory. You do intrigue me! Our marriage will be a good one, Krystyna." Fabian bowed now, as if he were excusing himself from a dance partner. "Forgive me for the impropriety of this visit. I'll not keep you from your sleep any longer. I'll leave the candle for you. I can find my way around the Nardolski museum blindfolded." He turned now and, like a ship into fog, faded away into the darkness of the sitting room, his footfalls so noiseless that she realized he must have been barefoot.

Krystyna moved forward and collapsed into a sitting position at the side of the bed. She sat staring at the candle flame, attempting to come to terms with what had just taken place.

Lord Fabian Nardolski had taken her by surprise once again. Initially, she had thought him inebriated. He was not. She had thought that in coming into her bedchamber he had only dark intentions. He had not. And up until now she had thought him with his air of frothy charm nothing more than a supercilious man about town. Not only had she been wrong on these counts, but he had wiped away in one brief and inappropriate visit, the reservations she had had about him and marriage into the Nardolski clan.

She leaned over and blew out the candle.

All but one reservation.

Sleep was slow in coming.

SEVENTEEN

Aleksy had gone into the lean-to tent very late and had difficulty getting to sleep so that he slept a full hour past his usual time to rise and go hunting. He slowly awoke to someone tickling the bottoms of his bare foot. The tent flap was letting in light. He grunted and retracted his foot. He longed to sleep a bit longer. "Ten minutes, Ludwik," he said. "Just ten." He settled himself once again on the pallet, but within a minute or two felt the unmistakable touch of a feather raking the bottom of his foot.

"Damn it, Ludwik!" he cried, lifting his head, any lingering sleepiness done in by annoyance. He sat up at once.

"Whatever it is, I am innocent!" Ludwik called from outside the tent.

He was not the perpetrator who leaned in, a pheasant feather in hand. Aleksy blinked, focusing now at the figure at the foot of his pallet, his overly large head protruding into the tent. "Idzi!"

"Idzi it is. Are you going to sleep the day away?"

Half an hour later Aleksy, Ludwik, and Idzi sat around the campfire sipping at tin mugs of chicory-infused coffee.

"They say," Ludwik said, "when we get to Vienna, there will be so much coffee that there will be no need to weaken the coffee with chicory."

"I tried the pure Arabian stuff at one of the stalls," Aleksy said. "They served it in the tiniest of cups but, by God, it makes your hair stand on end!" He turned to Idzi. "Now, as for you, just what are you doing here?"

"Lord Halicki requested my presence on his journey here. It was either me or your brother Damian. And your father felt I was more dispensable, I gathered."

"Don't go feeling sorry for yourself."

"I don't. You know I don't."

Aleksy smiled. "I know. How are my parents and Damian?"

"All good, but worried, like everyone, about the state of affairs."

"Has Lord Halicki been commissioned here—to await the king?"

"No, he's going from here to join his old friend, General Lubomirski who's to attach his forces to Adam Sieniawski's army and move toward Vienna from a different direction."

"I hope they are quicker about it than the king seems to be. And are you on your own time until you go back to Halicz?"

"I am! Free to lie about and see the sights."

"What's the master's business here, then?" Aleksy nodded toward the tent. "Here to check up on his sons?"

"No." A blank expression came over Idzi's face, at least one Aleksy could not decipher. Glancing at the tent that housed the sleeping Halicki brothers, his voice dropped to a whisper. "He's come to attend to some financial business because he's not staying for the wedding."

"Wedding?" Aleksy snapped, his head already reeling. "What wedding?"

"Why, his daughter's."

Aleksy was on his feet at once, turning away, blood rushing to his face. This was not possible. The ground beneath him seemed to move.

"Chrystus—you didn't know?" Idzi asked. "Ludwik here said you talked to her."

Aleksy kept his back to the others. He hadn't provided Ludwik with any details of the meeting. He spoke now in a tense, hushed tone. "She… she didn't say anything, not a word. Are you sure? Maybe it's Roman's wedding… or Marek's?" He was grasping at straws, he knew. Had it been one of the brothers, he would have heard about it.

"No," Idzi said cautiously.

"And the financial business—you mean the dowry?"

"Yes… I'm sorry, Alek."

Aleksy drew in breath, turned back to Idzi. Krystyna's behavior the day before made perfect sense now. "No need, my friend." He dashed the remainder of the mug's contents onto the ground. "I need to go about my hunting now. Care to join me, Idzi? Or are you tired from your journey?"

Idzi jumped up, swallowed down the chicory-coffee concoction, and handed his mug to Ludwik, whose face mirrored his in like concern for

Aleksy's unhappiness. He attempted a smile. "Me? When did you know me to be tired?"

The two left Ludwik to care for the camp and feed Roman and Marek upon their awakening.

We're not to meet again, she had said. *We can't.*

Aleksy never felt the need to lose himself in his archery skills more than at this moment.

Krystyna awoke early to the news that her father had arrived from Halicz. She greeted him with a smile and three kisses, gifting her mother and Lord and Lady Nardolska with smiles less genuine. Monika, the cook herself, saw to the breakfast buffet, supported by a young serving girl.

As the conversation turned to the war against the Ottoman Empire, Krystyna stayed silent, thinking about Fabian, who had already left the house. It was her duty to marry him. It was the way of things, as her mother had told her so many times. Love would come later. But—would it? Her thoughts kept being interrupted by the vision of Aleksy's face as she left him—so serious, so earnest. She had gone to sleep thinking that she would not meet him at noon. She couldn't bear another meeting. How could she tell him that the marriage was just days away?

But by the time she climbed the stairs to her room, she had made her decision. She would tell him herself. She would meet him a final time—and she would tell him.

At mid-morning Krystyna descended the stairs to the ground level, wondering why her mother had sent a maid to ask for her to come down. She opened one of the mullioned doors and entered the dining hall.

"What's all this?" she asked.

Her mother sat at the far end of the polished oak table that was scarcely visible now under a vast array of paper of all kinds, shapes, and colors, as well several scissors of various sizes, including sheep shears.

"We're to do *wycinanki* today, Krystyna."

"But—why? Christmas is months away."

"Ah, but your wedding is not!"

"Paper-cuts for my wedding?"

"Yes. Oh, Krystyna, with this wedding being done with such haste, so many of our beloved customs will have to be set aside—no groomsmen or bridesmaids. No young married ladies to laugh with you, prepare your bed and then test its strength by jumping on it."

"Mother, please! I don't care about any of that."

"But I do and you're the only daughter I'll see married off. I thought we could do some paper-cuts to decorate the house and the buffet table. You know, Lady Nardolska is planning a wonderful and delicious spread and vodka from Gdańsk—Goldwasser Vodka! They say it's the drink of kings!"

"Drunken kings."

"Now, Krystyna, come and sit down, will you? You hardly ate anything at breakfast. It's a case of the nerves, I told Lady Nardolska. I thought *wycinanki* would be just the thing for you to relax. You were always good at it."

Krystyna felt like telling her that she had done so much of it with the nuns at school she had come to dislike it. Instead, however, she glanced at the clock and sat down. "I'll work at it until half past eleven."

"Excellent!"

"But for a wedding—what subject? Certainly not two squirrels or roosters."

"A rooster and a hen!" her mother said with a laugh.

It was good to see a smile on her mother's face, so Krystyna could not help but laugh, too. She picked up paper and the shears. "I'll do a pattern on white paper for a man and then a woman. I'll place them against a simple black background."

"No color?"

"Simplicity is best, Mother."

"Very well—we can place them near the *kołacz*. I asked Lady Nardolska if we should send for Klara to make the wedding bread, but she said that was unnecessary and that her cook is quite capable. If she hadn't appeared insulted, I would have insisted. After all, Klara's bread has never cracked in the cooking, and you know what they say—"

"'If the wedding bread cracks, the marriage will crack, as well.'"

"Exactly! It's all in the quality of the ingredients, Klara says. I doubt that the Nardolski cook is her equal when it comes to fashioning dough to make the beautiful rosettes, crosses, swirls, and plaits for the top of it, but there *must* be a wedding bread. You know what else they say—"

Krystyna sighed. "I do, mother. 'Without a *kołacz*, there is no wedding.' Now you must let me concentrate."

"One more thing—I'm not leaving anything to chance. I'm going to address the issue with the cook today. Right now, in fact. I'm going to ask her to attempt a *kołacz* sometime prior to the wedding." With that little pronouncement, her mother left the room.

Two wedding breads, Krystyna thought. *I should probably think myself lucky.* But she knew she had no time for self-indulgence. The hands of the tall clock in the corner were moving just as surely as was the wheel of Fortuna. She could not let time slip by. She had to meet Aleksy.

And so Krystyna began to create the paper-cut of the woman first. Her shears commenced to clip at the white paper, starting with boots that would appear dark against a black foil and then a full skirt design with squares alternately black and white, a blouse of white, a white head scarf—its two scalloped ends resting on her back, like wings—small hands, face peering up. She imagined that later she would have time to create a tree as well as birds for the woman to be watching, but for now—the clock chimed eleven—she started work on her male figure.

She began with black boots again, white trousers with double black stripes moving vertically up to a short black and white coat, head uplifted under a simple cap, arms outstretched—as if to the woman—with one hand bracing a scythe that rested on his shoulder. And later she would fashion a haystack, dog, birds, and hints of a little house behind a picket fence.

Krystyna looked to the corner of the room. The clock read half past eleven. She would have to hurry. Her mother entered just as she pushed her chair out to get up.

"The cook has agreed to bake a trial bread. It's a relief to me.—Oh! Let me see what you've done!" Her mother came and stood behind her.

Some moments elapsed before her mother drew in breath to say, "Why the girl looks like a peasant, Krystyna, all nicely cut—very nicely done—but she seems to be dressed plainly, like a peasant. And the boy—with that scythe—"

"They *are* peasants, Mother. *Wycinanki* is an art created by peasants to decorate their simple dwellings and glassless windows. Were you expecting two of the *szlachta* in fancy clothes?"

"Well, yes, I imagine I was." She looked at the figures again. "Oh, well," she sighed, "we can talk about this later. Right now, we have to take a little walk."

"A walk?" Krystyna looked to the clock. "Mother, I don't have time."

"You have something better to do than select a material for your dress?—What, I should like to know?"

"You said nothing of this. How was I to know?"

"It was the cook that told me about this merchant at the Cloth Hall. He's there only until early afternoon. Now, hurry. Come get your hat. We don't want to miss him."

Krystyna was left standing at the table, blood thrumming at her temples. Aleksy would be waiting for her. *He'll think I don't care.* Her eyes rested on the male figure holding a scythe and suddenly she realized what she had done. She had created a paper-cut of Aleksy, one not so very different from the boy in the field she had seen that day from the carriage.

A full minute passed. *Perhaps it's best,* she thought. *Perhaps it's best if he thinks I don't care.*

"Krystyna!" her mother called.

With her left hand, Krystyna picked up the paper-cut of the young farmer, and her right hand retrieved the shears. Deftly, she cut and cut—until nothing was left but shreds upon the table.

Pivoting, she ran from the room.

At the deep sounding of the Wawel Cathedral bells for the noon Angelus, Aleksy stood, hopeful yet anxious, at the confluence of Grodzka Street with the Market Square—where he had begged her to meet him. And as the bells of the myriad Catholic churches in Kraków started to peal in support, people everywhere stopped, many falling to their knees in reverent prayer. When the tolling ceased and citizens and soldiers were stirred into movement again, he realized—with no help from a gypsy—that Krystyna was not coming.

Nonetheless, he waited half of an hour. He moved away then, passing the stone steps of the cathedral.

"No visit today, my young soldier?" Father Franciszek inquired.

"Not today," Aleksy said, barely able to get the words out. He did not turn, resisting eye contact because he could not return the priest's good humor.

"Have you had the miracle, Aleksy? I've been praying for it."

A lump came into Aleksy's throat. He could not respond. He kept walking, mindlessly so, for he soon found himself in the Cloth Hall, impervious at first to the jostling, noise, and commotion as people shopped and bargained, often in high, strident tones. Occasionally, a shopkeeper at his stall would nod at him, so familiar had he become in recent days. He thought of the time he had spent in his search. He had been so naïve, so stupid, he thought.

And then he saw her. Krystyna—dressed in blue—and her mother were at the far end of the building, inspecting bolts of cloth. He stood, still as death. Was he to go to her, mother or no? Or was he to turn and hurry away, obeying her voiced wish that they not meet again? Perhaps that was best, for her and for himself.

In retrospect, he would not remember making a decision, only that his feet propelled him forward.

He was but two stalls away when she noticed him. Her face blanched and her forehead perceptibly nudged back the blue bonnet. She raised her hand as if she were a witch empowered to stop him. At her gesture, he did stop. Her mother was caught up in haggling with the Persian shopkeeper.

Aleksy nodded in the direction of a nearby stall that was more of a tent, the side of which obstructed the view from the cloth merchant. She understood the intention but she resisted, giving a fearful shake of her head.

Aleksy called her bluff, moving several paces forward, his conviction clear. Fear flooded into her eyes. She held her hand up again. He halted, having no wish to speak to her in front of Lady Halicka.

Krystyna was now saying something to her mother, who, embroiled with the Persian in a bargaining over a bolt of ivory silk, waved her away. She took the opportunity to steal over to the tented stall where a potter sat cross-legged, turning a wheel, shaping a large bowl with his hands.

Aleksy joined her there. Immersed in his work, the old Polish craftsman gave them no more than a glance. They stood, face to face.

"Aleksy, I told you that we could not meet again." She spoke in a low, serious tone.

"But you didn't tell me everything, did you?"

"What?"

"The silk—is it to be your wedding dress?"

"Who… who told you?" She thought for a moment. "Oh, Idzi!"

"Why didn't *you* tell me?"

"I… I just couldn't. I didn't want to hurt you."

"Do you think running off and giving no reason hurts less?"

"All right, then! You're right to chastise me. I was taking the easier way out for me. But, Alek, don't think that makes my caring any less. And I did intend to meet you today, but Mother had other plans, as you can see."

This statement and the use of his diminutive took his breath away. "You do care?"

"Alek, it is impossible for us—"

"You do care? Answer me!"

"Yes!"

"Love?"

She nodded.

"Say it."

The emerald eyes locked onto his. "I love you, Alek."

"Then… how can you— ? "

"Do you think I have a choice? Do you?" Her face flamed red. "My parents promised me to this man when we were children. I won't go against them. I can't."

"And so you'll marry someone you don't love.—Jezus Chrystus! Who is he?"

"Lord Fabian Nardolski. I tried to demonize him in my mind, but I can't. He's a good man."

"A lord? With a wealthy family?"

Krystyna nodded.

"And a Pole."

"Of course."

"*Of course*?" Aleksy stiffened. "Certainly not a Tatar, then? So that's how it is."

Krystyna touched his arm. "That's not how I meant it. His *name* is what I meant, you goose! How could a man with a name like Fabian Nardolski be anything but Polish?"

"My name is Aleksy Gazdecki!—Deceiving, isn't it?"

"The point is yours, I admit. You're Polish in name and spirit."

"But not in appearance? Not in blood?"

"You should be proud of being a Tatar."

"I am proud!—But I'm not of the *szlachta*. No land, no title for me. That's a problem, too. Isn't it?"

"Perhaps not in the way you think. People like us don't marry for love, Aleksy. They don't." Her hand fell away. Her eyes averted his. "I need to get back to my mother."

"No!" Aleksy took hold of her hand and brought her close to him. "Don't do it, Krysia. Don't!"

"I have no alternative. The plans are in motion, as you see. Next week at this time, I'll be married."

"Not to him," he said through clenched teeth. Then louder: "Make different plans! Marry *me*, Krysia!"

Whether she thought him sound in mind or completely insane, he could not tell. In any case, she was struck silent.

Aleksy kissed her hand, looked up into eyes that bled tears. "Marry me," he repeated. "I know a priest. I can arrange it."

"And then what?"

"We'll forge our way—with or without your parents' approval. Can you live in a cottage with me or do you prefer a museum with your lord?"

Krystyna gave out with her little laugh. "That's just what he called his home—a museum." She paused and a kind of steeliness came into her eyes. "Listen, Aleksy, you're going off to war. How am I to live? You have no cottage and I couldn't bear to live at home even if my parents allowed it. No, we must face reality. They say this war could be a catastrophe for all of Europe. In the end, none of this may matter."

"I'll keep myself safe. I'll come back to you, you'll see."

"He said that, too."

"Good! Then in some ways he and I are on equal ground. I'll talk to the priest. We'll find a way. Now ask yourself, who do you want to see returning to you once the Ottomans are defeated?"

"You seem very certain of success."

"I'm Polish in spirit, like you said."

"Krystyna!" The high-pitched call came from Lady Halicka.

"I must go," Krystyna said, her face a mask of worry.

"Listen to me, Krystyna. I'll make the plans. I'll send you a note as to the time and place."

"Aleksy, I can't—"

"Krystyna!" Lady Halicka's voice registered panic. And it seemed very close.

Aleksy put his finger on her lips. "Don't speak, just nod. I'll send a note. Will you come to me?"

Krystyna's eyes demonstrated her love, her heart's wish, but did they show the derring-do his plan would require? If she were to decline, all would be lost. He would not attempt to see her again.

"Krystyna!" came the call. Lady Halicka was but a pace away.

Krystyna pulled away and in doing so, nodded. At least he would tell himself over and over that she had done so. Aleksy turned in the opposite direction and dropped to the ground, seating himself cross-legged opposite the pottery artisan, his eyes absently following the revolutions of the bowl on the potter's wheel.

"There you are!" Lady Halicka said, stepping into the stall. "You gave me a good scare. Did you not hear me calling?"

"I'm sorry, Mother. I was mesmerized by the potter's wheel."

Aleksy imagined Lady Halicka's eyes taking in the merchant—and the backside of a soldier's retainer who held his head down. He held his breath, afraid that she would surmise who he was.

"Come along, then. I've struck a good deal with that crafty Persian."

Aleksy waited a few minutes, his mind replaying that nod of her head. Had she been agreeing to his proposal—or had she nodded merely to effect an exit? When his eyes came up to meet the eyes of the potter—light blue under hooded lids—the man gave him a wide, toothless smile of approval. His wheel was stopping now and Aleksy realized that the clay bowl was hardening into a lopsided work of art. Evidently, he had been silently following the conversation all along.

Well, Aleksy thought, *at least we have the approval of one.*

EIGHTEEN

King Jan Sobieski finally arrived in Kraków on 29 July. Great jubilation in the city erupted upon the entrance of the royal cavalcade, the length, breadth, and color of which Aleksy could not have imagined. In the short time at Kraków he had learned, however, that there were a number of naysayers commenting on the king's tardiness, some Polish officers among them. Why had he waited so long to leave Warsaw? Why had he not gone directly toward Vienna, where the threat was centered, directing those at Kraków to meet him there? Why did he take his time coming to Kraków? Was a stop to pray at Częstochowa an absolute must? Was it necessary to bring the queen and her entire retinue? Aleksy learned that such dissonance among strong-minded Poles—relating even to a beloved king himself—was what was commonly called *the Polish Way*.

Following the arrival, criticism was again levied, this time because the king did not immediately take the great army on the road to Vienna. Censure grew as days passed. Word had it that the celebration of St. Laurence Day, 10 August, the day that ushered in the celebration of the harvest, would be the pivotal date and that they would leave shortly thereafter.

Aleksy was glad for the extra time and used it well. It took three meetings with Father Franciszek to convince him to perform the marriage ceremony and to do so in complete secrecy. It would take place in his rectory office immediately after the St. Laurence Day ceremonies in Wawel Cathedral. Father Franciszek had also been able to obtain placement in a convent for Krystyna should her family not accept her once she informs them that she has married a Tatar. She would need a safe harbor. Should it come to that, Aleksy prayed that the war against the Ottomans would be short and his return to his wife soon. His *wife*! The word made him shiver out of an abundance of emotions—pride, fear, anticipation, and amazement.

Certainty, he admitted to himself, played no part. During this interim, Krystyna went unseen. Neither Aleksy, nor Ludwik, nor Idzi managed to sight her out and about in the Market Square. Idzi, who was staying in camp—and enjoying his freedom—went on a little espionage mission to the Nardolski town house, where he learned from servants that Krystyna had been barred from leaving the house. Having been caught attempting to slip out, she now merited prisoner status and was closely watched. Other news was even more disturbing: preparations went on for her wedding; it was to take place on 12 August.

Well, Aleksy reasoned, they would take her to the celebration in the cathedral on the tenth. That was a certainty. At least he prayed so. Everything depended upon it. From there, he figured that she should be able to escape and go to the good Father Franciszek's rectory. The scheme needed to work as accurately as the great cathedral clock.

Aleksy's hunting skills had brought him a bit of money from others in the camp so that he could have hired a local scribe to write the instructions to Krystyna; he preferred, however, to purchase paper, pen, and ink from him and write them himself—and did so painstakingly. Not only did he want the handwriting to be his own, but he was also afraid to trust the contents of the message to a scribe, who might envision a much higher fee coming from Krystyna's parents. He sealed the letter with beeswax from a taper. That he had no signet bearing a family coat of arms gave him pause for a moment to reflect on the chasm that separated him from the Halicki family. Finished with the task, he realized his hands were shaking. Good God! Was he asking too much of Krystyna? Was he out of his mind to expect her to sacrifice everything for him?

Krystyna did care for him. She did! He managed to dispel his second thoughts and, at the entrance to Grodzka Street, he handed the letter over to Idzi, in whom he had confided the details of the scheme. The dwarf had some freedom coming and going within the Nardolski town house and would be able to safely deliver it.

"Do you think I am crazy for doing this, Idzi?"

Idzi looked up with his saucer-like blue eyes. "Crazy in love, as I told you once."

"But what about—this?"

"If the girl is willing, I always say—"

"Be serious, man!"

"Well, I also told you once there is the changeable and the unchangeable, and Alek, my friend, I think you are about to challenge that theory." Idzi gave a little bow. "If I were to find a hat of any substance to fit my oversized head, I would doff it now. Hats off to you!"

Aleksy laughed. "You are incorrigible. *Incorrigible Idzi* I should call you. Now, keep the letter well hidden in your *żupan*, Idzi," he warned, "until the moment you can safely manage to get it to Lady Krystyna."

"Of course."

"Should you be found with it, destroy it at once, no matter what happens."

"I'll eat it"

"Good lad!"

"I'm no more a lad than you are."

"Point made. Now, go."

Aleksy watched Idzi move down a busy Grodzka Street until his small form was lost amidst an oncoming crowd whose destination was the Market Square.

He sighed. *Will I be able to transform the unchangeable into the changeable?* By the time he had walked back to camp, he had shut out any doubts.

"Krystyna, come quickly! Hurry!" Krystyna's mother stood at her door, motioning her forward.

"What is it, Mother?"

"The *kołacz* that's what it is! You know!"

"The trial one?"

"Yes, yes, now come along."

When they reached the kitchen, a smiling and proud Monika took them to a side work table. As if unveiling a work of art, she withdrew a towel that had been covering the cooling bread.

"Oh, my! It's lovely," Krystyna's mother trilled. "Look, Krystyna, why the rosettes and leaves are perfect. And the top—not even the tiniest crack!"

Krystyna smiled at the cook; her mother's overt enthusiasm seemed quite enough for the occasion.

"Would you like to see tonight's honey cakes?" Monika asked, nodding at a table across the room, where her young assisting maid, Ruta, was working.

"Oh, yes. It's too bad we won't taste this tonight, isn't it, Krystyna? But that would be bad luck. We must wait for the official one which will be a bit larger. Still, Monika, I insist you bring it out after the meal to show everyone."

"Larger?" Krystyna asked Monika after her mother had sauntered off. "This seems a good size for what is to be a small gathering."

Monika nodded, whispering in a conspiratorial manner, "To accommodate the gift your father has brought. It's to be placed inside the bread."

"Gift?"

The cook covertly looked to Lady Halicka, who was giving high praise for the night's desserts, then leaned in to Krystyna, her deep blue eyes glistening. "Yes, and you didn't hear it from me."

"What is to be in the bread?"

Monika bent over the table and covered the *kołacz* with the towel. Her answer came in a whisper, hardly more than a breath. "A hundred ducats."

Krystyna aborted a gasp. Her dowry—or at least part of it.

Roman sat with his brother in the Nardolski dining hall. The entrée of ham stewed with cucumbers was a refreshing change from the typical fare of fowl and venison Aleksy provided at camp. Everyone was present—his parents, the Nardolskis, and Fabian—all but Krystyna.

At an opportune moment, when everyone seemed to be involved in conversation, Roman drew his mother's attention and leaned toward her. "Are you certain she's in her room?"

"She says she has a headache." Lady Halicka's thin lips widened and her stone-gray eyes gathered a bit of luster. "You needn't worry. We've done everything but place a harness on her.—But, Romek, are the streets so dangerous?"

"For young girls like her, yes."

It was true. Girls, pretty or no, could be snatched off the street by drunken soldiers or men who secretly and lucratively dealt in the Eastern slave trade. But, more to the point, Roman remembered finding Aleksy, forlorn at the top of the street, and he wanted to make certain there would be no more *happenstance* meetings—like at Halicz—with his sometimes foolish sister.

Dessert consisted of baked honey cakes emblazoned with reliefs of the Nardolski coat of arms—a wolf bearing a cross. A nice touch, he thought.

Once the cakes had been consumed, Fabian sat forward in his chair. "I want to say that we have more to celebrate than my upcoming marriage to Krystyna. A great honor has been visited upon your daughter and my future wife, Lord and Lady Halicki. My father will provide the details."

Lord Ryszard Nardolski smiled, something he should do more often, Roman noted, for the smile took attention away from the long, pitted face. He cleared his throat and in stentorian tones announced: "I have managed to attain for my soon-to-be daughter-in-law the honor of wearing the harvest crown on St. Laurence Day."

The table went quiet for a few moments. "In the cathedral?" asked Marek, voicing others' reactions. "With the king present?"

Lord Nardolski nodded. "Indeed. It will be the king himself who will accept her offering."

Lady Halicka gasped and her face flushed with delight.

"The poor dear was so taken aback when I told her, little more than an hour ago," Lady Irena Nardolska added, fingering the diamonds at her neck, "that she was too shy to come down to sup with us."

"And no wonder!" Roman's mother cried. As Roman turned to her, he caught out of the corner of his eye a small figure passing by the dining hall's mullioned doors. Was it a child? he wondered. And then as he tried to reprocess the image in his mind, he thought the figure might well have been Idzi. What would he be doing moving about the town house like a specter?

As amazement over the honor bestowed on Krystyna played out in lively comments and toasts, Roman excused himself from the table, passed through the glassed doors and moved toward the staircase. He took the stairs two at a time, coming up to the first floor just in time to see at the far end of the hall the figure move toward the shadowy servants' backstairs. Roman ran at once to the stairwell, but found it empty. He listened. There was no sound, nothing to indicate whether the small figure had moved down the stairs—or up. Had it been a child? Whose? Had it been Idzi?

In any case, Roman had been eluded by someone. He had no intention of searching the servants' stairwell. He could just imagine the Nardolski kitchen servants gawking at him. He turned back now, moving toward the main stairs. He would pass Krystyna's room and gave brief consideration to knocking at her door. As he moved closer, however, he chose not to do so; she was probably napping. Bearing out that theory was the fact that she had yet to retrieve a note that had been left beneath her door.

Returning to the dining hall, Roman found everyone silent, unusually so. "What did I miss?" he asked, seating himself. "What's wrong?"

"Oh, I'm certain it's nothing to worry about," Lady Nardolska said, her soft tone directed at his mother. "It won't happen a second time and that's when it will matter."

He looked to his mother, whose face had gone white as swan's down. She turned to him and nodded at the trial wedding bread she had exultantly told him about earlier. It seemed that the cook had only just unveiled it moments before. The cook stood nearby, her face fiery red. He leaned over to take a good look at the contents of the pan.

The highly decorative *kołacz* now displayed a wide crack, moving through its middle, from one end to the other, like a line of demarcation.

"Mission accomplished," Idzi said.

"You gave it to her?"

"Not quite."

Aleksy was instantly on guard. "What do you mean?"

"Well, someone was coming upstairs fairly close behind. I had no time to knock at her door. I pushed your letter under it."

"Then what?"

"I hightailed it out of there, down the servants' stairs this time."

"Good God! You used the family stairs to go up to her bedchamber?"

Idzi shrugged. "My friend Ruta—the cook's assistant, she is—said going the back way would raise some eyebrows among the kitchen help. Besides, the entire family was at supper."

"Then who was coming up behind?"

"Don't know. Sorry, Alek, if I didn't handle it properly."

"No, you did fine—I hope. Thanks, Idzi. And now we wait for St. Laurence Day."

"There's something else."

"What?"

"Well, after the family's supper, two of the maids collecting the dessert dishes came into the kitchen with some surprising news."

"What?"

"It seems your Lady Krystyna has been given the nod to wear the harvest crown."

"What?"

"I said—"

"By God's wounds, I heard you!—At the cathedral?"

"Seems so."

"Holy Chrystus!" Aleksy's head spun. St. Laurence Day traditionally opened the harvest season which featured the wearing of a harvest crown by a young maiden who would ceremoniously present it at High Mass. Aleksy felt the muscles of his stomach tighten. All eyes would be on her. How was she to get away and meet him at the rectory? Were the things that were unchangeable working against him? Would it always be so?

But the more he gave thought to this little twist in his scheme, the more he came to think this might be a good thing. At least he knew she would be allowed to attend. That had been no little concern.

NINETEEN

On St. Laurence Day, Aleksy arose long before dawn, put on his dark blue *żupan* which he had cleaned to the best of his ability the day before. His brown boots were well polished. For his own part in the scheme, his greatest fear was that he would be turned away from Wawel Cathedral, which most certainly would be packed to overflowing. The nobles—magnates and *szlachta*—ecclesiasts, and army officers would be promptly admitted, and it would not surprise him if there was but a little space left to the common people like him. He meant to be there early.

He left camp before anyone had awakened. He arrived at Father Franciszek's rectory as day was dawning but was told he had already gone out. Where could he be? Called to a family home, the nun who acted as his secretary said. So the first part of his plan—to confirm the priest's part in the scheme—had misfired. He had to trust that the priest would be true to his word. He would not wait for him to return. He had to find his way into the cathedral as early as possible so as to guarantee his not being locked out.

This part of his plan was a success. He was among the first, slipping into the still dark, cavernous building as cathedral servants were replenishing votive candles, placing fresh flowers upon the altars in the many side chapels, and rolling out a red carpet down the center aisle toward the main gilded altar, which featured a painting of the Crucifixion and a high canopy of black marble supported by four columns.

Aleksy moved down the side aisle on the north, passing the entrance to the clock tower and several chapels until he came to the chapel at the transept. Here he stopped, for this vantage point would provide a clear view of activity at the main altar. The dais holding the king and queen's thrones were on the south side, facing him. *Perfect!* He waited. Time passed slowly.

A muffled commotion of boots on marble arose. He turned to see more than a dozen men coming up the north aisle. They were passing him now, turning left toward the entrance to the Zygmunt Tower. Father Franciszek had told him it takes twelve to ring the five massive bells in that tower and still more—he could not recall how many—to ring the three smaller bells in another tower.

Stepping out from the side chapel, Aleksy tapped the last bell ringer on the shoulder. The heavy-set man turned about, his high forehead wrinkled in curiosity. "Have you seen Father Franciszek this morning?" Aleksy asked.

"No," the man said in a husky attempt at a whisper, "he's often at the door to see us start our day—but not so today." The man nodded and moved off to catch up with the others.

No morning masses were offered this day, not on the main altar nor in the many chapels. By eight in the morning the cathedral was being cleared of all visitors. This was as Aleksy anticipated. He quickly ducked into the entryway of the Zygmunt Tower and held his breath. Those servants evicting worshippers, making no exceptions, passed him by without notice.

Time dragged on with him huddled there like a thief, every fifteen minutes marked by the clanging of the eight bells. Soon, the cathedral began to fill with *szlachta* and citizens of some stature, as well as nuns, canons, seminarians. He returned to the little chapel area, making certain to look as inconspicuous as possible. Large areas were roped off for the later arrival of magnates, palatines, generals, bishops, priests, and anyone who held sway within the city or Commonwealth. Many of these would march in procession behind King Jan III Sobieski and his French wife, Queen Maria Casimire, to whom the people sometimes referred as Marysieńka, the king's sobriquet for her.

Citizens and soldiers were allowed in at ten o'clock and they filled every inch of the huge structure that had not been cordoned off. Aleksy fought to hold his viewing space behind the rope that separated the little chapel from the north aisle. People filled in behind him, tighter than a school of fish.

The procession began promptly at eleven. Led by a choir and an Italian prelate that Aleksy would later find out was Papal Nuncio Pallavicini, the king and queen entered, their bearing regal, their faces somber. No one spoke or even whispered. The only sounds came from the voices in the choir, clear and perfect notes pealing and splashing off the stone walls of the chamber. The royal couple moved slowly and with great pomp toward the main altar, then stepped to the right. After ten or twelve steps, the king aided his wife onto the dais. They stood in front of two carved chairs cushioned in red velvet as the nearly endless train of intelligentsia, military, and nobility filled the reserved sections.

Aleksy saw the Halicki family arrive, led by Roman. In their midst were an older, richly dressed and jeweled couple and between them was a young, handsome soldier. He immediately intuited that this was the Nardolski family. The handsome Polish soldier was the man promised to Krystyna. Like a wave of nausea, jealousy washed over Aleksy. How could he, with his dark looks and almond eyes, compete with such a specimen of the *szlachta*? He felt a fool.

His insecurity was forced aside for the moment by a greater concern. *Where is Krystyna?* She was not seated among her family members. Why? Of course, he reasoned, she might be placed elsewhere because of the role she was to play in the ceremony. But, on the other hand, what if she had refused to come? Perhaps she declared herself ill so that she would not have to face him. What if she had regretted at once that little nod she made at the Cloth Hall, agreeing to follow his directives, agreeing to marry him.

Breathe, he told himself. *Breathe. Believe.*

Aleksy attempted to allay his fears, focusing instead on the king. His armor, fitting for the occasion, covered the wide expanse of his chest and belly while the sleeves of his royal blue *żupan* went unarmored. Over this raiment he wore a long, black velvet *kontusz*, the shoulders swathed in red velvet. He carried a plumed helmet. The queen—his Marysieńka—wore a deep red brocaded gown with a matching hat that held black plumes. Her cloak was purple, trimmed with the whitest ermine. Her delicate features, framed by a mass of dark, dark hair, belied her years and seemingly numberless pregnancies.

Aleksy's attention returned to King Jan Sobieski, assessing him in light of the gossip that had preceded his arrival. He was indeed stout, his face full and fleshy. The receding, curly silvery-brown hair and the great drooping moustache brought Aleksy to conclude that he looked all of his fifty-one years. Were his fighting, triumphant years behind him, as he had heard Roman and others suggest? Judging by his stalwart and commanding stand, as well as that of his wife—who, people said, impassioned the king with strong national and personal ambition—he would acquit himself admirably.

At least Aleksy prayed it be so. The nation and Europe depended upon him to fend off the onslaught of Turks.

As the day began to heat, so did the swarm of bodies in Wawel Cathedral. Incense hung lifeless in the air and nostrils, inciting occasional sneezing. The Mass ran long, as High Masses do, and every so often a commotion arose when someone fainted and had to be carried out.

Where is Krystyna? Where is she? Aleksy fought off a cold wave of panic.

And then came time for the sermon. Gasps were heard as Papal Nuncio Opizio Pallavicini himself stepped forward to give it in a broken—but forgiven—Polish.

But where was Father Franciszek? Surely he had returned from his early duty. Was he somewhere in the background, stage managing this historic event?

"Pope Innocent XI sends his blessings to Poles and to all Christians on this heavy day," Pallavicini began. "The Holy Pontiff gives, this tenth day of August, 1683, indulgences to any and all men who go forth to battle in this Holy War against the Ottomans." Exuberant murmurs rustled through the crowd. As the sermon went on, warning of the Ottomans' threat to the entire continent while elucidating the tenets of Christianity, Aleksy felt electricity flowing through the crowd. The people were greatly moved, politically and religiously. After the sermon, the king and queen stepped down from the dais and processed to the altar steps. The Papal Nuncio, standing on the first step, blessed a very reverent and resolved king and weeping queen.

Then, as the royal couple returned to their places on the dais, a true tenor lifted his voice and began singing the Bogurodzica—*Mother of God*—a patriotic hymn sung for centuries at the installation of kings and often before going to war.

Virgin, Mother of God, God-famed Mary!
Ask Thy Son, our Lord, God-named Mary,
To have mercy upon us and hand it over to us!
Kyrie eleison!

Son of God, for Thy Baptist's sake,
Hear the voices, fulfill the pleas we make!

Listen to the prayer we say,
For what we ask, give us today:
Life on earth free of vice;
After life: paradise!
Kyrie eleison!

As the song went on, the beautiful tenor voice was tempered by the voices of thousands, and by the end of the age-old hymn, few eyes were dry.

It was at the Offertory that one of the Polish celebrants spoke of St. Laurence and a soft buzz of wonder among the crowd began at the distant vestibule, rippling forward in a wave parallel to the soundless steps of someone moving with a measured pace up the main aisle.

Aleksy could not yet see the figure, but he knew. He knew!

And then she came into view. She was taking one step, pausing, then bringing the other foot forward, continuing her slow solo procession until at last—as she came close to the altar steps—Aleksy could see her full profile.

She was dressed in a flowing white satin and tulle gown, like a divine bride. Were these materials that she and her mother had chosen at the Cloth Hall? The crown was a dome-shaped wreathing of ears of grain. Flowers and ribbons had been added so that she looked very much the bride.

Aleksy's stomach tightened with insecurity. Was it too much to hope she would be *his* bride? Was he not a fool, the biggest fool on earth?

She was turning now to the south and moving toward the dais where the king and queen sat.

The king stood. Aleksy's vantage point allowed for him to view the visages of the monarchs, but not Krystyna's. Her back was to him. Krystyna performed a deep curtsey, stood, removed the crown from her red-gold plaited hair and presented it to the king, who whispered something, turned, and handed off the crown to a concelebrant of the Mass, who then walked over and placed it on the altar, calling out for St. Laurence's blessing on the harvest.

The king now took a blue velvet purse, one that had some weight to it, and handed it to Krystyna, completing the custom that the maid be rewarded for her giving up of the crown. Playing her part now, the queen placed a white veil upon Krystyna's head.

Krystyna curtsied again, turned about, radiant as a rose, and began the slow retracing of her steps, steps accompanied by the approving buzz and mesmerized stares of the congregation. Her beauty and demeanor charmed them. For the briefest of moments now, her head came up, brow lifted, eyes seeming to scan the crowd. Was she looking for him?

It was only after she had disappeared from Aleksy's sightline—like the final burst of a comet—that the Mass continued. The dispensing of Holy Communion went on interminably in the oppressive summer heat. Several more worshippers fainted. Self-doubt shadowed Aleksy, like a phantom.

He felt a sense of dizziness, too, though it was not from the heat. Krystyna had been the darling of the congregation, favorably noticed even by the royal couple. She had been set to marry a handsome man of the upper echelon of the *szlachta* and who might one day attain magnate status. Did he truly presume that she would give all this up for him? Would she? The question stabbed at his heart. I *must* be a fool, he thought, to think she would forego everything coming her way for the life I am able to provide. He sensed himself going red in the face. His legs threatened to give way beneath him. The Nardolski family had everything to offer. *What do I have to give her?*

My love for her, he thought. And this Fabian Nardolski? It was not so much the changeable versus the unchangeable as it was the tangible versus the intangible. How likely was it that she would choose him, a poor Tatar, the intangible? He had goaded her into saying yes—no, she hadn't even done that. She had merely nodded. And might a random motion of the human head be mistaken as a nod?

What of his plan? This was the moment that would provide her the opportunity to escape the cathedral and make her way to the rectory. Would she do that, or would she wait for the congratulations of her family—and her intended's family?

His hopes were peeling away like threads from a torn garment.

"I am waiting for Father Franciszek," Aleksy told the nun who came to the rectory door. At the closing of Mass, he had been paralyzed, so lost in his dark thoughts that he realized too late that the cathedral was emptying out and so he was among the last group to leave. In the crush of the crowd there had been no sign of Krystyna or her family.

The old nun nodded as if she had been expecting him—a good sign. "This way," she said. She showed him in to the priest's office, told him to take a seat, and noiselessly withdrew, closing the door behind her.

The room was utterly still. He took several paces into the cavernous chamber with its bookshelves that smelled as if they were newly polished with beeswax. The opaque lancet windows let in little light, prompting his eyes to adjust. *No sign of Krystyna.* His heart dropped within his chest. The chair behind the large desk was empty. No sign of Father Franciszek. *No one* seemed to be in the room. What did this portend? His heart pace accelerated. He was about to turn back to the door and question the nun when he heard his own name.

Then the voice came again from a shadowy corner of the room: "Aleksy." A man's voice. But not Father Franciszek's. A voice that was somehow familiar.

Aleksy turned in the direction of the voice. A man was rising from a high-backed, hand-carved Bishop's chair. The rotund figure took several steps toward him. It was no ecclesiast.

Aleksy's mind became as blurred as his sight.

"Krystyna's not here," the man said.

And now he recognized both voice and man. It was Count Konrad Halicki. Krystyna's father.

The room seemed to fall away, sense and senses with it. How was this possible? Disappointment flooded through every pore of his being—even as he girded himself for Lord Halicki's anger, retribution.

What happened to him now mattered little. He had lost Krystyna. Forever.

Had the scheme been discovered—or had Krystyna revealed it to her family? Had she deliberately scuttled the plan?

"Father Franciszek was taken away on some business or other, Aleksy."

"What?... Why are you here?"

"I thought you needed an explanation."

They stood some ten paces apart, neither willing to move closer.

"That Krystyna didn't come is explanation enough."

"You know, Aleksy, I do admire you." Lord Halicki's words seemed free of sarcasm. Good God, were his character and meanings as quixotic as his daughter's?

"Why?" Where Aleksy expected searing, violent anger from Krystyna's father there seemed what?—Compassion? How could that be?

"You saw what you wanted and you did your best to attain it. I can understand that."

"I love Krysia!" The diminutive rolled off his tongue on its own. "And she—"

"Oh, I don't doubt that—or that she may for the moment return your feelings. But it is not to be. She's been promised to another."

"Someone more acceptable?"

"Fabian is a good man. He will be a good husband."

"And if she is unwilling?"

"Ah, this is the way things are done among the… it's the way things are done. It's Krystyna's fate."

"Unchangeable?"

Lord Halicki nodded. "You might say so."

"I don't believe it. I believe fates can be—"

"Ah fates! Your fate, Aleksy. Yes, I should like to talk to you about your fate. It is time."

What was he talking about and why—in Father Franciszek's study—did he take on the persona of a true parson, one who spoke as if he cared?

"Come, let's sit over here, Aleksy," he said, motioning toward two upholstered chairs that sat face to face under a lancet window. "Do you mind if I call you *Alek*?"

Aleksy, his mind a cobweb of confusion, absently shook his head and followed him to a chair.

"This must be a terrible disappointment to you—Alek."

Aleksy just stared.

"I know that your wish was be become a soldier. You told me so back in Halicz."

"A hussar."

"Indeed. It may be possible."

"I'm a mere retainer. Marek's retainer."

"Ah, yes. But I can make a recommendation to King Sobieski. I've done it before."

"Not for your own sons." He had overheard Roman complaining that his father had not used his influence with the Old Guard of the *Kwarciani*.

Lord Halicki's eyes widened in surprise. "Uh, no. You're right there, my boy."

"Then why would you do so for me? To the king? Why? To keep me at bay."

"No, within a week Krystyna will be married. I won't have any worries about keeping you at bay after that."

"Then why would you go to the king over a poor orphaned Tatar?"

A shadow passed over Lord Halicki's face, and after a pause, he said, "My conscience dictates that I do."

"Your conscience?"

"Yes. Aleksy," the count said, drawing in a long breath. "I've done you a wrong—a great wrong." He paused. "You know that your parents died during the border wars, yes?"

Aleksy nodded.

"And that your birth father died expressing the wish that his good friend, a Pole, take you into his care? That it was a solemn promise between two friends of different backgrounds but like minds? A binding oath? A sacrosanct promise?"

"Yes, my father has told me these things."

"It was the promise of a blood brother. There are such things between Poles and Tatars out there, east of the River Dniester and west of the Don, in the desolate Wild Fields." He paused now, his eyes holding Aleksy's. "Have you not longed for more details—about your parents?"

"Yes, but my father, or rather Borys—"

"I can give you those details. Your father's name was Abbas. He was a good man. In the old days we fought on opposite sides, but we found peace. We found friendship. He lived as a herdsman and served his tribe well as chieftain. Do you know what Abbas means?"

"Lion."

"Ah, Szymon taught you well. Yes, and a lion he was, Abbas your father, both wild and tame. He worried for you. And—yes, Szymon told me how he was teaching you some Tataric."

"And my mother?"

"Fazilet."

"I don't know that one."

"It means 'beautiful temperament, spiritual one'. You got your daring from Abbas and your looks and goodness from Fazilet."

"They both died?"

The count nodded. "They did."

"And the blood-brother—that was Borys, yes?" If such was the case Aleksy could only wonder why his stepfather had kept these things secret.

But Aleksy saw now that Lord Halicki was shaking his head, his eyes averted. "No, Aleksy."

"No?"

Lord Halicki's gaze locked onto Aleksy's, his eyes glistening in the dim light from the lancet window. "I was that friend—that blood-brother."

"You?" Aleksy sat numb, aware of the silence in the room but for the ticking of the mantel clock—or was it his own heart?

"I swore to Abbas—your father—that I would see to your care. I intended for you to be as a son to me."

"I don't understand."

"Neither did Zenobia—my wife. She wouldn't have any of it. You see, her first husband—Roman's father—was killed in the border wars."

"By Tatars?"

"Yes."

"So she couldn't stomach having me anywhere near?"

Lord Halicki gave a little shrug. "No, it's not something she's rational about." He let out a sigh, long and deep, as if he longed for years of guilt to go with it. "And so I asked Borys to fulfill that promise for me, to be my proxy. I knew in my heart it was wrong. I knew I had promised. And I failed to keep the promise of a blood brother."

"So the proxy secured a proxy."

"I hadn't thought of it that way... But I knew one day I would tell you."

"To relieve your conscience?"

"Yes—but also out of fairness to you and to your real father. Borys and his wife have raised you well, no? You've been happy—that is, until now—why, had it been up to me, Krystyna would be a sister to you."

This strange thought struck Aleksy like a thunderclap. His back stiffened. "But she's not my sister!"

"I know. She's been a... friend."

"More!"

"Perhaps, Alek, but she can be nothing to you now. Nothing." Lord Halicki stood, preparing to leave, his expression grim and unflinching. "I wish I had done things differently."

Aleksy sat, his eyes on a crucifix on the wall. *The changeable and the unchangeable,* he thought.

"I'll send my recommendation to the king."

"No need. I don't want it."

"I'll write it just the same and see that *you* get it before the troops move out. That way, it'll be your decision, Alek, whether you become a hussar. Yours alone."

"I don't want it!" Aleksy shouted. He shot out of his chair. "I'm a retainer and shall remain so!"

"Just the same, I'll write it," Lord Halicki said, undeterred. "Don't let pride stand in the way of your dream."

Aleksy stood rooted to the floor, seething, resolved not to accept the very thing he had wanted—the only thing—until Krystyna entered his life.

Lord Halicki stopped at the door, turned about. "Fate is seldom fair, Alek," he said. "You got caught up in currents too strong, currents that could drown you.—Oh, should you accept my recommendation and should the king follow through, as I'm certain he would, you would be eligible for officer status. The fact that you can read and write—very commendable, I might say—makes you eligible."

The sound of the closing of the door behind the count came as though filtered through a cave. After a while, echoing footsteps could be heard moving toward the door, Father Franciszek's. The trembling priest's first and oft-repeated words of apology came back only later—interspersed with details of how two young hussars had deliberately taken him from his duties that morning, detaining him on some ruse until that moment. Aleksy understood what the priest did not. He could well imagine who the two hussars were. He stood, silent and stunned. There would be time later to take in what he had learned about his true parents, but for the moment, all that he could deal with was the realization that Lord Halicki knew he could write. Somehow, his note to Krystyna had been found. Had the person following Izdi on his mission been the one to find it under her door before Krystyna could read it?

Or worse, had Krystyna herself surrendered it?

TWENTY

"It's tough luck, Alek," Idzi said, his legs pumping hard to keep up with his friend.

Aleksy was moving quickly through the forest, intent on hunting, intent on forgetting. "Tough luck?" he called. "Is that all you've got to say? Tough luck is when an arrow is loosed on course and manages to go astray."

"I slipped your note under her door. I did!"

"Maybe it was her father's door. You were to give it to her personally!"

"I told you that someone was following me. Hate me for it, I did what I could, damn it!"

Aleksy pivoted to see Idzi as he tried to step over the huge fallen oak he himself had just cleared with a bit of a jump. A protruding branch of the tree snagged the dwarf's leg and he fell. Aleksy made no move to help him up. Had he done so, Idzi would feel additional embarrassment, he knew—and yet, as he watched the little man right himself and clumsily clamber up over the tree, he knew he was giving way to a moment of meanness. His voice was sharp now: "Did you leave a bit of the letter showing outside her door?"

Idzi caught up to Aleksy, breathing hard. "I—I don't think so. That is, a bit might have been showing."

"There's only one other possibility."

Idzi looked up, his face reflecting the gravity of the other possibility. "That *she* revealed your plans to her family?"

"That's right."

"I don't think she would do that."

Aleksy stared down at Idzi for the longest moment, then, without a word, turned and headed into the heart of the forest. He didn't think she would do that, either.

Later, after a single arrow from Aleksy's yew bow took down a stag, they tied the legs to two birch branches and rested before heading back to camp.

Idzi dared to speak. "What are you going to do about the letter—Count Halicki's letter, I mean?"

"What—oh, nothing."

"Nothing?"

"Exactly that. I told him I didn't want it. It was an impulse of his to make himself feel better, that's all. He's probably forgotten it by now."

"And if he hasn't?"

Aleksy bent over to pick up the two poles holding the front end of the carcass. "Are you going to help, or do I have to drag it back to camp myself?"

Idzi bent to pick up the back end and as they set off, he said, "But he's offered you your wish to become a hussar! How can you—"

"As a replacement for the role he had promised my father he would play in my life. As a replacement for his daughter! No, I won't accept his offer. I won't ease his conscience!" Aleksy spat to the side of the path they were forging. "I'll play the role of the retainer." He cringed as he said this but he meant it. What made it more humiliating was that both Roman and Marek knew about the failed elopement. He could discern that they did by their deportment, especially by Roman's smugness. And yet they said nothing, did nothing. Why hadn't they overtly vented their hatred? Lord Halicki must have interceded. At last, he summoned his courage and asked, "And the marriage—what are the details?"

"It's set for noon on the holy day of Our Lady, the day you leave with the king's forces. It's to take place in one of the chapels in Wawel Cathedral."

"The king has ten as our departure time. Are Roman and Marek to miss her wedding?"

"They're to stay behind a day or so to witness the ceremony."

"And to celebrate, no doubt." Aleksy paused, attempting to exorcise his bitterness. "Oh, it won't be too hard for them to catch up. Queen Marysieńka is going, too, with all of her court and many wagons. We'll move like turtles. My God, you would think the Turks were still at the safe distance of their homeland instead of tightening a noose around Vienna at this very moment."

"It's a mystery, it is," Idzi said. "A royal one."

"And Lord Halicki?"

"He's leaving almost immediately to join his old comrade, General Lubomirski and the Sieniawski army. He's so set on being part of the action that he's skipping his daughter's wedding."

Aleksy stopped sharply in his tracks, his eyes on the horizon. Long moments passed as the two held to their burden. He drew a long breath, guessing that the silent Idzi behind him must have expected the next question. "And the young Nardolski?"

"After the—wedding—he and his retainers will join up with Lubomirski also."

"When?" Aleksy spat.

Idzi cleared his throat. "The—the next day."

After the marriage night, Aleksy thought. *After the marriage night.* He felt a weakness come over him as he recalled when he saw Krystyna in her attic chamber. Caught by surprise, she had unbraided her hair and it fell about her shoulders in rich, fluid red-gold waves. It was how she would wear her hair on her marriage night....

Idzi gave a little cough. "Do you—do you wish to know which chapel? In the cathedral, I mean?"

"God's death!" Aleksy dropped his hold on the carcass and turned on him, shouting. "Now, why would I wish that?" He glared at the stunned dwarf, daring him to say more. Idzi's lips locked. Aleksy pivoted, took up his end and started walking again, accelerating his pace.

"Sorry," Idzi mumbled. His breaths came harder, and he spoke now with some effort. "Don't walk so fast, Aleksy.—And why not accept Halicki's influence? You know wearing the wings is your dream."

"If you want me to slow, you'll finish this little outing in silence."

Much later, as they neared camp, Aleksy tried to rouse himself from the crushing disappointment and malaise that had seemed to take over his life. "What about you, Idzi? What are you to do?" He attempted an even tone. He had made his friend squirm enough.

"Me? No excitement for little Idzi. I gather I'm to return to Halicz with the Lady Zenobia." He let out a dramatic sigh. "Why, I offered to attend Lord Halicki. I'd like to see the action at Vienna. I want to take part! He wouldn't hear of it. Damn near laughed at me, he did. So I'm left to..."

"Left to—what?"

"Go back to my duties. Why does she dislike me so, Alek—your mother?"

It was true, Aleksy thought, his mother had always had an aversion to Idzi. "I don't know, Idzi." That, too, was true.

"My fate, I guess, and unchangeable it is."

And so, Aleksy was reminded that he was not the only one to face up to disappointment, to face up to prejudice. Idzi's sly attempt at a little lesson was as transparent as glass—and not completely ineffectual.

"You're leaving before the wedding?" Roman asked his stepfather.

"Chrystus! Not you, too?" Lord Konrad Halicki snapped in annoyment, his eyes coming up as his son entered the small music room of the Nardolski town house. "I just had this conversation with your mother. I came to Kraków to facilitate the betrothal and to my surprise it turned out I was needed to prevent Krystyna from acting foolishly, so I don't regret coming. But, as I told your mother, I should have gone directly from Halicz to meet up with my old commander and friend, Prince Lubomirski, whom you met at the wedding of his daughter. The king is the king, but he's moving slowly, according to all reports."

"It's the truth."

"Sit down, Roman.—I've had a long message from the prince. It seems Christian men have already engaged enemy Turks and allied Magyars. I need to be there."

"Krystyna understands?" Roman took the chair opposite.

"Seems to, but she's despondent."

"Over the Aleksy business? Good God, what was she thinking? The stupid little fool!"

"She was thinking she was in love."

"And now?" Roman asked. "She won't even open her door to me."

"She's resigned to her fate. She has no reason to dislike Fabian."

"Father, what is the situation at Vienna? What do we have to look forward to?"

"Look forward to? That's a strange way to talk about killing." Lord Halicki sighed. "But I think the experience will surpass anything you and Marek might have undergone had you been chosen for the elite *Kwarciani* guarding the borders at the Wild Fields. You do forgive me for not interceding on that count?"

Roman shrugged and forced a little nod of his head. The wound still festered, but with the prospects of excitement and glory at Vienna, it mattered little now.

"As of the message that came yesterday," his step-father began, "the Sultan's Grand Vizier, Kara Mustafa, has taken up position on the southern slopes of Vienna where evidently he can see the entire panorama of the city. Charles of Lorrraine, who leads the Habsburg forces, had the foresight to burn the suburbs around the city before he left it so as not to lend shelter to the Turks."

"But... why did he withdraw?"

The count shrugged. "Other fires to put out, I suppose. Emperor Leopold himself, his family and thousands of the citizenry fled the city. Those who remain are committed to fight to the death. As is often the case in sieges, a peace offer came from those besieging. Kara Mustafa offered peace to those who might stay, accepting Islam and living as Christians under the Sultan, and peace, also, to those who were free to leave, taking their goods with them."

"And should they resist?" Roman asked.

"Death—or slavery to all. The offer was declined, of course, and orders were given to wall up the gates of the city. The Turks then began their offensive with bombardment and the digging of trenches. Despite brave sorties out of the walled city by its defenders, the Turks moved ever closer. They also began digging underground passages and setting mines that opened up gaps in the palisading and parapets. The Viennese quickly shored up the openings and proceeded to countermine, but Vienna was fully surrounded by then—but for the River Danube which flows behind it. The Habsburg forces are begging for reinforcements from Saxony, Bavaria and, of course, Poland. My God, Sobieski should have departed days ago!"

"Sounds desperate."

"Oh, it is that," his father said.

"Damn!" Roman cursed. "And here we sit. You'll see action before we even arrive."

"Don't fret. You'll see your share, Romek. And when you do, don't be too impulsive—and do take care of Marek."

"What about his retainer? Isn't that his job?"

"Aleksy? Yes, it's his job in part, but he won't be in the front line of hussars with the two of you. Roman, you've not harmed him… and you won't, will you?"

"I promised as much, but I can't stomach him. He's not to be trusted."

"Idzi tells me he's never seen a better archer. He would come in handy, but as it is, it's possible he'll play a different role." Lord Halicki stood, moved to a nearby table and took up a sealed letter. Walking back to the seated Roman, he said, "Wait a few days after you've left Kraków for Vienna and give this to Aleksy. It might mean you'll no longer have to 'stomach' him. Can I trust you to do this? You are my eldest, Romek. Will you do as I ask? On your honor?"

"Yes, Father." Roman turned the sealed missive over in his hands. "You're mistaken, Father. You've written *this* letter to King Sobieski."

"No mistake. Just give it to Aleksy. He'll know what to do with it—or rather he will have to choose what to do with it."

"What's this all about? What's in it?"

"It's a request to be given to the king—at Aleksy's discretion—asking that he be outfitted with a horse, wings, and a lance—and be given a place in the husaria against the Turks."

"What?" Roman thought he had misheard. "A hussar?" Roman jumped out of his chair so that he stood eye to eye with his stepfather. "Are you crazy?" he dared to say. "A Tatar peasant? The Tatar who nearly absconded with your daughter?"

Lord Halicki ignored the disrespect. "That may be so, but she had a part in it, also."

"Why? For the love of Jezus Chrystus, you wouldn't speak up to the Old Guard about Marek and me, but you'll go to the king for a Tatar! Why, Father? Why?"

"There's more to it than that."

"I'll say there is! You neglected to say that Kara Mustafa has taken as allies a horde of Tatars!"

"What you say is true, Roman, and I've fought my share of them at the Wild Fields. Why, King Sobieski himself was born during a Tatar attack, and yet he is a man who believes in forgiveness and redemption. And now,

Romek, there are thousands of Lipka Hussars from Lithuania who fight for the Commonwealth."

"Dogs, I say, but fine, that still does not tell me why you should write the king to raise up one of our tenants' sons!"

"Will you sit for a moment?"

"No, I want to know!"

"Very well, I'll tell you, but *I* am going to sit."

Roman remained standing.

His stepfather seated himself, his steady eyes looking up, the fingers of his hands interlocking. "I spent many years patrolling the Wild Fields and had some success."

"You fought Tatars."

"Among others. They don't call it the Wild Fields just because of the desolate terrain. But when war with the enemy was done and peace was made with the chieftain, sometimes you liked the chieftain. Sometimes you became friends. Water was poured over the sabres signifying the end of conflict. This held off a recurrence of violence—and it also sometimes made for a genuine friendship. You've heard of this ceremony with the sabres?"

"Yes."

"The pouring of the water meant that the two were blood-brothers, bound together always. I had such a bond with a Tatar named Abbas, a good and decent chieftain. One day I came upon his settlement after it had been decimated by marauding Cossacks. A terrible sight, it was, Roman, terrible. The huts were burning, many dead, all valuables looted. His surviving people were routed or enslaved, I don't know. Abbas had suffered a mortal wound, but he lay sheltering his wife Fazilet, who was in childbirth. He died before he could see me bring his son into the world—but not before he pleaded that I see to the care of his wife and child. Fazilet died the next day. I could not stop her bleeding and I think she had lost her will to live."

"And the baby? That was Aleksy?"

"That was Aleksy. I should have raised him. I gave Abbas my word. But I gave him over to Borys to bring up."

"You would have brought a filthy Tatar into the house, knowing they had murdered my birth father? You would have done that to my mother?"

"Had she allowed it, yes."

"I thank God that she didn't allow a slant-eyed devil child into the house. He might have killed us all in the middle of the night."

Lord Halicki held to his composure. "I regret not keeping my word. I most regret it because he would have been raised as brother to you and Marek. You would know compassion and love. Had that been the case, you would feel differently about him."

"And as a brother to Krystyna?" Roman howled. "I think not. A cholera on the bastard! God knows she wouldn't still be a virgin today, if in fact she is!" He spit upon the floor.

Lord Halicki was on his feet in an instant, his arm in motion even as he took several paces. Sheer surprise held Roman still as a corpse while the blow across his face came with the sound and force of a thunderclap.

Roman's head spun, the room going momentarily dark. He struggled to stay upright. He took a step and leaned against the harpsichord, blinking, again and again, trying to bring the room back into focus. Slowly, the mullioned casement across the way took on definition. His stepfather had left the room. He had never struck him before.

Not so very far away, in the hall, came the plaintive words of his mother to her husband. "What is it? What's he done?"

Roman left the music room by a different door, one that led through the kitchen—but not before picking up what had fallen to the floor—the sealed letter to King Jan Sobieski.

TWENTY-ONE

On 15 August, the Day of Our Lady's Assumption, the entire camp was stirring and bustling long before dawn. Everything was to be in readiness. The trek to Vienna was to commence immediately after the ten o'clock Mass.

"Where's Roman and Marek?" Ludwik asked. "Out carousing all night?"

Aleksy and Idzi shared a knowing look. Aleksy turned away, so Idzi was left to tell Ludwik that the two were at the Nardolski town house in preparation for the wedding. He did so in a quiet tone, scarcely more than a whisper.

"All the cooking supplies are well packed," Idzi announced then in a husky voice. He had stayed in camp overnight to help organize and pack things. After seeing Aleksy and Ludwik off, he would place himself in the service of Lady Halicka—until their return to Halicz, whereupon he would resume his duties at the Gazdecki cottage under the eyes of Aleksy's mother. "All is ready for the road but this here iron frying pan. I'll stay and have some ham sizzling by the time you two get back from the Mass. You'll be famished and there will be little time."

"Indeed," Ludwik said. "There wouldn't be so much fainting in church if it weren't for having to keep the fast."

Aleksy and Ludwik stood just inside the crowded Wawel Cathedral, far from the altar and the dais upon which the king and queen sat. Mass moved along at a glacier's pace. The congregation listened to the prayers, as well as a sermon from the Bishop of Kraków, and to Aleksy the people seemed entranced by the seriousness of the moment. Their Commonwealth was at stake. Their religion was at stake. All of Europe and their very lives hung in the balance. It was a time and a day in history like no person of that congregation had witnessed. Every soul within those stone walls seemed to sense as much.

Aleksy, however, experienced the importance of the moment as someone watching from afar. It would be only later, on the road, as details about the situation at Vienna unfolded that he would recall and take to heart the words of the sermon, the king's strong call to arms, and the people's tears and patriotic fervor. He would vow to do his duty and do it well.

But for now, standing among the thousands in the morning heat, he could not keep his eyes from scanning the north and south aisles, nor his mind from the thought that could not be suppressed. *In which of these chapels within the time span of two hours is Krystyna Halicka to be married?*

Feeling like a caged bird, Krystyna paced her bedchamber. Her mother had just retreated, having left the ivory silk wedding dress lying across a chair in the sitting room. The Nardolski seamstress had delivered it at last. Even the most cursory glance revealed the exquisiteness of the needlework that had attached hundreds of pearls to the bodice.

Krystyna went to the window. There, below, were dozens of people hurrying toward the Market Square, eager to find places in Wawel Cathedral where the feast of the Assumption was to be celebrated. She looked to the mantel clock which read five minutes to the hour. She doubted that these tardy churchgoers would be admitted.

For some moments she had the strangest sensation. She imagined herself being lifted up, ascending right through the coffered ceiling and then through the roof and high into the sky. She levitated there, looking down on the Market Square, the Cloth Hall with its stalls and shops shuttered, and the great Wawel Cathedral and masses of people overflowing it, down the steps and into the square. At the very moment when she remembered she could not tolerate heights, her stomach dropped and she fell away, as did the vision.

Someone was lightly knocking at the door. Krystyna hurried to the door.

It was one of the Nardolski kitchen maids—Ruta, a thin girl with a high forehead and a sincere disposition. Krystyna took her by the elbow and brought her into the room, closing the door behind them.

"The stable groom has just returned, Lady Krystyna," Ruta said.

"And?"

"He says he delivered the verbal message."

"He found the right person?"

Ruta dared a little laugh. "No others like *him* in Kraków—at least that I've seen."

Krystyna handed over two złoty. "Give him one of these, then, and keep one for your trouble."

Ruta curtsied perfectly, for Lady Nardolska demanded perfection from her servants. "Thank you, milady," she gushed.

"Just make sure you bring him up the moment he arrives." Krystyna saw Ruta out and walked back into the sitting room, coming to stand at the window. The streets had emptied. She was jarred now by the clangor of the cathedral bells, tolling out the tenth hour. The Mass would be beginning. She shivered. At noon there would be another Mass in the Chapel of the Birth of the Holy Virgin Maryja. A nuptials Mass.

She thought now of the ancient legend of Queen Wanda, one that her governess had told many times. In the attic schoolroom as children, she and her brothers even created a little play detailing how this orphaned daughter of King Krakus was being forced into a marriage with Prussian Prince Rytigier, who longed to have Poland and to possess her—not as an equal, but as a trophy. Roman played the Prussian and Marek played her true love. War was not an option for Queen Wanda; it would bring ruin to Poland, for their army was ill-matched against the Prussian forces. She prayed to the old gods for a solution. Rather than give Poland and herself over to him, she made the ultimate sacrifice, hurtling herself over the escarpment into the River Vistula. Thus, Poland was saved from Prussian rule, and a burial mound was erected in her honor.

Krystyna smiled ironically to herself. The governess sometimes had peculiar notions of what stories were appropriate for the fantasies of the young. And no, *she* was no queen and there was no country to be spared by any such similar action. And yet—

A coded knock came at the door.

Krystyna opened the door and Idzi slipped in. "I'm ready," she said. "Did Ruta show you where the *kołacz* is?"

"She did. She said it was heavy. I asked how heavy bread could be, and then I lifted it. By God, she was right—it's damn heavy. Oh! Pardon me, milady."

"There's a reason for its weight. Is it *too* heavy?"

"No!" Idzi closed his hands into fists and lifted his arms. "I am stronger than people give me credit. I placed it near the kitchen door that leads out to the drive."

"Good—let's go."

Idzi laughed as they left her suite, his distinctive voice then going into falsetto song: "Without a *kołacz*, there is no wedding, no wedding, no wedding."

"Shush!" Krystyna hissed. She could not, however, stifle one of her own little laughs.

TWENTY-TWO

After setting up camp on the fourth day of tediously slow travel, Aleksy went into the forest to hunt. While there was enough on hand to eat—meat that had been salted and stored in some of the thousands of wagons that trailed behind—he felt the need to go off by himself and concentrate on finding game, losing for the moment the dark and unhappy thoughts that haunted him. It would take more than a dozen grueling days on dusty roads for Aleksy to begin to come to terms with the terrible, grinding grief he felt. How difficult it was to adjust to the unchangeable.

He moved deep into the forest so as to distance himself from others who were also searching for game. After an hour, he slowed and moved along quietly. Suddenly he heard a rustling some distance in the brush ahead. He halted immediately and silently positioned his bow and drew an arrow, nocking it at once. He waited. He thought he heard a twig snap somewhere to his left, but before he could turn in that direction a stag appeared in his immediate sightline, a little beyond a copse of bushes.

He let fly his arrow at once, just as the deer came alert and prepared to dash away, too late. The stag dropped.

Aleksy ran to the spot, pushing aside the bushes that shielded the body. The deer lay dead, but Aleksy's eyes widened at what he saw.

The stag lay with two arrows protruding.

The little mystery was soon answered when another voice startled Aleksy, a voice unfamiliar to him. "Well, my friend, how shall we divide the spoils?" The lightly inflected words came from his left.

A young man of perhaps twenty was pushing his way through the greenery. He was not a soldier, as evidenced by his cap and soiled brown *żupan*. He whistled when he viewed the deer. "It didn't know what hit him." He turned to Aleksy. "Bravo!" He directed a gaze of amazement at Aleksy.

"And to you." Aleksy wondered what brought a young civilian Pole to a forest occupied by soldiers.

"You embarrass me—or rather I embarrass myself. My pathetic arrow is in its hind end. And yours—my God!—is buried in its heart. No wonder it went down like a fallen tree."

He was right. Aleksy had already realized as much, but now he noted that the arrow in the hind had some small symbol on it. He squatted down and inspected it. Just below its feathering, a tiny white eagle had been meticulously painted. He stood, his curiosity aroused.

"My name's Piotr," the man said, offering his hand.

His hand was soft. He was new to hunting. "I'm Aleksy, Piotr—do you hunt for—"

"The king," Piotr said, smiling.

Aleksy's mouth slackened. "Sobieski?"

"Of course, but I'm afraid I make a better spy."

"A spy?"

"Of sorts. I managed to escape Vienna so I could get news of the city's plight to the allies, such as the king."

"Chrystus! You escaped the besieged city?"

"I did."

"Tell me something, Piotr. How close is the city to falling to the Turks? Are we going to make it in time?"

"It's true they're knocking at the gates at this moment. I've told the king that it's going to be a close call."

"I hope he took you at your word.... Tell me, how did a spy like you get collared into hunting?"

"I'm no more a spy than I am a hunter, truth to tell. But after my mission was complete, I asked one of his generals what service I could be and he handed me this bow and quiver here and told me to hunt. I think he just wanted me gone so they could talk strategy." He looked down in awe at the dead deer. "Won't he be surprised? We'll divide it up, of course, but—"

"You've never cut into one."

Abashed, Piotr shook his head.

"Ah, there's no dividing the deer, anyway. You have the king and queen to provide for."

Piotr shrugged. "Perhaps not for long."

"What do you mean?"

"I mean—between you and me—to speed up the campaign the queen is to be sent back to Kraków once we arrive at Tarnowskie, where we're to stop overnight tomorrow. That's the talk. The king has had an ambassador from Charles' headquarters."

"Are you able to speak of the meeting?"

A sly smile appeared under his sparse moustache. "Perhaps."

"Perhaps?"

"A quid pro quo. Hunt with me tomorrow! You give me some tips with the bow and I'll give you some royal tips."

"Done! The first lesson we'll call the safety lesson. When I heard you step on a twig a few minutes ago, I might have turned in your direction to let my arrow go."

"I think I learned that yesterday. I saw some bushes move and took my shot. What comes out of the bushes but a little man and he was quite irate, I can tell you. Swore at me up and down, the dwarf did. Damn good thing I was a lousy shot, he said. And he was right!"

The two laughed. For a moment Aleksy thought of Idzi, imagining that he was most likely well on his way back to Halicz with Lady Halicka, or Old Leatherface, as he called her. "Now, let me help you get this choice venison to the royal campsite."

"And there, if you take the lead, we *will* do some division of it. After all, Aleksy, if it weren't for you, this unlucky fellow would be running about with the indignity of my arrow sticking in his ass."

"Dog's blood!" Roman was grousing, "Why must we move so damn slowly?"

"For one reason," Marek, the voice of reason, responded, "the queen and her entire household is traveling with us. We can't go any faster than does her carriage and various wagons."

"I know that. Just tell me why!"

"Why she's with us? Because for Jan Sobieski the sun doesn't move in the sky but by her wish—or whim."

"Chrystus's thorns! Save me that kind of adoration!"

Marek laughed. "I doubt you'll ever be so troubled. As for the king, I expect he'll have to set her to the side when he thinks it time."

"When, pray tell? He left Warsaw late. He left Kraków late. It's as if he doesn't want to get to Vienna before the whole thing is finished.—And without us, it will finish up badly."

"I think he's still waiting for all of his troops to coalesce. We have forces joining us every day. He's got his pride and he wants to join Europe's other leaders with the greatest possible forces at his back."

"Some say," Roman added, "that the pride truly resides in the queen and that she wants him to arrive at Vienna in a position whereby he can take charge of all the allies, even those of Charles of Lorraine."

It was the fifth day out from Kraków and Aleksy sat with Ludwik at the evening campsite, listening to Roman complain and Marek explain. Aleksy was sorely tempted to say what he knew about the queen's impending departure but kept his silence. Neither retainer was invited to partake in the brothers' conversations. The brothers Halicki, in fact, did not speak to Aleksy at all, other than to bark orders.

Mysteriously, despite the slowness of the cavalcade, the brothers had not caught up to it for two days. "Must have been some wedding celebration," Ludwik had muttered before going silent at the sight of Aleksy's stricken expression. Oddly enough, too, Roman had not appeared triumphant or smug about his sister's wedding. Aleksy had fully expected some sort of righteous vindication and gloating. But—nothing.

What did it matter? Krystyna was gone, like a shooting star, radiant until it plummets from the night sky. Now here, now gone.

For the moment he kept his mind centered on the situation at hand. Roman's complaints were true as rain, Aleksy thought. They had lumbered out of Kraków, southwest through the Vistula Valley in an unwieldly manner—this menagerie of horses, mules, carriages, wagons, cannon, royals, *szlachta*, soldiers, retainers, and servants —and more slowly, he ventured, than those fleeing Egypt in the great exodus. And behind them wound an untold number of supply wagons, mules and all manner of camp followers.

"And this General Caraffa from Charles of Lorraine's camp, what do you make of that?" Roman asked of his brother.

"Don't know," Marek said with a shrug.

"He's here to deliver a plea to the king." The words were out of Aleksy's mouth before he could give them a second thought.

"Oh?" Roman asked. "You know something, Tatar? Marek, the boy thinks he knows something."

"Out with it," Marek said.

Aleksy told them now what he had learned from Piotr. "The plea is for the king to accompany his vanguard and push ahead of the slow-moving train without delay. The situation is dire. Vienna's garrison is weakening. The commandant has been taken ill. And the Turks' mining is bringing them ever closer to access."

Marek whistled.

Roman was on his feet at once. "Where would you get that kind of information?" He walked over to where Aleksy sat cross-legged and kicked at the sole of his boot. "Do we have a spy in our midst—or are you just talking through your peasant cap? You're lying, aren't you?"

Aleksy sprang to his feet and refused to cower. "It's true."

With the thickening of tension, Marek and Ludwik stood now. Roman shoved Aleksy, forcing him backward a foot.

Aleksy's nerve only increased. "The queen will be left behind at Tarnowskie."

"What?" Roman demanded. He pushed again.

"She and her attendants will return to Kraków."

"A font of knowledge, you are, Tatar! What is it with you? Do you have some seeing power?"

Ludwik spoke up. "It's just what we heard, Lord Halicki."

Roman pivoted to Ludwik. "Just gossip?"

"Could be." Ludwik said, seeming to seek a middle ground.

"Time will tell," Aleksy said, not without confidence.

Roman spun back to Aleksy. "Time will tell the end of you, Tatar!" His arm went up and back for a powerful swing, Aleksy's face its destination.

Marek had been on guard and with both hands caught his brother's arm at the crook of the elbow. "No," he cautioned when Roman turned his angry eyes to him. "Like Ludwik says, it's just what they heard around camp."

Roman pulled away from his brother, glared at Aleksy, and went into his tent.

Marek turned to Aleksy. "It's best if you keep things to yourself, Aleksy Gazdecki."

TWENTY-THREE

THE CAVALCADE HAD SHAMBLED INTO Tarnowskie on 21 August, at mid-day.

Dusk was settling in now as Aleksy and Piotr returned from hunting. They climbed down from their steppe ponies and walked toward Market Square, talking as they went.

"How'd I do, Aleksy?"

"You did fine, Piotr. Once you develop calluses on those arrow fingers, you'll do better.—You know, something's got to change. Six days of travel, and what, not much more than seventy miles?" He realized he was beginning to sound like Roman, but their tardiness in getting to Vienna was fact. The camp was tense with anticipation.

On the outing with Piotr, Aleksy had learned a great deal about the initial days of Vienna's plight. "Emperor Leopold seemed very relaxed at the start of July," Piotr said, "hunting he was, like he was carefree. But when word came of the Turks' crossing Hungary's plains, his mother left her villa and sought refuge behind Vienna's fortifications. I think that's when it dawned on the emperor what the risk was. That's when things got serious because the Imperial Army is not very large and much of it was elsewhere with Duke Charles of Lorraine. The Imperial family packed up, along with some sixty thousand citizens, and hightailed it west."

"Who the hell was left to defend the city?"

"Count Starhemberg was made commandant and given supreme command. I have to hand it to him: he put the remaining folks to work repairing the city's defenses. Good thing, too, because by mid-July, the Grand Vizier Kara Mustafa and his thousands of troops came upon Vienna, by God. One hundred forty thousand by most accounts, with one-third of them trained fighters. He sent out detachments that encircled the fortress. Scared the wits out of the witless—I can vouch for that. They had numberless horses and wagons with baggage. And camels! My God, Aleksy, have you ever seen a camel?"

"I have not." Aleksy felt very provincial. He would not tell Piotr that he had only just seen his first large city, Kraków.

"Marvelously mysterious beasts, they are! Humps on their backs big as you please. Well, once Vienna is pretty much surrounded, up comes a Turkish officer to our counterscarp—oh, we'd not been idle. We numbered maybe fifteen thousand. Commandant Starhemberg saw to the defenses as best he could. So this officer delivers a document for the commandant that calls out for the citizens of Vienna to accept Islam and live in peace under the Sultan's protection—*or* surrender the city and continue as Christians under the Sultan."

Aleksy let loose a whistle. "That last seems unlikely."

"Indeed. The offer was for citizens to leave peaceably with their belongings."

"And if one chose neither?"

"To stay? To resist? Death or slavery. Oh, the two were wrapped up in fine words, but that's what they amounted to."

"And the commandant?"

"He turned away the Turk and proceeded to wall up the gates. From the way the Turks settled in at some little distance, making a kind of tent city for themselves, it seemed they were in for the duration and that the Hofburg was their target."

"The Hofburg?"

"Leopold's palace. It's got hundreds of windows, a high roof, and timbered structures, plus rumors of great treasures within, so I suspect that's what tempted Mustafa. He assumed it must be the weakest point. That's when they started tunneling. The many tunnel entrances that we could see from St. Stephen's tower told us they had dug a warren beneath the stony ground, like rabbits. Their siegeworks were clearly aiming for the two particular bastions nearest the Hofburg. When they got far enough along, they started mining."

By now the two had arrived with the goods of Piotr's archery lesson—pheasant and rabbit—at an area in the Market Square abutting the inn where the king and queen were housed. "Ah, here's where tomorrow the king bids farewell to his Marysieńka," Piotr said. "Her carriage and all her retinue are slowing us, truth to tell. Now, you take most everything but this plump rabbit. It won't be needed here. The king and his folk will not be relying on my poor expertise this night, for they will be doing some high dining inside. At least as high class as one can get at a Tarnowskie inn. And besides, you were the successful hunter today, no surprise there. I'm responsible for only the rabbit, and if he weren't so fat and slower than most, I wouldn't have done that much."

"You think he'll do it, then? Send the queen back to Kraków?"

"I've heard him say so myself. Tomorrow, there's to be a review of troops. If you ask me, it's for General Caraffa's benefit, should he be sending word on ahead to Charles of Lorraine about our force and its readiness. The king will want a good report preceding him."

"What's this, then?" Aleksy asked, nodding to a circular stone pillar no more than four feet high. Flowers were placed all about it.

"I heard the mayor tell the king that it's a recent monument to plague victims. The plague ravaged this area just six or seven years ago before going on to Vienna."

"Probably traveled faster than we are," Aleksy said.

"They say a third of the townspeople are buried underneath it in a mass grave. It had to be done quickly. Oh!—What is the saying? 'Nothing is ever done well in a hurry, except running from the plague or from quarrels—'"

"'And catching fleas!'" Aleksy said, finishing the old proverb. He laughed heartily with Piotr, but each nonetheless made a quick sign of the cross to ward off the evil eye that was often thought to bring the plague.

Aleksy started gathering up the lion's share of the day's game. It would be enough to satisfy Marek and Roman.

"Oh, look," Piotr said, "there's someone who defied the evil eye!"

"Who?"

"There—across the square at the well, drawing water. It's that dwarf I told you about. Had he been a foot taller, I think my arrow would have pierced him through one temple and out the other."

"Skewered the little one, hey?" Aleksy's eyes narrowed as he stared across the square. While the Tarnowskie Market Square wasn't nearly as massive as Kraków's, it was still some distance from the one end with the column to the other with the well. Several of the townsfolk stood in line, but he was focusing on the dwarf Piotr was talking about. One glance told him he looked much like Idzi—the same height exactly, large hatless head, and body stance. Was it possible? Or was it that dwarfs tended to look alike?

"Did you get his name?" Aleksy asked.

"The dwarf's? No, I nearly killed him. I was all apologies, but we weren't about to become bosom friends."

"But he's Polish?"

"Of course."

Aleksy dropped his cache, turned, and started to walk toward the well, ignoring some question or other that Piotr was flinging after him.

As the dwarf, on tiptoes, drew water and splashed it into his bucket, his back was to Aleksy. About halfway to the well, Aleksy almost gave up in what he thought was likely a foolish conjecture. He would merely embarrass himself. Idzi couldn't be here in Tarnowskie. He must be in Halicz by now. But then he heard him speaking to a man waiting behind him. All dwarfs surely didn't have the same voice and speak in the same cadence. This voice was Idzi's.

At that moment the little man was turning about, preparing to leave the square with his water.

"Idzi!" Aleksy called.

The dwarf turned toward the approaching Aleksy. A shadow passed over his face. "A—Aleksy," he said.

Aleksy blinked in disbelief. "What are you doing here?—My God, you've run away!"

"No... no, Aleksy. I've been with you all the while."

"What? Travelling with us? What the devil—" Aleksy stopped short, for he saw that Idzi had given a person nearby a furtive look. It was a cloaked and hooded figure, not quite as tall as most men. A woman, Aleksy guessed.

He cast Idzi a suspiciously amused glance. "What—are you cavorting with the king's camp followers now? Truly? Why, my friend, how I *looked up* to you!"

His little joke—an old one—didn't elicit favor from Idzi. "Aleksy, I... that is, I—"

"I can't remember your being at a loss for words before. What is it?"

Through his peripheral vision, Aleksy now noticed that the hooded companion was slinking away. "Wait!" he called, turning toward her. "You there, wait a moment!"

The figure was moving faster and Aleksy had to run to catch up. He managed to catch hold of the cloaked arm there in the middle of the street that accessed the square. Both Idzi and Piotr were behind him, saying things he could not comprehend.

The figure pivoted toward him. It *was* a woman, her face in the shadow of the hood that she held forward, over her brow.

Aleksy's heart stopped. It couldn't be, he told himself. *It can't be!*

"Aleksy," she said, pushing back the hood with both hands, freeing up her long blond braids.

He stood there motionless, all breath drawn from his body as if he were drowning. "Krystyna," he heard himself say—and then he could not speak.

"She's the one that's run away," Idzi was saying. "And God help a poor dwarf for aiding her! My gallows won't take but half the usual allotment of wood. I told her it was insane for a noblewoman to go about like a common camp follower. An honest one, I admit, but nonetheless—"

Aleksy hadn't taken his eyes off of her. "You disguised yourself as a camp follower?"

"Well, you needn't take that tone with me, Aleksy," Krystyna said. "And it's no disguise at all. Did you think the worst? There are many virtuous camp followers, I can tell you—wives and children, victual sellers, men and women who cook and launder and nurse. They are not all of spoiled reputations."

"I'm aware of that, Lady Krystyna."

"Oh, you needn't start that either—like you don't know me."

"You ran away from your husband… and then caught up to us?"

"From Fabian? Yes!" Her face was reddening. "Only… only… oh, you tell him, Idzi!"

"She didn't marry Lord Nardolski, Aleksy. Conspired with me to get away is what she did instead. God help me, I'll have no home to go to after this. You might as well give me a lance—a short one, mind you—and point me in the direction of Vienna because—"

Both Aleksy and Krystyna turned to the talkative dwarf and said in unison: "Hush up, Idzi!"

He obeyed, but not without muttering about the crowd they were attracting.

Aleksy turned back to Krystyna. "You left him at the altar?"

"I left a note."

"A note? Holy Chrystus! Why, your brothers never let on that the wedding didn't go forward. No wonder there was no boasting."

"They didn't let on? For your benefit, no doubt. Bastards, aren't they?"

"Is this the truth?" Aleksy felt as if he were dreaming.

"Idzi can corroborate my story," Krystyna said. "Idzi?"

"The wedding was cancelled, Aleksy," his little friend said, "for want of a bride. We were off buying our way into a group of camp followers."

"But… why, Krystyna?"

"I couldn't stay in Kraków, now could I? And—"

"And?"

"I thought you could read, Alek, and yet you need everything spelled out." She took a deep breath. "Because the man I love is here."

"Here?"

"Before me, you ox."

"Prettiest speech I've heard today," Idzi offered. "Who might she be speaking of?" Nodding at Piotr, he said, "Keep in mind her amour is not this fellow here who nearly killed me the other day with a wayward arrow, and as for me—why, I'm not even on eye level with the lady.—Why, it must be you, Aleksy."

It seemed unreal. He *had* needed it spelled out. That she would do something so careless and risky for him made his head spin. He took her into a clumsy kiss-less embrace, then held her at arm's length. "You've been with us for all these many miles and days. Why didn't you show yourself? Oh, Krysia, when were you—" His questioning was cut short by a movement of her eyes, darkly green in the dusk. She had shifted her line of vision to something behind him, something that made her pale almost immediately.

"Oh, Sweet Jezus," she murmured, "this is why, Alek, this is why I dared not come to you."

Aleksy pivoted to see Roman Halicki bearing down on them, fire in his eyes, a stern-faced Marek trailing.

TWENTY-FOUR

"It's her," Roman bellowed. "It's Krystyna! And she's with the Tatar cur! A cholera on them!" In a split second Roman's hands were on Aleksy's *żupan*, pulling him toward him, wrenching him away from Krystyna. "You'll pay for this," he shouted as he started to deliver hammer blows to Aleksy's face.

Aleksy, taken so off guard, tried merely to fend off the blows. "He's done nothing!" Krystyna yelled at her brother. "It's my doing, Roman! Leave him alone."

A blow to the chest sent Aleksy to the ground. Idzi had joined in on the shouting, too, but he was easily pushed to the side by Marek. A small, curious crowd began to gather so that only later did Aleksy realize Piotr must have disappeared about this time.

Marek roughly pulled Aleksy to his feet. He and his brother were not finished with him. As Roman moved forward, Krystyna, screaming through tears, tried to intervene, stepping in front of her brother. He tossed her stumbling to the side.

Anger flared up in Aleksy now. He shoved Marek aside and threw himself on Roman. They fell to the ground, rolling and wrestling in the dirt, locked in what seemed an even match—until Roman came up atop Aleksy's chest. Just as he was about to deliver a blow to the face, Aleksy shifted his head and Roman's hand struck the stony earth. As Roman cried out in pain, Aleksy threw him off and their positions were at once reversed. He had no time to deliver a blow because Marek threw his whole body at Aleksy, sending them both careening. Aleksy jumped up and stood his ground as the Halicki brothers moved toward him. He would not back down.

Both Krystyna and Idzi made moves to come between Aleksy and the brothers, but they were thrust aside. The two did, however, work in tandem to keep Marek from interfering with the Roman and Aleksy contest that went on at some length.

"Stop!" The commanding voice came from the rear of the shallow crowd that had gathered. "Stop this at once!"

Aleksy turned around, toward the speaker, but had difficulty seeing. He wiped at a stream of blood that hindered the sight of his right eye.

The crowd parted as if they were cued actors upon a stage. A large, daunting figure in a scarlet *kontusz* stood over the three frozen forms. "What goes on here?" King Jan Sobieski demanded. "Our first rest in a real town is to be interrupted by ruffians! I think not! You will stop this, the lot of you, and you will explain yourselves."

The Halicki brothers stared in abashment, and Aleksy opened his mouth to answer—an answer as yet unformed—but it was Krystyna who spoke first. "I can explain," she said, curtseying demurely as if at court.

The large man, his face empurpled in the evening's dying light, turned to her. "You? Who are you? Are these men fighting over you?"

"Not in the way you might imagine, Your Majesty."

"You speak strangely well considering your attire." The king let out a sigh. "Very well, I'll listen. The rest of you," he addressed himself to the onlookers, waving his arms as if shooing away birds, "go about your business! Move along!" His stage magic seemed to work again.

Roman started to speak but one dark look from the king silenced him at once. Krystyna told her tale: how she was being bullied into a marriage she didn't want with a man she didn't love; how she and Idzi had become camp followers; how it wasn't more than a half an hour ago that her brothers had discovered her presence; how they mistakenly thought that Aleksy, their retainer, had engineered her masquerade.

"So you say that this one," the king asked, nodding at Aleksy, "didn't know you were here, either?"

"No, Your Majesty."

"But he is the reason for your attaching yourself to a war party instead of a wedding party, is he not?"

"Your Majesty?"

"God's teeth, girl! Is this the boy you love—or not?"

Before Krystyna could answer the question, a figure appeared at the king's side now. "Husband, the tables are set and we await your arrival in the hall before the supper can commence."

Aleksy had seen Queen Maria Casimire from a distance at the cathedral but not up close like this. Framed by long, luxuriant curls of raven black, her face, even a bit distorted now by her pique, shone with a luminescent beauty.

"I apologize, Marysieńka," the king said, the diminutive wrapped in warmth. "There's been a little scuffle over this girl and that boy there."

Aleksy drew in breath and held it. That the king referred to him as a boy and Krystyna as a girl was insulting, but he could do nothing about it.

As the king apprised his wife of the scenario in shorter time than Krystyna had taken—and not without a twinkle of amusement in his eyes—the queen's eyes became riveted on Krystyna.

"Husband," she said, once he had finished, "don't you recognize this girl?"

The king's forehead furrowed. "What do you mean?"

"This is the girl who brought up the Offertory gift in the cathedral at Kraków! I've never seen a girl with greener eyes."

"Is it, indeed? You know I'm not as good at faces as are you." He addressed himself to Krystyna now. "It was you who brought up the crown of grains, then?"

"Yes, Your Majesty."

"She's of a good family," the queen said. "She's not to be among common camp followers, by heaven. She needs to be sent back at once."

"To Kraków?" Krystyna implored. "Oh, please—"

Roman took a step forward. "If I may speak, Your Majesty—"

"Yes, very well," the king said. "What is it?"

"Your Majesty, If you would allow it, I would leave for as short a time as possible in order to return my sister to our parents. We're traveling not so fast that I couldn't find my way back before—"

"Another one to hector me about our speed! God's death, when will it end?"

"I only meant—"

"Yes, yes, I know what you meant. You're right—she should go home."

The queen now drew her husband to bend low so she could whisper in his ear. Aleksy studied Krystyna, whose face had gone white with despair, a despair that clung to him, as well. Was Roman to return her to angry parents? Might she still be forced to marry Fabian Nardolski? Had her brave gambit come to nothing? What was there in his power that he could do?

The king nodded in agreement to something his wife was saying. He stood erect now, making known his thoughts as if they comprised an official announcement from the royal dais. "There will be no need for you to leave us," he said to Roman. "You and your brother are hussars, yes? Well, we will need every lance, every man, every damn pair of eagles' wings." The heavy-set king's chest rose as he drew in a long breath, then said, "It's to be announced at supper—the supper I might add that you people are keeping us from—that Queen Marysieńka will be returning to Kraków tomorrow. She and her household will go well protected. In her goodness, she has asked that the young Lady Halicka accompany her and her attendant ladies, whereupon she will be returned to her family."

Roman's mouth fell agape.

Aleksy's inside knowledge about the queen's imminent leave-taking had proved accurate, but his thoughts were too tangled to lord it over Roman. He looked to Krystyna. She seemed no more relieved than if Roman had been given permission to escort her. And rightly so, he realized. She would likely be under guard until given over to her mother.

And they were to be separated yet again.

"Your Majesty, If I may be permitted to speak—" Krystyna ventured.

"You may not!" the king countered. "You're to accompany my wife to her rooms, and her ladies will see that you are properly dressed and attended for tomorrow's departure. Your life as a camp-follower, my sweet, has ended."

Krystyna's eyes went beseechingly to Aleksy. "Alek, I—"

"Now," the queen said, taking hold of Krystyna's arm and hustling her off.

"And, Your Majesty," Idzi piped, "am I not to attend Lady Krystyna?"

"I think not," the king said. "What to do with you, then? Is this Aleksy here not your friend?"

"He is, Your Majesty, and his greatest wish—well, one of them—is to be a hussar himself and not a retainer."

Holy Chrystus! Aleksy's mouth fell open at the little man's nerve. What had prompted him to such boldness?

The king's gaze fell on Aleksy. "Is this true?"

"It—it is," Aleksy mumbled, forgetting the proper form of address.

"You would like to be a lancer?"

"Your Majesty," Idzi persisted, "he's made his own lance and it's a beauty. He's also the best archer in camp."

"Fewer and fewer of those, to be certain," the king said.

"Your Majesty," Piotr interjected, "I can vouch for his expertise with a bow. He's been giving me lessons. That venison you so enjoyed the other day came only at his great skill as an archer. Took the beast right through the heart."

"Indeed?" The king took a hard look at Aleksy. "As you must have done that waif of a girl you were fighting over, yes?"

"Milord?"

"Don't stand there with your mouth open! You might wish to join my Tatar company, then? You are a Tatar, yes?"

Aleksy stiffened. "I am a Tatar loyal to Poland, Your Majesty." He could scarcely think. Krystyna had just been wrenched from him and yet, was his other dearest wish about to be granted him—out of the blue and the mouth of a dwarf? Had he not believed in Chrystus, he would swear that the old gods were having their fun with him.

"It can be done," the king said.

Aleksy knew that a few words from the king and anything was as good as done. But words of interference from Roman came as no surprise to Aleksy.

Roman spoke without permission. "Your Majesty," he blurted, "although my family is of the *szlachta*, we are not so wealthy that our father was able to provide the requisite three retainers each for my brother Marek here, and for me. Neither did he afford us two. Marek and I have but one retainer apiece. And if you take Aleksy we will be at a sore disadvantage."

"Ah, I see."

Aleksy felt his stomach drop in disappointment. He could think of nothing to counter the argument. What could he say—that the Halicki brothers hated him? That they might murder him in his sleep? What? He said nothing.

What did it matter? Superseding everything was the reality that he had just lost Krystyna yet again. Idzi started to speak, but a subtle hand signal from the king hushed him at once.

"Well," the king said, "your point is well taken. I will allow you your retainer here—and the little man into the bargain."

For the briefest of moments he had almost broken free of Roman Halicki, but the king's words rang in his ears like the clanging of a prison door.

Before leaving Aleksy and Idzi in the custody of Roman and Marek, the king bound the two brothers to an agreement that no harm whatsoever would come to their retainer and his little friend.

Still, Aleksy thought how in the chaos of war, it would be so easy for them to deliberately place him in danger—or to kill him themselves and claim it was the enemy. Safety while in the hands of Roman? Perhaps. But the thought did not buoy any hope in Aleksy. He had lost his one brief chance at becoming a hussar. And he had lost Krystyna.

His life seemed little enough of importance.

The next day, 22 August, a grand review of the troops, wagons, and cannon was held with King Sobieski and General Caraffa officiating on a raised platform. Cavalry—including hussars—and infantry were estimated at thirty thousand. While the cavalry was supplied by and included noblemen, their horses, raiment, and accoutrements richly varied, colorful, and impressive, the infantry was that much less so with its attempt at uniforms stymied by faded, threadbare clothing and paper-thin soled boots worn from other campaigns. The infantry was kept the farthest from the viewing stand and from General Caraffa, who would send ahead to Charles of Lorraine assurances of the Polish army's readiness in numbers, expertise, and equipment.

Aleksy stood to the side with Ludwik and Idzi, shielding his eyes against the morning red glare of the sun. Only later would he learn that in a more private moment the king had said goodbye to his Marysieńka and her retinue of ladies, servants, and soldiers, who along with carriages and wagons, were being sent on their way to Kraków. He learned, too, that Krystyna was seated in the queen's fine closed carriage.

So short had been his reunion with Krystyna that only now did he recall how his heart had swelled at the sight of her, how his future had glittered before him in rainbow colors. But he had not been allowed even a moment alone with her—for an embrace or kiss—before hope was crushed.

His last memory of Krystyna—Krysia—would be of the queen hustling her quickly away from him.

TWENTY-FIVE

"WHAT'S KEEPING THEM IF HE'S so damn good with the bow?" Roman asked. Aleksy, Ludwik, and Idzi had gone hunting. The sky was quickly darkening. Campfires began to dot the ruined fields like the appearance of stars in the night-sky.

"Game could be scarce when thousands are out foraging," Marek said. "What, do you think he would desert?"

"Don't you?"

"No, and I don't think you do, either."

"He's a Tatar, isn't he?"

"Roman, did you believe Aleksy when he said he had nothing to do with Krystyna's jilting of Fabian—or that he even knew she was disguised as a camp-follower until that moment we came upon them?"

"I believe nothing from him. And you?"

"He seemed credible."

"And you're gullible, brother. But what does it matter? One way or another, he'll pay. Somehow."

"What do you mean? Remember, he's my retainer, not yours. I need him! And you promised the king—"

"The king? He certainly manages to get decent lodgings, doesn't he? This is the second monastery in a row. His bed will be soft, and you can bet those monks are kowtowing to him as I speak."

"At least we're moving a bit faster by day."

"You're right on that count—*a bit*." He spit into the campfire. "And as for retainers, my lord brother, if Father hadn't been so tight-fisted with every złoty, we'd each have at least two."

"Two złotys?" Marek asked, smiling.

"Retainers, you bastard!"

Krystyna sat in the moving carriage dressed in an elegant pink gown and satin-covered slippers that the queen's Mistress of the Robes, Madame Heloise, had commandeered for her from the youngest lady-in-waiting. She would gladly wear the peasant garb she had been forced to give up if she could somehow change the outcome of the events a few days before. Her yearning for Aleksy had not abated. What future was there without him?

She watched Queen Marysieńka—in blue brocade—dozing on the bench across from her. The carriage trundled on, minute to minute, hour to hour. How much time had passed—two, three days? They were endless. Highest ranking of the queen's ladies present in the coach, Madame Heloise shared the bench with the queen, while two ladies-in-waiting bookended Krystyna now, to no little discomfort. Conversation was in French and Krystyna mentally gave a reluctant thanks to the nuns for the strong foundation she had been given in the language that was spoken in the courts of most of Europe's capitals. However, the queen's ladies spoke very little. Their silence and sour faces bespoke their resentment of the interloper. In daylight they worked at their embroidery so silently and intently that Krystyna thought she would go mad. She had been offered a hoop and had politely refused. How she hated embroidery, always had, ever since her convent confinement when it had been punishment for her erring ways.

The carriage proceeded, rocking on imperfect springs, perpetrating a vibration within the coach that no seat cushion could mitigate. A wheel struck a hole now, jolting the queen awake. Krystyna studied her eyes. Were they blue—or were they merely reflecting the brocade?

Krystyna became determined to shake off her despondency and break the silence, the hum-drum boredom of hooves and wheels, jouncing and jostling. "Your Majesty," she said, "may I ask a question?"

The queen's back stiffened slightly as she roused herself. "Mademoiselle?"

"I see that your eyes are almond-shaped."

Though Krystyna sensed a sudden tenseness in the coach, she repeated her observation. Pinch-faced Madame Heloise let out an audible gasp.

"It was just something I noticed, Your Majesty. Do you have any Eastern blood?"

"Mademoiselle?"

The women on either side of her ceased their embroidery.

"I ask because Aleksy has almond-shaped eyes much like yours, except they are dark as pitch. Of course, he's a Tatar."

"Indeed. I can assure you, Mademoiselle Halicka, that I am entirely French—and Polish by marriage."

Krystyna knew she had overstepped her bounds but regretted it not and stepped further out onto the ice. "You were married once before, yes?"

"Ouch!" Madame Heloise cried, having stuck herself with her embroidery needle. "Mademoiselle, you are not to interrogate Her Highness. *C'est inapproprie*. Shame!"

Krystyna knew that Madame Heloise was correct in calling her forwardness a breach of decorum. Mother Abbess Teodora would no doubt be horrified. *You are a reckless girl, Krystyna Halicka!*

Not so the queen, who said, "Calm yourself, Hellie, Krystyna means only to pass the time. I'm thankful for that." Her eyes came to Krystyna's and she started speaking fluent Polish. "Yes, child, I was married before—to a man of great wealth and position, but of little ambition. I had set out in life to achieve something, for me and for the man whom I would marry. That was an unfortunate alliance."

Krystyna knew that she was speaking of Jan Zamoyski, the Prince of Zamość.

"His official title at Court was Cup-bearer, a humble title as court titles go, and also ironically fitting, for he was often in his cups." The queen laughed, as did Krystyna, and when the other ladies kept a deadpan silence, Krystyna realized that they were unable to follow the queen's quick tongue of her adopted country. A tête-à-tête had been the queen's intent—but *why* was the queen speaking to her of such personal matters?

"There is another irony, too," the queen continued. "I had met Jan Sobieski before I met my first husband. He was a Jan, also. I loved the first, and yet I chose the second one. What fate, eh? Who was it that called Lady Fortuna a strumpet?"

"The Roman goddess?" Krystyna gave out with a little laugh. "I often blame her myself, Your Majesty."

"Yes, she would spin her wicked wheel without regard to whom she gave —or withheld—her favors."

"You were too young at the time for... your current husband? Or was he not interested?"

"No, he was interested, as you say, and so very handsome but his family was against the match. I was, like you, precocious and headstrong and yet, to my regret, my first husband, his fortune, and a good many diamonds won me over. I thought I could spur on his ambition. Alas, he could be spurred on only to his wine. To complicate matters, the two Jans were friends."

Krystyna smiled, suppressing the urge to ask about the rumored infidelity with the second Jan, who would one day become king. *That* would be reckless.

"And you, my dear," the queen said, turning the tables, "you have had two suitors to consider, as well."

"Yes." By now, Krystyna saw through to the queen's motives in speaking to her as if they were equals. She was attempting to use her own private history to prove Fabian the better choice.

"One noble and one—not, yes?"

Krystyna nodded.

"And you chose—for the moment—the Tatar. A daring choice."

Was this a question or an accusation? She could not be certain and did not reply.

"The noble suitor," the queen continued, "is he old or ugly? Is his face marred by the pox?"

"No, Fabian is young enough and quite handsome."

"Does he lack ambition, my dear?"

"I don't think so. He is seeking a military career as an entrée into the Sejm."

"Ah, a politician... And the Tatar?"

"Aleksy."

"Mademoiselle?"

"Aleksy, his name is Aleksy. I sometimes call him Alek."

"And does Aleksy have ambition?"

The question startled Krystyna. She had to pause and think about it. "Why, yes, I think he does."

"And that is?"

"He... he wishes to be a hussar."

"A lancer with the wings. An ambition with danger. The glory Polish soldiers seek on the battlefield—I am familiar with it. And—what does this mean for you?"

"The ambition is to fight for Poland—for you, Your Majesty, and for the king. Is that not enough?"

The queen gave a half-smile. "A point—you score a point, my dear."

Krystyna felt hot tears suddenly spring into her eyes. Aleksy's dream made sense to her now. Yes, he sought freedom for Poland and all of Europe, but he also sought the field of glory.

The queen persisted. "You are likely to regret your first refusal. A girl can be too headstrong for her own good."

"Pardon me, Your Majesty, but it seems you regretted not being strong-willed enough to marry the love of your life at the first." Suddenly the words were there, said and done. *You are a reckless girl, Krystyna Halicka!*

Madame Heloise let out another gasp. Had she managed to pick up enough of the Polish to follow along?

The queen turned her head to the window, and it seemed as if she were looking off into the horizon. Then, almost inaudibly, she whispered, "Another point, my dear."

On 24 August, after the cavalcade crossed the River Oder at Ratibor, the king and his magnate companions were being sheltered and fêted in grand Saxon style by the Obersdorf family. The bill for the non-monastic hospitality, however, was being footed by Emperor Leopold himself. As mere members of the *szlachta*, Roman and Marek were excluded. They had managed to secure a bottle of brandy and repaired to their own tent to lubricate their damaged pride.

Rain was spattering onto the canvas of the lean-to attached to the tent. Inside, Ludwik lay lightly snoring on the pallet parallel to Aleksy, who lay awake, wondering about Krystyna. How close was she getting to Kraków? He knew her father had left to take up duty with General Lubomirski, but what of her mother? Had she returned to Halicz or did she remain in the city? And what of the Nardolskis? When Krystyna reappears, will they still nourish hopes of securing a union with their family? The thought brought a thrumming to his temples. And what of Fabian?

"Aleksy?" The whisper came from Idzi, whose little pallet was placed width-wise at Aleksy's feet.

"Yes?"

Idzi slithered his way up through the narrow gap between Aleksy and Ludwik so that his voice would not carry through the canvas partition. Aleksy had not heard the voices of the Halicki brothers for a good half hour and so he assumed they had gone to sleep.

"A secret?" Aleksy asked.

"A concern."

"What is it?"

"You need to be careful." Idzi's's expression was indecipherable in the dark, but his voice reflected earnestness. "Roman is nursing real hatred for you."

"Old news, that is."

"You went hunting tonight by yourself. Don't do it again."

"Is that an order?" Aleksy spoke lightly. "What do you know?"

"Only the way he looks at you. Oh, I know what the king told him—to treat you well—but it's as if he's planning something."

"You must have gypsy blood. I'll make sure you or Ludwik are with me. But I think my supplying their metal camp plates with good game will help keep me safe."

"Perhaps," Idzi said, unconvinced.

Ludwik had come awake now and made his offering. "There's another reason, too, that they might not try anything. That is, if they're smart,"

"That much is debatable," Idzi countered.

"What's that?" Aleksy asked.

"They want you at hand with your bowstave when they finally don their feathers and pick up their lances. Remember, they have yet to go up against their first enemy."

"As do I."

"True, but you are an expert archer," Ludwik persisted. "You have that to commend you."

"They'll use you," Idzi said, "and think nothing of placing you in harm's way."

"I expect as much.—Thanks, the both of you."

Idzi moved back to his place and within fifteen minutes his even breathing could be heard, as a delicate counterpoint to Ludwik's snoring.

Something in their conversation had given Aleksy pause. It *would* be his first battle. In his position as a retainer, he would likely have to kill a man—or be killed himself. To date, neither brother had addressed the duties of their retainers during a battle. He'd been secretly practicing with a sabre, but he had no experience with firearms. And although Szymon had provided a modicum of practice with a lance, he could not expect to be afforded the opportunity of using one at Vienna.

But to kill a man—what would it feel like? He had longed to be a soldier, a hussar. He had thought it would happen somehow, as if God willed it. But had he really thought about hand-to-hand combat? About taking a life? He had not killed animals for sport, thinking that a wasteful business. He killed to put food on the table, his own or others'. Of course, at Vienna he would be killing for his faith, freedom, and for Poland, his adopted country. Valid reasons, he decided, although the question nagged at him: What would it be like to take a man's life?

Before sleep came, his thoughts swam back through these dark thoughts to days of light, the three prized occasions he had spent with Krystyna at Castle Hill.

TWENTY-SIX

While Roman and Marek had not merited invitations to the Obersdorf entertainments, they and their party were included among the three thousand who accompanied the king on 25 August as he struck out for Vienna ahead of the main army. The smaller cavalcade made better time so that they arrived in Brno on 28 August and in Ober-Hollabrun on 31 August. It was there, amidst a raging and sultry storm, that a war conference was held. While Roman and Marek revealed none of what they might have heard, Piotr, who served the king and kept his ears open, had much to say on the subject when he visited Aleksy, Idzi, and Ludwik at the campsite, as he did with some regularity.

"Did you hear?" Piotr asked as he entered the lean-to tent. "Prince Lubomirski has arrived with his forces! A good many, too."

Idzi and Aleksy exchanged glances. They knew that Lord Halicki had followed his old commander back into the field. Aleksy's blood ran cold. Now that Halicki knew his daughter's marriage had been aborted out of her love for a commoner—and a Tatar—how would he treat Aleksy? He had heard that troubles seldom travel singly and that they come in company of threes. Not only would Lord Halicki have accompanied General Lubomirski, but Lord Nardolski, Krystyna's would-be father-in-law would be in camp now—as would Fabian Nardolski, the jilted bridegroom. That made for three. His head spun.

Piotr dropped down and sat cross-legged in the circle of friends and continued with his news. "Oh, and Charles, Duke of Lorraine, was full of fine compliments for our king—how he was pleased to learn the art of war under his stewardship, and the like. These two were joined by Prince Georg Waldeck, who is commanding Franconian and Bavarian forces. The king was asked to formulate the plan whereby the three armies would proceed in the twenty-five mile march to Vienna."

"And..." Ludwik asked, "who's to have the baton of commander-in-chief?"

"It certainly seems like it's to be Sobieski," Piotr said.

"They say," Ludwik said with a wink, "that had Marysieńka been allowed to remain on the march, her husband's baton would be a foregone conclusion."

Piotr chuckled and continued. "At least he's the one to lay out the plan going forward. The Saxons and part of the Austrian Imperial infantry and cavalry are to take the easiest route, along the Danube. Charles and the rest of the Imperial forces, supplemented by Waldeck with his Franconians and Bavarians, are taking the center."

"And us?" Aleksy pressed.

"Ah," Piotr said, as though he were saving the best for last, "we, my friends, are to take the right flank through the forested highlands of the Wienerwald and follow the high, long, long ridge of the Kahlenberg."

Idzi spoke up. "I thought the Kahlenberg was one of the highest peaks, not a ridge."

"Well, it is that," Piotr said, "but the entire ridge of the Vienna Woods—the Wienerwald—is referred to as the Kahlenberg."

Ludwik gave a high whistle, his visage revealing vexation rather than approbation, for talk had gotten around by now of the difficulty of negotiating the Kahlenberg route. "Damn, we're in for it now. Beautiful country the Vienna Woods, all streams, hills and low mountains, pretty as you please, but dragging wagons and cannons up there in the heat of summer is going to be hell. The king has managed to gain for us the worst of the bargain."

Aleksy had put Lord Halicki and the Nardolski father and son out of his thoughts. Neither was he thinking of the climb up, arduous as it might be; he was thinking of how magnificent the descending formation of the winged hussars would look to the people of Vienna, those long encased in the citadel who were praying for a last minute miracle. He was also thinking of how terrifying the Polish formation would look to Grand Vizier Kara Mustafa and his troops, who, it was said, feared the hussars more than any other force. The Ottomans had yet to win a battle when pitted against Sobieski and his hussars. It was also put about by spies that he did not believe Sobieski would come to Vienna's aid so that the sight of the king's feathered hussars flying down in formation, stirrup to stirrup, would be doubly terrifying.

Aleksy felt a stab of jealousy at the heart when he thought of Roman and Marek—in their leopard skins draped over polished armor and chain mail—tearing down from the ridge, their feathers singing in the breeze, the sound and sight inciting terror in the Ottomans and spooking their horses. And how the Viennese would rejoice to see their freedom at hand. All Europe would sing the praises of the Polish hussars. Oh, he would have his part to play. He and other retainers would come afterward, in the wake of the hussars, on steppe ponies or horseless, striving to both help their wounded lords and perhaps wield some blows, as well. But the glory of being a hussar—that was for others, like the Halicki brothers.

"Do you know," Piotr said, looking pointedly at Aleksy, "that one of the king's most serious concerns was that of the Tatars that fight for the Ottomans?"

"War must be in the Tatar blood," Idzi said, winking at Aleksy.

Ludwik spoke up now. "Well, he's got his own elite Lithuanian Tatars—the Lipka—to counterbalance those from the Wild Fields."

"I should like to see them," Idzi said, "but they have yet to arrive."

It was an unsettling feeling for Aleksy to think that Tatars like himself would be fighting on each side, perhaps brother against brother. On whose side would his father—blood brother to Lord Halicki—have stood?

"Of course," Piotr said, "Duke Charles and Prince Waldeck wanted to know how the king beat the Ottomans in the past even though his forces were always greatly outnumbered."

"And?" Aleksy pressed.

"He said *speed* and the fact that he would never allow the enemy to collect in one place."

Divide and conquer.

"And..." Aleksy said, feigning an offhand question, "has the king had word about the queen's progress toward Kraków?"

"No," Piotr replied, "too soon for that, my friend."

"Of course," Aleksy mumbled, a bit embarrassed. Piotr's tone revealed that he saw right through to his real concern: Krystyna.

Piotr stayed longer than Aleksy would have wished. He longed to put his head down and lose himself in sleep.

It was after midnight that they heard loud voices in Roman and Marek's adjoining tent. Aleksy and his three friends fell silent and listened. He could discern four voices: Roman's, Marek's, Lord Halicki's and one other.

A single questioning expression directed at Idzi brought the answer. Idzi mouthed the name: Fabian Nardolski.

Aleksy's heart caught at once, but there was no time to assess his feelings, for the tent flap was thrown back and Roman reached in, grasped hold of Aleksy's cotton shirt and dragged him out into the rain. "Someone to meet you, my would-be soldier.—Fabian, meet your competition!"

Aleksy stared at the tall figure, his handsomeness evident despite the rain-soaked uniform and wet ringlets of hair. Water ran from the end of his fine nose like from a spout. Like Roman, he was drunk.

"Krystyna fell for this—this Tatar?" Fabian asked dumbly. "You cost me my marriage, Tatar? Speak up!"

Aleksy didn't know how to respond. He was unafraid and even surprised himself with a feeling of compassion for this man, who—like him—had lost Krystyna.

Roman moved behind Aleksy and took captive his arms at the elbows. "The lieutenant is addressing you, Aleksy. Treat your betters with respect—answer him!"

Idzi threw back the flap and started to come out of the lean-to. Roman kicked him now, propelling him back into the tent.

Aleksy fought an urge to pull free from Roman. "I did not ask Krystyna to follow me. It was her choice."

"Choice, Tatar? Choice?" Lord Fabian Nardolski sputtered. "She had no choice. The marriage had been arranged."

Aleksy felt Roman's hold on him tighten like steel. He knew from Fabian's momentarily averted eyes that some signal was passed from Roman to him. Fabian stepped forward and brought his fist up like a hammer into Aleksy's face. All went black for some moments and as he sank back, Roman released his grip and he slipped into the mud.

He sensed a stir around him as his friends exited the tent to come to his aid. And then came the voice of authority. "What's going on here?"

Lord Halicki thundered. "Roman, I can't even go off for a piss and you're at Aleksy's throat!"

"Not I, Father. I've kept my promise."

Aleksy looked up to see Lord Halicki's gaze move from his son to Fabian. Was he making some allowance for the spurned lover? Then he looked again to Aleksy, who was being helped to his feet by Piotr and Ludwik. "Help him into your tent, men. By God, you'll all catch a death of cold in this downpour—and then where will we be for the coming battle?"

As Aleksy was brought to his pallet, he heard Lord Halicki chastising Roman before calling out, "You should have given the letter to the king, Aleksy, do you hear? Too bad you didn't."

Letter? Aleksy thought. He remembered at once the count's promise of a letter to the king, but he had been given no letter and wanted to tell Lord Halicki as much, but the pain of his jaw precluded his raising his voice above a whisper.

He lay back on his pallet. No covering was needed in the dense and sultry air. Piotr left now to return to the king's campsite, and Ludwik and Idzi settled themselves in their respective places.

As usual, Roman had meant his mischief, but Aleksy—empathizing with Fabian and his aborted marriage plans—could almost forgive the forsaken groom.

Sleep came eventually despite the pain, a pain assuaged by the realization that with Lord Fabian Nardolski involved in the saving of Vienna, no marriage to Krystyna could occur. That knowledge was worth a broken face.

TWENTY-SEVEN

KRYSTYNA HALICKA PACED BACK AND forth, forth and back, across the intricate arabesque of a luxurious carpet created in Constantinople and the irony was not lost on her. Hundreds of miles away, Polish and other European allies were converging at Vienna in order to halt the Ottoman Turks' takeover of an entire continent. So many that she loved were caught up in the effort to hold Christian Europe. Her father, her brothers Roman and Marek—and Aleksy. God protect Aleksy from the Turks, she prayed—and from her brothers.

Two guards armed with halberds stood posted outside of her castle chamber door. Ostensibly, they were there to protect her, but she knew better. They were there to see that she did not attempt to flee. On the return from Tarnowskie to Kraków, the queen had been fussy about where the royal party spent the night so that often they took circuitous routes to wealthier homes and better inns, making the long journey interminable and that much more exhausting. Sometimes—if the queen developed a rapport with her hosts—they stayed an extra day. But they were in Kraków at last, the city that had been the Commonwealth's capital before Warsaw laid claim to the title, and Krystyna found herself all but a captive in Wawel Castle.

Upon their arrival in the city, the queen sent word to the Nardolski household, only to learn that Krystyna's mother had returned to Halicz. Despite Krystyna's tearful plea to refrain, the queen wrote to the countess at once, instructing her to come and *collect* her wayward daughter. And so Krystyna waited for the sword of Zenobia to fall. It would be some days before her mother's arrival, but in the great scheme of things, that was of little importance. What mattered, truly mattered, was whether King Jan Sobieski would triumph at Vienna—and whether Roman and Marek and Aleksy would survive. Even if her mother and father went against her, even if she was forced to marry another, she could not enjoy a breath of life if Aleksy were to die at Vienna.

A knock came at the door. Before she could call out, the door opened and—impossible as it was—for a moment she thought her mother had arrived, for that was very much her signature entrance.

Dressed in a drab blue gown, Madame Heloise stepped in. Krystyna smothered a little laugh because it occurred to her now that this woman with her humorless demeanor could provide a fairly accurate proxy for her mother.

"Her Majesty Queen Maria Casimire," the Mistress of the Robes announced, haughtily stressing the queen's French name, "wishes to know if you have settled in—?"

"I have, Madame."

"Is there anything you wish?"

Krystyna affected sincerity. "How very sweet of you to ask."

In return, Madame Heloise rendered the facsimile of a smile. "It is the queen who asks."

Krystyna returned an expression in kind. Of course she knew that. At least the woman took no credit for any sweetness. "I'm wondering if the queen has had word from her husband."

"His Majesty, the King, you mean?"

Krystyna suppressed a sigh and took the correction in stride. She just wanted the answer. "Yes, His Majesty, King Jan Sobieski."

"She has."

"And?"

Madame Heloise pursed her lips as if unsure whether she should relay such information.

"Madame Heloise, he and my father fight for the future of the Commonwealth, and my brothers and—my brothers are with him." Later, she wondered why she stumbled, why she hadn't said Aleksy's name. After all, the woman knew about the scandal of her running away to follow a young peasant Tatar. She was no doubt the talk of the castle. Krystyna locked eyes with the Frenchwoman. "*Please* tell me if there is news."

The woman shifted from one black leather pump to the other. "They were very close to Vienna when he wrote. They may be engaging in battle as I speak."

Krystyna lost her equanimity for the moment and a hand went to her mouth. She turned away and looked out the lancet window, her eyes focusing absently on the high walls of the barbican. The defensive wall and tower made her think of the encounters with Aleksy at the castle ruins at Halicz. Several moments slipped by. She spoke then without turning about. "Thank you, Madame Heloise, for looking in on me."

"Lady Krystyna," the woman said.

"Yes?"

The woman gave a little stage cough. "Her Majesty Queen Maria Casimire has invited you to sup with her."

"What?" Krystyna pivoted to face the fish-eyed woman, quickly wiping at a tear. Throughout the entire journey, she, the unexpected passenger, had taken her meals by herself at the inns and noble houses as if she were a pariah, a leper. Now she was being asked to share a meal in the dining hall of Wawel Castle? How was it possible?

Madame Heloise read her silent wonder. The woman shrugged and said with a voice destitute of expression, "Her Majesty took a liking to you." She turned now and went to the door, adding at the last, "I can't think why."

Aleksy worried. Days passed without word coming back of the queen's retinue. Surely Krystyna must have arrived in Kraków by now—and yet no news had come.

The immediate military plan was for the three armies to go their separate ways and converge at Tulln on the other side of the River Danube. For the Poles, the route first ran through marshes and lowlands to the south bank of the Danube. There, with the participation of the three forces, pontoon bridges were built—with the loss of three valuable days—but Sobieski's fear that Ottoman Tatars would waylay them during this process did not materialize. They were now close enough for the Poles to hear the bombardment of Vienna. Aleksy brooded that they might not arrive in time. He was not alone.

By 10 September, Aleksy's hunting forays were days long past. They had to rely solely on what supplies were provided by the army stores carried in the scores of wagons that lagged behind, often breaking down in the uneven, ever-rising terrain. Before dawn Sobieski's army started through the Wienerwald, the Vienna Woods. These rolling, richly forested highlands would take them up to the Kahlenberg ridge.

Aleksy and Ludwik took the climb on foot, carefully leading their steppe ponies while nearby Idzi—who occasionally played relief driver for Bogdan and Jacek—drove one of the Halicki wagons, the one that held the Halicki armor and camp equipment. They moved along the path newly made by the king and the vanguard, Roman and Marek among them. Occasionally they halted in order to urge a horse forward or to help men of the infantry push forward one of the cannons.

"Piotr told me that the Kahlenberg is sometimes called Bald Mountain," Ludwik said, an hour into the climb.

"Hey," Idzi called out, "how is it that we can we be so close to Vienna and yet we see nothing?"

"Don't worry, my friend," Ludwik shouted, "I'm told we are but a few miles away. Were it not for the denseness of the trees, we could see the city."

"But the cannon fire," Idzi persisted, "it sounds as if it's many miles away."

Here Aleksy's yeomanly skills came in handy. "The forest with its many trees, mostly still in leaf, mind you, mask the noise. Ludwik's right. The city is closer than it sounds."

Idzi grunted. "How does the proverb go? 'Hunger will lead a man out of the forest'."

"In our case," Piotr said, serious as a monk, "it's a hunger to hold on to Poland and to Europe."

"That it is," Aleksy agreed. "That it is."

"They also say," Idzi said, inflecting a pointedness that escaped Piotr, "that 'the forest can't be without its jackals'."

"Indeed! You are full of sayings today," Aleksy said, making light of another warning of Roman's intentions, but nonetheless wondering whether Roman would one day play the jackal.

"Perhaps, Alek, you don't get the drift," Idzi said.

"And they say," Aleksy retorted, "'Don't go near a dwarf because God Himself hit him on the head with a hammer'."

"What's this?" Piotr asked. "What drift, little man?"

Idzi's complexion now went beet red. Aleksy realized that his original proverb and Piotr's solicitous epithet "little man" doubly stung his friend. "Never mind, Piotr," Aleksy said. "Just know that as far as intelligence goes, Idzi is as tall as either of us."

Idzi mumbled something and quickened the pace of the wagon so that Aleksy could not tell from his visage whether his quick repair had any effect.

Not a day went by that Idzi did not warn Aleksy of danger from the Halicki brothers, Roman in particular. Of course, Roman was a jackal, but he was a jackal being watched by a royal lion, King Sobieski, who had taken notice of Aleksy—and hadn't he been named "Lion of Poland" by the Turks he and his hussars had defeated in numerous battles? Would Roman dare take his revenge? Aleksy thought not. He would be too afraid of the king's reaction. Any revenge vented on Aleksy would likely end Roman's ascent in the husaria.

Unless... unless Roman were able to mastermind an accident no one would question. A fall? A drowning? A hunting accident? He thought again. No, they had gotten too close to Vienna now for Roman to attempt something. The focus was on what was to come, not on avenging a sister's honor. Not with the battle but hours away. *The battle!* At the thought, Aleksy's hair on the nape of his neck stood on end. He could imagine such chaos and confusion that Roman, atop Flash and with a sabre sharp as a razor, could cut him down in an instant and have no one the wiser. Or a pistol shot would be even quicker and less likely to be noticed.

The imagery was not easily put to rest. Aleksy fought off a chill that ran though him. Idzi was right. He would have to watch his back even as he battled Turks. What was it Szymon had called Roman?—Slyboots.

Krystyna sat, waiting, waiting, as if for the executioner rather than for an escort to the royal dining hall. The clock on a pedestal near the ceramic stove ticked loudly. She sat on an uncomfortably prim white stool, pushing the fingernail of her index finger along the map-like lines of minerals in the predominantly white marble that formed the top of the boudoir table. Below, one of her borrowed silver slippers tapped nervously at the parquet. Not so many months ago she would have been mesmerized by the interior of Wawel Castle. Oh, Roman and Marek bragged about their visit to the

Royal Castle in Warsaw, but they had never stepped foot in Kraków's Wawel Castle, much less been welcomed into a room of their own. Wouldn't they be surprised? How would she describe the color of the walls and the gold-trimmed bed hangings that framed the moderately-sized bed in the alcove? A purplish blue, she thought, and so very rich in the candlelight emanating from the crystal chandelier above her and the wall sconces on either side of the gold-gilded mirror. The resplendently royal color, juxtaposed with the paneled door and wainscoting of white enamel deemed the chamber fit for a princess—and yet Krystyna was numb to her surroundings. It might as well have been the meanest, rat-infested cell at convent school.

She could think only of Aleksy. What had become of him in the days since their very brief reunion? Had the army reached Vienna? Had the fighting begun? Would he survive it? The pace of her heart leaped, bounded. He must, she prayed. And there was danger for him in the persons of her own brothers, too, especially in Roman. What might he do to Aleksy? He would attempt retribution if he thought he could do so with impunity. She cursed herself for her untimely appearance at Tarnowskie, forgetting for the moment that it was an accidental discovery. She had gone under the guise of a camp-follower because she wanted to be near Aleksy, just to be near him. She had hoped for what would seem a serendipitous meeting, away from her brothers, away from everyone—not the catastrophic one that played out in front of townspeople and a royal audience.

She heard footsteps coming now to the door, stopping. When the knock came, Krystyna stood at once and brushed at a crease in the satin gown. *"Entrez-vous,"* she called.

She had no idea whether to expect a soldier, servant, one of the queen's ladies, or the queen herself. She thought the last possibility unlikely.

The door opened in, allowing entrance to a woman in a ruffled rose gown.

"Ah, you are ready, mademoiselle?"

"I am," Krystyna said, facing up to the queen's one servant she detested. Nonetheless, she smiled, praying she would do her French schooling justice.

Madame Heloise clucked her tongue. "I see you are wearing white."

Krystyna's spine tightened at the implied insult. "Your vision is excellent," she said. "It is what the queen's dresser sent me."

"Ah, then if you are ready—"

"I see that you are not."

"Not, mademoiselle?"

"Wearing white." Krystyna paused for effect, then added, "That shade of red is very beautiful. Daring—but you have the years to carry it off well."

Confusion fell like a mask onto the woman's face. She didn't know whether she had been complimented or insulted.

Krystyna didn't wait for the revelation. She made for the door and brushed past the guards.

Madame Heloise dogged her steps. As they walked a long, lighted hallway lined with portraits of royal predecessors, Krystyna could not help but ask for a hint of what the evening held in store. "Are there many guests this evening?"

"Many? No. When the king is away, the table consists mainly of Queen Maria Casimire and her ladies." Her head turned toward Krystyna, an odd sparkle in her eyes. "You were hoping for some gentlemen company, perhaps?"

Another barb. "No!" The word flew out of her mouth like spittle. Clearly, Madame Heloise had at last felt the bite in Krystyna's earlier retort and so now wished to turn the tables.

"Ah, well, that's to the good, then. In the carriage you talked of your interest in a Tatar, didn't you? Here we have no such young men. Tatars—isn't their culture primitive and barbaric?"

Krystyna stifled her anger. She would not be netted like an easily-caught woodcock. She maintained her silence as they came to a staircase, descended, and moved toward a dining hall that glittered in the light of hundreds of flickering tapers. She could well imagine herself the maligned subject of gossip among the queen's ladies. Since their arrival in Kraków, she had had two private conversations with the queen, during which she had implored the monarch to shield her from her parents. She could only wonder now if the queen had discussed her with her many ladies. She might have told them everything; indeed, she might be very free with how she shares important information and gossip because, after all, the queen had once been a lady-in-waiting to a Polish queen of bygone days, and what did such ladies have to amuse themselves? Certainly not needlepoint.

Ah! What did it matter if they all knew of the bride that ran away to be a camp-follower of a mere peasant—and a Tatar at that? Krystyna's mind sought a different path, one well-worn these past few days: *What are her plans for me?*

They entered the great hall to find the queen already seated at the far end. All the many other chairs that populated the long varnished table were vacant. Only one other place had been set with bone china, polished silver, and gleaming crystal goblets.

"Come along, then," the queen said, waving her forward. "Come along with you."

Krystyna turned to see that Heloise was taking in the scene—the empty chairs, the two place settings—and was perhaps more surprised than was Krystyna. The other ladies must have been sent away. The woman's mask of confusion appeared once again, but by the time they arrived at the queen's side, a false, bitter smile had replaced it. Heloise had taken stock that no place had been set for her.

"Sit there at my side, Krystyna, so we may have our little tête-à-tête." The queen glanced up at Heloise and smiled neatly. "You are dismissed, dear."

Upon sitting, Krystyna looked up as Heloise's head turned slightly, her dark eyes holding Krystyna's for a moment, the beautiful rose-red gown reminding Krystyna that the woman had dressed for a supper from which she had just been excluded. The contempt in the woman's gaze brought home to Krystyna the fact that she had made a lasting enemy.

"I do hope you will like the wine, Krystyna," the queen said, even while Heloise was in earshot. "Indeed, everything laid before you today is a favorite of mine: the pâté, the onion soup, the Black grouse in blackcurrant and beetroot sauce, mustard-glazed salmon, potatoes mashed with cheese and garlic—oh, and whatever fresh fruits are still in season this September. While the ingredients are Polish, of course, the cooking is French. It's my heritage. The king's tastes are a bit more prosaic. 'Prosaic and Polish,' I tell him. He laughs, as you can imagine."

Krystyna could not imagine the king, whom she had met so briefly in Tarnowskie and under such strained circumstances, laughing at much of anything.

The queen nodded toward the wake left by Heloise. "Gossip needs no carriage," she said, now lifting the delicate goblet of white wine to Krystyna.

Krystyna was at once buoyed by the queen's intimation of privacy. She lifted her own goblet, sipped and said, "Très bien." The queen had something important to say to her. Krystyna's heart raced with hope. Was it possible she would take her side?

"Good! I'm glad you like it. You know, when he's on campaign, I treat myself to French cuisine and drink. It's not that I spent much time in France, mind you. Why, I came to Poland at the age of five to be raised as lady-in-waiting to another French-born Queen of Poland, Maria Louise Gonzaga. Five years old! Can you imagine?"

Krystyna could not.

"So very few Poles know that before I married Jan, I was Maria Casimire Louise de La Grange d'Arquien. And why should they? A tongue twister, yes? Some prefer the Polish, calling me Maryja Kazimiera, but most have learned well that *he* calls me his Marysieńka. I rather like it." She sighed now, a bit dramatically, Krystyna thought. "Well, here I am, a Frenchwoman sent back from the road to war so that I can handle the matters of the country while the king is off on yet another campaign. Ironic, no? You do know, Lady Krystyna, the stakes they are playing for at Vienna? The stakes for all Europe?"

"I do. Please tell me, Your Majesty, has there been any word?"

The queen shook her head. "Nothing recent." She sighed again. "I pray we hear something soon." The queen was lifted into a loquacious mood so that as the supper with its parade of dishes commenced, Krystyna barely had time to finish one when another appeared, her hopes in a state of ebb and flow, while the queen managed to talk of matters of state and finish her portions in good time.

Krystyna guessed that the queen's chatter was a guise for her worry about her husband and the future of the Commonwealth. By the time dessert was to be served, Krystyna's stomach had tightened in discomfort, not from the fine food, nor the dour possibilities for Christian Europe should the Grand Vizier Kara Mustafa triumph. The source of her discomfort was the fact that the queen had yet to address her predicament.

A single bowl of green grapes was set before them to share. A second server brought small individual bowls of bilberries in thick cream. "We started with wine made from the grape, didn't we?" the queen asked. "And now, how apropos that we finish with the grape. You know that the season for fine fruit has come to an end when the assortment has been reduced to grapes and bilberries."

"At least one has the choice of two," Krystyna said.

"As in suitors, yes?"

Krystyna felt blood rush to her face. "I… I made my choice." The subject was broached at last. Her gaze went to the queen's visage. The smile was indecipherable.

"You did, it seems. I, of course, made a poor choice in my first marriage. One must take great care in choosing."

"I followed my heart."

"Ah, Krystyna, you must weigh the positives versus the drawbacks. The young Tatar is good-looking. Fetching in a romantic sort of way—that dark allure that he projects. I saw that. Opposites *do* attract, it seems.—And you say the Lord Fabian Nardolski is handsome, as well?"

Krystyna nodded. Her head was spinning. That the queen somehow knew the full name of her jilted fiancé put her on high alert. *How* did she know?

"And both of your options are young, is that not so?"

"Yes," Krystyna said, her voice tentative.

"An even score, as they say. The king is more than a decade older than I, but so was my first husband, who left me widowed. Ah, you are so young, Krystyna, you must gird yourself against the heartache you are to sustain."

Krystyna found and held the gaze of the queen. "What is it you are telling me?"

"I am telling you that you must always be ready to have your heart broken. I was widowed so young. Do you know I had three children—all girls—by my first husband? None of them survived."

"I'm so sorry, Your Majesty."

The queen waved her hand dismissively. "Oh, I've lost several of Jan's children, also. One learns, one faces defeat. How one faces defeat determines character, Krystyna. Fifteen pregnancies, all in all—or is it sixteen? While I'm forty-two and the risks of childbirth may be behind me, I must still stand like a pillar. You know, my son Jakub fights side by side with his father." Her eyes began to mist. "Sixteen years old he is and he rides with the king at great risk. My God, such risk. I could lose both husband and son. It is the Polish Way, I know." The queen's eyes had filled, and yet she stared unblinking, disallowing a single tear to fall. "And so much is asked of us women, too."

Krystyna worked at finishing her bilberries and cream, allowing for a few minutes to pass.

"You haven't taken any grapes," the queen said. "They're quite delicious."

"I made my choice," Krystyna said pointedly.

The queen peered up over her half raised spoon and seemed to fend off a smile.

"Your Majesty," Krystyna pressed, "I want to ask you—"

"Ah, we have strayed from the topic, haven't we?"

Strayed? Krystyna thought not. She was certain that the queen was very deliberate in the way she directed the conversation. Despite the wine, she was as precise with her words as Aleksy was with his arrows.

"Your Majesty, after we arrived, you implied that you would help me."

"It was no implication, child. I mean to help you."

"How?"

The queen released a long sigh. Was she at last at a loss for words? Her hands reached diagonally across the table and drew Krystyna's to her. "My dear, I've heard Poles say that love is like a head wound. It strikes hard and violently, it makes you dizzy and in the absence of it, you think you will die. But you recover."

A servant entered to collect the dessert dishes, interrupting the conversation. The queen seemed to look past Krystyna. The moment hung fire for what seemed an awkward eternity.

Krystyna cleared her throat once they were alone, drew strength, and asked, "Have you heard from my mother?" She felt an immediate quiver in the queen's grasp. "You have, haven't you?"

"I have, Krystyna."

"You're going to give me over to her, aren't you?" Krystyna was already trying to formulate a plan of escape.

"I don't have to do that, child."

Krystyna withdrew her hands. "I am *not* a child!"

"No, of course not."

"When is she coming?"

"Tomorrow."

Krystyna gasped. "Sweet Jezus," she whispered. When she looked next at the queen, she saw in her pained expression that there was something more. "What is it?" Krystyna demanded—too boldly, she knew, as if from a friend and not from the queen.

Queen Maria Casimire straightened in her chair, drew back her hands and allowed them to fall in her lap. "You're to be married tomorrow, Krystyna."

Krystyna closed her eyes and it took some moments to process the thought and as the words echoed in her head, the room began to spin around her. "How… how is that possible?"

"Your mother has made the arrangements."

Krystyna opened her eyes. "To… Fabian?"

The queen nodded.

"Sweet Jezus! He wouldn't want me now." Krystyna felt the floor dropping away. "The Nardolski family wouldn't want me, surely!"

"It seems *he* does—and therefore, *they* do."

"But—why? And why tomorrow?"

Gaze intent, the queen leaned forward slightly, as if to impart a secret. "Because you made quite an impression on him—and because there is some sense of urgency."

"Urgency?"

"Your mother writes that Lord Fabian visited you in your bedchamber one night before you disappeared." The queen was scrutinizing Krystyna's reaction. "Is that true?"

Krystyna's shoulders drew back against the velvet cushioning of the chair. She felt blood rush to her face. "So far as that statement goes, yes. It is true."

"Ah, then—"

"But nothing happened."

The queen smiled solicitously.

"I tell you, Your Majesty, nothing happened! My God, is he so besotted with me—and his family so eager to have an heir?"

"I imagine he loves you."

"And I love another."

"Just as my son Jakub—so close to you in age—marches with his father, we have our roles to play."

Forgetting herself, Krystyna abruptly stood, the back of her legs forcing the chair to scrape against the marble floor. The crystal chandeliers blurred as the room began to spin again. She drew in a deep breath. "Did he not *choose* to march with his father?"

The queen rose, the quintessence of equanimity. "He did—and in so choosing he bowed to the expectations of his class and family. He chose duty and honor." The queen's expression flickered for a moment as if she was regretting that choice, those expectations of a boy just sixteen. Then the royal gaze fastened again on her subject. "You are upset at this news, I know. Please remember, Krystyna, what I said about steeling yourself against the heartbreak that comes to us all."

The queen went on in this vein for a few minutes and while she did so, Krystyna, holding to the back of a chair, latched on to a thought that would certainly make marriage on the morrow impossible. The dining hall came into focus. "Your Majesty, Lord Fabian was to march in the effort against the Turks. He is with General Lubomirski and they have likely joined up with the royal forces by now. So—how can he possibly be here tomorrow? How? And if he does show, will you allow me to marry someone who has shirked his patriotic duty? Someone who has deserted the warfront? Will you hand me over to a coward?"

As she spoke, confidence grew where there was only despair. Here was a stand she could take. Here was hope.

The queen's expression softened in the most cloying way, as if she were trying to explain the unexplainable to a simpleton. "Lord Fabian *is* doing his duty, Krystyna, as is his father and your father. You are correct. He *is* marching with General Lubomirski. Tomorrow you will do your duty. Your mother and the Nardolski family will arrive with a proxy."

"A… a proxy?"

"Yes, dear, tomorrow you are to be married to Lord Fabian by proxy—a young cousin of your Fabian. Awfully young, though, he's just ten."

TWENTY-EIGHT

FOR THE POLISH FORCES, THE route through the thickly green and majestic Wienerwald soon gave way to the unimagined difficulty of ascending the series of mountains known as the Kahlenberg. The day dragged on painfully with the climb, the efforts of everyone expended in moving their cumbersome cavalcade along—wagons, cannon, horses, bag and baggage, upward, ever upward, through impossible terrain, navigating through pine, beeches, oaks and hornbeams, as well as streams, briar, and stony ground. The rolling heights were steeper than anyone thought possible and dragging artillery carriages and wagons proved to be back-breaking work. It took at least two dozen men on two ropes to successfully manage the climb towing a single cannon carriage, with other artillery men turning the wheels by hand, spoke by spoke.

The evening's dusk found Sobieski and his forces settling in at last near the top of the Kahlenberg ridge. The reverberating sound of the enemy cannon could be heard clearly here. Aleksy and Ludwik joined Idzi on a small, treeless overlook. "I can't see a damn thing," Idzi was complaining. "And I'll throw the first person off this cliff who says it's my height. We're on a mountain, for Chrystus's sake. I shouldn't have to stand on someone's shoulders."

"It's the smoke, Egidiusz," Aleksy said teasingly, knowing he hated the name, no doubt because only Aleksy's mother called him that—and in an impersonal way. He shot a conspiratorial wink at Ludwik as they approached him, chests heaving. Breathing at this height was difficult enough, but it was made more so because the thin air was wreathed with acrid smoke from cannon fire and the mines the Turks were employing in the tunnels they had burrowed in the earth leading to the city walls of Vienna.

As if on cue, a gusty mountain wind took away the cloud of smoke that had been obfuscating the valley below, affording now an eagle's eye view. The three took in the sight. To his left Aleksy saw the mighty River Danube, looping its way like a great liquid belt around the northern perimeter of Vienna. From the near center of the walled city rose one significant building: St. Stephen's Cathedral. The layout of the city walls brought to Aleksy's mind the image of a star, but one with triple—or more—the number of protruding points. It sat stolidly on the plain, its well-designed defense against assault making it seemingly inviolable.

A great explosion occurred at that moment. "Look there!" Ludwik said, pointing to smoke that was billowing up from the ground near one of the bastions the Turks were attempting to destroy so that they could have better access to one of the gates they were attempting to breach.

Behind two bastions, thick walls, and sealed gates sat Hofburg Palace, focus of the siege. Had its size and magnificence lured Kara Mustafa to that location? Aleksy wondered. Was the Grand Vizier imagining the wealth that was likely housed in its many wings and estimated two thousand rooms? Was he salivating at the gold, silver, jewels, art—and Christian slaves—that he would bring back to the Sultan?

Aleksy's companions on his right had been silent for what seemed a long time. He turned his head toward them and read amazement, horror, and fear upon their faces. Idzi's square jaw had fallen slack. He realized at once that their lines of vision, unlike his, had started from the right and moved left. Aleksy's eyes shifted now to the area of the valley in front of the city walls. A tremor started at his middle and sent a strong shockwave through him. He let out an involuntary gasp. As other soldiers moved out onto the outlook and along the ridge in both directions forming a phalanx of lookouts many men deep, Aleksy heard other gasps—and then curses, profanity, and oaths to the saints and to the devil.

Below him, the Ottoman encampment on the plain unfolded, providing a spectacle of colorful tents, animals that included horses, buffalo, the camels Piotr had mentioned, and a great tapestry of Ottomans—one hundred and forty thousand, someone guessed—some working siege guns that were ripping at the city walls and gates of Vienna, causing the earth to shake and smoke and flames to flare up into the sky. Some of those moving about like ants or working within the tunnel system below ground were Christian slaves who must be praying for their release. Closer to the

Wienerwald were a myriad of Tatars—loyal to the Sultan—guarding the length of the foot of the Kahlenberg.

Roman pushed his way to the front, and in so doing came between Aleksy and Ludwik. "Just look at that mob of Tatars," he grumbled. "Maybe some relation to you among them, huh, Aleksy?"

Aleksy felt his spine stiffen but said nothing.

"Well," Roman announced, his chest inflating with resolve, "here is what we've come to do at last. We'll mow them down on the morrow."

Roman's comment had cut into Aleksy. Those were his people down there. They were related by blood and ancestry but not by circumstance and experience. He was strangely discomfited by the realization that he was to assist in mortal combat against men of his heritage.

Ludwik, who had observed the exchange, came around to Aleksy's other side, nudging Idzi aside. "Remember," he whispered, "the Lithuanians have the Lipka on the king's side—all Tatars loyal to the Commonwealth, my friend."

The reminder tempered the vexation Roman meant to incite, and Aleksy was grateful for the comradeship of Ludwik.

Aleksy had no more time to dissect his feelings on fighting his own people, for as he tilted his head downward, his line of vision moved away from the main of the Grand Vizier's camp and passed over little valleys and villages and came upon—with no little sense of fear and dread—the terrain that would have to be traversed in the morning. "Holy Chrystus!" he blurted.

By then everyone had seen it. He caught his breath as he surveyed the land directly below. There was no gentle sloping to allow the hussars to orderly and grandly descend, the mere sight of the lances and eagles' wings sending fear into the hearts of the infidel. Below them was an impossible checkerboard of woods, vineyards, cliffs, brooks, and gullies, crosscut by hedges or stone walls. It would be no easier for the infantry or artillery, either—or retainers, such as Ludwik and himself. Only much farther down did the landscape start to level onto what would be the fighting plain.

But for a brief blast of a whistle from Idzi, the sight brought upon the wide throng of men an eerie silence—.

Later, Piotr would say that when the king saw the descent ahead of them, his face went scarlet and he swore a blue streak.

The men now turned their backs to the harrowing sight below and took to their tasks of making camp, polishing weapons, and doing what needed doing on the night before a major battle.

"Aleksy!" Roman called.

Aleksy, Ludwik, and Idzi halted and turned toward Roman.

"They call the next mountain over there Sauberg because there are sows that run wild. Have you ever killed a wild pig, Tatar?"

Aleksy nodded.

"Good. Then take Ludwik and go pick off one or two. We'll stage a pig roast up here tonight and go into battle with full bellies. Now go. Put that bow of yours to work again. It's been idle long enough."

"I'll go, too," Idzi said.

"The devil you will!" Roman countered. "Back to our wagons, dwarf! I've got work enough for you."

It took no time at all to find traces of wild boars. Sauberg was populated with a forest of oak trees and the boars feasted on the plentiful acorns. Finding one to shoot was another matter. Deep into the night, two hours passed with no sign. "Their sense of smell is vital to their self-preservation," Aleksy whispered to Ludwik. "They're very much aware of our presence up and down the Kahlenberg."

"So they've taken to hiding?"

"No doubt." Aleksy stopped abruptly. "Look there!" He pointed to an area where the shrubbery had been crushed and lay in a heap. "That's a nest, it is. And it took a huge sow to make it."

"How big?"

"Some can weigh two hundred pounds."

Just then they heard an unidentifiable noise some distance away. "Come on," Aleksy whispered, a finger to his lips. He took the ash arrow he had despaired of using and nocked it to the bow cord. They continued up the mountain, stopped, listened, and moved on. They were nearly at the top when they realized they were hearing voices, human voices. They were unable to discern the language. Friend or foe?

They moved carefully, softly, fearfully. Aleksy had to hold his balance with just his feet for his hands were occupied with his bow, the arrow still nocked.

They came to a little overhang and knelt down. They realized they had come to a perch higher than the men who were speaking in hushed tones. Aleksy peered down into the dark and he could make out a nest, but it was no sow's bed. Three men in Turkish garb with dark turbans had made a nest of their own. This was an outpost of the enemy. One held a telescope to his eye, searching the area below them, undoubtedly observing the Poles putting the finishing touches on pitching camp.

Aleksy sensed Ludwik's body go tense next to him. His friend had good reason to worry. After all, Aleksy was known as the marksman with the bow; Ludwik had brought a dagger to gut the pig, nothing more. The weapon was useless in this situation: one needed close contact to work with a dagger. Nonetheless, he withdrew it now and looked to Aleksy as if to say, *This is your call. Make the move.*

Aleksy ruled out attempting to take the Turks prisoners though the vision of proudly presenting them to the king played momentarily in his head. No, there was but one path. He had worried over his first kill. And now the moment was here. He trembled. It was here and there were three of them. *Three! God's bones!* If he could not do this quickly and with his best accuracy, his life and Ludwik's would be forfeit.

His left hand held tightly to the well-used thick center of the bow. He had made ten or twelve bows since Szymon pronounced him a brilliant bowyer some ten years before. This one was the best of the lot, fashioned as it was from the best yew woods in Poland. He had become an expert at creating the arrows, too, perfectly straight they were, with meticulously glued goose feathers at the ends to guide the steel arrowheads to the target.

This was the first time, however, he found himself taking aim at a man. His mouth went dry. He knew how to bring down a great stag at a run, a rabbit hidden in a thicket, or a pheasant in flight, but this was different. This is war, he told himself, taking in the three turbaned targets. He touched the cross that hung from his neck. He recalled Lord Halicki saying, "Remember—it's the cross that will prevail in Europe, not the infidels' crescent."

This is why I am here! Pulling back on the cord, Aleksy shifted slightly so that his feet were placed shoulder width apart, but in so doing, he dislodged a small stone which slid down the incline, making the slightest noise. Aleksy's heart paused, only to pick up moments later and begin to pound. His breath held.

The three had heard the sound. They turned in Aleksy's direction, faces upturned.

It was not a matter of aiming; Aleksy had learned how to concentrate and think his arrow to the target. He drew to the ear and loosed. The arrow flew true. One Turk cried out and pointed, but it was the one who had a pistol at the ready who took the first arrow—right to the heart.

Aleksy immediately nocked another to the cord, and within seconds of loosing, the crier went down, silenced at the throat.

Quick as lightning one more arrow went to the cord. At that moment Aleksy picked up on a noise behind them so that instead of loosing it on the third Turk who was clambering over the front of their outpost in an effort to escape, he instinctively turned quickly around, ready to loose.

It was nothing more than a fraction of a second in which the brain sent the message to his hand that saved the life of Roman Halicki.

"What—are you going to kill me, Tatar?" he grunted. "Where's our supper?"

It was Piotr who brought the news of the escaped spy to the king. He returned to assure Aleksy the king was thankful for what action he had taken. The Turkish spy mattered little, for another abandoned outpost had been found. Kara Mustafa knew by now from multiple sources that the Kahlenberg was a hive of enemy activity. "So be it," the king had said. "Let him stew over it. He'll have a bigger surprise when he sees me coming down at him."

If Roman felt any remorse for the blunder that botched Aleksy's third shot, he gave no evidence of it.

Supper was a modest mess of rations.

Piotr brought other news, too. The queen's safe arrival at Kraków had been confirmed, bringing much comfort to the king. Relief washed through Aleksy like the first rays of sun. This news surely meant his Krystyna was safe, as well. A great weight was lifted from him. Now he could accompany the Halicki brothers into battle with a clear mind knowing that she was protected. And knowing that, he could die content just having crossed her path. No, just having loved her. Aleksy looked up into the night sky and gave thanks.

Not long into the night, after the rain temporarily abated, King Jan III Sobieski witnessed rockets flare up into the dark sky from St. Stephen's Cathedral, clearly a clarion call to the relieving army and no doubt a last recourse, a final hope for those within the walls who must have been imagining the rape, death, and slavery that would follow a break in the wall.

The king had rockets at the ready and, one after another, several were sent flaming high into the sky above Kahlenberg. In minutes these were answered with three fiery flares from St. Stephen's.

Alone, the king walked out to the overlook. He raised his eyeglass to Vienna and to the tower of St. Stephen's. His vision was no longer perfect, but he saw movement there, shadows in the night. He imagined a group of men leaning out over the tower's parapet—the commandant of Vienna, Rütiger von Starhemberg, among them—staring up at the Kahlenberg, cautiously excited by the rockets that promised relief and the masses of soldiers camped there. Their liberation was at hand if only God would allow it.

The night quieted for those on the Kahlenberg, but cannon roar coming from within and without the city walls was incessant, punctuated by occasional explosions of mines within the tunnels the Turks were digging. Later, he would learn that countermining was going on, as well. Some of his men were able to sleep, but the king remained at the outlook, the mantle of responsibility heavy on his shoulders.

The sight below gave reason for trepidation, of course. No doubt, Grand Vizier Kara Mustafa and his men had watched the fiery communication between city and camp. He would be making preparations.

And yet the king saw cause for optimism. At Tulln he had told several nervous generals, "We shall conquer him easily." It was not just bravado. He knew wars were often won by the missteps of leaders. Tulln was just fifteen miles from the Turkish camp and yet Mustafa had done nothing to prevent the raising of a bridge over the River Danube by allied forces there, affording his enemy access to the mountain range upon which they now perched, ready for the coming battle. More than that, it took twenty-four hours for the king's men to assemble on the other side of the bridge, easy pickings for a Turkish leader with a military brain. Mustafa had missed a golden opportunity. Having beaten Turkish forces with his husaria several times, the king knew that his hussars were feared equally by the Janissary infantry, the mounted Sipâhis, and their most exalted leaders, such as Kara Mustafa himself. He could only conclude, then, that Mustafa did not believe Sobieski and his husaria would come to the relief of Vienna. It would prove a fatal error, he told himself. *I am here. We are here, Mustafa, an unpleasant surprise for you.* Perhaps some good had come from the delays in marching to and from Kraków, for which he and his forces had been well criticized.

And then, too, his battle plan that placed Lorraine's Imperial and Saxon forces on the left flank and the rest of the Imperial Army, reinforced by Franconians and Bavarians, in the center meant that the Polish armies had been delayed by the roughest and most precipitous terrain of the southeast Kahlenberg. In addition to the forces he led, he placed great faith in those of Adam Sieniawski and Stanisław Jabłonowski, each of whom he had named hetman, the highest rank of military commander after the monarch. The conjoined Polish forces had arrived at night, he mused, so his men had less time to prepare, and yet their arrival under cover of night was fortuitous because the Turks would have noted all the Imperial allied activity along the center and northeast of the ridge and would not prepare for the significant charge that would come from the southeast face of the mountain—the Poles with the husaria in the vanguard.

The king continued his assessment. That the two bastions upon which the Turks were focused fronted the Hofburg Palace clarified the Grand Vizier's intentions. He was waiting for surrender and the relinquishing of all the booty that the palace and other buildings housed, as well as the slaves he would conduct back to the sultan. He demurred at the prospect of a full and general assault that would lose much of the riches to destruction and to the greedy plunder of his own men. And dead slaves brought no coin. Avarice won the day. But would it be a winning gamble? Based on the grim intelligence reports of spies from the city detailing the injuries, deaths, widespread dysentery—and despair—he had received over the past ten days, the king was certain that a general assault would have given over the fortress of Vienna to Turkish forces. A missed opportunity for Mustafa, he thought.

Much of the morrow's outcome, the king conjectured, would depend on how Kara Mustafa conducts himself as a military leader. To his knowledge no Eastern general had ever had to contend with assaulting a fortress while fending off a significant relieving force. The king and all of the allied generals along the Kahlenberg did have this experience. This was, then, Christianity's less-than-secret advantage.

King Sobieski left the outlook now, going off to his tent to write what could possibly be, he knew, his last letter to his Marysieńka.

Upon returning from yet another trip to the overlook, Aleksy came upon Idzi and Ludwik removing large grain sacks from the Halicki wagon that had been driven by Jacek. "What are you doing?" he asked. "What's in those? It sounds like enough pots and pans for a regiment."

He pitched in to help, and when the contents had all been laid out, the three stood agape at armor that—even in the tree-filtered light of the moon—showed itself fully in need of polishing. Ludwik scratched his head. "This isn't the Halicki armor we've been polishing with vinegar and sand for these past weeks."

"No, and it's in need of just that," Aleksy said.

"Then what's it for?" Idzi asked. "When we were tossing things out of the wagon to lighten it on the climb up, Marek wouldn't let me near the bags."

"Confused, boys?"

The three turned to see Roman approaching.

"You best get to work on it," Roman said. "It won't polish itself. The king wants our armor to blind the Turks and Tatars as we descend. Hope you weren't all planning on getting any sleep."

"Who's it for?" Aleksy ventured. "Yours and Marek's are in perfect condition."

"You flatter your own expertise, you do," Roman said. "But as I'm sure you've noticed, there are two of everything—helmets, mail shirts, ribbed breastplates, combat sabres and war hammers." He flashed a strange grin. "Not of the best quality, I admit."

"Who... who are they for?" Ludwik asked.

Aleksy had already made the deduction. "They're for us," he muttered in amazement.

"Indeed!" Roman snapped. "Your own trousers and boots will have to suffice."

The three stared at the inventory. "Then we're not to follow with the infantry as aides or medics?" Aleksy asked.

"No, Aleksy, you will have your chance to play soldier, as was your wish."

"My... my lance?"

"You'll have it. Oh, and you needn't thank me for this. It was my father's idea. He insisted although I can't say I disapprove of the idea of placing you front and center against the infidel." Roman gave out with a guffaw.

"What about me?" Idzi blurted.

Roman looked at him in faux astonishment. "Yes, Idzi, what about you?"

It was a question meant to humiliate and terminate the inquiry, but Idzi pressed further. "I want to fight!"

Aleksy cringed at the hurt Roman was inflicting with nothing but the weapons of words.

"We have nothing your size, Idzi," Roman intoned as if he were speaking to a dolt. "You're to stay with the wagons. If your friends here fall, you can go pick up the pieces."

Even in the dark, Aleksy could see Idzi's face had gone scarlet.

Idzi drew breath. "Well, where are their wings?"

"Wings?" Roman was as surprised as Aleksy at the dwarf's nerve. "Wings? Do you think hussars are made from the likes of them, little man? Plucked from the peasantry? Do you?"

"But you've given them armor and weapons."

"My father has!" Marek announced appearing on the scene laden with brushes, rags, vinegar, and sand. "Aleksy and Ludwik here will ride with the lighthorsemen, behind the husaria. They will have their chance to prove themselves."

Roman scoffed. "Maybe they can deliver the finishing touches to unhorsed and wounded Turks."

A lull ensued.

Then, as if suddenly remembering something, Marek spoke. "Lord Brother Romek," he said, employing the affectionate epithet in a staged tone, "the same rider who brought the king news of his wife's arrival at Kraków brought Father a letter, too."

"Indeed? Good news, also?" Roman asked.

"Good news indeed, Romek. Within a day—or perhaps it's already done—our sister Krystyna is to marry Fabian Nardolski."

"That is wonderful news, Lord Brother Mareczek!" Roman's eyes went to Aleksy. "Perhaps we'll be uncles before our tour of duty is done. Of course, Aleksy here is very happy for her. Aren't you, Aleksy?"

Roman's lilting use of Marek's diminutive removed all doubt. They were acting out a scene to provoke him. Aleksy would not rise to the bait. And yet—could the content of their exchange be true?

Another lull.

"I know his thoughts, Marek. He's thinking a marriage to Fabian is impossible because Fabian is somewhere along the chain of mountains here, attached to General Lubomirski's forces."

Aleksy stiffened. This was exactly his thought.

Roman snickered and continued. "No, what Aleksy doesn't understand is that among the nobility there are time-tested ways of doing things. You see, Aleksy, when a noble cannot appear for his wedding for whatever reason, a proxy is sent in his place. And the wedding goes forward." His exaggerated smile went wide and he snapped his fingers. "Just like that!"

Aleksy swallowed hard. He looked to Marek.

"He's right, Aleksy. Our sister is to be married by proxy to Lord Nardolski."

In Marek's straightforward confirmation, Aleksy thought he sensed a fleeting trace of empathy, just a trace for a heart that was breaking.

"Of course," Roman said, sans empathy, "our friend here could always pray that Fabian gets skewered by a Turk so *he* might have a chance at the widow. But I doubt that he would do that. What think you, Marek? You're too good for that, aren't you, Aleksy?"

Again, Aleksy ignored Roman. He knelt instead, picked up a brush and began polishing a ribbed breastplate.

"Marek," Roman said, moving away, "you're handy with a razor. See to it that this one and Ludwik have the sides of their heads shaved so that they might at least resemble warriors."

Once he was out of earshot, Idzi spoke: "I'll do it, Lord Marek."

Marek turned to him, tilted his head in thought, and shrugged. "Have at it, little man."

Long before dawn, Krystyna was awakened by a rough shaking. A woman stood to the side of her bed. "What… what is it?"

"It's time to rise, Krystyna."

The throaty voice belonged to Madame Heloise. Krystyna shuddered.

"Why, for heaven's sake?"

"Heaven, indeed. Your mother has arrived."

Krystyna's heart plummeted. Oh, there was love for her and a bond with her, this woman who had sent a husband and two sons off to war, but Krystyna certainly did not want to be given over to her, like a piece of baggage. The queen had said her mother would *collect* her, as if she were a nonentity.

Krystyna drew herself to the side of the bed and sat. She looked up at Madame Heloise through the dimness. "I suppose I am to pack what few things I have?"

"No."

The woman's attitude unnerved her. "Are you here then to make certain I take nothing that the queen has given me? You needn't bother."

"I have no such orders other than to get you into that gown."

Krystyna looked to a nearby chair. Draped upon it was a dress she recognized, its ivory whiteness glowing in the dark chamber, the beaded pearls of the bodice glittering. Her heart raced. "Where did it come from? It—it's—"

"Your wedding gown." Madame Heloise produced a broad smile, displaying her teeth, small and widely spaced. "Your mother sent the veil, too, very sheer, it is. But perhaps it is inappropriate, yes?"

Krystyna knew that the veil symbolized the virginity of the bride ever since the days of the Crusades, but she ignored the insult, bolting out of bed and drawing away from Madame Heloise and the dress. "I won't wear it. I won't." She felt as if her world were closing in. She had told herself that a proxy marriage would never materialize, that her mother would never force it upon her, and that the Nardolski family would not wish to welcome her into their clan after she had jilted Fabian.

And yet this woman who seemed to enjoy being the harbinger of bad news had picked up the dress and was moving toward her, her face dark and serious as an owl's.

"I won't!" Krystyna cried, holding her ground, "I won't put that on!" She pivoted now in an attempt to approach the wardrobe for her day dress.

"You will!" Madame Heloise dropped the dress onto the bed, moved right up to her and took hold of her wrists.

To think the equivalent of a servant—her connection to the queen notwithstanding—would lay hands on her shocked Krystyna and she recoiled for just a moment. "How dare you!" she cried now, attempting to pull free.

The Mistress of the Robes' resolve was not shaken. "Come in, come in!" she called out.

The door flew back and three of the queen's ladies hurried in, as if they were minor stage characters whose moment had come.

All of her flailing and fighting went for naught so that in less than half of an hour, Krystyna was fitted out in dress and veil like a fish for a king's platter and ushered into the royal chapel, Madame Heloise and the three ladies-in-waiting hovering about her like Swiss guards. Krystyna looked toward the sanctuary. Waiting there in the aisle was her mother, along with Lady Irena Nardolska. A cluster of others she guessed to be of the Nardolski clan stood stationed nearby at kneeling benches. One was a pimply-faced, rotund boy of no more than ten. She held back a gasp. Was this to be her proxy? Her heart revolted at the thought, at the image of standing side-by-side with him.

Krystyna pushed back the veil from her face. Lady Halicka was moving down the aisle, toward her. "Look happy, Krysia," she whispered, taking both of her hands in hers. "For the Nadolskis, look happy."

"I'm not happy, Mother. I won't do this."

"You will," her mother said, the facsimile of a smile vanishing, her grip tightening and pulling her closer. "You will do this for the family. That—that boy you were obsessed with is gone. You have no reason not to marry Fabian."

"By proxy? I won't." Krystyna withdrew her hands. "And Aleksy is fighting for the Commonwealth, just like Father and Marek and Roman."

"He won't come back," her mother hissed.

"You don't know that! Perhaps Fabian won't come back—" Krystyna went silent. She had seen her mother's eyes covertly glance at Madame Heloise in a most peculiar way.

"You haven't told her?" her mother whispered to Madame Heloise.

Ice formed about Krystyna's heart. "What? What hasn't she told me?"

Lady Halicka turned back to her daughter. "The boy—"

"Aleksy!"

"Yes, Aleksy." Her mother reached out and drew Krystyna's hand into hers. "Krystyna, the boy will not be coming back. Like many of the soldiers we've heard about, he died of the dysentery. It's not uncommon at all."

The chapel—altar, pews, lancet windows, statues, people—moved vertiginously about her. She could not speak. She had not heard correctly. Someone would shake her from her dreams, for that was what this was—a dream, a nightmare.

People about her were chattering, but to her it was gibberish. Finally, her heart slowed, the vertigo ceased. She turned to Madame Heloise for corroboration.

Madame Heloise nodded sadly. "It's true, mademoiselle. It's true."

Was she playacting? "How could you know? How could—?"

"The news came to the queen with His Majesty's letter yesterday. It seems your brother wanted you to know."

"The queen—where is she?" Krystyna asked, her voice faltering. "Why isn't she here?"

"She has shut herself up in her private chapel, I'm afraid," Madame Heloise replied coolly. "We have every reason to believe the battle at Vienna is going on now—at this moment—and she wishes to fast and pray."

"I want to see her!"

Lady Heloise's voice hardened. "You can't."

Some slight noise and movement emanated from the area near the altar, claiming everyone's attention and eliciting hushed tones from the small congregation awaiting the ceremony. The priest was entering from the sacristy.

Lady Halicka took hold of her daughter's upper arm and looked into her eyes. "There is no choice for you, Krystyna. No choice." Suddenly her mother was walking her up the aisle. "You cannot escape your fate."

Krystyna wanted to lash out with curse words at the shopworn proverb.

Instead, she heard herself ask, "Is it to be that fat and pimpled child?" Her will was weakening.

"I think it is, yes, dear. Remember he is just a proxy for handsome Fabian."

They came to the little crush of Nardolski relatives. Now came the introductions, the feigned joy her mother and Lady Nardolska tried to exude. Had Fabian taken to her so much that he had engineered these nuptials from afar?

Krystyna was introduced to Count Maksymilian Balicki, Lady Nardolska's widowed father, an ancient soldier in his dress uniform of another time. With a flourish of his helmet in his hand, he bowed, deep and long. Rising, he said, "Irena has been singing your praises, my lady."

Krystyna curtsied, wiped away what some dim attendees might have taken for tears of joy, and said, "Tell me, Lord Balicki, would you honor me by being Fabian's proxy?"

Krystyna smiled demurely, quietly enjoying the gasps that came from those who heard her, little satisfaction indeed for a life signed away.

The old man straightened, his face brightening.

TWENTY-NINE

ALEKSY LIGHTLY FINGERED THE SHAVED sides of his head. While he was not a hussar, he had become a warrior and a certain thrill streamed through him.

The many campsites along the ridge that night settled into an eerie silence, as if inhabited by ghosts. Everyone—magnate, *szlachta*, soldier, retainer, servant and camp-follower—seemed to know instinctively that the morrow would determine whether Vienna and Europe to the west would remain Christian. In contrast, the reverberating explosions of the Ottoman cannons above ground and mines below continued. The stakes were enormous. The morrow would bring the battle of the century.

Aleksy slept little. The scene from the previous night played in his head. The battle had not yet been joined and he had killed two men. Roman had sent Aleksy and Ludwik back to their camp with orders to direct Marek to the Turkish outpost. An hour later, Roman and Marek came back to the ridge having stripped the bodies of anything of value, and when Marek, out of Roman's sightline, offered Aleksy an orb of blue glass with a black center that one of the dead had worn on a gold chain as a talisman against the evil eye, he declined. He had killed the enemy for God and for country—not for booty. His hand went to his breast bone, where he wore the gold cross Lord Halicki had given him. That was enough for him. Through the night he wrestled with his mixed feelings. He had wondered what it would be like to kill someone and now he knew. He had done it as quickly, smoothly, and effortlessly as he had done myriad times when hunting rabbit, deer, or wild pig. He wondered whether the two men he killed had wives, children. And yet—paradoxically—he felt exhilarated. This was not the field of glory men talked about; it was the capture of an outpost and attacking men by surprise. And yet, facing up to the truth, he realized the act of killing still provided a sense of power and euphoria. It had been done with ease. Is this what they call bloodlust, he wondered. It was puzzling. Tomorrow he would go into battle leaning forward with the seventeen-foot lance he had fashioned. Perhaps it was good to already know what it was to take a life. Perhaps it would be his salvation in the battle line when there would be no time for thinking. Instinct is all.

Never far from these thoughts was his anxiety regarding Krystyna. Had she been married by proxy to Fabian? Did her brothers speak the truth? They were certainly playacting to heighten the effect on him. But was the essence of their little scene true? He scolded himself now. Wasn't it good enough that she was safe, that the queen's retinue had returned to Kraków unharmed, that the queen herself had taken charge of her? Shouldn't he breathe more easily, knowing she was safe?

In any case, if he was to survive the next day or two in battle, what chance would there be for them to share a life? What chance? Their circumstances remained unchangeable. She was lost to him.

The camp began to stir more than an hour before the sunrise at half past six. Aleksy spoke little as he and Ludwik helped Roman and Marek into armor before aiding each other with their less than perfect gear. Aleksy wondered if Ludwik was nervous, fearful. What about Roman and Marek? This was their first conflict, too. That they spoke little seemed indication enough that they were apprehensive.

When they were all suited up, Marek walked directly up to Aleksy and handed him a sprig of hay. When Aleksy's eyes questioned him, he said, "It's what the Lipka hussars wear in their helmets so as not to be taken for enemy Tatars. You know, the dark Lithuanian Tatars that fight for the Commonwealth."

"I've heard," Roman added, "that the Lithuanian forces with the Lipka Tatars have yet to arrive." He spat upon the ground. "Wouldn't you know it? It looks like it's to be Poland, Austria, and a collection of Saxon princes against all of the Ottomans and the Crimean Tatars. No Lipkas this day. Let's go."

Aleksy placed the sprig in his pocket.

"At least we know they want you alive at the start," Ludwik whispered.

"I wouldn't count on it," Idzi chimed.

The five climbed to a higher point on the mountain, just below the summit, where an altar had been set up for Mass near the ruins of a monastery. The Army Chaplain, Father Marco d'Aviano, officiated and the king himself acted as altar server. How many of the seventy thousand allied forces spread out from peak to peak could actually see or hear the ceremony, Aleksy could not imagine. He himself had no clear view and could barely hear the priest even though the men were silent as the oak trees. Holy Communion was dispensed first to the sovereigns, princes, and generals, but there was neither time nor blessed bread enough for the thousands girding themselves for a fight to the death.

The ceremony seemed to go on interminably. "What's happening?" Aleksy whispered.

Marek, who stood on a good-sized boulder and had something of a view, heard him. "The king's son Jakub is being knighted. It's his first battle."

"Like us," Idzi said. "How old is he?"

"Sixteen," Marek replied, jumping down.

Aleksy was thankful Marek didn't mock Idzi for his *like us* comment.

After several minutes, the chaplain called on God to bless the day with a victory for Christianity. Then, from atop Palasz—his bay stallion—and in view, King Jan Sobieski held aloft a cross and spoke in his loud, clear voice: "Let us ever fix our eyes upon this sign, and let us remember that by it *we shall always conquer.*" The words of the priest and king were abbreviated, Aleksy surmised, because playing in counterpoint from below were the repeating and shrilly reverberating shouts of "Allah! Allah! Allah!"

"Go with God!" the priest cried in a final, full-throated voice.

And then the men turned away and within a quarter of an hour the movement of horses and seventy thousand men began to flow down, slowly, relentlessly, and deadly—like lava from a volcano.

His brother at his side, Roman directed Flash down the steep hillside, the brothers part of the first line behind the king. He knew the king's orders and he bristled with contempt.

Word came that at the northeast of the Kahlenberg ridge, the Duke of Lorraine and part of the Imperial Army had begun to descend, with

Nussdorf, the village nearest the River Danube, the target of the left flank. Roman knew that the front line of these Austrians carried a white flag with a scarlet cross, a flag that must be visible to those awaiting relief on Vienna's walls.

Further inland, the center forces—Bavarian, Franconian, and Imperial—began negotiating the downgrade, pulling behind them their light guns, their sights on a wide swath of Ottoman-held redoubts.

Both the left and the center Christian allies had shorter distances to travel and this was the source of Roman's irritation. *They* would likely engage the enemy well before the arrival of the three armies of Polish forces on the right flank because the Poles were left with the most difficult of descents.

According to the sun's position in the eastern sky, Roman was gauging the time at 8:00 a.m. when Marek whispered something and directed Miracle to halt. It was not a difficult thing to do, for the lines were ragged because of the folding terrain. "Listen, Roman!" he hissed. Roman drew up Flash. Others were pausing, too, in the long, circuitous, and painstakingly hazardous descent.

From the far left came the sounds of guns. Roman doubted that a Christian general gave the order to fire, conjecturing instead that the Ottomans must have staked out positions on the lower slopes and were initiating a series of skirmishes. Exclamations could be heard on the wind now, wind that carried the smoke from the guns and cries of "Allah! Allah! Allah!" The proximity and strength of the returning salvo of "Jezus, Maryja!" led him to believe both left and center forces were under fire.

As they resumed their descent, Roman cried out, "Chrystus's wounds!" He ignored a caution to be quiet from Marek, little caring whether the king would hear him and note his displeasure. "We're not even close to the plain yet! Why should we be the last dog to the fight?"

By mid-morning the sounds of the skirmishes had become louder and without respite. King Sobieski maneuvered Palasz to the front of his forces. He raised his hand and motioned his men forward.

The front line of hussars moved in formation, the Halicki brothers among them. "Roman," Marek began, "about Aleksy—"

Roman's head whipped around to his brother. "What about him?"

"You're not going to do anything to him, are you? Your threats—"

"It's Aleksy that poses the threat to our family, my brother." He swiveled about in his saddle to see Ludwik and Aleksy, who were riding with the last line of cavalry. Aleksy was trying to balance his lance atop the little steppe pony. "What is it they say? People can only become a threat if you let them. I don't intend to allow that to happen. He'll not see Kraków again."

"But, Roman—"

Roman raised his open hand to his brother, a signal for silence. "Look there, Marek!" They had come to a little shelf of land in the hills, hills that rolled and dropped, dropped and rolled. From here they could see the Grand Vizier's Tatar forces and they seemed as numberless as the grasses, even more than the twenty thousand the king had estimated. And they were waiting just below. He heard Marek give out with a little gasp. "Those are Aleksy's people, Marek—we're not. It looks like they will provide our first contact. Ironic, isn't it? I may have to do nothing to Aleksy. Do you think he—with his lack of battle skills—will survive against his fellow Tatars?"

"He's good with his bow."

"Damn his bow! He's a filthy Mongol!—And when did you start defending the Tatar who brought dishonor on our house? First Father—and now you!"

"And would it not be dishonorable for you to take matters into your own hands?"

"I told you—his own Tatars will finish him off unless he's coward enough to remove that sprig of hay you gave him and turn traitor. Has he placed it in his helmet?"

"He has.—I hardly think—"

"Dog's blood! Don't think, Marek, and have done with this subject!"

The sounds of the skirmishes far to their left had become louder as the Christian allies clashed with the Ottoman Turks.

"You're brooding, Roman," Marek said, his head turned toward the tumult of battle. "We are the most important part of the Holy League. We'll have our chance."

Roman scowled at his brother. "We have reason to brood."

Aleksy looked down the steep mountainside at the camp peopled by thousands of Tatars. They wore caps and many were coated in sheepskins with the fleece sides worn out for summer, making them appear like great woolly beasts upon their steppe ponies. There were those with lances, sabres, war hammers, maces, muskets, and pistols. Unlike the majority of the Christian forces who had abandoned the bow, nearly everyone below—to a man—carried one. These were the recurve bows about which Aleksy had heard a great deal. The Tatars were positioned on the very part of the plain upon which the Polish forces would soon find themselves. His hand absentmindedly moved up to lightly touch the sprig of hay attached to his helmet, his protection from being misidentified as an enemy to the Christian soldiers.

Earlier he had heard Roman and Marek complaining of the extra time it would take to descend this part of the Kahlenberg and that the Imperial forces, buttressed by Saxons, Bavarians, and Franconians, would make it to the plain long before the Polish. He felt the same sense of frustration. What if the Poles came too late to savor the victory? Or worse, what if they came too late and the cause was lost because of their tardiness?

However, seeing the massive display of Tatars below brought him up short. These were men of his background, his ancestry. What a turn life had made for him seventeen years before when his family's tribe had been decimated by Cossacks and he had been taken in by Polish Christians. His dying Tatar father had made that choice, but Aleksy himself had chosen to be baptized and to accept Catholicism, just as he had wholeheartedly accepted his new Polish identity. How could he know that one day he would face Tatars in war? He could see that they were making preparations for their defense now. Clearly, he would have to kill Tatars—or be killed by them. It was an unsettling thought. And that many of them relied on his weapon of choice—the bow—further clouded his emotions. He should be happy that one bowman against another could be a level playing field—but what of the difference between the bows? He had once asked Szymon if the recurve bow was superior to the European longbow.

"Ah, boy," the stable master had said, "the Mongols' recurve bow is a clever one. It has tips that curve away from the archer when the bow is strung. The extra curve isn't natural-like because of that backward bend, but it's just that difference that gives the weapon a dash of extra speed, you hear? So—why didn't I show you how to make one of those? It's because the longbow has more stability. Its single bend is natural. It doesn't have that extra bend that can sometimes cause just a little wobble and throw your shot off kilter. That's why. Oh, the Mongols are masters of the thing, but I'll suffer a bit of speed to be more certain that my bow is stable and my shot flies true."

"You were right, Roman," Marek said. "Word's come down that the Lithuanians with their Lipka hussars still have not arrived. They are to miss the action."

Roman spat upon the ground. He recalled the swagger of the Lipka at the wedding reception. All the dark faces—like Aleksy's. He grunted. "How many of them would have gone over to the Turks' side?"

"Some, I suspect," Marek said.

Roman looked to his left, where color and movement had drawn his eye. He caught Marek's attention and pointed down at the plain. Ottoman cavalry reserves were being moved to the area surrounding the village of Türkenschanz, southwest of the Nussberg, known as "Wine Mountain," and precisely in line with the descending center troops. A scarlet tent was being set up, and in front of it, the Standard of the Prophet. The Grand Vizier himself would rally and direct his men from there.

"It could mean," Marek said, "that they are unaware of us. What a blessing that would be. What do they call Sobieski—the 'Lion of Poland'? We would come at his left flank from the rear."

"A lance in Kara Mustafa's backside?" Roman laughed. He turned in his saddle now to view behind him the descending hussars with banners flying from the ends of their vertically-held, seventeen-foot lances, then the *pancerny*—the light cavalry with their bows and shorter, solid lances—then the infantry and twenty-eight cannons of three Polish armies as they moved over ground that sloped, flattened out, and sloped yet again, allowing for the flow of men to appear, disappear, and appear in a seemingly unceasing stream. "No, brother, look behind us. They're not likely to miss this sight. To them it must look like the mountain has released endless currents of soldiers—and hussars into the bargain!"

Marek turned about in his saddle. "Chrystus Almighty!" he cried. "Endless is right."

"Yes, but too slow. Just too damn slow." Roman looked to the sky. "It's an hour from noon and we've heard fighting for—what?—four hours? We can't leave it all up to the Duke of Lorraine on the left, and to the center with his hodgepodge of princes, for God's sake! And here we are picking our way through tangled brush and vines and watching for rocks and gullies and streams." As he had at the Lubomirski wedding reception, Roman went on to question the king's leadership abilities, pointing out that he was now a commander whose age and girth slowed his ability to lead on the battlefield. In years past, he had had extraordinarily good days—winning days—on the battlefield, but those days were behind him, Roman insisted.

The descent continued under searing heat of high noon. Aleksy was soaked with perspiration as the Polish forces moved down from the heights on either side of the Alsbach, a tributary stream. He was finding out just how difficult it was to wear armor. He wondered how the hussars must be dealing with the heat, for over their armor they wore additional coverings of tiger and leopard hides, meant to both reflect their status and incite fear.

At an hour past noon, the Sobieski forces were descending close to the village of Dornbach, and although they were not yet on the plain, the forest and hills were thinning, and they could see Hetman Jabłonowski's column to their right and Hetman Sieniawski's column to the left—and beyond that the Christian allied forces stretching the length of the Kahlenberg to the Danube. And as those forces became visible, so too did three Polish columns, hussars at the front, become visible to the other allies, who were no doubt buoyed by the appearance of the Poles and from whom a great round of cheers went up. All eyes went to the Vienna walls and ramparts now, for the cheers were being seconded by the survivors of the long siege, who waved banners from the tower of St. Stephen's, their hopes for their salvation revived by the fluid might the great Kahlenberg ridge was releasing.

The lances of the cavalry bore the pennants of the national colors so that when the black and gold pennants of the husaria appeared on the hilltops it became clear to the enemy that—against speculation—King Jan III Sobieski had indeed arrived.

"Oh my God," Ludwik said, half an hour later, his mouth open. "Look!"

Aleksy looked to where his friend pointed. Below, in the Tatar camp, something was stirring among the twenty thousand. Men were mounting their horses, but—oddly—their tents were being struck, wagons were being made ready and camp followers and slaves organized. Even to novices, none of this fit a battle plan so that Aleksy and Ludwik were initially at a loss to understand. "Holy Chrystus!" Aleksy whispered, looking to Ludwik, whose mouth still gaped.

The entire Sobieski force hesitated, too, in fascination at the sight. Murmurs ran through the columns of men. And then a strong voice from the front line shouted: "They're leaving—the devil be hanged—the Tatars are leaving!" Aleksy recognized the voice as Roman's. "The Tatars are not going to risk their lives against the hussars to save the hide of Mustafa!"

A great cheer went up from the three Polish columns, but as the first wave of it died, the king's voice could be heard. "No cheers!" he called. "No cheers! Let's leave their tails where they are—between their legs. We don't want to provoke them into staying."

"Is he joking?" Ludwik asked.

"Not certain," Aleksy said. "But I think he had a smile, ear to ear."

Only after the battle would it be learned that the Tatar leader, Khan Murad Giray, had gone to the Grand Vizier's tent and berated his superior for not having taken his besieging army away from the mining operations in the tunnels and shored up the forces posed to fight the descending Christian forces. "I can tell you," the Khan said, "that Sobieski leads them all. And do I need to tell you that in recent history Sobieski and his damn hussars have run their lances through us at every battle?" The Khan knew that his speaking so was insubordinate and that he was risking his own head.

When Kara Mustafa assured him that the Tatar forces would repulse the Poles, the Khan left the tent shouting back that he had no intention of staying to test the matter. "Sobieski wins," he shot back. "Sobieski always wins!"

Thus, as the Poles resumed their slow, painstaking descent, they watched in awe as the train of twenty thousand Tatars left the battlefield and proceeded to march in a southeasterly direction—toward the River Vienna and a friendly Hungary. Aleksy gaped at the prisoners who were placed in tow, tied to the horses' tails.

Another hour passed and as the amazement of the Khan's betrayal lessened, Polish leaders threaded their way through the ranks in an attempt to allay over-confidence, assuring the hussars, the cavalry, and the infantry that this would still be no easy win. The Turks still vastly outnumbered the Christian forces.

The Polish forces painstakingly picked their way downward so that by mid-afternoon the shelf of the plain spread out before them. Roman took note that after the retreat of the Tatars, the Grand Vizier did shore up the forces that awaited the Poles with numberless Sipâhis and Janissaries.

The Sipâhis were the most elite of the Ottoman cavalry and looked menacing. The richest and most highly placed among them were fully armored, as were some of their horses. They seemed lightly equipped with sabre, shield and pistols. The infantry—the Janissaries—provided the Sipâhi support and some of their muskets were reportedly of the latest design and deadly in accuracy. They were also armed with sabre and shield and a good many carried a bow case and the Mongolian recurve bow. Head gear was a mix of caps and turbans. Long coats or vests were worn over loosely draped pants which fit into boots or soft leather shoes with upturned toes. These were uniforms they wore, Roman assumed, but colors depended upon battalion and rank so that the field was a stationary rainbow, baited and waiting to go into a dancing prism of motion. Nearly everywhere, on both tents and staffs, flags and pennants featuring the Ottoman symbol of the crescent undulated in the hot breezes.

Contact with the enemy was now imminent.

On a jutting shelf of land, King Sobieski wheeled his horse around, urging it to rear up in front of the first line of the husaria. The men drew up their mounts, silent as the skies, tense as stalking tigers. Roman could not explain it, but had to admit to himself that the king's great girth somehow made him seem even more impressive upon his massive stallion.

"Ten years ago next month," the king called out, "some of you were with me at the Battle of Chocim. Remember the glory of that day! Do you hear me? Answer me—do you remember?"

From his veterans came a great volley of affirmations.

"I hear you, my men, my patriots! On that field we defeated the Turks in resounding fashion!"

Great cheers went up all around.

He waited for the cheers to die away. "I was your hetman then and you followed me with God-given courage!"

Cheers again.

"Today—here at Vienna, I am your King. The crown came through you and through the courage you showed at Chocim!" He paused, allowing for another round of cheers, loud enough to travel down the mountainside. "But today," he continued, "you fight for a different king. You fight for the King of Kings and for all Christian Europe. You fight for the Chrystus! You must endure, you must summon your strength, you must *win*!"

An eerie few seconds followed another round of cheers, and then came the drub of drums and the staccato thump and dull repetitive clang of metal weapons upon wooden shields.

The king waited again. "For those of you young bloods who were still at the hems of your mothers' dresses ten years ago, this is your chance, this is your time—your time for glory!"

A stillness descended on the troops, an unexpected and poignant moment of soul-searching.

The king called now for ten volunteers from the hussars to fill the positions of absent men in the Prince Aleksander Company, so named for his infant son. At the required number of one hundred fifty, the unit would make the first sortie.

Marek was one of the first to shout his intent, raising his lance point to the sky and waving it.

Roman knew the battle tactic; it was typically Polish—send in a voluntary force to test the terrain and ascertain the enemy's tactics and strength. On this mountainside there were specifics to be gleaned. How far did the grapevines stretch? To what extent were the stone fences impediments and likely hiding places? Had the enemy dug holes so that the horses would break their legs upon stumbling into them? How confidently and with what measure of force would the enemy react? He knew, too, that some of the volunteers would be sacrificed. They would not return.

Lord Halicki had warned of this type of volunteer mission and had elicited a promise from his sons: should the hetman ever call for volunteers for such a venture, only one of them was to volunteer. He would not lose two sons on the same perilous mission.

Later, Roman would question his own initial reticence but once Marek had spoken up, he turned to his brother. "Let me go, Marek. I'm the elder."

"So what?—I was the quicker to speak. The king nodded to me before he moved on toward the Sieniawski column."

"He won't know the difference if we switch."

"But I will!"

"Damn it, Marek! Then I'll go with you."

"No you won't! Father made us promise."

"He doesn't have to know."

"Chrystus, he's in there among the Sieniawski column somewhere. And he'll know if neither of us comes back."

"I can run a lance better."

"Oh?" Marek spoke sarcastically. "Like when we were being considered for the *Kwarciani* and your horse stepped out of line. I do believe your lance faltered."

Roman felt the blood rushing to his head. He deserved the verbal cuffing. He had walked right into it. He glared at his brother.

Marek knew he had bested him. He snuffed out a smirk and called for Aleksy to accompany him as retainer.

"No," Roman said, as if by instinct. "Take my retainer—take Ludwik."

Marek lifted his noseguard, his eyes questioning.

"Aleksy will want to use his damn lance at the general charge," Roman explained. "We have those extra pistols Ludwik can carry along with his sabre and war hammer."

Marek shrugged, as if to say he had won the better part of the argument so his brother could have his way in this. Roman surmised, however, that Marek suspected the truth: that he wanted control over the fate of the Tatar, whom he so hated.

Marek turned to Aleksy, who had ridden forward. "Go tell Ludwik to get the two guns from my wagon and ride up with me. He's about to see action."

"But, Lord Marek," Aleksy said, "it's my place to attend you, not—"

"Do as you're told," Roman commanded.

Aleksy looked from Roman to Marek. Marek nodded and Aleksy used the pressure of a knee to turn his horse and direct it through the lines of hussars and cavalry to the retainers, who rode or marched behind.

THIRTY

"I heard the sound of their wings, like the roar of rushing waters, like the voice of the Almighty, like the tumult of an army."

—Ezekiel 1:24

ALEKSY WATCHED AS THE ONE hundred and fifty hussars on their heavy Polish-Arabian combat horses mustered into position and a smaller number of retainers, mostly on standard cavalry steeds or steppe ponies, made ready to follow. He had thrown his arms around Ludwik before helping to hoist his armor-heavy body atop his steppe pony. His friend had been given only the most cursory lesson with the pistols. Along the route from Kraków, Marek had given them both tutorials in the use of the sabre and the fine-pointed war hammer meant to pierce the enemy's helmet, but neither he nor Ludwik felt adept at them. That there was no bow to give Ludwik mattered not, for he had volunteered that his aim was cursed. "I'll thrust and parry and cut with this rusty old sabre," he told Aleksy, "and chop, too, when it's called for. Don't worry, Alek."

Aleksy did worry. "It should be me that's going with Marek."

Ignoring the comment, Ludwik waved his double-edged sabre and sang a little ditty they had learned from the cavalry:

Hungarians cut directly,
Muscovites cleave from above,
Turks whip roundabout,
And Poles slash criss-cross!

Aleksy did not join in. He could see that the Turkish forces directly in front of them were thick and colorful as an old forest in autumn plumage. Intelligence came back that the reinforcement Sipâhis and Janissaries that were arriving now to face the Polish armies after the Tatar betrayal and retreat had come from the Grand Vizier's right wing. This was good news on two counts: The Duke of Lorraine's Imperial column would have an easier time of it in their descent to the plain on which all would be decided. It also meant that the Grand Vizier had not pulled men from the tunnels and ramparts facing Vienna's walls. His forces were still divided into two armies.

However, for the hundred and fifty men being placed in a square formation now and staring into untold numbers of the enemy, the wheel of fortune seemed to be turning a different way—a darker way.

With a voice that could rival the strength of a trumpet, a King's Guard called for silence.

The volunteers raised their lance points to the sky and sang the centuries-old Polish hymn "Bogurodzica," "Mother of God." By the second verse all the Polish forces behind them had joined in.

Virgin, Mother of God, God-famed Maryja!
Ask Thy Son, our Lord, God-named Maryja,
To have mercy upon us and hand it over to us!
Kyrie eleison!

Son of God, for Thy Baptist's sake,
Hear the voices, fulfill the pleas we make!
Listen to the prayer we say,
For what we ask, give us today:
Life on earth free of vice;
After life: paradise!
Kyrie eleison!

The thrill of hearing the three Polish armies sing out in their deeply masculine voices in the open air under the blue vault of heaven made for a wondrous experience Aleksy took in and stored away. A chill ran along his spine and the skin on his arms went to gooseflesh. He could only imagine what fear this fervent hymn was reaping in the hearts of the enemy below.

But there was no time for imaginings or thought. Two unarmored trumpeters in blue *żupans* and matching caps bordered with sheepskin rode forward and took up positions on either side of the volunteer company. Twin blasts from the trumpets now cleaved the air, compelling Aleksy's spine to stiffen.

"Secure your hats!" This order was for those men without helmets. The volunteer hussars sat tall in their saddles, armor and mail glinting in the sunlight.

"Draw together knee-to-knee!"

"Sabres on sword knots!" This command was for the lancers so that their sabres, attached to their left wrists, would be easily drawn once their lances had been used and discarded.

"Draw sabres!" Those without lances, like Ludwik, drew blades and the scraping of scabbards momentarily broke the silence.

"Dalej!" March on!

The hundred and fifty moved forward at a quick trot. When they came to within the prescribed one hundred paces of the enemy, they halted. The sound of the final order was shouted out and carried on the air back to the silent, breathless watchers, King Jan Sobieski among them: "Złożcie kopie!" *Lower your Lances!*

Aleksy looked to the front of the square and watched as the lances—with black and gold husaria pennants, each with a white eagle flying near the point—were lowered and for leverage and support were tucked into the toks, the boots attached to the saddle. Here they would stay until impact. In his mind Aleksy was rehearsing his own first charge. He recalled Szymon's directive to aim at the approaching enemy's spleen. The thought at the time had made little impact on him, but now he was close to carrying out the directive against a human being. Today he would know the cost of war, the cost of bravery.

The order to charge was unheard to those watching from a distance, but it had come, clearly, for the lancers were galloping across the field now, holding their lances parallel to the horses' heads, their speed accelerating by the moment. Aleksy watched carefully as they thundered away, noting that the formation loosened a bit, no longer stirrup to stirrup so as to facilitate movement, or even change direction slightly if necessary. A small retinue of retainers followed.

With the resounding salvo "Jezus, Maryja," the square smashed into the awaiting Turks and the lances did their work, impaling a good number of the Sipâhis. The watching Poles cheered, for the attack bred chaos in the Turkish ranks. Bodies of the Sipâhi fell from their mounts and Janissaries on foot were trampled before their sabres could strike. The Janissaries carried bows, too, recurve bows that Aleksy had only heard about until now, but in close quarter fighting, pistols, muskets, double-edged sabres, and war hammers were the weapons of choice. For an archer like Aleksy, this was a worrisome situation.

There seemed to be space opening up ahead and the hussars forged on. The sounds of gunfire, metal clanging on armor and thudding on wooden shields blended with the crack and splintering of lances, many with the weight of Ottoman bodies.

Were these Turks preparing to turn tail, much like the Tatars had? Eyes focused and spine rigid in his saddle, Aleksy hoped that the case, but for a single square of hussars, no matter the fierceness, to incite such fear seemed unlikely—unless it was the unnerving presence of all the Christian forces standing together and stretching from the bottom of the Kahlenberg at the River Danube the five miles to the Polish columns at the southeastern end.

Now, however, came the reversal of fortune as the Turks formed up and a triple line of Sipâhi closed the opening that the Polish square had carved out. How would Marek, Ludwik, and the other courageous volunteers find it possible to extricate themselves from this enclosure? The war whoops and screams of *Allah* rose to a deafening fever pitch, sending a chill down Aleksy's spine.

He thought he would be sick. He drew in breath and fought the tears that brimmed in his eyes. Three lines ahead he saw Roman turn his head, that part of his face not hidden by the nose and cheek guards of his helmet had gone ashen gray.

Roman watched, listening to the rising crescendos of pistol fire, the cracking of lances, and the shrill cries of "Allah! Allah! Allah!"

The Poles—his brother Marek among them—were being set upon as if by wolves baying at the sky and shrieking for blood. The thought brought him up short. He recalled the time he and Marek were heading back to camp from their manor house. Marek had challenged him to a race, but Roman was occupied with other thoughts and allowed him to go on ahead. In the forest that night he had heard the shrieks of a wolf pack and was consumed with fear and guilt that he had allowed his little brother to go to his death. As it turned out, Marek had taken a different direction and he suddenly appeared in perfect health.

Roman's heart thumped. He knew in his soul that Marek would not suddenly appear today. He would not come smashing through that line of Sipâhis. This time the wolves would triumph.

On that previous occasion in the forest, when he had thought the worst, his biggest concern had been what he would tell his mother and step-father. Now, after the long and grueling journey to the Kahlenberg and to the siege at Vienna, he had no such thought. His single-minded concern was for Marek. They had bonded on this mission so that if Marek was lost, he would deeply grieve for the half-brother who had become a true brother.

"Dogs' blood!" he cursed under his breath. "Harm a hair upon his head and you will pay. I will make you pay!"

Aleksy was relieved to see another unit of hussars ordered into the melee so as to effect the retreat of the first. He saw two hussars struck from their horses, but the Sipâhi line opened, allowing for the retreat of a good many of the volunteers. Nearly seventy-five, he guessed. One was immediately shot dead, but the others made it back. As they went to rejoin their company, Aleksy scanned the group for Marek—to no avail.

He waited, breathless, longing to see Marek and Ludwik escape through the breaking in the line, wishing for it, imagining it, praying for it.

Half of the party was lost. Just those seventy-five survived. A few were escorted to the king so as to relay information about the lay of the land and strength of the enemy. No retainers came back. Ludwik was gone, one of the first men sacrificed. Marek, rest his soul, had volunteered for the mission. But Ludwik, a poor farmer and no soldier, had not. Aleksy held his tears at bay.

Such was his introduction to war.

God's teeth! What had come of this mission? Why had the king ordered it? Why were men allowed to die with their compatriots looking on? He could not understand it.

Time passed slowly now. Aleksy guessed conferences among the Christian leaders were going on or messages were being exchanged. The Duke of Lorraine's Imperial left, as well as the center flanks that included Imperial, Bavarian, and Franconian forces, were now aligned with the three Polish armies of the left flank. No doubt the leaders were laying out the plan of attack. Men and horses waited in the hot sun.

The Christian forces faced one hundred and forty thousand Ottomans. Another twenty thousand continued to assail the walls of Vienna in the hope that the city would fall and be taken this day, assuring an Ottoman victory. Against the hundred and forty thousand, the hussars numbered three thousand with another fifteen thousand Polish, Saxon, and Austrian cavalry. Infantry and retainers brought the Christian forces past the eighty thousand count. Among the Poles, no one complained about the numbers—it was not the Polish Way. He had heard the army motto more than once this day: "First we kill the enemy, then we count them!"

"Idzi!" Aleksy called, withdrawing from his hidden pocket the pink ribbon Krystyna had given him. Idzi hurried over. "Take this," he said, dropping it to his friend, "and tie it around my wrist."

Idzi gaped at it, the intuitive blue eyes widening, then casting a look of shared confidence even though he had not seen it before. "Best keep it hidden under your gauntlet, Alek. You wouldn't want Roman to see it."

Aleksy grunted and offered his left arm. "Hardly a time and place for him to make a scene, no?"

Time. Looking to the western sky, Aleksy gauged sunset as just two hours away, and yet the blistering heat of the afternoon seemed not to lessen. The sense of readiness permeated the air, a nervous readiness. The warhorses sensed it, neighing, snorting, stamping—and readying. The hussar blocks—arranged in Sobieski's favored checkerboard pattern—tightened. While dragoons flanked the hussars, the cavalry stood behind both, and behind the cavalry came the mounted retainers and, finally, the infantry and retainers on foot.

Idzi handed Aleksy his lance.

Aleksy held the weapon vertically, his right hand slippery with sweat, his mind astir. Since he was not a hussar, the national colors of red and white, rather than the black and gold of the elite corps, were attached to the lance's end, near the point. When he created the lance, so long ago it seemed, lovingly fashioning it with a boy's dreams of glory on the field, had he truly thought he might one day be preparing to actually use it? Had he imagined then the long and grueling march, the discomforts of camp, the heat, the blood of foe and friend, and the longing for home—and for Krystyna? His back straightened at the thought of her.

The sweet thought of the girl in yellow was short-lived, for the Poles were once again singing the battle hymn "Bogurodzica." It resounded on the Kahlenberg Mountain all about him, insistent and yet silvery, as if he were in the midst of an army of angels. He cleared his voice and joined in. No gooseflesh this time. Just tense readiness. He was no longer a boy.

At the conclusion of the song, Polish kettle drums and then trumpets drowned out the distant but relentless drums and piercing war cries of the Ottomans.

The drums and trumpets ceased. Aleksy's heart seemed to lose a beat. He reached up and touched the gold cross about his neck.

Then came the orders he had heard before.

"Secure your hats!"

"Draw together knee-to-knee!"

"Sabres on sword knots!" Aleksy had a sabre in a wooden scabbard, but he had his bow strapped to his back, as well. He determined that each situation in which he found himself would dictate the use of one over the other. And then there was his war hammer, too, strapped to the saddle.

"Draw sabres!" He held to his lance, listening to the rasping release of countless blades from their scabbards.

"Dalej!" March on!

The drum Aleksy heard now—and felt—was the beating of his own heart. The hussars fronted some six or seven thousand horsemen. The Turks most certainly must be recalling the consummate courage that the hundred and fifty volunteer hussars had shown in crashing into numbers far greater than their own. Are they trembling? Aleksy wondered.

The hussar squares moved first at a light trot. The light cavalry followed and behind these, the retainers on horseback. Aleksy was one of the few retainers with a lance. The infantry and various retainers lagged behind.

At the requisite hundred paces from the enemy line, the troops stopped and the squares tightened.

"Złożcie kopie!" *Lower your lances!*

Aleksy had lost sight of Roman but kept his square in view. What was his order of priority—fighting the enemy or aiding Roman, his lord? He had no experience at this. *My lord*, he thought—what twist of fate this had been! Was Roman to be trusted any more than the deadliest Turk on the field?

He had no time to consider the twist, for the charge had come and the hussar blocks were tearing down the slopes, the trot quickening into a canter, hooves thundering on the earth, the feathers of their high winged apparatus vibrating in the movement. What a harrowing vision it must be, Aleksy thought, for both the enemy and their horses, to see these death machines flying down the field with points sharpened to skewer them like pigs on a spit. He listened to hear whether the feathers sang out an eerie death song, as some hussars contended, but the hussars were too far to the front to make a determination, and the cavalry that rode after them created their own thunderous noise.

He spurred his steppe pony and it moved into a gallop now. "Jezus Maryja!" Aleksy called out, careering into the storm of death.

The bow was his weapon, he had to admit, not the lance that he had so lovingly fashioned. Had he fully realized in creating it that it was a seventeen-foot instrument of death? And none too easy to handle. He had had so little practice with it, and yet he had to use it. These were no maneuvers, no games of riding at the ring, like he had seen done by the local hussars from his own little outpost on Mount Halicz. This was life or death.

The enemy had already been engaged by hussars and cavalry by the time Aleksy entered the fray. It came home to him suddenly that those at the front had the advantage of having a clear sightline on the person they meant to pierce. Coming several lines behind as he was doing now meant he was coming into a wild and frenzied melee. He knew that he had to choose his target quickly before his steppe pony was slowed or halted by massive warhorses and men who meant to kill him.

The thunder of the Turks' cannon aimed at Vienna's gates receded as reports of rifles and pistols exploded in his ears. Acrid fumes of gunpowder washed over him. Time expanded and life blurred red with men, horses, and glinting, death-dealing sabres as a white turban came into focus. Set against the dark face, angry white teeth shone as the Janissary infantryman stood in wait, snarling prayers or oaths unheard in the din of battle. Aleksy saw the one-handed curved sabre being lifted in readiness. Aleksy swallowed hard, steadied the lance in his tok, and held tight as his pony scrambled forward between bodies and broken lances.

The moment of impact came. The Janissary's single-edged sabre came down, striking and cutting clean through the hollowed-out wood of the lance. Aleksy pulled his portion from the tok and discarded it. For the enemy it was too late. He fell to his knees, the sabre still in his grasp, the front portion of the seventeen-foot long weapon buried in his chest. Aleksy's horse stepped past him. The long-treasured lance had served its purpose.

Only later would Aleksy learn that Janissaries had been culled from Balkan Christians who had been forced to accept Islam. Those wearing the white turban, like Aleksy's adversary, were signaling their elite status as warrior-martyrs.

THIRTY-ONE

A LANCELESS, BLOODIED ROMAN CAME TO a clearing behind an undefended hill, the clearing where many of the volunteer hussars had sacrificed their lives. The ground was nearly invisible so covered it was with bodies and dead horses. He saw him then, recognizing in the helmet the distinctive orange-dyed plume their mother had given him. He directed Flash in and among the fallen, drew up and dismounted.

Marek's body lay there on his side as if he were sleeping even though he had suffered numerous wounds. On the ground a pool had formed beneath a fissure in the chest plate mail, darkening the grasses.

Roman sucked in breath and knelt, heedless to the chaos that surrounded this recently deserted spot. He picked up and held his brother's hand. It was cold. He lost track of the seconds and minutes as his life with Marek passed before him.

Slowly, he became aware of a war shout, and he looked up to see a horseless Sipâhi rushing toward him. It came home to Roman that the man in the pointed conical helmet had lost his mount and meant to kill him and take Flash. The response in drawing himself from the reverie was slow—too slow for his initial defense, he would remember later. His mind had been made sluggish by what he had seen this day, by what he had done, by his brother's sacrificial death. He ordered himself to stand against this warrior. He could do it. He had killed half a dozen Turks already. He must draw himself up now to...

Suddenly, however, an arrow thudded into the unarmored Sipâhi, striking him clean in the heart. His dark eyes went wide and he dropped like a stone. Roman had noted by now that no man truly expected a fatal blow, and every Turk he had dispatched this day had looked at him with utter surprise.

Roman was in such a state he didn't question the source of the errant arrow. It was as if he had observed the Turk's death from a distance. His eyes went back to his brother's body.

"Oh, Mareczek, my lord brother," he said, using the diminutive he had used when they were children. He said a prayer, and a minute or two must have passed before he heard the voice behind him.

"I'm sorry, Roman."

Roman stood, pivoting toward the speaker. "It's Lord Halicki, lest you forget, Tatar."

As Aleksy stared at Marek's lifeless form. Roman read his expression. "What do you know, Tatar?" he shouted. "About war? About the Polish Way? I'll tell you—Nothing!"

Aleksy seemed about to speak but fell silent.

"Their sortie, dangerous as it was, provided the king with information. We found out invaluable information. The Turks had had time to shovel out trenches, set up palisades, dig holes in which our horses would break their legs. But did they?"

Aleksy shook his head.

"No, they did not! It was information we needed. And just as important, when they saw the courage of a single block of hussars descending on them with eagles' wings attached to their backplate and with nerves and weapons of steel, the wisest among them knew the battle was fated to go against them. For the rest, they pissed their eastern trousers."

Roman didn't expect a response. That he had swung from sharp criticism of King Sobieski to his defense of him for the benefit of Aleksy did not strike him as ironic. He picked up his sabre and was mounting Flash, his face red with anger, his veins gorged with bloodlust. "There are enemies beyond that hill, Aleksy. There's still killing to do. Are you here to take a nap?"

And then he was gone.

Aleksy came to stand over the fallen Marek, enough bloody wounds about him to attest to a ferocious struggle. Ludwik's body lay nearby, a single red gash incised into the newly-shaven side of his head. Aleksy had thought that sending just one unit into the midst of the enemy was senseless. He wanted to ask Roman what the suicide mission proved, what good had it done, but to do so would have been telling him that his brother Marek died at the king's whim and because of his own foolishness in volunteering. The question must have been on his face, however, for Roman had spoken directly to that unvoiced query.

Trenches? Palisades? Holes? No, the Turks had not taken these precautions that would have so benefitted them. Aleksy recalled now that as he had crossed into the enemy line, there *was* fear in the Turks' eyes, and a kind of resignation in some of their expressions as they fought.

Roman was right. The volunteer mission had been worth it. And Marek and Ludwik had their parts to play.

Aleksy moved to Ludwik's body now, knelt, and closed the lifeless blue eyes. Even as he said a quick prayer for his soul, his own eyes moved to Marek's wings. The apparatus seemed intact. He thought of Idzi's theory of the changeable and the unchangeable. Was it unchangeable that he was barred from wearing the wings of a hussar? And then he was merely doing, not thinking. He gently moved the body one way, then the other, and the steel backplate that held the wings came free. Aleksy stood now, and with some difficulty, strapped it on. It was surprisingly light.

Later, he would question his thought process in making this decision. Had he taken on the wings to carry on the fight in Marek's place? Or had he done so to force his own dream of becoming a hussar to come true?

Wings in place, Aleksy mounted his steppe pony. Holding high in the air the unsheathed sabre should it be needed, he directed the animal through the morass of bodies, human and beast, moving toward the little hill beyond which Roman had disappeared. He came to the crest and stopped. He felt for a moment like he was home on that little shelf of land that jutted out of the side of Mount Halicz. And this time it was he who wore the eagles' wings. But the panorama before him was not one of entertaining maneuvers—it was one of unspeakable gore.

Aleksy made an instinctive decision now. He placed the sabre in the scabbard. He reached back and removed his bow from its case. With the weapon made from the finest yew, he felt whole now. Oh, he had seen some of the Janissaries use their recurve bows but, for the most part, the fighting here was sabre on shield, war hammer on armor. The single-use lances lay strewn about, some broken and already turning black with blood, others embedded in the guts of the enemy. While the din of battle continued, the sharp report of rifles and pistols diminished, for they were clumsy to reload and prime in such close quarters.

He placed an arrow on the cord and drew back as far as his ear. Sighting a Turk who was battering the shield of a Polish cavalryman, he took aim and loosed. The arrow flew true, avoiding the armor and winging its way into the Turk's neck. His sword hand stopped in mid-strike, paralyzed. His left hand instinctively reached for the shaft and ripped it out, allowing for a geyser of blood to spew forth like a fountain, spattering his opponent until his stiffened body fell forward on his mount. Oddly, the Pole spurred his horse away without searching out his benefactor.

Aleksy took no time to probe the oddity, for he already had nocked and loosed a second arrow. The shot ran wild and clear of its target. What had come over him? It wasn't that he was one to take a great deal of time in aiming and loosing. During a thousand hunting outings he had learned that he had to think his arrow home. This was the secret of a great archer. He would see and feel the arrow strike and then allow his arm, hand, fingers, and sight to work instinctively. The arrow came from the quiver, went to the cord, its goose feathers pulled to the ear and released–all in one seamless movement. Unless the animal was especially quick, Aleksy's method always worked.

And so now, from this little hillock, he allowed his instinct to rule. One after another, he drew the shafts and loosed. It seemed easy for the body, this killing—hands, arms, chest and shoulder muscles needed for the pull—but for the mind a kind of numbness set in. Or was it madness? Was this what it meant to be a soldier?

Aleksy killed and killed again.

Fifteen minutes passed before he looked up to see that a Sipâhi had taken notice of this lone sniper on the hillock. He was spurring his horse toward Aleksy, the sunlight glinting off the tightly knitted rings of his mail shirt.

This, then, was a perfect target, Aleksy thought, his confidence bolstered by the accuracy of his recent shots. He was as good a marksman as any on the field. But when he reached back for a new shaft, he found the quiver empty. There was no time to cut the lace on one of his two remaining sheaves attached to the saddle. Neither was there time to discard the sprig of hay on his helmet that proclaimed him an enemy in the unlikely event the Turk had not witnessed Aleksy's kills. The Sipâhi was moving up the hill and advancing on him at a fierce gallop so that first contact would favor the enemy.

In a clumsy move to place the bow in its case, Aleksy dropped it and it fell to the ground. "Dog's blood," he cursed as he unsheathed his sabre, his eyes on the opponent. The Turk was much larger than he and clearly a veteran. He was grinning, Aleksy realized. *Grinning!* A scar in the shape of a crescent moon—no, it was a tattoo!—ran from his forehead to the corner of his mouth. He was nearing the crest now. How many battles had he already seen? Survived? How many Christians had he already killed this day?

Aleksy had no time to touch his gold cross or assess his loss of confidence, just time to reach for his shield with his left hand and tighten his grip on the sabre in the right. The Turk—twice the brawn of Aleksy—was upon him now, sabre coming down with great force.

Aleksy was ready and although his shield deflected the blade, the force nearly knocked him from his mount. He directed the steppe pony to turn about. He saw that the Turk's huge stallion below was turning on his haunches in preparation to climb the hillock for a second pass. Aleksy would not sit and wait. He had the advantage of moving downhill and so he took it. He spurred his own horse into a lope, then a canter.

As the Turk approached, murder in his black eyes, he held his sabre in the same way as before, but the move was the feint of a skilled fighter so that when Aleksy lifted his wooden shield, the Turk's sabre slashed below it. Aleksy instinctively directed his steppe pony away, but the blade nonetheless sliced into the side of his upper leg. His own attempt to strike had been brushed away.

The pain was sharp and stinging. Aleksy turned and halted the horse at the bottom of the hill, struggling not to let the hurt show. They were some forty or fifty paces apart now. Atop the hill, the Turk was looking Aleksy over, the dark eyes beneath the helmet narrowing. "Tatar?" he growled. He had taken note of Aleksy's complexion and eyes.

Aleksy nodded.

The Turk drew up in his saddle. His teeth shone as he screwed his mouth into an ugly smile and unleashed some curse—and spat. He directed his warhorse down the slope and had it circle Aleksy's steppe pony in a kind of prancing gait... once... twice. He was taking full measure of Aleksy, who recognized the word *boy*. Another curse and then he withdrew, moving off many yards, and for a moment Aleksy thought he was abandoning the fight, but he turned the horse and sat, watching. No more than a minute passed before he began his charge.

Aleksy thought better of putting his horse in motion. He wanted to be in full control of his weapon and so he waited for the next contact. He was no boy and he would not allow this man—this veteran soldier—to kill him. He would not. He prepared to strike. His chest and arms were strong, as were any good archer's—and Szymon had deemed him the best. He would watch for the feint this time. Perhaps he would stage a feint himself.

But he had not imagined the ploy this opponent had in mind.

The Turk's stallion was in full gallop now and coming straight at him. Aleksy waited, his voice calming the horse, shield ready, sabre poised. He would strike under the Turk's arm at a gap in the mail and drive the long blade into his body. He had the strength. He needed the precision—and the opportunity.

The Turk came forward cursing in his tongue. His sabre came down in a chopping motion—not upon Aleksy, but upon the neck of the steppe pony, fatally wounding it.

The animal shrieked and dropped to his front knees. Aleksy had the presence of mind to jump from the horse before it could roll over and pin him. He leaped to his feet beside the dying animal.

The Turk had ridden some distance before turning to watch the scene he had created unfold. He laughed then, no doubt assuming the match a foregone conclusion.

This seasoned enemy was playing with his prey and enjoying it all the while. His mind racing, Aleksy determined to use the time. One of the sheaves of arrows attached to the saddle was within reach, but the bow was many yards away, atop the knoll where he had dropped it. He retrieved his sabre but knew it would not save him.

The Turk was grinning again, fully assured he had his wounded, horseless quarry. But—blessed be God!—he had yet to spur his warhorse.

Pain be damned!—everything Aleksy did now had to be one fluid movement—swift as quicksilver—if he wanted to live. And he did. He drew in a deep breath, took two paces, used his sword to slash the lacing on the sheaf of arrows, and quickly withdrew two shafts. He turned now and ran toward the crest of the hillock, racing for the bow, racing for his life.

He took no time to check the Turk's reaction, but the laugh came again—as did the hollow thudding of the horse's hooves across the field, no doubt leaping over bodies, racing, coming for him.

Aleksy's feet propelled him forward, his eyes scanning the grass, slick with blood. He panicked. Where was the bow? He was a dead man without it. *Have I missed it?*

And then he spied it. He darted three feet to the right. He dropped hs sword. Setting one arrow down, he kept one at the ready as he picked up his prized bow. He thanked God the cord was intact and taut. The arrow kissed the string before he turned around to see the Sipâhi nearly upon him.

There would be no time for the second arrow. No second chance.

He felt the feathers of the shaft tickling at his ear and then they were off, stinging past the folded fingers of his other hand once loosed.

He started to reach down for the second shaft although he knew he could be cut down before he could nock it.

But the first flew true, and the steel tip had been so sharpened and the distance from the Turk so close that it pierced the mail and buried itself in the man's chest. The force threw him fully back onto the cantle of his saddle, his arms going limp, sabre and shield falling to the ground.

Aleksy jumped to the side and the stallion thundered past him, down the hill and slowing as it entered the melee from which the Turk had come. He watched as a Pole pulled his body from the horse now, allowing it to fall upon other corpses, so that he could commandeer the animal. An ignominious end for one with such a wealth of bravado.

Aleksy looked to his own horse now and descended the hill. The steppe pony lay near death, breath coming fast and hard—and even though Aleksy was seeing men cut down this day, something stirred inside him for this poor beast who, like a thousand others, had given up its life for the machinations of men. He put the palm of his hand upon the horse's chest, heedless that the animal might bite at him. The steppe pony attempted to lift his head at the touch, as if to look at Aleksy, but the wound was too grievous. The head fell back upon the ground and Aleksy's hand went still as the rise and fall of the horse's chest ceased.

Aleksy stood, divested himself of the backplate and wings, and picked up his bow. He filled his bag with arrows, then bent to collect the partial and full sheaves. He would carry them. He reclaimed his sabre, placing it in the scabbard on his sword knot, and was debating whether to remain on foot where his aim might be better than on horseback. But on foot he would be too easy a target. He had to confiscate another horse.

Though he had yet to use it, he would likely need the war hammer, he knew, and was bending to take it from its leather strap on the saddle when he heard a commotion.

A Polish soldier, dressed in elaborate cavalry gear Aleksy had not seen before and riding a huge warhorse, was descending pell-mell into the narrow field already abandoned by the living, but for Aleksy. Moments later, one of the Sipâhi flew over the crest, a war hammer in his hand, his horse galloping down in pursuit.

Aleksy determined that Fate was directing him. He withdrew an arrow, dropped the rest, removed and flung aside his helmet, and unslung his bow, but before he could set the nock of the arrow to the cord, the Turk struck the soldier's shield with such force that he was thrown head first from his mount. The Sipâhi holstered the war hammer as his knees directed the horse to turn for another pass. In drawing his sabre to finish off the boy, the Turk gave Aleksy all the time he needed.

Aleksy loosed—once, then twice. The first shaft hit the Sipâhi's chest at such an angle that it glanced off the metal plate.

The startled Turk looked up, his eyes finding Aleksy. But there was no time for reaction of any kind, for the second arrow flew with blistering speed, striking the man above the mail at the collarbone. The effect was nearly bloodless—but deadly. The man's dark eyes bulged with astonishment before rolling back into his head. And then he fell from his massive horse.

Aleksy ran to the supine form of the Polish soldier and knelt. He removed the helmet, revealing a mass of wavy black hair and no wounds. He saw that he was a boy, slight and younger than himself, perhaps even fourteen. He had been dazed by the fall, but he was quickly regaining his senses. He opened his eyes with a start at the sight of Aleksy, who realized at once the boy's fear came from his Tatar dark looks.

"I'm Polish," Aleksy said in their common language. "See, my wings are lying just over there." He went on to allay his fears and assure him the Sipâhi was dead.

But there was little time for introductions, for a noise drew Aleksy's gaze to the crest of the hill. Two Sipâhi had drawn up their horses there and they were peering down.

"Were there others chasing you?" he hissed.

"Yes." The boy started to lift his head.

"They're watching. God's tongue, stay quiet."

Aleksy stood up. If the boy had thought him a Tatar, so might they. Aleksy waved his arm dismissively, as if to say, *Go on your way; this deed is done.* He prayed his Polish style trousers and boots were bloodied enough that they would not look closely. His very life relied now on his appearance.

The boy started to stir and Aleksy quickly put a boot on his shoulder, as if he were a hunter taking credit for his kill. "Don't move," he ordered through clenched teeth, "or we'll both be dead."

One soldier was saying something to the other.

"Ölmüş?" the one shouted.

Aleksy hesitated.

"Ölmüş?" the other demanded, louder. He drew himself up in his saddle as if preparing to descend the hill.

"It means 'dead'," the boy-soldier whispered.

"Ölmüş!" Aleksy cried, pantomimg a slash across the throat and waving them on. Through clenched teeth he whispered, "Go! Damn you, go!"

They seemed convinced and were about to leave when one of them looked behind them. Aleksy could hear and feel the hooves of a good many horses approaching.

In but the blink of an eye the two men vanished.

Assuming the arriving force were Christian allies, Aleksy bent to help the boy get to his feet.

In moments a Polish force of five was flying down the hill toward them. Suddenly fear shot through Aleksy. They, too, would assume he was Turkish or one of the Grand Vizier's Tatars.

The boy stepped in front of him just as the *rotmistrzr*—a company commander and almost certainly noble—jumped down from his mount, hellfire in his brown eyes, sabre in hand.

The boy held up his hand to protect Aleksy. "Polski," he said simply. "He came to my aid."

The commander's intense face slowly softened and then he finally nodded.

Relieved, Aleksy nodded in return, guessing the commander was the boy's father. He retrieved his helmet now, making sure the sprig of hay was still secured in the pocket used for plumes. He wanted no one else thinking him the enemy—except the enemy. He went then to pick up his bow and the sheaves of arrows.

The boy was atop his horse by now, as was the commander, who pointed to the dead man's stallion and said, "Take the bastard's animal!"

Aleksy nodded.

"Thank you, Tatar!" The boy called as he rode off, flanked by his posse of five.

After retrieving and strapping on the wings, Aleksy went to take hold of the warhorse, thinking that the commander must be the boy's father.

He could waste no time. He had to search out Roman, as was his duty. It wasn't till he threw his leg over the dead man's horse that the pain reminded him of his wound. "Chrystus Jezus," he whispered. The movement had deepened the slice in his thigh and it was bleeding, badly. He went to rifle through the enemy's saddle bag for bandaging. He gasped at the sudden realization that he recognized the saddlebag. He was sitting upon Marek's horse Miracle. It was not the first time he deemed the horse aptly named.

Marek rode with him. He was convinced of it.

Enraged with hatred and anger, Roman spurred his horse from one combat to another. He left no Turkish challenger alive. He was angry about his brother's death, angry he had so badly mishandled his lance in his first exchange that it broke into three pieces, and he was angry about Aleksy. How he wished he would just die—that some Turk would skewer him like a goat steak. Better him than Marek. As a retainer, Aleksy was to keep him in sight, but Roman shrank at the thought. He hoped never to cross paths with the Tatar again. He cursed the day his father returned from the Wild Fields with him.

He drew in breath and stiffened in his saddle, readying the sabre in his right hand, directing the horse with his knees. *Better to deal with this dark devil in front of me*, he thought, as he ran his double-edged blade through the side of a Sipâhi who was getting the best of a mounted Saxon cavalryman. He moved on, allowing the Saxon to finish him off. "Bastards!" he screamed, charging toward another Sipâhi, slashing the throat of a Janissary infantryman as he rode before quickly dispatching the horseman. His targets had taken him toward the Danube and parallel to the Kahlenberg ridge, and in so doing he realized that he had passed from the bulk of the Polish forces into the midst of a good many Imperial and Saxon troops. They parted for him, nodding their respect for the Polish uniform and especially, he guessed, for the wings he wore. He had the impression he increased the intensity of the action around him and he reveled in it. As for the Turks, just one in five dared to view his winged figure as a target while the others kept their distance. Roman saw to it that those who took their chances with him came to regret it in short order.

Roman had effectively disappeared into the swarm of warriors. Aleksy thought little of the leg wound he had bound, the noble's son he had saved, or even the whereabouts of Roman, for the chaos that was war roared on. He sat upon Miracle, holding to his bow, his fingers—despite the calluses—raw and red with blood from the quantity of shafts and their goose feathers flying through them. He kept his distance where he could so as to have the stillness of the horse for his aim. Few Janissaries wore helmets or mail coats so that he could work more efficiently than he had imagined. These were not animals quick to sense danger and run. These were soldiers pledged to stay for the duration, pledged to embrace death if such was their fate.

Three mounted Sipâhi spied him now. One turned on him with his recurve bow. Szymon's comment that recurve bows had the advantage of speed over longbows rang in his ears. Aleksy drew an arrow from his case, nocked it, and loosed. No time to aim, only time to think it to its destination—as he had learned to do.

The arrow flew to its target. Before the Turk could release his arrow, the steel point of Aleksy's shaft slammed into the man's turbaned forehead. The red stain on the white turban was scarcely more than a little circle about the embedded shaft when the man dropped to the ground, his eyes wide as an owl's.

The other two had not taken notice of their fallen compatriot. Their horses were climbing the incline toward him, the Turks cursing Aleksy in their language. Aleksy had another arrow nocked in time and he sent it into the closest man's cursing throat, knocking him backwards so that he tumbled from his mount. There was no time to nock another arrow, for the third man was but yards away. In one movement, he placed the bow upon his back and drew his sabre. Holding little hope the horse would take direction, he pulled on the reins and—blessedly—the horse reared. The movement startled the Turk's horse, which thundered by, out of striking distance. The Sipâhi directed his stallion to pivot and without delay came after Aleksy again, sabre raised. Aleksy maneuvered his horse, turning its head and neck away from the downward strike of the deadly curved blade meant to take down the animal and thus unseat its rider. He had learned that move.

Aleksy tugged again. The horse reared and as it came down, twisting in a semi-circle, Aleksy drove his sabre into the unprotected chest of the Turk.

There was no time for self-congratulation, he realized, when he looked down to see the bandage undone and his thigh wound once again awash in blood. He felt himself growing weak, dizzy.

THIRTY-TWO

The Kraków night air was cool, and Krystyna stood hugging her elbows at the open window of her sitting room in the Nardolski town house. The city below was quiet, eerily so. Talk all day along Grodzka Street had been of the effort to halt the Turks and save Vienna. Folks said the enemy had been engaged. But how could they know? Krystyna wondered, fending off tears. Vienna was so very far away. Had the queen been informed by special messenger?

The heavy bells of Wawel Cathedral tolled now, their deep sonorous sounds rolling like cannon booms through Market Square and out into the spider web of Kraków streets. Krystyna placed her hands on the windowsill which vibrated slightly with the report of the bells. The tolling came as a jolting, and perhaps unnecessary, reminder for the citizens to pray for Christendom's victory. No one was likely to forget, for it came hourly. Krystyna wondered if it would continue through the night.

The bells of the Wawel Cathedral reminded Krystyna of St. Laurence Day, just one month earlier, the day she processed down the main aisle wearing the harvest crown that she presented to the King of the Commonwealth. The day she was to have wed Aleksy in the cathedral's rectory. Too late, Idzi had told her of the contents of Aleksy's note, the note that had fallen—by way of Roman—into her father's hands.

Aleksy.

Was it possible that he was dead? Was it? Had he sickened in those days after he left Kraków? She could not accept his death as fact. She would not. It didn't feel right. In her heart he lived.

And yet, in that moment, at the castle, she had accepted it. She had allowed herself to be fitted into the Nardolski clan with little more effort than it took for the queen's ladies to fit her into a wedding dress. And so now she was Countess Krystyna Nardolska.

She shivered, thinking of the man she had married by proxy. Fabian Nardolski… what was his fate? What if he is wounded in battle? What if… what if he dies? It could happen. It could very well happen. What then? She would still be married to the Nardolski clan. The guilt set in at once. She didn't wish Fabian dead. She wished Aleksy alive.

Her next thought served only to enlarge the guilt many times over. What if Aleksy were to return and not Fabian? What if it were in her power—by wishing or praying—to make the decision?

She became dizzy at the thought. It was an evil thought and she attempted to stamp it out as if it were a small fire that might grow into a great conflagration, one that would sear her soul.

Krystyna turned back to face her little sitting room, lighted by wall sconces, and the attached bedchamber, still dark. She doubted that she would sleep. Her body told her of its hunger, had been telling her. She had begged off going down to supper, complaining of a stomach ailment. She supposed that her mother would bring a plate up to her room, but for once she proved not so predictable. She was most likely in her room taking pains to pack for her trip home to Halicz, leaving her unhappy daughter to fend for herself in the Nardolski household.

Krystyna decided to go down to the kitchen herself in order to find something in the cupboard that would hold her over until morning. She did much the same thing at the convent school, stealing down to the cold room to appropriate something sweet. That seemed a lifetime ago.

She was halfway down the front stairway when she realized she should have taken the servants' stairwell so as to avoid running into Lady Nardolska. Nonetheless she stealthily pushed on.

She came to the bottom and moved toward the kitchen, but as she did so, she heard whispered voices coming from the dining hall. She sidled along the wall until she stood very still near the open double doors. The voices belonged to her mother and Lady Nardolska.

"You're welcome to stay, Zenobia," Lady Nardolska was saying.

"No, what with my husband and the boys at war, there are things to be managed at the estate." Her mother paused. "Besides, the marriage is a fait accompli. What is there for me to do here?"

"But your daughter Krystyna… I'm concerned how well she will adjust. She refused to come down to supper. And I've heard her crying in her room."

"Her fate is sealed. She knows that, so there won't be any trouble. She will adjust. I'll talk to her tomorrow morning before I leave."

Krystyna's heart seemed to catch between beats. Her fate *was* sealed, indeed.

"But that boy that ruined—"

"The Tatar?" her mother asked. "He ruined the planned wedding for certain, but Krystyna is still a maiden."

"But she seems to still care for him."

"Not to worry, Irena. Krystyna will get over him."

Krystyna thought how wrong her mother was, how distant mother and daughter had become.

"But if he should—"

"Survive and come back?" her mother interjected. "Not likely. If news of the marriage isn't enough, Roman will dissuade him from any kind of intermeddling in quick order. That is, if the little upstart Mongol hasn't been eliminated by his own kind."

Krystyna flattened her back against the wall, heart thumping in her chest. *Sweet Jezus!* They had lied to her about Aleksy's dying. The two of them had schemed together in order to get her to agree to the marriage by proxy. She had been duped—and by her own mother. There was a rushing, pounding sensation at her ears. She felt as if her life were in freefall. As if she were plummeting to earth and no one was there to aid her. Nothing to break her fall.

She was certain she was about to pass out when one thought superseded all others.

Aleksy was alive. Alive!

It was a sweet, sweet thought. Bitterness followed, for the incontrovertible truth was that they were set on different paths. If he survived the war, they could never marry. They might never see one another again.

But this, just knowing he was alive, even if he were on the other side of the earth, this was enough for her to go on, for her heart to go on. Aleksy was her heart.

Krystyna drew in breath and returned to the stairway, the thought of food far from her mind.

Aleksy awoke slowly. For the moment he had forgotten where he was, forgotten the danger, the killing, the slaughter.

He lay on a strangely soft and luxurious pallet. A lamp burned close by. He was in a tent, he came to realize, one like he had never seen. Two men his size could stand atop one another in the center and not touch the roof. The walls of the tent were not a mere coarse canvas, as he had been accustomed to, or even the fine weave of Turkish canvas employed on the exterior of the enemy tents. These walls glittered with rich materials of purple and crimson, its Islamic arabesques sewn with thread of gold.

Am I a captive? Dog's blood! The question hit him like a war hammer.

He was alone. His attempt to rise from the pallet was foiled by the pain in his thigh. He lay back, recalling the wound and how the bandaging had fallen apart while he was atop his horse. He was losing blood, so much blood. He could remember a profound weakness, then slipping from his mount into what seemed a vortex of animals, men, sabres, gunfire, cries of war and of pain—and finally the muffled thud of what could only have been his body striking hard earth. Then—nothing.

He reached up now to touch the gold cross that lay on his breastbone. That it was still there on the leather lacing surprised him. His soiled and blood-stained white linen shirt had been untied at his neck, and his armor, *żupan*, and boots had been removed. He looked down to his leg now. The trouser leg had been torn open and his thigh had been tightly bandaged. When? By whom?

Outside pandemonium reigned. Shouts, cries, running. Did the battle still rage? In those last moments of consciousness, he had watched the allies gain the upper hand. The Turks were panicking, turning tail and running pell-mell. Was the rout a mere tactical maneuver? Had they gathered forces and returned? It was just such a maneuver for which they were famous. He felt the hairs on the back of his neck rise at the thought. *Am I a prisoner?*

I should pray, he thought. But no prayers would come to him. He remembered now what Szymon had told him about prayer: "I do pray when I breathe, my boy. And when I breathe, I pray." It was still a mystery to him.

He noted that except for his bandaging, he was not bound in any way. Motivated by equal parts curiosity and fear, Aleksy pulled himself up into a sitting position at the side of the pallet just as the crimson flap was pulled aside and a small figure entered.

Idzi.

"My God!" Aleksy cried. "You're in one piece—"

"I am, indeed," he said with a wink. "My size increased the odds."

Aleksy laughed. "God's bones! For a minute I thought I was a prisoner—oh, my God, Idzi, you're bloodied from head to toe!"

"Not my blood, Alek. Some belongs to a Turk who thought me an easy target. And some might be yours that got on me while we tried to patch you up. Seems *your* Turkish dance partner sliced into one hell of a vein."

"You bandaged me? You found me?"

"You didn't think I'd let you out of my sight no matter how far behind we trailed the hussars."

"You and… ?"

"Piotr. He and I lugged you into this fine tent. I expect it belonged to one of Kara Mustafa's favorite minions, yes? Pretty fancy, eh?"

"Where is Piotr? He's unharmed?"

"He is. He's gone to rejoin the king's staff. I've been standing guard outside to keep looters at bay, as well as keep an eye on Miracle. Holy Chrystus, how did you come by him?"

"Pure happenstance—where is he?"

"Piotr took him for safekeeping."

"Good—so, we've won? It's over?"

"The battle for Vienna? Yes, it's done, quick as you please."

"Sweet Jezus!—What time is it?"

Idzi shrugged. "An hour or two after midnight."

"The king?"

"Sound as a bell."

"Roman?"

Idzi shrugged. "Don't know."

"And the situation? The Turks did not return after the rout?"

"To face the hussars? No, they knew that was the way to hell. It's yet to be decided whether the king chases them down."

"And the Grand Vizier?"

"Injured in his eye, we're told, but he escaped. Carrying his Holy Banner, he was." Idzi snickered. "No doubt between his legs." His face sobered now. "Do you know, even with our winged offensive coming down at him from the Kahlenberg heights like avenging birds from the heavens, he allowed his considerable forces to continue the siege of the city. It was a catastrophic military decision."

"God's mercy! Putting them against us would have made the victory more difficult."

"Yes, and word has it that they were within half an hour of laying enough explosives in the tunnels to breach the wall."

"Ah, if they had gained access to the city, the tables would have been turned."

Idzi nodded. "No doubt about that. Before he fled, Kara Mustafa did order a retreat for those still in the siege trenches, and so some managed to save themselves. He also mandated that any equipment be destroyed, and that was done to a great extent, but the worst of his orders was for the captives to be executed."

"My God!—Christian captives?"

Idzi nodded. "Yes, at least many of them, but the order came late enough that it was not fully carried out. They did a better job of killing their own."

"What do you mean?"

"The slaves and women they left behind, whether camp entertainers, prostitutes, lovers, or wives—all were butchered rather than be left to their enemy."

Aleksy felt his stomach tighten with disgust. Victory was sweet, indeed, but the price was extreme. Was this the field of glory he had imagined?

Idzi moved toward the pallet. "Now, lie back down and let's take a look at the wound. You lost a good deal of blood."

Later, as things outside quieted, they slept the short night away, Aleksy on the pallet, Idzi on the ground, curled like a snail into a fine Turkish blanket.

"Time to rise and look pretty!"

Aleksy opened his eyes. The voice—at once jocular and stentorian—wasn't Idzi's, and yet it was familiar.

With some effort, Aleksy sat and pulled his legs to the side of the pallet. Nearby, Idzi was wiggling out of his blanket.

The tent was dark, the speaker a mere shadow near the entrance.

"Who goes there?" Idzi demanded, his voice all snarl, like that of a small dog that surprises one with a strong bark.

"Ah, here we have it," the speaker said. He had found and was lighting a Turkish lamp. "It's Piotr, Idzi, who else?"

"Could have been Roman," Idzi said, echoing Aleksy's thought.

"Good to see you, Piotr," Aleksy said, wiping the sleep from his eyes. "I hear that I have you both to thank for finding this little palace for me."

"Think nothing of it. Now, you've both got to make yourselves presentable."

"Presentable?" Idzi grumbled. "Chrystus, we're at war."

"At this hour?" Aleksy asked. "Presentable for what?"

"Well, as fate would have it, last night I was witness to a tale told by a young man to his noble father about a hussar—a Tatar, in fact—who had saved his life by pretending to be a heathen who had just taken the life of the young man in question." He paused nodding toward Aleksy. "Does this scenario sound familiar to you, Aleksy? The description fit you down to your sprig of hay."

Aleksy felt hot blood rushing to his face. "Did the boy say I forced on him the indignity of playing dead rather than playing the hero certain to die?"

"He did." Piotr paused, smiling. "So it *was* you, blessed be the saints and King Krakus, too! It's good I spoke up, then."

"You spoke up? You told them what?"

"Who you are, of course. The boy wants to thank you. Indeed, so does his father. I gave a good description of this tent—why, it's just spitting distance from the Grand Vizier's pavilion. Easy enough to find. They shouldn't be too far behind me." Piotr retrieved Aleksy's boots from his pile of belongings and dropped them in front of him.

"God's wounds, can't this wait?" Aleksy asked. "Who needs this now?"

"There was no putting them off."

Aleksy had no sooner pulled on the darkly-spattered yellow boots than he looked up to see someone pushing aside the tent flap and entering. It was the boy Aleksy had saved.

With some effort, Aleksy managed to stand, weak and unsteady, all the while taking in the figure before him. A smile stood in place of the dirty and pained visage of the day before. A full head of curly, coal-black hair framed the thin, pale face that tapered to a pointed chin. He stood tall in a relatively clean officer's uniform.

"You've been hurt," the youth said.

Aleksy shrugged. "I've been told I'll live, eh, Idzi? Good to see you upright, too."

Aleksy turned to see that Piotr had just bent to whisper something into Idzi's ear. Idzi's gaze flashed to the figure of the youth and his mouth fell agape.

"What is it?" Aleksy asked.

The youth spoke before Piotr could reply. "I am here to render thanks, Aleksy Gazdecki."

Aleksy nodded. "You've been told my name, I see. And yours?"

Piotr cleared his throat and spoke now. "Aleksy, this is Prince Jakub Sobieski."

At first Aleksy smiled widely, thinking it a silly joke, but a glance at Piotr and then at Idzi told him otherwise. Their faces and demeanor were serious as the plague.

"Prince Jakub?" Aleksy asked, his voice thin and tentative.

The youth nodded. "My father's come, also. He's outside. Are you able to walk?"

Aleksy felt the blood draining away from his face. "Yes… I think so." The weakness he was fending off wasn't completely physical.

"Good, come then." The young lord turned and left, followed by Piotr. Idzi—his huge blue eyes all wonder—silently held the tent flap to the side and waited for Aleksy, who limped forward, heedless of the pain.

Outside, dawn was breaking, a mist clearing. At the center of a semicircle of eight or ten soldiers stood Lord Jakub, his corpulent father to his side, King Jan III Sobieski. He had shed his armor and was robed in a red *kontusz*, lined in blue and fitting his stout form like the bowl of a bell. He wore no hat or helmet.

Aleksy felt his heart contract.

The king recognized him and smiled. "Ah, it's you," he said, genuinely surprised. "What little mystery we must have here! Unravel it we will, in time. But first, our thanks to you, young Tatar, our deepest thanks."

Aleksy was at a loss as to how to receive the gratitude of a king. He nodded slightly before making the appropriate bow.

"Aleksy, is it?"

"Yes, Sire"

"I've not forgotten our first meeting. What was the name of the girl of whom you were so enamored?"

"Krystyna."

"Very pretty, too. Now, my son has told me how your posing as one of the enemy Tatars deflected attention from him and allowed his escape."

"I'm afraid I used force to make him play dead, Sire. I am sorry for that."

"Sorry?" The king sniffed, as if at an unpleasant odor. "He was at a disadvantage and outmanned, yes?"

"I was," Prince Jakub interjected.

"We have much to be thankful for this morning, Aleksy. Just as Vienna and Europe have been spared, so has my son. There is the reward to consider."

"Your Majesty, I had no thoughts of—"

The king held up his hand to shush his subject. "I'm sure you had no thoughts of reward. In fact, judging by your reaction this victory morning, I would venture that you had no idea whom you were aiding. Is that correct?"

Aleksy nodded. "It is, Sire."

"All the more reason for an appropriate reward," the king announced, his voice rising and his head turning to those behind him. "Wouldn't you all agree?"

Several voices called out in the affirmative. Only now did Aleksy notice that a small crowd had gathered about the king and his men.

"Now for the mystery, Aleksy… ?" The king was prompting him for his family name.

"Gazdecki."

"Aleksy Gazdecki, then. When we first met—somewhere along this long road to victory—you were a retainer for two hussar brothers, I believe. Is my memory correct?"

"It is, Sire."

"Ah! And yet your derring-do yesterday was done in the guise of a hussar, was it not?"

Aleksy could feel a great heat rise and burn in his face. He knew he had turned scarlet. His temples throbbed. "It was, Sire."

"Now everyone around me knows the skills required of a hussar, the length of time it takes for training, and the obstacles one has to overcome to be initiated into the elite corps."

Aleksy stared at the king. Of themselves the words were accusatory, but the king's attitude was hard to decipher.

"How is it," the king was saying, "that in the matter of a few days, a young retainer is able to leap over such requirements and become one of my beloved and valued hussars? How is it you were wearing the wings of a hussar?"

Sweet Jezus, Aleksy thought. *I'm not to be thanked here. I'm going to be placed on trial. I had no right to be wearing the wings.* He took a deep breath. The king hadn't even mentioned that he had stepped outside of—and above—his class. Was he to be accused of impersonating nobility?

"Aleksy," the king was saying, "how is it possible?"

"I can answer that!" The voice came from behind the King's Guard.

All eyes turned toward the soldier pushing through the small crowd, taking little care to avoid jostling soldier or citizen. In moments he stood before the king and Prince Jakub.

Roman!

Aleksy's throat tightened. Was he here as friend or foe? Roman shot him a quick, indecipherable glance before bowing to the king. "I can explain, Sire."

"You? Why, you were the one this young man was brawling with the other day."

"I was."

"Your name?"

"Roman Halicki."

"Well, what do you have to say for yourself?"

"My brother Marek was there that day, too. He was one of the hundred and fifty hussars who made the initial sortie into the Turkish center... He did not survive it." He paused, allowing time for his words to be digested.

The king's manner softened. He nodded. "His service to country will be celebrated. Now, go on."

"I gave the wings to Aleksy here," Roman continued, "so that he could take Marek's place. I thought well and good if he could kill just one of the enemy, Sire. I could not have imagined that he would save the life of Lord Jakub."

Indeed not! Roman was lying to the king. Aleksy had taken it upon himself to commandeer Marek's wings. He instantly saw through to Roman's motivation. If rewards or glory were to be handed out this day, Roman was expecting to be lauded also for what he saw as his part in saving the king's son. Why else speak up for the Tatar he so hated?

"I see," the king said. "How can even a king question your decision? You are to be commended for putting in order the elements that led to Jakub's rescue."

Aleksy saw Roman's spine tighten at the compliment, his shoulders lift, his lips attempt to avoid a full-out smile.

"But," the king went on, "this moment belongs to young Aleksy here." The king's small, deep-set eyes turned from Roman to Aleksy, who witnessed a flicker of disappointment in Roman's face. The semi-smile had fallen away. "Now, Aleksy, what is it that a monarch can do for you?"

Aleksy stared.

"Come now, Aleksy Gazdecki, what is your wish? Don't prevaricate. You are no Aladdin and I am no genie."

"I—I don't—"

"What is your dearest wish? It is to be a hussar, yes? You want to wear the wings? Piotr has vouched for your archery skills, I can tell you. You've supplied meat for the royal table more than once, he assured me."

What was he to say? His gaze went to Roman, who glowered back at him. Now his eyes went to Idzi, who was tugging on the skirt of the king's red *kontusz*. The king bent low to give his ear to the little man. Idzi cupped his right hand and whispered. The king, with slightly widening eyes, watched Aleksy as he listened.

A minute went by. The king asked Idzi his name, then straightened. "Your friend Idzi tells me you have *two* wishes, is that correct?"

Aleksy's eyes went from the king to Idzi and back again. The moment hung fire.

"Tongue-tied?" the king pressed. "I don't have all day. He tells me you would wish for the girl—Krystyna."

"Sire, that's not possible," Roman blurted.

The king held up the palm of his hand to Roman, who cut short his speech.

Turning back to Aleksy, he said, "The girl Krystyna, do you love her?"

Aleksy nodded before he could even give thought to the question or consider Roman's reaction.

"And does she return your love?"

"She does, Your Majesty."

"I see. And—on the other hand—you've longed to join the ranks of the hussars?"

Another nod.

"Well, there we have it," the king announced. "The young Tatar here has a decision to make. To be a bridegroom or a soldier." Then, louder, in a stage-like voice: "To make love—or make war!"

The crowd laughed. The king had drawn them into the little drama, and they peppered Aleksy with advice. Some called for him to take the girl while others urged that he take the hussar wings. One called out: "Take the wings and many girls will follow."

More laughter.

"Well, Aleksy?" the king persisted.

Aleksy burned with one part embarrassment, one part pressure. He surveyed the crowd of twenty or more. Was his future to be decided on the spot and in public? As a little diversion? *So be it.*

"Lady Krystyna Halicka," he said, even as his gaze fell on Roman and he remembered the hopelessness of the situation. "But, Sire..."

"What is it?"

Aleksy drew in another breath, but before he could get words out, Roman spoke.

"Your Majesty," Roman said quite forcefully, his face dark, "what Aleksy wants to say is that the Lady Krystyna—my sister—has been spoken for. She has been married to a *true* hussar."

Murmurs of disappointment swept the crowd.

"Against her wishes," Aleksy spat. "She went so far as to dress as a camp follower to follow me. She loves me!"

"Nonetheless," the king said, "if she has been given to another, there is little even a king can do. You will have to make do with your second wish. Once we return to Warsaw, I will see that you train properly to become a hussar."

How was it that being granted such a wish could now resound with disappointment? Aleksy forged a smile.

Idzi once again tugged on the king's *kontusz*. The king bent down, listened, his eyes seeming to brighten slightly.

"Idzi tells me," the king said, bringing himself to full height, "that Lady Krystyna's marriage was a marriage by proxy." He turned to Roman. "Did your sister marry this other hussar—what's his name?"

"Count Fabian Nardolski, Sire."

"Ah, did she marry him by proxy?"

"She did."

"And this soldier—Fabian—fights with us—here?"

Roman nodded.

"Did she marry willingly?"

Roman seemed surprised by the question and two or three heartbeats—Aleksy's—went by before he answered. "She did."

The slight delay had not been lost on the king. "Were you there, Lord Halicki, to lend credence to that fact?"

The color left Roman's face. "No, Sire."

"I see. Then, what it comes down to is this. Just days ago the girl seemed as enamored of Aleksy as he clearly is of her. I myself bore witness to that. Further, this proxy marriage has not been consummated. There may be things, after all, that a king can do in such a situation. In point of fact, I am writing to Pope Innocent himself today to let him know Vienna and Western Europe has been spared. He can only be pleased with the results of our great victory. If I ask for the annulment of this marriage by proxy, I doubt that he will refuse. It would be an easy quid pro quo, wouldn't you say, Lord Halicki?"

"But, Your Majesty—" Roman began and was silenced by the king's hand as surely as if he had been clouted by his military baton.

The king turned back to Aleksy. "How is your wound, soldier?" he asked.

"It has been well tended, Sire."

"I trust that it will heal, but at least for now your days as a soldier are done. I'm sending you back to Kraków. A convoy is being organized that will carry some of the wounded, as well as some of the spoils of this victory. It will be well protected and you are to accompany it. I suspect that by the time you arrive I'll have a message waiting for you at the castle as to the disposition of the request I make of the pope."

"Sire, I ask permission to accompany him," Roman said. "Aleksy is a retainer from our estate."

The king turned, eyes narrowing in appraisal of Roman. "To protect him? To keep him safe, no doubt." A certain sarcasm coated his words. "He seems quite capable, Lord Halicki. You look all of one piece. Tell me, did you sustain any wounds?"

"No, Sire. Nothing serious."

"Did you kill many?"

"Indeed, Sire. Very many."

"I see. You are to be commended. We could not do without your killing skills. In the coming days, we will be chasing the devil pillar to post, and I will need every man. Your request is denied."

"I have no retainer if he is to go."

"I'm not so sure you can't do without." The king thought and his gaze shifted down, then back to Roman. "Is Idzi here from your estate?"

Roman's face was screwed into that of a loser at high-stake cards. "He is, Sire."

"Then take Idzi. He seems the nervy sort. I'm certain his courage is big."

Idzi's chest rose as he took in breath and his eyes widened.

"Idzi, can you ride?" the king asked.

"Yes, Sire."

"Ah, good! Roman will make certain you get a fine steppe pony, won't you, Roman?"

Roman stared at the king, then Aleksy, then Idzi. By the time his gaze went back to the king, his visage indicated defeat and he voiced agreement—and yet Aleksy sensed defiance brewing beneath the surface.

While Idzi took his fortune with one part disappointment, one part aplomb, Roman's face reddened with impotent rage. If he was capable of serious mischief, Aleksy was not prepared to think about it.

His own head spun with the events of the morning, and his heart pulsed with hope.

The next day Piotr told Aleksy that the king did, indeed, write to Pope Innocent XI requesting the annulment of the Nardolski marriage. Further, Piotr told him, with no little excitement in his voice, that the king wrote, "I came, I saw, God conquered."

THIRTY-THREE

THE DAYS WENT BY SLOWLY, time passing like delayed drops of water in a water clock. Krystyna spent most hours of the day in her rooms, pacing, fretting, praying. She took her meals with Lady Nardolska, comporting herself with cool politeness, nothing more. She saw no gain in revealing to the countess that she knew she had been lied to concerning Aleksy's reported death. She would bide her time. The day would come when she would disclose that she was no longer the little fool others thought her to be.

How long would it take for a messenger to ride the two hundred and eighty-seven miles to reach Kraków with news of the battle at Vienna? Four days? Five? The citizens of Kraków, faces grim and mouths nearly mute except for the hourly prayers the cathedral bells adjured, walked about carrying out their tasks and errands as if in a daze. Everyone in the household—Lady Nardolska and the servants—were on tenterhooks, as well, wondering when the news might come, hoping for the best, fearing the worst. Lady Nardolska's temper with her servants ran short with regularity. She held her tongue in Krystyna's presence, but from her rooms Krystyna often heard the countess railing at her steward, maids, and other domestic help.

Krystyna shared the countess' anxiety. An Ottoman victory could mean the end of a Christian Europe, the end of countless cultures, the end of Poland as she knew it. The Ottoman Sultan and his Grand Vizier, Kara Mustafa, meant to supplant Christianity with Islam, destroying cities and lives, martyring those who resist conversion. What was to become of their way of life? Her family?

And Aleksy. *Maryja, Mother of God, keep him safe.*

Then, one day, the heavy bells of the cathedral rang and rang continuously. The Market Square erupted in a frenzy of noise and activity. News had come at last!

The queen had received word from Vienna. It took a little while for those citizens coming to the doors, windows, and balconies on Grodzka Street to discern that the great clamor was one of joy. The steward was sent out to learn the news. Upon his return, Krystyna, Lady Nardolska, and the entire staff shared in the jubilation, the countess ordering up a small barrel of fine Hungarian wine from the cellar. The Turks had summarily been defeated by King Jan Sobieski and his allied forces in just the nick of time. The enemy had been but minutes away, it seems, from breaching the walls of Vienna with their deadly mines.

Tears in her eyes, Lady Nardolska pressed Krystyna to herself. Krystyna, her grudge notwithstanding, held her and wept, too.

The next morning a heavy rapping came at the front entrance. Lady Nardolska nervously went to the door, shooing away the maid whose duty it was to see to callers. Krystyna moved quickly, shadowing the countess. Could it be news of her brothers or Aleksy? Or—almost in an after-thought—Fabian?

When the countess pulled open the door, Krystyna could see a mature servant dressed in a blue uniform; embroidered on his collar was the white eagle. Krystyna's heart raced. She recognized the livery as belonging to Wawel Castle. He had been sent on a mission from the queen. What could it portend?

Krystyna stood behind the countess, who positioned herself in the half-opened doorway so that it left little room for another. She strained to listen to the soft words of the messenger, thinking at one point that she heard her own name.

The countess' figure seemed to stiffen as she fired several questions at the messenger; none of his whispered responses yielded a satisfied word or gesture from her. As the man pivoted to descend the few portico steps, Lady Nardolska turned about and seemed almost startled to find Krystyna there. The woman's face had gone white as porcelain.

"What is it?" Krystyna asked, preparing for bad news.

The countess placed one hand on her heart. "It's the queen," she whispered, "we're to have an audience with her at ten tomorrow morning."

Krystyna could not sleep. Why were they being summoned to Wawel Castle? Were they to be informed of deaths on the battlefield? Whose? Count Nardolski's? Fabian's? Her own brothers'? Her father's? Wouldn't this be an unusual way of doing so? As for Aleksy, she knew that his death would warrant no such attention.

A carriage arrived to collect them at half past nine in the morning.

Neither she nor Lady Nardolska had been able to eat at the very silent and tense morning meal. The nearly sleepless night had revealed no insights as to the queen's order.

The drive to the castle was thankfully short.

Madame Heloise—the queen's Mistress of the Robes and the one woman Krystyna had hoped never to see again—was waiting for them at the drive entrance.

"What is this about?" Lady Nardolska demanded even before the footman had the drop-down steps in readiness. She descended now, Krystyna following. "Is this about my husband or my boy? Are they injured? Are they—"

Madame Heloise spoke with her usual curtness. "This is not about injuries or deaths, I can assure you, Lady Nardolska. As yet, no casualty list has been forwarded to the queen."

"Then what does it concern?"

Madame Heloise ignored the question. "As a matter of fact, the messenger must have muddled the request."

"What do you mean by that?"

"The queen wishes to see only the young lady."

"Krystyna?" Dumbstruck, Lady Nardolska looked to Krystyna, then back to Mistress Heloise, confused but choosing to play the game. "Very well, you may announce us."

"Alone."

"Excuse me?"

"The queen has asked to see Lady Krystyna alone."

Lady Nardolska paled considerably. A twitch below her right eye caught Krystyna's attention. It was a tic she had noticed before.

"Alone—why, for God's sake?"

Madame Heloise turned her back to give directions to the driver, instructing him to return the Lady Nardolska to her home on Grodzka Street. The footman came near to help her ascend the carriage steps.

"No—I will wait," she said, her demeanor stiffening.

Madame Heloise shook her head. "Lady Krystyna is to have luncheon with the queen. It is best you return home."

"Luncheon?" Lady Nardolska asked in a kind of gasp.

She was no more surprised than Krystyna, who stood as a silent witness to her mother-in-law's befuddlement.

The countess drew herself up in a ruffle of poorly hidden anger. "I will wait."

Madame Heloise shrugged. "It is not something I recommend, my lady. The streets can be rough these days with merrymakers and the like."

Lady Nardolska's eyes fairly bulged. The implication was clear: she was not to be invited into the castle.

"Good day to you, my lady." Madame Heloise took Krystyna by the elbow, directing her toward the entrance.

Krystyna dared not look back until they were entering the doorway. She saw then only the dark blue of her mother-in-law's dress as she stepped up into the coach. She had no love for the humiliated countess, but somehow she felt a small measure of pity.

At the long, carved oak dining table, Krystyna sat to the side of Queen Maria Casimire, much as she had done once before. Madame Heloise had left them alone.

There was a sly ebullience in the glitter in queen's eyes as she gazed at Krystyna. What is it? she wondered.

The queen picked up her fork. "The news from Vienna has been good, as I'm certain you know, my dear. So far, at least. Let us eat now."

"So far?"

"The fighting is not over."

"No? The city was saved; we were told it was."

"Indeed, it was spared. But the king is following in the wake of the Turks' retreat. More battles are expected."

"Oh." Krystyna attempted to eat. Her thoughts, however, went first to

Aleksy and then to her brothers and father. "Has there been news of... my family? Madame Heloise said no casualty lists have been sent."

"Hellie is accurate. I'm not sure when the lists will be sent."

"I see." Krystyna picked at her luncheon plate, a kind of chicken stew flavored with rosemary and a white wine.

"It's one of the French dishes I love. This is called *Coq Au Vin*. Do you not care for it?"

Krystyna arranged her mouth into a smile. "It's very good, Your Majesty."

"Ah! You're wondering why I've brought you here, yes?"

Krystyna nodded. She felt her stomach tightening.

"Well, you see, my dear, it's about that young man you were infatuated with a good while ago."

"A—Aleksy?"

"Yes. Well, my husband, that is, the king had some news. He has sent the boy back here to Kraków."

Krystyna grew faint. "I—I was told he was dead—that you had a letter come saying he had died of dysentery."

The queen blinked in surprise. "Who told you this?"

"Madame Heloise—no doubt at my mother's urging."

The queen's expression soured. "She'll pay handsomely for that indiscretion. Your marriage ceremony was arranged while I was shut up in the chapel. I had no knowledge of this great lie they told you. But now, more to the point, the boy is alive, Krystyna, but he has been wounded, you see, and—"

"Wounded?" Krystyna's heart leaped in her chest. "How—"

"Do not worry. He is on the mend, and like I said, on his way back here. Now I don't think I have to ask you this, but the king says I should."

"What?"

"Do you love this boy, this Aleksy?"

"Yes, oh yes, I do. But he's not a boy, Your Highness—" Krystyna felt the room spinning about her. And then the tears came.

The queen reached out and placed her hand over Krystyna's. "You're right—war has a way of separating the wheat from the chaff." She let out a sigh. "But you've been coerced into the arranged marriage. That's the problem and not a small one, is it?"

Krystyna's head was down, her long braids falling forward, tears splashing onto the white silk table cloth. "No." Her voice was little more than a breath. "Not small."

The queen squeezed her hand. "Look at me, child. Look at me."

Slowly, Krystyna lifted a tear-stained face to the queen.

"Listen to me Krystyna. Your Aleksy has saved our son Jakub's life. My son's life."

Krystyna could only stare.

"I can tell you that the king has some ideas about your... circumstances. Yours and Aleksy's. He thinks he can be of help. Here, take this napkin and wipe those tears away, while I tell you how both my husband and I will see that you find happiness."

The queen thought it best to wait two more days before telling Krystyna of the ultimate sacrifice made by her brother Marek.

Aleksy lay awake in the open air, staring up into the twinkling September stars, breathing, just breathing. It came to him now—not with a thunderclap but with a soft breeze—he was *praying*. Inexplicably, Szymon's words were no longer puzzling. He understood. Each breath taken in and released there under the winking heavens was a prayer. He was at one with life, with God.

With a great sense of wonderment, he thought how his stars had aligned to place him here. While the greater number of the wounded were being cared for in the Turkish tents at Vienna, he was one of some twenty wounded who were being taken back to Kraków, escorted by a contingent of Sobieski's Royal Guard, soldiers that were to return to the king after the duty was carried out. Luck was with him, too, because his wound had been bandaged well enough that he was able to ride horseback rather than being transported by wagon like most of the others. In the morning, as the wagons and wounded had been assembled, the truth about the mission of the convoy came home to him. There were many more wagons than needed for a handful of wounded unable to ride. Most of the vehicles were stuffed with the magnificent Turkish tents, confiscated weapons, and trunks that one guard had confided were loaded with enough jewels and treasure to build two cities like Kraków. The significantly high numbers of the well-armed military detail corresponded to the value of the cargo. The Turks had long ago applied the epithet "Lion of Poland" to King Sobieski, Aleksy knew, so it seemed fitting that he had taken the lion's share of treasure.

Aleksy watched as a dark whirl of clouds scudded across the sky silhouetted against the moon. How many nights would be spent in this way? Ten? More? They were promised a town and possibly real beds for the third night, but he would not assume such a luxury as a given. A bed would make no difference. What made for his discontent was that travel was slow, painfully so. Why, his old plow horse Kastor had seemed to move faster. Oh, he knew the pace was necessary; caravans moved as slowly as sap, especially one with wagons carrying patients, as well as booty. Of his own volition, Roman had allowed him to take Miracle. With such a horse, Aleksy had thought briefly of riding alone, but doing so would put him at risk of being set upon by bands of Turks or enemy Tatars.

He had had two days to rest before the caravan set out from Vienna. He spent the time recuperating in the Turkish tent where Idzi and Piotr had placed him and was thus saved from having to deal with Roman. Idzi managed to slip away from Roman just before the King's Army was to set out after the fleeing Turks. "Stay clear of him," Idzi had warned, "he's mad as I've ever seen him, Alek. They say anger's like an old snake skin that needs to be shed. Well, that fits him just fine."

Aleksy laughed. "I should be warning you. You're the one who has been given the unhappy post of playing his aide. So, it's Roman the snake—?"

Idzi didn't laugh. "He's a deadly one, Alek, and as long as the king has set you on the path to Kraków and Krystyna, he'll not shed that skin. It'll grow tighter and tighter. Don't think lending you Miracle is a good deed. He just wants Miracle home safe in the stable at Poplar House. You've got to watch yourself."

"I have some fancy protection." Aleksy took up a dagger that lay on his pallet. "Yesterday Prince Jakub gave this to me." He removed the dagger from the exquisite gold sheath and placed the hilt in Idzi's small hand.

"Good God," Idzi cried, his voice sliding up an octave. "Are these stones real?"

"You've seen the loot around here, Idzi. Do you think Kara Mustafa would prize fake rubies? Go ahead look at them closely—six on either side."

Idzi turned the dagger over. "This is protecting you in style." Sighing, he picked up the previous thread of thought. "Roman and I are going after the Turks and you are going to Kraków, so there's distance between you two now, but that won't always be the case. And snakes have friends, Alek." He handed the dagger back to Aleksy.

"Your point is taken." Aleksy replaced the dagger in its sheath and laid it on his pallet. "Now, let me tell you what else the king has done."

Idzi looked up, his high forehead furrowing. "What?"

"He's giving me land in the Kobryn Province. That's where he settled a number of loyal Tatars on Crown estates a few years ago."

Idzi's mouth fell open. "You're to be a land owner? My god! Is this true?"

"It is. A modest estate. Fifty acres or so."

"Then… then you're to be a lord!"

Aleksy laughed and shrugged. "He said I must have something to offer the daughter of Count Halicki."

"Do you think that will smooth things over?"

"With Roman—never! But I'm hopeful it will with the count and countess. A king's wishes are hard to ignore. And, after all, Lord Halicki's family was not always of the *szlachta*. At some point, someone raised them up."

"Where is Kobryn?"

"I'm told it's some two hundred sixty-five miles due north of Halicz."

"Not so close to the in-laws, then? Lucky man!"

"Or to Roman."

Idzi rubbed at his square, stubbled chin. "You would be closer to Warsaw, I'm guessing?"

"Maybe a hundred fifty miles east of it."

"Valuable land, Alek, unless it's a mountain," he said with a laugh. "The king must set great store by his son Jakub's life—to be so generous with you."

"Prince Jakub could be king one day. Listen, Idzi, I'll want you to come live there, too. You must."

"We'll see."

"What do you mean? You're not bound to my parents."

"Oh, your mother won't miss me a bit, but your father might. And he's the one who offered me a home."

The night darkened now as clouds—black as tar—eclipsed the moon. Aleksy lay in the chilled quiet, thinking back on that comment of Idzi's. He had always hoped that his mother's dislike for the dwarf had not been as evident to his friend as it was to him. He had regularly tried to shield him from her comments and sour face by making excuses for her unfriendliness. But something in Idzi's voice told him that her condescending attitude and efforts to disinclude him had not gone unnoticed. His mother's dislike had seared its way into his tender heart like a poker freshly reddened in the fire at her kitchen grate.

Guilt added to the dead-of-night, for he knew that it was as his surrogate that Idzi had been asked—in effect, ordered—by the king to accompany Roman on a most dangerous mission. King's request or no, he himself should not have allowed his friend to be his surrogate. He should have gone instead.

But in the briefest of moments he had made the most momentous of decisions. He had turned away from the opportunity of becoming a hussar. Was that not his dream? Had it not been his obsession for years? And then, when the moment miraculously arrived, in the person of the King of Poland no less, he allowed the occasion to pass.

Only now did he try to sort through his reasons for doing so. There was Krystyna, of course. Not long after meeting her, he came to value her as much as his dream of becoming a winged warrior. And then—suddenly, incredibly, the king presented him with his choice of futures. Life as a hussar—or life with Krystyna. His answer came in a heartbeat. He chose Krystyna. He did so even though he doubted whether the king could work his magic with Pope Innocent and have her proxy marriage annulled. It was a roll of the dice.

And he *had* been a hussar—unofficially—for one day and on the occasion of the battle of the century. He would always have that. And, in some ways it had lived up to expectations. The thrill of being part of the force of the winged hussars descending like birds from a vengeful heaven—even in his initial role as retainer—would stay with him the length of his life. Then, wearing Marek's hussar wings as he engaged the enemy brought his dream to life in the most spectacular fashion.

And in some ways the fields fronting the walls of Vienna, bloody as they were, were fields of glory, indeed. The Christian forces—pieced and hammered together by King Jan Sobieski—won the day. However, amidst the triumph, Aleksy witnessed such death and butchering of animals and men, friend and foe, as to defy imagination or description. His dream of becoming a hussar had not allowed for the sight of miles of torn flesh, a darkening lake of blood seeping into the ground, the piling of bodies to be burnt like so much rubbish.

It was not fear that made him decline the king's offer. Once he was in motion—moving into the thick of the fight—his fear dissipated like a mist at noon. He took to battle as if he were taking part in a village marksmanship contest, but instead of striking the archery butt, he was killing, killing, killing. It was the feeling of elation that ran through his veins like quicksilver that frightened him—not then, but in the aftermath. It was, he knew now, bloodlust, and it was not something of which he could be proud. He had been overcome with the appetite for violence. Is this the way of most soldiers, he wondered. He hated himself for it.

And so, the choice the king presented was not a difficult one. It came with some ease.

Krystyna.

THIRTY-FOUR

6 October
Párkány, Hungary

"Dog's blood!" Roman cursed. They had camped the night on the outskirts of Párkány, and he rose now before dawn. He had done nothing but curse, it seemed, since leaving Vienna—at last—on 17 September, the Poles under King Sobieski leading and followed by the Imperial forces led by Charles of Lorraine. A full five days had elapsed since the rout at Vienna, allowing the Ottomans too much time to escape and recoup. The delay allowed for a litany of things with which he took issue. Squabbling went on among the victors regarding credit for the victory and shares in the spoils. Arguments, as well as lethal illnesses Hungary was known to host in the fall season, caused the Saxons and others to return home rather than pursue the enemy. The number of Polish and Austrian forces to make the pursuit was placed at thirty-five thousand, a number that Roman feared could prove insubstantial. Further complicating the chase, a circuitous route was decided upon to avoid land that had been laid bare by previous foraging of friend and enemy forces, a route that also necessitated lag time because of waiting for boats at river crossings. All of this was enough to put Roman on edge, but there was more: beneath his frustration boiled his hatred for Aleksy and repulsion at the special treatment shown to him by the king. Kicking at the gravel, he growled out another curse: "God's arse! May the Tatar die before reaching Kraków—and my sister!"

Roman pulled from the campfire a small pot and poured into a metal cup Idzi's chicory concoction, wondering the while where the dwarf had run off to.

Idzi. Another bone of contention. Some hussars still had their three retainers to aid them, tending to their weapons and seeing their betters properly armed on battle days. He had but half of a retainer and one not to be trusted.

A red dawn was breaking. He stood now and took up his telescope. An Ottoman camp, its numbers unimpressive, was situated below guarding the pontoon bridge that spanned the River Danube, the sole access to the town of Párkány. The glass swept the panorama. To the right and to the left of the camp, the land lay flat as a board and empty.

He pivoted now, directing his telescope beyond the encampment of Sobieski's vanguard and toward the way they had come, surveying some five thousand Polish hussars and cavalry. As of the day before, the king said they were to rest and wait for the remainder of the Polish and Austrian forces to catch up. He raised his telescope. The horizon was empty. Roman turned and spat. "Only God knows when they will arrive," he mumbled. More lost time.

Idzi appeared. "You'd best get into your gear now," the dwarf said.

"Why? Are the others close? Has he had word?"

Idzi shrugged. He was already laying out Roman's armor. "We're making a move today."

"Who says so?"

"The king."

How was it that this little man always caught wind of events before others? "What do you do, sit under the king's table?"

No response.

"It's that Piotr that supplies you with information, isn't it? I thought we were to wait for the Austrians and the rest of our men."

Idzi was running a sharpening stone up and down the edge of Roman's sabre. "The king's spy said there's but a small number here at Párkány. He's not one to wait."

"Really? Not one to wait? You could have fooled me." Roman began the laborious process of donning his war-gear.

Holy Mass had been abbreviated. Roman declined Communion, as well as Confession offered by a chaplain. He was saddled upon Flash, anxiously waiting, his armor in place, the twin arcs of eagle feathers attached to his back. His sabre hung on his sword knot, his two pistols and war hammer were holstered. He wordlessly took hold of a new lance Idzi handed up. The night before, Roman had cut Marek's name into the wood.

The captain of his company of one hundred fifty hussars had announced that they were to be among seven companies of cavalry in the advance formation, with the king and the remainder of the five thousand following in support. Roman's company was to ride in the lead position of the right wing. Some soldiers whispered concerns as to why the king was not waiting for the arrival of the rest of the Polish and Imperial forces—cavalry, infantry, and artillery. Others wondered aloud. Company captains assured their men that word had come back to the king that the Ottoman force situated before Párkány was small and easily assailable—no more than one thousand. The Grand Vizier, Kara Mustafa, was thought to be at Buda attempting to reorganize the bulk of his disjointed—and some said insurgent—army. Intelligence had it that the meager Turkish forces present for the purpose of defending Párkány were under the command of a young pasha, Kara Mehmed. They were thought to be very vulnerable.

Young did not necessarily mean incompetent, Roman thought. And yet, he gave the king the benefit of the doubt: he found himself in agreement—that it was better to strike at once—before Ottoman reinforcements arrive.

He prepared himself for the killing that was to come, clearing his mind to the best of his ability. It had been difficult to do at Vienna because his brother had just given up his life in the initial contact with the enemy. It was difficult to do this day, too, for the fire of hate he had for Aleksy burned at high heat. He could not forgive the king for his meddling. Still, he made the attempt to find focus. The enemy lay ahead.

Idzi stood nearby, looking up. "Go with God," the dwarf said, nodding, as if in encouragement, but the valediction and gesture went unanswered and Idzi had to step lively to avoid Flash's flank when the horse pivoted and moved away. With the pressure of his knee, Roman directed Flash to his place in the advance party. It was to be a mere skirmish today, they were assured, easily fought, easily won. He assumed that was the reason why the Polish hymn "Bogurodzica" was not sung. Neither were there many more than a few sentences pronounced by the king, words that called for a swift victory over the heathen forces protecting Párkány. Confidence reigned.

Then came the usual orders.

"Secure your hats!"

"Draw together knee to knee!"

"Sabres on sword knots!"

And for those cavalry without lances: "Draw sabres!"

And finally, *"Dalej!" March on!*

The advance cavalry—more than one thousand—lances pointed upward with black and gold pennants flying—eagle feathers fluttering on the backs of the hussars—moved out and onto the way to Párkány. The advance to combat began.

The thousand moved at a gentle trot. In the lead company, Roman kept his eyes on the flat terrain, scanning ahead for the enemy. In no time, he could see that the Turks were mounted and ready. The pasha might be young but he was going to make his stand. Their numbers were not intimidating, and yet Roman could remember his father's many warnings about becoming too complacent, too confident of victory.

He recalled that during a fencing match with his brother at the Officer's Training School he had become quite full of himself, so certain was he that he would score the necessary hits. After all, Marek could not match his speed nor skill. What it was that took his attention, his focus, he could not recall. Someone's face in the audience? A loutish catcall from the side? Whatever it was, it allowed Marek to press forward with the winning hit. It was a lesson well learned.

Afterward, he had to go to some length to convince his brother that he had not thrown the match. *Marek, sweet Marek! Come be with me this day, Lord Brother Mareczek.* He would stay on guard.

Suddenly, Roman noticed to the right of the enemy and at a surprisingly close distance there was a multitude of colored splotches upon the field that up to that point had been only brown with a bit of green woven in. The hussars' trot seemed to slow as everyone became aware of what lay ahead to the right. At once, the riotous display of color seemed to exhibit movement. And then it came home to Roman, as it must have to everyone. This was not a field of flowers blowing and undulating in the wind. What they were seeing were waves of multi-colored turbans and other Eastern headgear of the Ottomans.

Roman's eyes grew wide even as his stomach muscles contracted.

Frantic curses went up all around him as the right wing prepared for a deadly engagement.

Their dark faces were coming into view. Their force—and it was a massive one—had been positioned below, completely hidden in a basin curtained by reeds. The fine horses—Arabians with a concave profile, arched neck and high tail carriage—were climbing the incline now and in no time the Sipâhis were placed level on the field with the Poles, falling into line with the pasha's thousand. The Poles were outnumbered, badly so. The Ottomans immediately gave spur and advanced, quickly moving into a full gallop, like a band of vampires loosed from hell. "Allah! Allah! Allah!" came the high-pitched, deafening and demonic cries. Their numbers were many more times than intelligence had figured.

"*Złożcie kopie!*" Roman's captain called out, but his call to lower the lances and the orders of the other captains were largely lost amidst the pandemonium of the panicking Poles.

Heart thumping, Roman lowered his lance, and along with a number of his company, moved forward in an uneven line, for there had been no time to form the true and tight battle formation of Sobieski's signature square. The surprise had been too great, the reaction too disorderly. Those who had fought at Vienna and lived to tell of it gathered their wits and brawn and made ready for the onslaught, and yet there were lancers who were not quick enough to lower their lances with the confidence and skill required and other soldiers who had no time to light the match-cords of their muskets.

Roman had the base of his lance secure in its tok, its length leveled horizontally, poised for his first kill. He spurred his horse into a gallop even as he watched the looming faces coming forward at twice the speed. Well aware that his lance could break upon impact with an enemy in breastplate, his focus settled on a Sipâhi swathed in orange and white. Some Poles were likely to thrust their spears into the enemies' horses so that the allied cavalry coming behind could cut down the fallen riders. Maiming and killing the warhorses caused great chaos and could work to the aggressors' advantage, but something in Roman revolted at slaying the animal. He felt that skewering a man on a lance was more effective in engendering fear and destroying morale. But he knew that whether the Turk or the horse was the target, large numbers on both sides would not be killed in the initial contact. The battle would turn on the hand-to-hand combat that followed.

"Allah! Allah! Allah!" the Turks shrieked and fell upon the stunned Poles.

"For Chrystus!" "For Maryja!" the Poles responded. "Strike hard!"

The Turk in orange and white was well fed and proved an easy target for the seventeen-foot lance. "For Marek!" Roman screamed. The enemy was fully impaled before he could wield his curved sabre. Roman allowed the lance to fall to the ground with the body. The weight of the enemy precluded a second skewering.

Roman would not trust muskets. He had always thought them a dicey weapon in the heat of battle. He quickly removed his sabre from the sword-knot on his left wrist, an action done none too soon, for he was suddenly in a swarm of enemy. It was obvious to him that the Polish advance had failed badly; they had been surprised and had no time to properly assemble. Orders came in a haphazard fashion and reaped little response. He fought now, calling on the spirit of his brother, doing more fending off than killing, even while he witnessed Poles being toppled from their mounts—some headless—in growing numbers.

The Ottomans were upon them like a frenzy of flies. Even while slicing and jabbing as he held off blow after blow, directing Flash to pivot and pivot again, Roman was preparing to die. There would be no way out of this. Just one second's inattention to the swirling maelstrom about him would bring his end. He should have made his confession in the morning. He prayed for his parents, for Marek's soul, and for Krystyna. Ah, Krystyna, he had not always treated her well. He regretted that. *God forgive me.*

Suddenly, he became aware of a surge of more Polish uniforms about him, providing him with the briefest of respites. He realized that King Jan Sobieski had come to the front with the rest of his forces behind him, some four thousand. The king himself was not far off, a forbidding figure atop Palasz, his powerful bay stallion, hacking and thrusting while calling out encouragement to his men and oaths against the heathens.

The king attempted to call for battle formation, but despite the influx of all available support, the chaos and panic did not abate. The order went unheeded, for they were but a hundred paces from the thickest contingent of the enemy, whose numbers had suddenly swelled to double that of the Polish. Instead of generating fear and panic in the enemy as hussars were wont to do, they themselves were infused with dread and despair. Roman had unleashed scathing criticism of the king throughout the trek from Kraków, and he thought even now as he fought for his life how the king had woefully mishandled today's maneuver.

The king had violated one of the most basic rules of military tactics, one that had been drummed into every cadet's head in basic officer training. He had forged ahead on emotions and hubris—without having any forces in reserve—not cavalry, not infantry, not artillery.

Good Poles were being cut down in front of Roman now—like so many stalks of wheat—by an enemy who exulted in the forward flush of victory. To them, the day was theirs. "Allah! Allah! Allah!" they shrilled with chilling glee. Nonetheless, those who were managing to fight off the Turks were called now by the king to penetrate the enemy line. "Forward!" Sobieski bellowed. "For the Chrystus!" Finding his options limited, Roman obeyed. A small force followed suit. He doubted he would survive the foolhardy gambit.

The charge succeeded for the moment, but it soon became clear that the sheer number of the Turks was causing the better parts of the Polish center and left wing—those who had not as yet met the enemy—to break off and retreat.

Roman found himself close to the nine who guarded the king. Little by little they were becoming enclosed on all sides by the enemy. One of the company commanders rode forward and beseeched the king to forsake the cause and flee. The king refused, instead ordering the commander to rescue the prince from the melee. While trying to convince Jakub to obey his father's request, the officer was fatally shot in the neck. Sidling his horse in toward the blood-spattered boy, one of the King's Guards managed to marshal a more compliant prince to an opening in the fray that might lead to safety. In no time they opened up to a gallop.

Meanwhile, Roman fell in with the King's Guard. He thought he heard Sobieski cry, "Welcome, Hussar!"

The king called afresh for a charge and galloped into a fairly wide opening, one which led deeper into the enemy. In but minutes they were forced to slow to a trot by a tightening line of Sipâhi horsemen. Roman thought Sobieski had become unhinged by his arrogance and questioned his own good sense for joining his guard because a quick survey of the masses in front of them indicated that to persevere meant an ignominious death.

He realized a full retreat was necessary to keep the king from being killed or taken prisoner. The monarch and his guard seemed to come to the same conclusion, for they veered right—nearly stirrup-to-stirrup now—and urged their Polish-Arabians into a canter. Escape would be no easy task, for the Turks pressed in around them, their dark faces as fierce as their cries, their horses hemming in the King's Guard, slowing them to a near standstill. Instinctively, Roman moved his sabre to his left hand and had only just grasped his war hammer in his right when a Sipâhi, hell-bent on taking the king, propelled his warhorse into their midst. One of the guards engaged him in swordplay, but was not nearly quick enough and suffered a grievous wound to his torso. The Turk withdrew his spattered sabre from his victim, and Roman saw his focus go to the king, but before he could sidle up to the king, who was already engaged with a brute of a Sipâhi, Roman's war hammer slammed into his steel helmet, splitting his skull and knocking him from his horse.

The king managed to dispatch his assailant, but two more of the King's Guards were lost before the group could extricate themselves. So it was that Roman was one of just six who, along with the king, now found an opening and forged a mad gallop.

The chase went on for nearly eight miles over rough and furrowed ground, the six and the King of Poland himself racing for their lives. As their own battered and recouping forces came into view, so too did the standards and pennants of the long-awaited Imperial and Polish Armies, which had only just arrived. Roman turned in his saddle to witness the pursuing Ottoman warriors—more than a hundred, he guessed—halt and take stock of the allies' freshly-arrived forces spanning a rolling hillside. They turned back. Roman would learn that more than a thousand brave Poles died. But the prize of taking the King, the Lion of Poland, had proven elusive.

He sighed aloud.

It would be some time later that he learned the fate of Kara Mustafa. For his failure at Vienna, the Grand Vizier's execution was ordered by Sultan Mehmed IV. He was strangled by a silk cord, the manner in which high-ranking persons in the Ottoman Empire were put to death.

THIRTY-FIVE

Kraków

THE LONG AND GRUELING JOURNEY from Vienna was coming to an end. The caravan of soldiers and heavily-laden wagons had never moved as slowly as it was doing now, snaking its way up the incline of the limestone bluff known as Wawel Hill and passing through the gated archway that led into the courtyard of Wawel Royal Castle. Aleksy had been ordered to ride at the tail's end, so he would be the last to witness the triumphant arrival of the spoils of war, as well as the welcome to a few victims of the combat that made victory possible. The sight of Kraków, belted by the River Vistula shimmering pink at dusk, quickened the pace of his heart. The debilitating fatigue of the interminable journey just completed fell away as he watched the great red walls of the fortress move closer, and every muscle, sinew, and vein in his body were alerted to the moment. He had every reason to believe he was about to see Krystyna.

The wagons were being systematically assembled in the large, irregularly shaped courtyard by the time Aleksy directed Miracle through the entry arch.

He remained mounted, surveying the commotion. While the wounded were being helped to what seemed to be several offices in the arcaded ground level, dozens upon dozens of men in royal livery were attending to the wagons containing the valuables. No time was being lost in cataloging and conveying the Turkish treasure to another ground level room that Aleksy guessed was the Crown Treasury. Swifter than thought, his hand moved to the sheath at his waist that housed the ruby-encrusted dagger. He took care to make certain that it was concealed by his *żupan*. What if one of the officials were to question him about it? He had nothing from the king to prove it had been a gift. And other than the bejeweled dagger and the monarch's unwritten promise of a small estate, he arrived in Kraków destitute.

His eyes moved upward now to the beautiful arcaded galleries of the second and third levels. It was this third level, this uppermost floor, with its soaring height under a steep, hipped roof that drew his attention now, not for its architecture, but for the activity there. Women, in a colorful profusion of finery, like tropical birds vibrant even at twilight, were filing out of the private royal rooms there, coming at once to the arcade railing, their faces alight with curiosity. Aleksy looked from face to face, searching.

And then he spied her. She was dressed in cornflower blue, her beautifully plaited hair piled high and decorated with a matching ribbon of the same hue. Almost simultaneously, Krystyna saw him and her hand gave a little wave, then it went to her cheek as if in disbelief. She immediately pivoted and made for the stairwell. A middle-aged woman dressed in brown silk—certainly not the queen Aleksy had seen on the road to Vienna—turned toward the retreating figure and called out something, her face grim in the gloaming. Clearly she meant to stop Krystyna—to no avail.

Aleksy dismounted and had only time to secure Miracle to a ring on an arcade column before she stood before him, a vivid blue figure perfectly framed by the arch. "Alek," she said, her voice nearly lost amidst the tumult in the courtyard. The moment lengthened as he stared, stricken silent. She was in his arms then. He would not recall later which of them had bridged the few paces between them, but he would remember how her body trembled next to his, her heart beating fast, her breath at his neck—and how time was held suspended. There was no kiss; the embrace was all.

Finally, gently, he took her upper arms and held her at arms' length. Tears were brimming hot in his eyes, but words were scarce. "Krysia," he said. He had imagined this moment every night of the trek back from Vienna.

"You're here—but you were wounded."

"I'm in one piece," he said, pulling a smile and wiping at the tail of his right eye. "It was a little cut to my thigh. It's healing nicely now."

"Thank God!—And you know about the king's request of—"

"The pope?" Aleksy asked. "Yes!"

"Isn't it wonderful?"

Another voice, sharp and unfriendly: "Unlike your decorum!"

Aleksy's eyes shifted right to see that the woman in brown was at

Krystyna's side, her hands capably dislodging Krystyna from his embrace. "You must come back, Krystyna."

Krystyna shook herself free. The woman was more than an annoyance. "Madame Heloise, this is Aleksy Gazdecki."

The woman shot Aleksy a cursory glance, her scowl deepening. "I have my orders. The queen said you are to wait."

"Wait and wait and wait, I know."

"Now, come away."

"Wait for what?" Aleksy interjected although he thought he knew the answer.

"For the letter from Pope Innocent XI," Krystyna said. "It's due any day."

"And until then," the woman said, "you have been remanded into my care."

"Just a few minutes, Madame. Please, just five—what could that hurt?"

"You, if you know what's good for you!" The woman tugged at Krystyna.

"I do know what's good for me!" Krystyna cried, pulling back.

"And what is that?" came another voice.

So focused had Aleksy been on the little drama that he hadn't noticed a stir of softened voices and movement among those nearby. He looked up to see the dark-haired woman who had stood beside the king on the road to Vienna. He blinked in wonder at Maria Casimire Sobieska, Queen of Poland.

He wore no hat to doff, but he bowed now, following suit to everyone who had taken notice of the queen.

The queen's hooded eyes were assessing him. "So this is the young hero, yes? A bit dirtied from the road, I see, but here in any case."

"My apologies, Your Majesty."

She raised her hand. "Not necessary, young man. You will have what befits the king's remembrance—and mine—for Fanfan."

Aleksy became confused. "For—"

"Fanfan. Oh, it's a silly name. I told Jan—the king—as much, but it's what he calls Prince Jakub—Fanfan." She smiled. "We are grateful, Aleksy."

Aleksy could only nod.

"Now, the letter we are all waiting for has yet to arrive, so until then Krystyna is to be chary with her presence. I'm certain you understand."

Aleksy nodded although he did not understand.

"Krystyna, you may have two minutes. We will wait for you by the stairwell. Just two minutes or I will send the guards. Do you understand?"

Krystyna gave a hesitant nod.

"Goodbye for now, Aleksy," the queen said and turned before Aleksy had finished his bow. "Come, Hellie," she said.

Her face a mask, the woman followed in the wake of the queen.

"Chary," Krystyna said, "it means stingy—stingy with my presence."

"I see."

Krystyna let out with a sigh. "Sweet Jezus and Maryja! You've only just arrived and we must part. Now, don't look so sad, Alek! The letter will arrive soon—perhaps even tomorrow!"

Aleksy was crestfallen. What was he to do now? He hadn't thought beyond the reunion with Krystyna. Did he expect a storybook ending, one in which they were married immediately and set on their way to his yet-to-be-seen estate?

"It's a temporary disappointment," Krystyna said, as if reading his mind. She took his hands in hers, her emerald eyes locking onto his.

"How am I to know when the letter comes?"

"I'll send word immediately. Where are you staying?"

He had no place to stay, no money for a room even. He drew himself up. He could not tell her that. "I—I will be near the river, in the area where the troops assembled before leaving. Send for me there. If I'm not there, have someone ask the old gypsy who has a wagon and tent at the water's edge. I'll keep her informed."

"A gypsy?" Krystyna's eyes widened.

Aleksy nodded. "A long story—for another time."

Krystyna flashed a smile, one that kept him rooted to the spot. "I must go now. The queen has been good to me."

"And the other one?"

"Madame Heloise? She's Mistress of the Robes and mean enough to steal the złotys from a dead man's eyes."

Krystyna and Aleksy shared a laugh. She took a step toward him now and they embraced. He held her tightly but could not fight off the sudden dread he was experiencing. Somehow, he felt things were amiss, that things were not about to go right for them. What if Fabian Nardolski showed up and claimed her? And what if Roman arrived? Even with an annulment of the Nardloski ceremony, he would not allow his sister's wedding to a Tatar to go forward. Without the king present, how would the queen handle the situation?

"It's time," Krystyna was saying. She withdrew from him. "I must go."

He nodded and forced a smile.

And then she was moving down the arcade, the swaying blue dress fairly floating away from him. *Is this to be the way of it always?*

Aleksy directed Miracle down to the great open space by the river. It was not even two months but seemed a lifetime ago that the coalescing troops sat in camp awaiting the king's arrival from Warsaw so that they could proceed to Vienna. He felt the pace of his heart quicken now as he prayed that he could locate the old gypsy woman. He had paid her four złotys: two to learn if he would ever become a soldier; two to learn what might become of his love for Krystyna. She had predicted he would see action—and he had. As for Krystyna, the old woman had been less than revealing, warning him that he would have many working against him. It did not bode well. What might she say today? But today he had no money at all. He cursed himself. The ruby dagger was treasure enough, but why hadn't he thought to ask someone for money? He should have sold the damn thing.

Aleksy drew reins. The field before him was empty except for the scattering of a few campsites of travelers or homeless peasants. His heart paused. What if she isn't here, he thought, his fear rising not from anything that she might tell him, but from the knowledge that he had told Krystyna to contact him through her. What had possessed him? And the gypsy might very well have moved on to a more populated place. What money was to be made in this open space now?

And then he saw her box-like and weathered wooden wagon. He sent Miracle into a trot, the hooves beating in time—so it seemed—to his heart.

In but minutes he dismounted and walked his horse toward the gypsy who sat on a wooden stool in a well-worn gray dress and a new-looking scarlet scarf that attempted to hold captive her wild white hair. Smoking a pipe, she watched him approach.

"You've become a soldier, I see," she said. The bowl of the pipe glowed red as she drew on the bit.

"A soldier of sorts," Aleksy said, surprised that she remembered him.

"You took your chances with a lance?"

"I did."

"I expected as much." She stood, imbibed a final time, released the smoke and struck the pipe against her wagon to dispel the remnants of ill-smelling herbs. She smiled then, revealing her few teeth. "You've come about your other wish."

Her statement brought him up short. How was it that the old crone could see into his mind? "I have no money," he said.

"Ah, a charity case. Tell me—?" She paused.

"Aleksy."

"Tell me, Aleksy. Did you kill Turks?"

"I did."

"Many?"

Aleksy nodded.

"The Turks have taken much from my family," the gypsy said, a tremble in her voice. "Land, my home in Hungary… and many lives. Poland has been good to me. And also to you, a Tatar?"

"Yes."

"Come sit on the ground near me." For the first time, there was a hint of a smile.

Párkány, Hungary

It was night. While Idzi lay sleeping in the tent, Roman sat cross-legged on the ground nearby, his mind laden with thought. The second engagement with the young pasha, Kara Mehmed, played out very differently on 9 October than it had two days previously. The combined forces of the Poles at nine thousand and the Imperial troops at nearly seventeen thousand put the odds soundly in their favor over the pasha's eight or nine thousand. When Kara Mehmed saw the number of Christians, he could only have figured his best chance lay in an attack. Working to his distinct disadvantage was the fact that he chose to meet the Austrian-Polish forces with a line of hills on his right, the River Gran to his rear, and the bridge over the River Danube the only way to withdraw. His attacking forces were repelled and, in turn, set upon by the allies. Their retreat was chaotic, made more so when the pontoon bridge collapsed, sending hundreds into the river and trapping thousands on the wrong side of the river.

The Christian victory seemed pre-ordained, and although Roman acquitted himself well, killing a score of Sipâhi and Janissaries, it was not the day's triumph that he was savoring; rather, it was the memory of the ignominious defeat on Sunday that plagued him.

King Sobieski's impulse to attack without waiting for the Imperial troops and the rest of the Polish forces had cost a thousand Polish lives. It would have cost the king his life, too, had it not been for Roman and five others who marshalled him to safety. Afterwards the king faced a crisis: a significant number of his men rebelled, demanding to go home or seek winter quarters, rather than risk a second encounter. Charles of Lorraine saved the day by calling attention to the fact that this time the numbers greatly favored the allies. The would-be rebels bowed to the king's orders and stayed to fight. The king, however, also acquiesced in that he turned over command to Charles, whose forces took the lead. It was the king's personal price of redemption, Roman thought. He wondered whether it was at all voluntary.

Roman was drawn from his despondency by the simultaneous approach of boot steps and a familiar voice.

"They say the king has written to Marysieńka calling today's victory greater than that of Vienna."

"Has he, indeed?" Roman asked his father, jumping to greet him. "Thank God, you're all right."

"And you, son," he said, pulling Roman to him in an embrace. "Wounds?"

"None to speak of. It's the good that die young." The memory of Marek's sacrifice struck him before the words were even finished. Even in the campfire light he could see the hurt flicker across his father's face. He could think of nothing to repair the faux pas.

Mercifully, his father picked up his original thread of conversation. "It does seem an exaggeration, the king's boast."

Roman offered his father a little makeshift folding stool, then sat upon the ground. "He's hoping the news will offset what occurred on Sunday."

"When he nearly met his maker? A very close call, the way it was described to me... You were one of the six, I heard."

"From him?"

"No—others."

Roman grunted and looked away. He could feel his father's eyes assessing him.

"Roman, has the king not acknowledged your—service?"

"No," Roman growled.

"He will, I'm certain."

"He's had two days, Papa." Roman jumped up, facing away from his father. "I fended off an attacker as we made the escape. I saved his life, for Chrystus's sake!"

"I see."

"Oh, I'm not looking for some reward—or—"

"The kind of recognition he gave Aleksy?"

"That filthy Tatar! No—just a word would have been enough. Dogs' blood!"

"The man's not without hubris, Roman. I think it goes with being a king."

"And the man's alive because of me!"

"I'm proud of you, Romek. You have no idea how proud." He paused. "Now, tomorrow I plan to ask permission to go to Kraków."

"From him?" Roman cried, pivoting back toward his father, the veins at his neck suddenly pulsing.

"Of course."

"You're not to say a word, do you hear? Not a word, Papa!"

His father stared. "If that is your wish."

"It is—swear you will say nothing of Sunday." Roman thought that he might indeed say something out of regret for not having recommended his sons for the elite *Kwarciani* corps.

His father nodded. "As you say, son."

Roman felt the blood to his face ebb. And then the sense of his father's request of the king came home to him and it flared again. "Kraków! You mean to stop the devil from marrying Krystyna. By God, I'll go with you!"

"I want you to go, but—"

"But what? If the king says no, I'll go anyway!"

"That's not it, Roman. I'm not going to stop the marriage. And neither are you."

"You're going to allow Krysia to marry the Tatar?"

"I am."

Roman stood silent. How was this possible?

"It's what she wants, Roman."

"She doesn't know what she wants... What about Fabian? He's here someplace, isn't he? Isn't he going to fight for her?"

"He is here. I saw him not an hour ago. He's got a nasty shoulder wound. And," his father said, shaking his head, "he's not going to go against the king and Pope Innocent. It seems the king appeased him with the hint of some promotion after all this is over. I suspect he will get the royal nod for a seat in the Sejm. That's been his goal."

"The dog! A cholera on him!"

"Best to find out about his character now."

"To hell with him! Lord Father, we can't allow Krysia to do this!"

"She loves him—she's gone to great lengths to prove it to me. Listen, Roman, I was not much older when I fell in love the first time."

This declaration caught Roman by surprise. "Before Mother?"

"Yes, before. It can be real."

"What happened?"

"I was not a fit candidate—according to her parents. And she—she was an obedient daughter."

"That's not like this, Papa. The Tatar will ruin her life. If we stop her, she'll get over it. Do you really want Tatar grandchildren? What of mother? Surely she is not of the same mind?"

"No, she is not. I guess too many years have passed for her to remember what it was to be young and how she must have loved her first husband—your father. No, Roman, she and I are not in agreement. She will not be at the wedding, or so she writes."

"Neither will I, Father." Roman turned and spat upon the ground, then turned back. "The only reason I would attend would be to call the devil out to duel—or kill him outright in the church."

Lord Halicki stood abruptly, knocking the stool over. "You will not!"

"And why not? He may be a master archer, but he can't *duel* with a longbow, now can he?"

"Nonsense! You're to stay here with the king, then. I won't hear any more of this kind of talk."

"And I won't have a Tatar as a brother-in-law—I won't! I'll die first!"

"Listen to me, Roman! I told you once Aleksy was to have been raised as your brother."

"You did," Roman snarled. "And does the Tatar know of your promise to the chieftain?"

"He did not—until I intervened in the elopement plans in Kraków. I told him then."

"I see… so he must consider himself a privileged person?"

"You mean like us? No, I don't think so." Lord Halicki's eyes held Roman's. "But *I* consider him as privileged as you and Krystyna."

Roman's head swam with confusion and anger. "What?"

"I did Aleksy a terrible disservice in not being true to my oath. He should have been raised as brother to you and to Marek and to Krystyna."

"I thank God that Mother didn't allow him in our home."

"And I ask God to forgive me."

Roman spat again. "So he thinks he has found a way into our home through Krystyna—Chrystus Jezus!"

His father's expression became screwed into one as stern as Roman had ever seen. "You will accept this, Romek," he said.

Roman saw tears at the tails of his father's eyes. There was no changing his mind, and so he let the subject drop. After some minutes of uneasy silence, they sat again, and they discussed the campaign against the Turks. It had not ended with Vienna or the recent victory at Párkány. The task was not finished. King Sobieski was determined to thoroughly rout the Turks. No battle would match the magnitude of the Vienna clash, but father and son were in agreement on this one point at least: more battles were to be had.

His father hugged him before leaving, but Roman stood like stone, unwilling and unable to respond. After some moments, his father held him at arms' length. "You'll come to accept this," he said, "you must. She is your sister and she deserves to be happy."

Roman was left standing alone, as if paralyzed, reflecting on his father's words and intention to allow the marriage to occur, his anger refueling and building within him like the promise of a great storm. "Dogs' blood!" he cried aloud. *Damn you, Father! And damn you to hell, Aleksy Gazdecki!* He cursed his brother Marek's absence. He cursed his father's oath and created his own as he stared up at the moon—half-hidden behind a screen of feathery clouds—vowing to die before he would see Krystyna marry the dark-skinned Tatar.

"Dogs' blood!" he cried again, kicking out at the earth, sending up dust and pebbles.

Suddenly he heard a noise behind him. He whipped around, blood pumping, his hand going for his dagger, ready to strike.

Without any need to stoop, Idzi was just exiting the tent. He looked up at Roman, his sharp blue eyes registering surprise to see the poised dagger, but fearless just the same. "If you must kill me, aim true, milord," Idzi said. "I don't want to linger."

The dwarf's drollness often entertained Roman—but not today. He had forgotten he was sleeping in the tent. "Don't tempt me. Tell me, what did you hear?"

Idzi stared for a moment, considering his response, then said, "Between you and your father?"

Roman realized at once that he had heard everything. He drew himself up as if to make a display of looking down at Idzi. "You're to keep your mouth shut, do you hear?"

"I do," Idzi said, unblinking. "I wish to go, too, Lord Roman."

"What?"

"I wish to go—with your father."

"What, so you can attend the ceremony? So you can stand witness to your Tatar friend's marriage?"

Idzi's steady gaze was his answer.

"You can forget that. The king has other battles to fight until the Turks are run out of Hungary altogether."

"You can manage for a short while, Lord Roman. I'll return."

"A short while!" Roman let out a great guffaw. "You should be the king's clown."

Idzi weathered the insult.

"No, my little dwarf-friend, you'll not be going anywhere."

"You've told me I'm of no use to you."

"It's slight enough, I'll agree to that, but you're all I have, what with the dark devil gone off."

Idzi stepped closer to Roman. "Your father thinks you're bitter that the king hasn't shown you any kindness since you helped him escape a bad situation."

"A bad situation?" Roman snarled. "Death himself on a pale horse was all but upon him!" He drew in a long breath. "I don't want anything from the king!"

"Ah, it seems to me, Lord Roman, that you have something in common with the dark devil."

Roman felt his spine stiffen. "What did you say, dwarf?"

"That Aleksy did more than save Prince Jakub."

"Indeed?"

"And like you, he received no thanks."

Roman felt a strange tightness somewhere about his belly. "Go to bed, Idzi. We're done for the night. You shouldn't believe any rubbish the Tatar tells you."

"I was there, Lord Roman."

"What?—Where?"

"On a hill overlooking the field where you were bent over your dead brother."

"You lie."

Idzi shook his head. "You were too filled with grief to notice the Turk coming at you."

"I saw him. I was just getting up to engage him."

"Too slowly, milord, too slowly. An arrow to the Turk's heart saved you."

"You *were* there?"

Idzi nodded. "He wore the pointed helmet of a Sipâhi warrior and he had the advantage."

"So what? Someone's arrow got in his way. I remember little of the battle. Luck was with me then—and other times, too. That's the way of it."

"Did you not see the ash arrow and gray goose-feathers?"

"I did not." Roman closed his eyes. Truth was there behind the closed lids. He *had* seen the familiar feathered shaft. He had. But he did not turn to see the direction from which it came. Such was his choice, and in the weeks since, he was able to distance himself from that day, recalling only the loss of his brother. Not the person who had saved his own life. Not…

He opened his eyes after a time to see that Idzi had walked over to the fire, passing him by. The dwarf was staring at him with round, knowing eyes. "I see that you do remember."

Roman felt his jaw tighten, his teeth cutting into his lower lip. Idzi's presumption galled him, as did his nerve and sense of righteousness. He spoke now through clenched teeth. "Know your place, Idzi. Now, go to bed. And take your pallet outside the tent. Tomorrow we talk."

It was the sort of intense order that the retainer knew not to disobey. Idzi seemed to assess the situation and words died in his throat. He nodded and started to retrace some twenty paces to the tent.

As Idzi passed, Roman stretched out his leg, sending him sprawling.

Roman turned at once and walked out into a moonlit vineyard well-trampled by horses and men. At the end of a row of crushed vines he came to a large rock and sat down. He could hear the spirited voices of soldiers at their campfires telling their stories of war.

War, he thought. There were those who hated it and could not wait to go home and there were those who adapted well to it and were ready for the next battle, the next charge, the next kill. He belonged to the latter group. Oh, he had been confident that he would be a good soldier, but he had not expected the rush of blood that pulsed through his veins and made every part of him feel alive when the hussars formed up and the command was given: "Lower your lances!"

He fought for a Christian Europe and for king and country, as well as for family, but he had come to learn this about himself: he fought for the love of fighting. His only regret was allowing Marek to volunteer for the first and most dangerous of sorties. He blamed himself for not disobeying his father's request that they would not both volunteer for such a suicidal mission.

He thought of Marek lying there, mortally wounded. The scene replayed in his head as it never had before: the white and lifeless face against the brown earth and the blood, the red Halicki blood, darkening and seeping into a field far from home. Idzi had seen through his lie. Yes, he *had* seen and recognized the arrow that killed the Turk that day, as effectively as the one that had stopped the heart of a rabbit a Tatar had poached on Mount Halicz. He spoke of luck to Idzi. A strange thing, luck, he thought. He had ordered Ludwik to accompany Marek and kept Aleksy behind so that he could put an end to the boy once the battle commenced. His stomach contracted. Had Aleksy gone, he might very well have protected Marek. Instead, Marek was gone, buried deep at Vienna, and he was alive, saved from certain death by the Tatar, Aleksy Gazdecki.

Luck! Aleksy was off to Kraków to marry Krystyna. Roman felt his pulse rush in ways far different from those at the front lines of battle.

Kraków, he thought, and a marriage performed under the auspices of the King and Queen of the Commonwealth. He spat and cursed.

What was there to be done?

THIRTY-SIX

Kraków

Queen Maria Casimire had forbidden Krystyna to leave the castle. *For your own benefit* she was told in the most solicitous way by Madame Heloise. And so the days ticked by in anxious anticipation of a document—the letter from Pope Innocent XI. The queen and her ladies at court assumed that the marriage to Fabian Nardolski would be annulled, given the circumstances: namely, that a proxy wedding had been imposed upon the bride, that consummation had not taken place—and most importantly, that the Pontiff was likely to look favorably upon any request from the king who had successfully done his bidding. How could he do otherwise? After all, people were already calling Pope Innocent XI the "Savior of Europe" for having initiated the Holy League—with King Jan III Sobieski at its head—that was seeing even now to the expulsion of infidels from Christian Europe.

Days went by. Krystyna wondered about Aleksy. Was he as impatient as she? How was he to be informed once the document arrived? Was a messenger to take it to him? She longed to be the one to tell him that their path had been cleared, that they were free to marry. What a blessed day it would be. Would the queen allow her—chaperoned, of course—to find this gypsy he had spoken of? To tell him face to face that they were to forge a life together?

Aleksy became the procurer of fish and game for the gypsy and for a number of others—mostly women with children and old men—who lived in shabby tents and lean-to's in the fields trampled and ruined by the king's coalescing army just months earlier. The gypsy provided him with a net and other fishing gear, and he had his bow. It was primarily small game he hunted, for he had to carry it back to the makeshift settlement by himself, but he came to enjoy once again losing himself in the hunt. He considered himself blessed in that the concentration it took to use the bow effectively blocked out all other thoughts and anxiety. Days passed and no word came from the castle situated in the fortress towering above, no message from Krystyna.

The gypsy herself had been a blessing. Among a huge pile of belongings left behind by the soldiers was a serviceable tent that she gave over for his use. Aleksy had slept in the open that first night and in the morning busied himself with successfully erecting what would be his shelter for more days and nights than he had imagined.

It was on that first morning when he arose from his blanket on the hard earth and turned to see the woman climbing down from her wooden wagon that he realized—when he went to address her—that he didn't know her name. She had simply been "the gypsy" to him in his mind and when speaking to others of her. It struck him now how some people back in Halicz had called him "the Tatar." They had this in common. Did she find it hurtful to be identified merely by her appearance, her heritage, in the way so many had identified him?

"I don't know your name," he admitted to her. Had he told her his name when they first met? He couldn't remember. In any event, he felt oddly shamefaced in having to ask her.

She smiled, as if to say, *so few ask me my name*. "Some call me "Gypsy." It is a name, but it is not my name." She shrugged and he saw a history of sadness in the gesture.

"And yours?" he asked.

"I am Nadya."

"Nadya," Aleksy repeated. "I am Aleksy."

"I know. If you get the fire lit, Aleksy, I'll heat up some chicory for us."

Aleksy nodded. Had he told her his name at some point? He must have done so.

"My mother told me it's a Ruski name," she called out as she retreated to the wagon.

"It's a lovely name," Aleksy pronounced.

The old woman turned and gifted him with a grin. "Hope," she said. "Nadya means *hope*."

An insistent knocking brought Krystyna from her dreams. She sat up at the side of the bed and called, *"Entrez-vous."*

Krystyna was relieved to see that it was not Heloise or one of the queen's French ladies-in-waiting; rather it was the chambermaid Berta, a middle-aged, plump Pole who tended the fire in the tiled fireplace. "Oh, Lady Krystyna, you better be getting dressed. The queen sent me to bring you to her."

"Really? How early is it? Why, the sun's not even come up yet."

"It is early. No later than four, I would hazard. Why, the queen's ladies are still abed."

"What did the queen say to you?"

"Nothing, other than to get you moving." Berta started to cross the room to the fireplace. "But there was some kind of hubbub in the courtyard not long before, someone arriving, I spect. Maybe news from Hungary."

"Or Rome." Krystyna flew out of bed. "Berta, help me dress at once."

The woman's eyelids flew back, accentuating the roundness of her face. "Oh, Madame, I'm not the one. You need a proper lady's maid."

"Never mind that. Just get me out of this nightdress and into that blue day dress."

The queen's expression was opaque as Krystyna entered her anteroom. She was sitting at a small desk cluttered with papers but stood now and beckoned Krystyna with a motion and a little smile.

Krystyna stepped forward and was directed to sit. By the time the queen seated herself opposite, the smile had broken.

"I am afraid, Krystyna, that we have been hasty in our evaluation."

"Evaluation?"

The queen nodded. "Of Pope Innocent XI."

Krystyna's heart began to race.

"You see," the queen continued, "in the seven years of his pontificate, he's been like a hermit in that he embraces a simple and austere lifestyle.

He rejected the luxurious apartment of his predecessors for the most basic apartment in the Vatican, and he wears cassocks until they are threadbare and falling apart. In his fastidiousness to restore piety to the Vatican he resists even a scent of nepotism. Why, he even informed a nephew—a cleric—that he is to expect no promotion within the Church."

"He would not sign an annulment?" Krystyna heard herself ask. The words were hers, but she felt oddly removed from them.

"He would not."

Krystyna paused to let the news sink in. "But—why? This isn't nepotism."

"Oh, he told us why at great length. The papers are on my desk. Sweet Maryja, his explanation is as long as a papal encyclical."

Beads that had been forming in Krystyna's eyes began to spill now.

"Oh, he went on and on about the sanctity of marriage, how the vows are not to be broken in any circumstance, even if the union has not been consummated. I'm certain his scribe must have had a sore hand by the end of it. And at its conclusion, I'm sad to say, Krystyna, he did refuse and you are still seen in the eyes of the church as married to Fabian Nardolski."

Krystyna choked back a sob and sat back against the chair. "So the king's winning the war against the Turks made no impression—none?"

"Well, he was impressed and grateful as you would expect, as we all expected, the king especially. He went on for a page or two about that.... However, he chose to see the thanks he would 'rain down' on Poland and on my husband as a separate issue from the favor of an annulment of a sacred bond because of what he called 'a minor countess's wishes'."

"Then the marriage is to stand?" The words escaped her lips even though the question had already been answered.

"I'm afraid so, dearest. I pray it's for the best." She reached out and took Krystyna's hands in hers. "You and... the Tatar boy would have faced other obstacles."

Krystyna pulled free and stood, the room revolving about her. The queen's mouth continued in speech, but Krystyna had gone deaf. Later, sitting in her room as dusk fell, having sent away all nourishment, she would not recall leaving the queen's presence. Had she even curtsied?

What did it matter? *What does anything matter now*, she thought, *except for getting the news to Aleksy?* Until Fabian came to claim her, she was no more than a captive in the castle. And she was not about to allow

Madame Heloise to take the message, knowing the woman would gloat over her undoing.

And then she remembered Berta.

By the time Berta arrived the next morning to sweep out the ashes and place fresh wood in the grate, Krystyna had spent a day and a night searching for options and then writing and rewriting the note to Aleksy, destroying two because the paper was stained with tears. The beeswax candles that kept the night at bay had guttered by the time she finished.

Berta had seen the gypsy's wagon down by the river and agreed to take the message. When Krystyna attempted to give her two złotys for the errand, the woman declined and Krystyna had to drop the coins into her apron pocket and scoot her out the door.

Aleksy was at the river fishing with a net a short distance down from the gypsy wagon when Nadya came to tell him a woman had come to see him.

A great rush of optimism took hold of him. "What does she look like?"

"A bit on the fat side, graying hair, round face."

His hopes did not fade. He was not expecting Krystyna herself to come tell him the pope's document had arrived. He waded ashore, dropped the net and hurried barefoot up the grassy slope.

He found her sitting on Nadya's stool just outside the wagon. The woman pulled herself up with surprising agility.

"You've come from Krysia—er, Lady Krystyna? Yes?"

The woman was eyeing him—from his hatless head to his worn clothes to his bare feet—with no little surprise. She was speechless.

"You've brought me news?" he persisted. "Are you not from the queen's service?"

"I am," she nodded, collecting herself. "Forgive me, you are Aleksy Gazdecki?"

"I am."

"I am Berta, milord. I've brought you this letter."

Aleksy took the proferred paper and broke the seal.

"My task is done," Berta said.

"No," Aleksy countered, "stay until I read it."

The woman nodded but remained standing. Aleksy read the letter, felt his heart drop a little with each line, allowed his hand to lose grasp of it, picked it up, read it again.

Nadya had come up from the river while he was reading and stood behind him. "It's not what you hoped, young Aleksy?"

"It's not," he said, turning toward her and drawing in a large breath. "The pope has denied the king his request. The marriage is a good one. I have no hope. None."

He looked to Berta now. "Did Krystyna give you any spoken message?"

The woman shook her head, her eyes widened by Aleksy's reaction.

"What else does she write, Aleksy?" Nadya asked.

"She says," he blurted, "that we should run away, that she will slip out of the cathedral on Sunday next after the nine o'clock Mass."

"And then what?" Nadya asked.

Aleksy shrugged. "She's not thinking clearly. There's no place we could go. Her family and the man she married by proxy will not let this go. We can't just disappear into the forest."

"Indeed," Berta said.

Both Aleksy and Nadya turned to the servant woman, who looked aghast at what she was hearing. It was obvious she had no idea of the letter's contents. "I should go," Berta said.

"Stay," Nadya said in a gravelly, authoritative voice.

"I won't tell anyone," Berta said, growing more uncomfortable by the moment.

"It's not that," Nadya said. "What was the woman's state, her emotions, when she sent you out on this errand?"

"She had been crying and looked tired, she did. Like her ladyship hadn't slept."

"She doesn't know anything," Aleksy said. "There's no point in questioning her."

Nadya ignored him, addressing Berta. "Did she hand you this message herself—from her hand to yours? Speak up!"

"Um—yes, that she did."

"Give me your hand."

"What?"

"Give me your hand."

The woman reluctantly obeyed.

"Nadya," Aleksy pressed, "what do you think you are doing?"

"Shush, Aleksy, now hand me the letter. In my other hand."

Aleksy obeyed.

Nadya stood there, eyes tightly shut, holding onto the servant with one hand, the letter in the other. Aleksy looked to Berta's face and had no doubt that her blank, incredulous expression was mirroring his own.

What seemed like two or three minutes went by. Dusk was descending fast.

Nadya's eyes opened slowly, like twin curtains.

"What did you hope to discover?" he asked, convinced the effort had been in vain.

"I did not know, young Aleksy. Certainly not what I learned. Her love for you is true."

"I knew that. You needn't have gone into a trance to learn that."

Nadya glanced furtively at Berta, then drew Aleksy several steps away, out of earshot of the servant. "That's not what I learned," she whispered.

"Then—what?"

Nadya's eyes came up and held Aleksy's. "The young woman is not married."

"What? I told you it was a proxy marriage," Aleksy said in a low hissing voice. "You don't understand. Our church allows it. She was married to Lord Fabian Nardolski by proxy."

Nadya shook her head. "Not a proxy wedding. It was sham marriage. Deception was involved. Terrible deception at the ceremony. Wicked!"

Aleksy stared at the gypsy for several heartbeats. "Are you saying she is not married?"

Nadya nodded. "She is not."

He would question her powers later, but for now there was something in her conviction and aura that made him believe her.

He pivoted and went to Berta. "I know you don't have time to wait for a written message, but please bring my words to Lady Krystyna. Will you?"

"Yes."

"You promise?"

"I do."

"Then tell Lady Krystyna I will meet her at the cathedral as she asked. It is only to talk. During Communion time she is to find me in the crypt of St. Leonard."

The woman's eyes bulged. "The crypt?" she mumbled, trembling slightly.

"Yes. The entrance is on the left side of the nave not far from the entrance. And she is not to do anything. Is that clear?"

"Yes, in the crypt at Communion time."

"And she is not to follow through on any plans she might have."

"Yes, only to talk, milord."

Aleksy waited in the shadows of a pillar near the entrance. The cathedral was packed to capacity. It had been filled with thankful, prayerful citizens, elbow to elbow, he was told, for every ceremony since word of the victory at Vienna had come back to Kraków. It was nearly nine o'clock; he had taken up his station well before so that he could observe the crowd arrive. Krystyna had yet to appear.

The past two days had gone by slowly, Aleksy's thoughts in ferment. He had time to play out in his mind the scene with Berta and Nadya. Doubts were abundant. He had heard of the magical powers of gypsy women, and Nadya's deductions at their first meeting had been eerily true. But was this notion that Krystyna's marriage was not a marriage true? How were they to find out?

He saw Father Franciszek coming down the main aisle now and froze, bile rising from his midsection. He had not seen him since the day Lord Halicki showed up in the rectory instead of the priest, a day of heartbreak and humiliation.

Aleksy moved behind the column so that he would not be seen as the prelate passed. When Father Franciszek did not make his way past, Aleksy peeked around to see that he had entered one of the nearby side chapels where he was preparing to say Mass. Preparations were being made at the main altar, as well, so he suspected that someone of higher rank, a bishop or cardinal, would celebrate there.

He turned back now to watch the flow of the crowd through the main entrance, worrying that the distraction with the priest might have caused him to miss seeing Krystyna. Ten minutes passed and the number of arriving worshippers dwindled. Suddenly, he caught sight of her entering amidst a crush of ladies-in-waiting and the queen herself. He was certain she glimpsed him as they processed up the aisle, but one of the women whispered to her, drawing her attention away. He prayed that the servant had gotten the message right about the crypt.

A few minutes later, the celebrant, along with a half of a dozen clergy and attendants, came from the sacristy and slowly processed toward the front altar. Aleksy recalled Marek's pointing the cleric out in the square once in what seemed a lifetime ago: it was the Bishop of Kraków, Jan Małachowski. Aleksy judged him to be sixty although his hair had not whitened yet. He had an unassuming sort of face, but his gait and bearing reflected his noble background. Marek had said his nephew was Governor of Poznań.

The Mass began and Aleksy managed to find a spot in the shadow of another pillar, well out of Father Franciszek's sightline. Soon the strong fragrance of incense—cedar-based, he thought—wafted throughout the cathedral, chafing his nose and throat. The bishop seemed to be in no hurry. The Mass dragged on, the bishop moving so slowly, as if its end would be his end.

Holy Communion time came. Aleksy drew in breath, his breath a prayer, one that would bring Krystyna to their rendezvous in the crypt of St. Leonard. He moved quickly to the cellar entrance and descended the stone steps.

It was musty and dark, but a few candles had been lighted near the St. Leonard tomb. Not the best meeting place, he thought, laughing to himself as he remembered how Berta had gone wide-eyed at the notion.

Time seemed to expand. Had Krystyna not been able to leave the others? What if she could not meet him? When would they have a chance again? He was certain he would not be welcome at the castle.

It was then that he heard her soft slippers moving down the steps.

Krystyna was in his arms then and they kissed. They held each other tightly, clinging as if they might never do so again. Then Aleksy held her at arms' length. "Even in this weak light, Krysia, you are so beautiful."

"Perhaps it is *because* of the weak light," she said, tossing off the little laugh he had so missed. "I don't have much time, Alek. I'm sure to be missed.—Now, why didn't you want me to make preparations—"

"Listen to me, Krystyna. I've learned that your marriage may not be valid."

"From your mouth to God's ear." She paused but a moment. "No, I'm afraid it is valid. Even the pope—"

"Tell me, was the queen involved in the arrangements?"

"No, she had locked herself away in her chapel. She believed the fighting at Vienna was occurring at that very moment."

"So who planned it?"

"My mother and Fabian's mother, Lady Nardolska."

"How badly did they wish for the marriage to take place?"

"Speaking for my mother, very badly. She saw the marriage as a rise in fortune for the whole family."

"And a way to keep me at a distance for good?"

Krystyna nodded. "They said you had died."

"What about the banns?"

"They said the bishop had given us a dispensation. Because of the impending battle."

"So there were none?—Who officiated?"

"Why are you asking these things? Who have you been talking to?"

"Who officiated, Krystyna?" Aleksy persisted. "Tell me!"

"Father Franciszek."

"From here—at the cathedral?"

"Yes, so he said. Aleksy, who is it that gave you these doubts? Berta went on and on about the gypsy. Was it she?"

Aleksy felt his face flush and wondered if it was visible in the dim and flickering candlelight. He was embarrassed to admit he had taken Nadya's words seriously. What could she know? Even though Father Franciszek had—unwittingly or not—been involved in the scuttling of his elopement plans, Aleksy had no cause to think the proxy ceremony performed by the priest was anything other than valid and ironclad. He sensed tears in the tails of his eyes. His arms dropped to his side, defeated. Nadya was wrong.

"Listen, Alek, I ran away once to follow you—and I'll do it again."

"No, you won't. What kind of a life would we have? I won't allow it. And you know as well as I that they would come for you."

They went silent now, realizing how very still it had become upstairs. The Communion chant and the shuffling of feet on marble had ceased. The Postcommunion prayers were being offered now.

"You must go now, Krysia."

"When am I to see you again?"

"I don't think that would be a good idea. You were right that day on Grodzka Street. We should have parted then. You have a different path."

"Don't say that, Aleksy." Her eyes streamed tears. "Don't say that."

"Go up," he said, his voice breaking.

"No."

Knowing how willful she was, he took hold of her upper arm and ushered her up the darkened stairwell.

The bishop was giving the people his final blessing. Aleksy meant not to say a word when they emerged from the crypt, but at that very moment he noticed Father Franciszek across the way. He had finished his Mass and was just leaving the side chapel.

A dormant hatred suddenly rose up in Aleksy. "There's our unsuspecting culprit," he said in a hiss.

"What?—Who?"

"There—just leaving that chapel. The prelate your brothers lured away from the rectory." Aleksy turned to Krystyna to make certain she was focusing on the priest.

She was. "Who is it?" she asked.

"Father Franciszek," he whispered. He could see the queen and her ladies recessing down the aisle now. He needed to send her off to them at once—before they were discovered.

Krystyna was taking a close inspection of the priest. "Sweet Jezus," she said.

"What?—What is it?"

"Aleksy, that is not Father Franciszek. That is not the man that performed the wedding."

One of the women in the queen's entourage sighted them now.

Aleksy wanted to tell her to go, but her statement had stolen the words. If Father Franciszek had not married them, then who had? *Is this the deception Nadya spoke of?*

Krystyna drew herself up now and her facial expression took on an understanding, as if she was taking the measure of something—or someone.

"Krystyna—"

She turned to him and spoke quickly. "Listen to me, Alek, go now. I will get to the bottom of this in short order. Let's pray that your gypsy is right. I'll send word."

Aleksy waited for the cathedral to clear out before making his exit. His intention was to talk to Father Franciszek. This was not the first time that he had thought about confronting him regarding the day Lord Halicki usurped the prelate's place in the rectory. He had not done so because he had no wish to revisit that memory. He had his doubts at first but, in time, came to accept as truth the priest's contention that the Halicki brothers had taken him away from the rectory on some ruse.

No—that was water already over the falls. What Aleksy wanted to know now was the identity of this *other* Father Franciszek. Where was he to be found?

Emerging from the cathedral into the light, Aleksy sighted the priest off to the side at his usual station, selling his little medals of Saint Stanislaus. He had a throng of well-wishers and people wishing to purchase holy keepsakes surrounding him, a crowd that seemed to grow as the time for the next service grew near.

Aleksy stood there a long while, impatiently awaiting his opportunity to speak to him alone, an opportunity that did not come, for the priest suddenly reentered the cathedral. Aleksy guessed he would say yet another Mass.

He turned and headed for the river.

Krystyna lay in wait. Berta knew to arrive at the queen's rooms at mid-morning when the ladies-in-waiting would be gathered in her reception room sewing, reading, and talking quietly. She would ask Madame Heloise to come to Krystyna's room. If she balked, Berta was to say Krystyna's health was at stake.

The day before, after she joined the queen and the other ladies as they left the cathedral, she spied the priest who Aleksy had identified as Father Franciszek. He was selling medals. Deliberately guiding the Mistress of the Robes over to the priest, Krystyna made a show of buying one.

"Wouldn't you like one?" Krystyna asked Madame Heloise.

"No!" the woman snapped. "Hurry or we won't be able to catch up to the others."

Krystyna had positioned herself between the priest and Madame Heloise so that she could surreptitiously observe her reactions. The woman was always in full control, of the servants, of the other ladies, and even seemed to have special latitude in the queen's presence. But there, at the front of the Wawel Cathedral, Krystyna took note of another side of her. She had paled considerably and a little tic manifested itself at the corner of her mouth. She shifted her weight from one foot to the other. The priest unnerved her—why?

Krystyna paid the priest and turned to Madame Heloise. "There—finished."

"Good—now come along."

Krystyna obeyed. She had the knowledge she wanted.

And so now she waited.

A knock came at the door. *"Entrez-vous!"* Krystyna called.

Berta pushed open the door and allowed Madame Heloise to enter. Having done so, she curtsied and backed out of the room.

The abrupt closing of the door caused Madame Heloise to look back, but it was the clicking of the lock that threw her off guard.

"What has that woman done?" she cried. With a quick, worried look at Krystyna, Madame Heloise rushed the few steps to the door and attempted to open it—unsuccessfully.

"She has locked the door," Krystyna said in a perfectly modulated tone. "I gave her the key. You needn't fret. She'll open it when I ask her to."

"Then do it now!" the woman ordered.

"No, we are going to have a little tête-à-tête, Heloise."

The Mistress of the Robes stiffened at Krystyna's familiarity. "About what?"

"About Father Franciszek."

Her eyes grew large and had she been wearing a cap, her forehead would have pushed it back an inch. She had no words.

Krystyna went to her dressing table, picked up the medal of Saint Stanislaus, pivoted back to Madame Heloise and held out the medal. "That nice priest who for a small pittance gave me this was named Father Franciszek."

The woman's eyes widened slightly. "Yes—so?"

"That is also the name of the priest that officiated at my wedding."

Madame Heloise's face flushed pink. "So there are two." She shrugged. "It's a common name."

"The priest with the medals lives in the cathedral rectory, as does the other Father Franciszek, or so he told me on the day of my wedding."

The Mistress of the Robes drew herself up, her face a mask. "Ask that woman to open the door."

"Not until I have some answers."

"Have her open it or I shall scream down this castle."

"Stone by stone, no doubt. But you should not be too hasty. You're privy to secrets, I'm certain, and I'll have them out before you leave this room."

"Is that a threat?"

"Take it as you wish. Who is this other Father Franciszek—this phantom priest?"

"Your mother and mother-in-law arranged the ceremony."

"And you played no part in this?"

"No."

"You're lying! Was he even a real priest?"

"Of course."

"Another lie! I can see it on your face. I was made to sign something—what was it? Was it a certificate of marriage?"

"You should talk to your mother about this."

"She's in Halicz. No, you're going to tell me. Who is this other Father Franciszek?"

"I will say no more to you." The woman turned for the door.

Krystyna grasped her by the shoulder and spun her around. "Did the queen play a part in this? She had been sequestered in her rooms and chapel, praying for her husband and the relief of Vienna. What did she know about *this*?"

"Nothing! She knew nothing."

"Ah, there we have it, don't we? It was a phony ceremony cooked up by you, my mother, and Lady Nardolska."

"Listen to me, Krystyna, they assured me they had your best interests at heart."

"But you never did, did you? You've treated me with disdain ever since that day in the carriage. Still, they must have paid you handsomely."

"Ask the woman to open the door now."

"After you tell me the man's true identity."

"I can't do that."

"You can and you will. You are the Mistress of the Robes, yes? The senior lady in Her Majesty's household? The faithful one to whom the queen seeks for company when her beloved is gone? Perhaps you even offer comfort and advice? Although she seems strong-willed—oh, and intolerant of deception, wouldn't you say? How will it go for you when she hears of this? When she hears that her husband has made a fool of himself by asking the pope himself for the annulment of a marriage that never was? There's no telling how she will react, is there, Heloise—or what is the pet name the queen has for you—Hellie?"

The woman was trembling and starting to sob. "You would tell her?"

Krystyna pulled the vanity stool over to her and handed her a cloth for her tears. "Sit, Hellie. We are nearly finished."

Before dawn even broke, Aleksy arrived at Market Square, where carts were being rolled in from adjoining streets and local vendors were starting to set up their wares in the areas surrounding the Sukiennice—the Cloth Hall—where a good deal of local and international trade was carried out.

The message from Krystyna had come by way of Berta the night before. It was cryptic, as if it was written quickly. "The marriage is no marriage. Look for a man named Feliks at the Sukiennice, a man who knows Latin and Russian. He is the key."

"A man named Feliks," Aleksy muttered to himself, entering the hall. It was a common enough name in Polish or Russian. There could be dozens of men in the mammoth hall with that name. Its extraordinarily long walkway featured dozens upon dozens of trading stalls on either side. The Cloth Hall was the bartering place for much more than textiles. The oddly aromatic mixture of the scents of leather and spices wafted through the open air building as he walked among Polish merchants who dealt in grain, livestock, fur, lead, iron, copper, marble, and salt from the nearby Wieliczka Mine, as well as a varied array of fabrics and textiles. Foreign purveyors were preparing their showcases of leather goods, tools, tapestries, wax, silk, wine, beer, and fragrantly exotic spices.

By the time Aleksy had made two full passes up and down the walkway, most of the merchants were at work within their stalls. He drew in breath, fortifying himself with the stamina he would need and began asking the merchants or their helpers if they had any knowledge of a man named Feliks. By the time he finished his search on one side of the hall, he had located four men by the name of Feliks. Two knew no Russian, one could speak a little but knew no more Latin than what he heard at Mass, and one was fully Russian yet lacking knowledge of Latin.

Aleksy turned about and began his questioning of the other side of the hall, wondering just what Krystyna had learned. Might Father Franciszek provide a clue? Would his time be better served by seeking out and questioning the priest? He looked about the increasingly busy Cloth Hall, determining that if this quest proves fruitless, a visit to the cathedral rectory would be in store for the afternoon.

The morning dragged on as he canvassed the other side of the Cloth Hall. Here he ran into fewer men named Feliks but more people intent on bending his ear because they were merely being genial or hoping to sell him something. He found that merchants—men and women—could be tenacious and downright cloying. This side took a good deal longer than the other one, and to no better end. No one seemed to know the person Krystyna had described.

He determined that he would go directly to the cathedral and pivoted now to walk the length of the hall for the final time, hoping to avoid the eyes of the most talkative merchants. He was at the middle of the hall when a woman he had already questioned called him over. Marzena, a plump older lady with long, wild silver hair, oversaw a jewelry stall that showcased amber jewelry, as well as raw amber. It took little time to realize she merely wanted to make her first sale of the day. He felt a bit sorry for her and allowed her to recreate her line of persuasive gabble, insisting that such a young, strapping young man must have a lady and that an amber ring set in silver was just the thing to bind up her heart. The ring she showed him was a beautiful thing, he admitted, and it was while he was considering its purchase that his eyes wandered to one corner of the stall where he sighted a stool and a high desk, the type he imagined one might find in an office. On its slanted top he could see books or ledgers of some sort. Certainly this woman could not read and write.

"That desk over there, Marzena—"

"Oh, my boy, tain't for sale, that."

"Who uses it? Your boss?"

"Not him. No, my boss is who rented the stranger the space."

"The stranger? Does he have a name?"

Marzena shrugged. "Calls himself 'the scholar' hoping to impress folks, I guess. Doesn't deign to talk much to me."

"What is his business?"

"He translates sometimes. Sometimes he writes letters for those who can't write. Or he reads them documents they can't read."

"Can he speak Russian?"

She nodded.

"Does he know Latin?"

"I don't know. It wouldn't surprise me none."

Marzena picked up the amber ring and was about to revert to her sales pitch when he felt someone pass closely behind him. Marzena's focus had been drawn to the passing figure, too, and she cursed under her breath.

In just moments the figure was ducking under the counter at the far end of the stall. Once inside, he glanced briefly at Marzena and Aleksy before going to the high desk and hoisting himself up onto the stool. Dressed in the robes of a scholar, the man was bald, plain-faced, and well-fed. Aleksy judged him to be about fifty years old.

Wihout even a conscious thought, Aleksy strode to the end of the stall, slipped under the counter, and proceeded toward the tall desk.

Marzena started to call out something, but one look from Aleksy silenced her.

"You are Feliks, yes?"

The man was genuinely startled. "Yes, yes. Do we have an appointment? Do you need a translation?"

"Latin?" Aleksy questioned. "Can you translate something into Latin?"

"Ah, yes, of course." He was recovering from his initial sense of caution. Like Marzena, who stood to the side watching, he was perhaps generating coins in his head.

"And tell me also, Feliks, can you work from a Russian document?"

"Naturally, my son. My mother was Russian, you see, but that carries little weight around here, I can tell you.... Now, what do you have for me?"

Aleksy smiled. "A surprise, perhaps."

Feliks smiled—but his face had folded into a question.

"I need a marriage certificate. Can you create one?"

Feliks's eyes widened. "Ah, one without the auspices of Mother Church, is that it?" He winked.

"Yes."

"I shouldn't ask the circumstances?"

"No."

"I am curious," he whispered so as not to allow Marzena to hear. Her attention, however, was taken up with a customer.

Aleksy shrugged.

"You are a glib young man. If we are to do business—"

Aleksy coughed and feigned embarrassment. "The young lady is to be led to think it is a real document."

"A faux marriage, I see," he whispered, hand to the side of his mouth. "I won't ask for the details. Yes, I can do that. It will cost a sum, I can tell you."

"I can pay. Are you able to show me a sample of your work?"

"You can read?"

"No," Aleksy lied.

Feliks smiled, his expression seeming to say, *I thought not.* He stood up now, pushed the stool aside, and opened the top drawer. He shuffled through a number of documents and withdrew a short stack. "Ah, here are several copies that should recommend me."

Aleksy took the oversized documents. They were written in a florid script in what he assumed was Latin. It was the fourth one of the six or seven that yielded even more than what he had hoped for. "This one," he said, "is signed by a Father Franciszek. Who is he?"

"Ah, you read that much, huh? He is the priest who married those two." He pointed to the names Lord Fabian Nardolski and Lady Krystyna Halicka.

"A genuine priest?"

Feliks flashed the smile of a well-sated fox exiting a hen house. "*I* am that priest. I played the part of Father Franciszek. Maybe you need the same *services*?" he asked, clearly enjoying the pun.

Aleksy turned away for a moment and called to Marzena, who had been unable to hold on to her customer. "I'll have that ring in a moment, Marzena, if you'll get it ready."

He turned back to Feliks before she called a happy affirmative in reply and he picked up the previous thread of conversation. "No, I don't need such services, but I do wish to repay you for your services in attempting to ruin the life of this young girl." Aleksy pointed to Krystyna's name on the parchment.

Feliks cast his eyes down, his expression screwing into one of wonderment, but as he lifted his face to Aleksy, a fist crashed into it with absolute force. He dropped like one of Aleksy's deer kills.

THIRTY-SEVEN

Krystyna nearly fainted to find her father at the door to her chamber, led there by a servant. It took no more than fifteen minutes for her to open her heart to him. She found him surprisingly compassionate about the "marriage" perpetrated by her mother and Lady Nardolska. "Father, I am so happy you are here!" she exclaimed, once the story was out. "Why Queen Maria has arranged everything—who would have thought? She was horrified when she heard about the first ceremony and the deception that went on, but she was genuinely happy for me and Aleksy. She dearly loves the king, so I think that is why she understands us, Aleksy and me.—Do *you* understand, Father?"

"I do."

Krystyna hugged her father, lamenting Roman's absence and Marek's death. When she looked up into her father's eyes, the tears came. "And Mother—Mother refuses to come for my wedding." She shook with sobs as her father held her.

"There, there, child. Do not blame her too much. She cannot help herself."

"Is it because of her part in the charade of my first ceremony? I've written to her. I don't blame her."

"Sweet girl—I will try to follow your example."

"Is it because Aleksy is not noble? You know the king has given him a small estate? He is no longer without means."

"I know."

"Is it that? Or is it his skin color? That he is a Tatar?"

"Perhaps it is that, my Krysia. Perhaps it is these reasons, as well as others. However, it is best to put it aside. This is your day."

"Am I never to see her?"

Her father considered her question. "I'm sure you will.—Just wait until you and Aleksy present us with our first grandchild."

"Will she accept him? Or her?"

"I have a feeling she will insist on the fastest team of horses we own to bring her to you. Think of that today."

Krystyna swiped at her tears. "I will, Father. Thank you for coming!"

Nadya adjusted the collar of Aleksy's newly-made *żupan* of Egyptian blue and looked up, her eyes shining with pride. Aleksy noticed for the first time that her eyes were as dark as his. In the few weeks of living next to her wagon, he had become quite attached to the gypsy. She appeared businesslike and even gruff to those meeting her for the first time, but that was the outer shell she wore, like a turtle, as protection; in her case a shell that shielded her from anyone who might take advantage of a gypsy woman living alone in open, often foreign and dangerous surroundings. Her heart, he learned, was wide as the sky. He had found the material for the long wedding coat at the Cloth Hall, but no seasoned tailor would agree to have it ready on short notice. Money was not the issue, for he had gotten a good price for the ruby-studded dagger. He could not help but wonder if their responses would have been different had he not been a dark-skinned Tatar. He let that thought go. Nadya had come to him, confessing that she was adequate with a needle and thread, and she proved it to the extreme. The cut and details of the *żupan* were perfect and the blue shimmered like a dark lake in winter. Beneath it he wore a white cotton shirt with a stand-up collar at the back. Nadya had embroidered with white thread the collar, cuffs, and the center laced opening that dipped to the middle of his chest.

"I want you to come to my wedding, Nadya." It was his third such request. "My parents and brother have come from Halicz. I should like you to meet them."

The gypsy waved her hand dismissively. "The sash is next," she said, working about him the black and gold embroidered sash, arabesque in design. "Turkish cloth?" she asked.

"Polish!"

Nadya laughed. "It is odd, I think, how the Poles wear clothing styled by their current enemies. Ah, think young Aleksy, how the world would be if there was exchange between peoples in all things."

"We might have peace."

Nadya nodded as she pulled the sash tight and tied it. "A good length, Aleksy—for when you are lord of your manor house and have much to eat."

They both laughed.

"Now, let me help you into your *kontusz*."

The russet cloak with its open sleeves fit nicely over the *żupan* and draped to the new yellow boots of fine leather.

"Do come, Nadya. I never would have been prepared for this day if not for you."

"Nonsense." Nadya gave a little laugh. "And what would I wear to the Royal Castle? Me—among all those women in their fine silks—and in a Catholic chapel?"

"You won't reconsider?"

She shook her head. "It is not my fate, Aleksy. It is yours."

An hour later, Aleksy set out on foot for the castle, sporting a *kolpak*—a hat Nadya made from the blue żupan material, lining and trimming it with black fox fur and for the special occasion a fan of peacock feathers at the front. The gypsy's words about fate still sounded in his head. Idzi had told him there was the changeable and the unchangeable. He had not forgotten. Despite his skin color, despite his peasant status, he was about to marry Lady Krystyna Halicka. Who would have thought it possible? That it was not unchangeable? Perhaps there was no such thing as the unchangeable.

Thinking about Idzi brought him up short. Guilt still weighed upon him for leaving him to the devices of Roman. It was not the first time he chastised himself for abandoning his friend. Was he being kept safe from the continuing battles with the Turks? Who was there to keep him safe from Roman? Had Idzi's fate been unchangeable? He said a quick prayer for him as he entered the fortress and headed for the golden dome of Zygmunt's Chapel, which adjoined the southern wall of the Wawel Cathedral.

Coming to the stone and marble façade, he passed through the gates of wrought iron grillwork and quickly moved to the heavy doors, heart racing like that of a Polish greyhound. He paused, hand on the door, knowing his life was about to change. He recalled now that same presentiment at Castle Hill in the moments before he met Krystyna for the first time. He drew in a deep breath and entered, removing his hat. Coming in from the sunny outdoors, he found the narthex dark and strangely oppressive. That this chapel was King Zygmunt's resting place made it an unlikely site to begin married life, but the choice had been Queen Maria Casimire's, not his.

His eyes began to adjust as his father, mother, and Damian approached him, tightly embracing him, one and then the next, all full of excitement, smiles, soft laughs—and tears. They had arrived from Halicz the night before and the queen had seen that their accommodations at the castle were superior. They were all dressed in their Sunday church clothes, humble by comparison to denizens of the city, but not one of them seemed to care.

"Oh, Alek," his mother cried. "Thank Our Lord Savior, you're safe home from Vienna!" Tears splashed down her cheeks. "And now you're to be married. Who could believe it?"

"I do." Damian said. "Aleksy's bow and fancy arrows weren't about to let him lose out to a devil-Turk. And, by the way, brother, come next month I am to be married, too!"

"I see you're not going to be outdone, Damian," Aleksy said, laughing. "Who is the happy girl? The one from Horodenka?"

"Yes—Lilka!"

"Ah, Lilka. Congratulations, Damian." Aleksy hugged his brother again. "You are in charge of this," he said, slipping into his hand the silver-mounted amber ring meant for Krystyna.

Aleksy's father, who stood by and had said almost nothing as if overawed by the unfolding scene, touched Aleksy on the shoulder and whispered, "Lord Halicki and his daughter are arriving."

Count Halicki was dressed in a captain's dress livery, a detail Aleksy would notice only later, for his eyes immediately took in Krystyna, who glided toward him like an angel in gold sunshine. She was a girl no more. The braids of a maiden had been unplaited so that her blond hair fell loose under a small wreath that held in place a long ivory veil that draped behind her. Leaving her shoulders bare, the brocaded satin dress featured a snug embroidered bodice that flared from her middle in a V configuration that called attention to the reveal of a décolleté and large, puffy sleeves cuffed at the elbow. As she moved, the tips of her matching gold slippers appeared beneath the voluminous folds of the gown.

He knew her smile must be reflecting his own as she approached him.

"I know how you commented on my yellow dress," she said, "so I sent home for it, but Mother refused to send it. When the queen's ladies stepped in to see to the details of the wedding, I requested a yellow gown.—Did they go too far?"

Aleksy produced a full smile. "No, it's beautiful, Krysia. You're beautiful."

"I'm going to miss my hair," she said, giving forth with that little laugh that had often confused him. He knew that after the ceremony, her hair would be cut short and she would be fitted with an intricately designed wedding cap, symbolizing her entry into the circle of married women.

Aleksy smiled uncertainly. "I'm sorry, Krysia."

Krystyna waved her hand dismissively. "And you are giving up your soldiering, so I care little about my hair." Her eyes moved to the hat he held in his hand. "What is this bow tied about your peacock's feathers?"

"Must you ask?" He himself had used the pink ribbon she had given him upon going to war.

Her hand moved to her breast. Somehow he expected one of her little laughs, but so overcome was she that she could manage only a little shake of her head.

Aleksy thought his heart would burst and was about to embrace her when his father gave a warning cough. "There are some traditional formalities to attend to," his mother cautioned in a whisper, "before the queen and the others arrive." She directed the couple to a small table covered in a white linen cloth. On it were a small dish of salt, two small pieces of rye bread, and a dainty glass of red wine. Aleksy's father, brother, and Lord Halicki joined his mother as witnesses to the union. "The bread here is present to banish any future need or hunger," his mother said. "The salt is to remind you that life will have its struggles and that you must cope with the hardships that may come your way." She paused for effect. "Now, Krystyna Halicka, which do you choose—bread, salt, or the groom."

Krystyna knew the prescribed answer. "I choose the bread, the salt, and the groom to make the money for it."

Everyone laughed.

When Aleksy and Krystyna ate the bread, Lord Halicki presented the glass of wine to Krystyna, saying, "May you never thirst. May you always have a life together of good health, cheer, and company of good friends."

Krystyna took the glass, drank, and offered it to Aleksy. When the glass was drained, there were kisses all around, three, on alternate cheeks, one right after the other. Aleksy and Krystyna were the last to kiss, and only they kissed on the lips.

The doors were opened now by palace guards, allowing in daylight and a small parade of the queen's ladies. With smiles, nods, curious glances at Aleksy, and an occasional wink at Krystyna, they filed past the two families, followed by the queen herself, who stopped to congratulate the couple and family members. "I only wish the king were here today," she said, her eyes on Aleksy, "you do know this young man saved my Jacob from certain death at the hands of heathens."

Aleksy burned with embarrassment as the others nodded or spoke a few words.

When she swept away, moving up toward the front of the chapel, his mother whispered, the amber specks in her blue eyes glittering, "What a wedding this is to be!"

Light caught everyone's attention again as the palace guards opened both doors for the entry of the priest.

Aleksy stepped forward. "This is Father Franciszek," he announced. After introductions were made all around, the priest said to Aleksy, "So, you have your heart's desire after all is said and done, my most fortunate boy." He turned to Krystyna now. "In time, my dear, you will know how fortunate you are."

Aleksy saw his mother swipe at her tears and turned to see pearls brimming at the tails of Krystyna's eyes.

"Now," Father Franciszek announced, "once I am at the altar, the families will process to the front. Aleksy and Krystyna come last, of course. Now, let's get on with God's work." The priest turned and moved up the aisle toward the awaiting queen and her ladies.

No one had thought of music, so there was none. Aleksy's father urged his wife to accompany Lord Halicki up the aisle so that he would not have to walk alone. As the two started their march, Aleksy glanced at Krystyna, whose face betrayed her longing for her mother at her wedding. He took and squeezed her hand. Her tears held back and she drew herself up, preparing for her march.

Now Aleksy's father and Damian were moving forward.

Aleksy and Krystyna were left behind. "If you care to change your mind," Aleksy said, "now is your chance."

The emerald green eyes widened at his words. She grasped and squeezed his hand, but only after she had delivered her enigmatic laugh.

For once, Aleksy deciphered that nervous giggle. His heart brimmed full. He took Krystyna's hand, and as customary, they began to process together toward the awaiting priest.

They were not yet halfway to the front when Aleksy heard a commotion behind them, at the doors. They kept walking, but the noise and voices persisted, grew louder.

The guards were denying entry to someone. *Who?*

Aleksy stopped, dropped Krystyna's hand, and pivoted to face the half-open doors.

It seemed a soldier was arguing with the guards, demanding entry to the wedding. Before Aleksy could take a full reading of the scene, he noticed a small figure squeeze in between the guard and the man he was holding off with his halberd.

The figure raced into the chapel, his foreshortened legs doing double time. Aleksy took several long strides toward the little man, who stopped abruptly, realizing at once with no little shock he had the attention of everyone in the chapel.

"Idzi!" Aleksy cried. "What is it?"

"It's Roman," Idzi said, catching his breath. "They won't let him in—and perhaps they shouldn't."

Either Krystyna heard her brother's name or she recognized him from afar. She swept past Aleksy and Idzi now in a gold blur of movement, gliding toward the doors.

"What's his intention?" Aleksy demanded, his heart racing. "Why has he come?"

"That's just it, Alek. I don't know. He's said nary a word. In Hungary, I thought I had talked sense into him."

"How?"

"I told him the truth—that he was alive because one of your arrows flew true."

"How did you know?"

"I saw it. I saw the whole thing, Alek.—And after I told him off, he decided, all sudden-like, that he was going to follow his father here to Kraków."

"And he's said nothing?"

"He shut up tighter than a clam."

Aleksy suddenly realized that Krystyna was drawing near, hand in hand with Roman. His spine stiffened. Church or not, his first thought was for a weapon, but he had none. Nonetheless, he was prepared for a confrontation.

"I see we've arrived just in time," Roman announced, heedless of the audience.

"In time?" Aleksy asked, heart at double time, nerves ready for anything.

"Indeed, Aleksy, indeed." He shot a glance at Krystyna. "For my sister's wedding!"

Aleksy knew that he could muster but the weakest of smiles.

"Doubt it not," Roman said. Stepping forward and gripping Aleksy's forearms, he leaned in and delivered the three prescribed kisses on alternating cheeks. When Roman released him and stepped back, he said, "Aleksy!—once again I have a brother!"

Aleksy tried to assess the midnight blue eyes. They were laughing, he was certain, but beyond that he was at a loss. Had *this* unchangeable become changeable?

A smiling Lord Halicki joined the little circle now, hugging his son. "Welcome, Roman. I am glad to see you have come to your senses."

Time and place blurred for several moments, and then Lord Halicki was ushering his son up to the front, and the chapel that had been echoing the soft murmurs of shock and surprise fell into a hushed silence. Idzi, too, found a place up front, near Aleksy's parents.

Krystyna took hold of Aleksy's hand. He turned to see her smiling. "They're waiting," she whispered.

It was the face, the smile, and rather than the gold of today, it was the yellow of the dress that he had seen what seemed so long ago.

Breathe, he told himself, *breathe*. He took in breath and—for now—let go of thoughts of Roman.

Aleksy and Krystyna processed toward the awaiting Father Franciszek.

READING GROUP GUIDE

1. Is 'love at first sight,' as in *Romeo and Juliet*, a possibility in real life? Although Aleksy is stricken by the appearance of the girl in yellow at first sight, their relationship develops over the course of four meetings. What moments are particularly poignant and key in that development?
2. After the initial physical attraction, might the deeper and enduring relationship between Aleksy and Krystyna evolve because each recognizes the rebel in the other?
3. Love encounters obstacles when it blooms between members of different social classes, cultures, or religions. Consider the attitudes and actions of Krystyna's parents and those of Aleksy's adoptive parents regarding class and culture.
4. What does the story underscore about religion? History?
5. Might someone today relate to the theme of the changeable versus unchangeable in the same way as Aleksy does?
6. Szymon tells Aleksy that Kystyna seems to enjoy making a "fuss." What are some of the instances? What does the character trait reveal about Krystyna? Do the instances prepare the reader for her jilting of Fabian?
7. Szymon tells Aleksy: "I do pray when I breathe. And when I breathe, I pray." Much later, Aleksy thinks he understands. How would you characterize Szymon's philosophy of prayer?
8. What is it that would prompt someone like Aleksy to think he could become a hussar? To think he could marry a nobleman's daughter?

9. The theme of prejudice plays out through Aleksy and the world into which he is adopted. How does he deal with prejudice? How does Idzi supplement the theme? And Nadya?
10. Is Roman's change-of-heart credible? Do you think he is sincere in his acceptance of Aleksy?

THANK YOU for reading ***The Boy Who Wanted Wings***! I sincerely hope you enjoyed it. If you did, you will also like **The Poland Trilogy**. Check it out: https://goo.gl/93rzag

PLEASE sign up for an occasional announcement about freebies, bonuses, booksignings, contests, news, and recommendations. http://jamescmartin.com/announcements/

LIKE me on **Facebook**: James Conroyd Martin, Author https://www.facebook.com/James-Conroyd-Martin-Author-29546357206/

Follow me on **Twitter:** @JConMartin

Follow/add me on **Goodreads**:
https://www.goodreads.com/author/show/92822.James_Conroyd_Martin

E-mail me at: JConMartin@gmail.com

Made in the USA
Charleston, SC
02 November 2016